The Devil's Lapdog

STORMY R. SIMS

Dedicated to my amazing family that put up with

my delusional ass for so long.

Chapter: 1

Her right eye twitched in annoyance as she attempted to keep the false, shaky smile that painted her delicate porcelain face. Faye felt black, beady eyes ogling her features as though she were nothing more than a piece of meat. Tapping her foot anxiously, she knew every second she was stuck in this overpriced hell was just another opportunity granted to her cheap slip on flats to destroy her feet with blisters. And while her elegant dark blue dress showed off every good curve on her body, it also hugged her bosom a little too tight, forcing her to sit with her arms over her chest so as not to give the man an accidental show.

She'd rather not give her date that type of satisfaction, seeing as he was the son of some scumbag politician or some big shot criminal. Faye could not find it in her heart to give a single damn which one it could be or even who he was as a person, especially when this disgusting man had been nothing but rude to her from the start. All she wanted was to get this awful date done and over with so that she could return home to her loving cats and loose fitting clothing.

In fact, the only reason she had agreed to meet up with this sad sack of human waste was at the insistence of her longtime friend and mentor, May Saken, who had promised the young woman a favor later on if she could do this one small task for her. Apparently, the older woman had found herself indebted to some top dogs, and they will call her debt paid if she talked Faye into the date. At least she only had to last two hours with this jerk, be non-confrontational, and peck him on the lips one time for the transaction to be completed. As dreadful as that sounded, it would at the very least be worth it, so long as he didn't mistake her for a prostitute.

He kept going on and on about himself, now and then throwing in some shameless comment about Faye's overall appearance. She stopped bothering to engage a while ago and had been simply biding her time until the two hours were up. He hardly seemed to notice her clear irritation with him, as he was far too caught up in his own hype to even question it. This man was apparently God's gift to the world and had women everywhere flocking to him in numbers. She should consider herself lucky a man like him even bothered to give her the time of day, even though she was the one that had to be bribed into attending this dinner. If this situation hadn't been so uncomfortable for her, she would have found humor in the whole thing.

Faye had been poking at her salad for the last ten minutes when the man cleared his throat. "Not hungry?" He smirked at her with crooked teeth she wanted to knock out. "Maybe we could cut to the end of this little dinner and make our way back to my place instead." Faye had to swallow down the bitter taste of bile, as her face wrinkled in disgust at his audacity.

"Not interested." She said blatantly, attempting to remain polite. The man choked a little, taken aback by her answer. "Oh, come on, baby." He slowly crept over to the irritated woman, refusing to take his eyes off her. "My father paid your boss good money for you. The least you can do is have some fun with me."

The arrogant man child said that last part so unreasonably loud, it drew the attention of the whole restaurant, causing all eyes to fall on the irritated woman. He slithered his arm around her waist with the grip of a python, nearly suffocating her. Her eyes flashed over to the large steak knife that sat unused by her plate, wondering for a moment if prison really was as terrible as people made it out to be.

She shook her head at that thought, knowing it probably wouldn't be worth it. Instead, she mustered up the iciest glare she's ever given, freezing the creep in his place as realization set in that he may have pushed a little too hard. Sucking in a deep breath, she calmed her nerves and quelled her rage so that she wouldn't completely ruin the rest of her evening by saying something a little too harsh.

"Alright, let's get a few things straight. May is not my boss, she does not own me and your daddy didn't pay a single dime for me because I'm not for sale. I came here on my free will and have absolutely no obligations to stay with you. Second, part of the agreement is that I spend two hours with you and remain polite, so long as you remain polite with me. You were told upfront not to touch me. Ever. And yet you're disrespecting that one boundary we had put in place, and on top of that, you turned us into a complete spectacle. I will forgive these idiotic little blunders and finish this date, but you may not disrespect me like that again. Do I make myself clear?"

The man quickly removed his arm from her waist, as though her skin was made of lava. Sulking back over to his seat, he sunk down a little in his chair after having his ego crushed so badly by the feisty young woman. Faye simply rolled her eyes before sitting back down in her spot. If the mood wasn't ruined before, it sure was now.

The rest of the evening went by with no further issues, and it seemed all the other guests had lost interest in the bickering 'couple' as they had gone back to their own conversations. Faye could still feel eyes burning into the back of her head as though she were the only thing left in the universe for them to look at. It made her feel a little uneasy.

She pushed past that uneasy feeling and wrote it off as some lowlife goon who worked for her date. The jerk probably hired him so he could keep track of her and make sure she didn't run away. As nice as running away sounded, she held a little too much pride and patience to pull off a stunt like that. Besides, as long as he remained polite, there would be no need for her to run away. She wanted her favor after all.

A loud alarm echoed from inside her purse, bringing all attention back to the two, but Faye didn't seem to mind it this time around. She let out a deep sigh of relief, silencing her phone as she gathered her belongings together. His beady eyes hovered over her with a look of curiosity, wondering what her next move might be.

Slowly and carefully, she stepped over to the man, the smell of wine and cheap cologne plunging into her nostrils, practically suffocating her. As disgusting as this was, she needed to complete the deal, so, holding her breath, she leaned in and pecked the man on his thin, chapped lips, quickly moving away from him so she could contain her gag reflex.

His mouth curled back into an arrogant smile, showcasing just how much his dentist did not like him. "Does that mean you're up for another date?" He wondered, attempting to shoot his shot. "Absolutely not! I hardly date to begin with, but this has just been fucking terrible. You are a miserable sack of shit, and I can't fathom spending even another minute with you, let alone a whole night. I just needed to finish up my end of the deal and I'll be out of your hair."

She did not hold back, feeling no obligation to do so. He sat there in his chair, with his eyes wide as he crossed his legs, his hands covering the zipper on his pants. She scrunched her nose in disgust as she turned to flee from this freak, her head held up high. "I'm going to go home and gargle some bleach now." She announced, rushing out the door.

Once outside, Faye took the long walk of shame through the parking lot, making her way over to her old, beat-up car she prided herself on keeping running for all these years. Opening up the car door, she sat in the driver's seat, resting her head on the dashboard. She wanted to take a moment and debrief from the experience, but out of the corner of her eye, she caught sight of a tall figure slowly making its way over to her vehicle. Panic and paranoia quickly set in as she started up her car and peeled out of the parking lot, not wanting to give them a chance to make any moves on her.

Halfway into her drive home, her stomach growled, reminding her that the only thing she ate that night was a small salad, courtesy of her arrogant date. She made a last-minute decision to get something actually satisfying to eat before driving all the way back home. Faye pulled into a MacBurger's drive-thru, trying to decide whether she should splurge on the apple pie, when her phone rang, May's name lighting up the screen. She let out an irritated huff before hitting answer. "What the fuck do you want, you red-headed bitch?" Faye grumbled, not in any mood for her friend's nosiness.

Laughter sounded from the other end as a thick Danish accent spoke up, greeting her back. "Was it really that bad?" she asked, referring to the date and the fact that Faye completely skipped all pleasantries with her. "I don't know, you tell me? I'm over here, in my car, sitting in a MacBurger's drive-thru because some arrogant prick decided a small side salad was more than enough to satisfy me. I feel bad for any woman that has ever slept with him." She sneered, pausing her rant to ramble off her order to the poor employee working the closing shift. "In fact, the only time he even acknowledged me was so he could drool over my body and tell me all the nasty things he wanted to do with me. I'd rather suck off the barrel end of a shotgun than let that bag of used needles anywhere near my privates."

Faye was not holding back on her insults, feeling as though she had every right to be angry with the man. "Jeez, that sounds terrible. At least you kept him off of you." May attempted to say out of comfort. "Yeah, I did. Almost beat that fucker with the closest blunt object, but I controlled myself. And he thought he was so fucking slick bribing the server into dumping wine all over my chest. How dumb does he think I am? I could clearly see him hand the dude some cash and tell him to spill it while pointing at my boobs. May I swear to God you would have had to bail my ass out."

The more she ranted, the more guilty the older woman felt putting her friend in such an uncomfortable situation. "He also somehow got the notion I was one of your whores, so that kind of sucked." She handed over her debit card to the cashier, who now seemed completely invested in this story, probably wishing she'd put it on speaker so he could hear the other side of the conversation.

"The fuck? I told Mike that his sleaze bag son was going on a date with my niece, not one of my girls. How in the hell did that get lost in translation?" She asked in frustration. "No idea, but either way, you'd still be wrong. Not your niece," Faye said pointedly. "Okay fine, daughter." She teased. "Hell no!" she retorted, grabbing her bag of food as May chuckled.

"Well, you sound like you had a pretty rough night. I'm sorry for setting you up on a date with a loser, but I'm super grateful you stuck it out for me." May sighed, relieved her friend wasn't too mad at her. "Yeah, yeah, just sign the damn book and stop setting me up with creeps." Faye laughed nonchalantly. "Oh, come on, I don't always set you up with creeps. Besides, I figured you could use a little more excitement in your life." She said playfully.

"My life is plenty exciting, thank you very much." She retorted, rolling her eyes. "Honey, you are pharmacy tech for an animal hospital. How is that exciting?" "You don't know the shit I've been through! Those dogs are fucking crazy!" Both of the women let out a good laugh before finally bringing their conversation to an end. After, Faye pulled out of the drive-thru and made it back on the road, heading home before it grew to be too late.

Chapter: 2

A few weeks had passed since the awful date with a creep, and she had all but forgotten that terrible night. Keeping true to her word, May did indeed sign off on Faye's book, making her obligated to owe her a favor. Because it wasn't an actual contract, May didn't legally have to pay her back, but there was still the moral obligation. Those on the outside might see it as a childish concept, but it was the best way for Faye to keep people from taking advantage of her. It especially came in handy when dealing with some of May's acquaintances, who saw her as a young and easily manipulated girl.

The concept of her having a book of favors was actually thought up by May, who hated seeing her friend get treated like garbage. Faye wasn't too fond of it at first, thinking it was ridiculous to expect something in return for being nice, but she was quickly shown the hypocrisy of her ideas.

Whenever Faye reached out for help, she was met with rejection or with people wanting things in return. "There is nothing wrong with knowing your value," May would say, attempting to convince her to keep track of people who continuously reach out.

Faye humored her and started off small by keeping track of who borrowed money and why, having them not only sign off on the amount, but put in writing exactly why they needed it. Because she still felt weird about asking for the money back, her close circle would often have to convince her it was okay to both want and demand that she be paid back. "But I feel like a loan shark." She would joke awkwardly. "Faye, I love you so much, but you would be the worst fucking loan shark." May pointed out. "They make people pay back their loans."

In the past two years, she eventually became more active in keeping track of people and shutting them down when they ask for too much. Many people surprisingly took the favor system pretty well, finding it rather fun and amusing. She even gained a few favors from some more well-known figures she met through May. After all the positive feedback she got from different people, Faye just went with it, figuring it might come in handy one day.

After signing off on the book, and parting ways, May went back to settling all her debts and selling off her many businesses. Lately, the sex scene had been undergoing some severe issues. While it had always been a risky business, it had gotten worse over the past few years. There was already a mafia that ran the city and, although they were a pain to deal with, they weren't entirely unreasonable.

She could deal with paying her dues, knowing it would be standard in any city that turned a blind eye to her work, but what she couldn't handle was all these small gangs popping up randomly trying to take claim to her properties. They had been bullying and harassing her for far too long, and she was sick of it. The nail in the coffin was that a lot of her prostitutes have gone missing. The threats left behind were more than enough to clue her in on where they were, and while she prided herself on being strong and not taking shit from anyone, she couldn't help but be a little shaken up over it, worrying for the safety of her loved ones.

Her grandmother had recently reached out to her, giving her the opportunity to move back to her home country and leave behind her shady line of work. Because of that, her husband put in a request to work internationally, which luckily had been approved, but it would take a year before they could actually make the move. In the meantime, she wanted to tie up loose ends and make sure her girls were all taken care of.

She was cautious about who she told about her plans, knowing that if it got out that she was leaving, gangs all over would fight tooth and nail to steal her clubs and brothels. That didn't mean that everyone was left completely in the dark. May was almost certain the mafia that she paid off had been well aware of her eventual departure. That thought alone is what brought her to this place.

May stood outside of a strip club feeling a pit of dread in her stomach as she debated on whether she should actually go inside. She knew it was inevitable that she meet with them. Refusing to do so would bring nothing but trouble to her and her loved ones, but that didn't make it any easier for her. The reality was that she was terrified of them, well more so she was terrified of their leader, the one she would meet with.

He was a devious man by the name of Elio Eclisse, who had been known for his terrible temper. While his men mostly ran all his businesses, he was still heavily involved in every bit of their work, especially when it came down to issuing cruel punishments and putting out hits. If Elio wanted someone dead, they would be dead, and if he had to do it himself, many would be dead. Whether it be man or woman, senior or child, he didn't discriminate, and would hunt them all down equally.

She found it suspicious that the mob boss wanted to personally conduct this meeting. Normally, all her dealings with this gang would go through one of his high-ranking members. Her business was in sex trafficking, after all, so he had no reason to waste his own personal time with her. 'It's just a simple deal.' She thought to herself. 'Go in there, sell him whatever clubs he wants to buy and get the fuck out.'

She didn't even care if he ended up low balling her so long as she could wash her hands clean. Thinking back now, she was grateful Faye chose not to follow her lead and work with her. While giving all her properties to the young woman would be the easiest way to get out of the industry, she would practically hand Faye, someone she's worked so hard to protect, over to the cruel crime lord who probably wouldn't appreciate her unfiltered words and unapologetic attitude.

"Are you coming in, or are you planning to stand there and look stupid?" A man snapped, catching her completely off guard. May quickly pulled herself back together, putting on her usual stoic expression as she nodded her head, following the man inside. She glanced around, happily surprised that the place wasn't too unkempt. While it certainly didn't live up to her standard of cleanliness, it looked as though time and effort was put into the upkeep. At least she could be assured her pride and joy would be left in capable hands. "In here ma'am." The gangster grumbled, pulling her into a room hidden near the back of the club.

As she entered the private room, her heart racing a mile a minute, she couldn't help but hold her breath, fearing for what awaited her. Elio wasn't the type to be taken lightly. He was a large, well-built man, towering at a height of 6'8" and weighing around 250 pounds. There wasn't an ounce of fat on his body, only muscle. His sun kissed skin had the perfect tan to it, dissolved of all blemishes, excluding a deep burn mark that ran through the right side of his face. Oddly enough, it was the least interesting feature on him as his deep, fiery orange eyes outshined it in every way. They held a level of threat to them that could make the most stoic of men tremble in fear.

While the room had been dimly lit with a few neon lights giving a small glow, Elio was still very easy to spot. He sat on a large leather couch with his arms and legs stretched out. His short, reddish-orange hair had been perfectly slicked back so that not a single strand fell out of place. It shaped his face nicely, giving him a very mature look.

Normally the crime lord had on a large brown overcoat, but he seemed to have taken it off long before she arrived, hanging it neatly over the sofa. Currently, he was wearing a dark red button-up shirt with the sleeves rolled up to his forearms, the bottom of it tucked neatly into black slacks. He tapped his well-polished chestnut colored dress shoe against the ground, impatiently waiting for the red-haired woman to speak.

"Hello Elio, thank you for taking the time to meet with me. I know you must be extremely busy, so I promise to make this brief." May greeted, swallowing down her nerves. She knew better than to show any signs of fear around him. "No need for that. I have my whole schedule cleared for this meeting. I have other things to discuss besides your little clubs." He retorted, his voice deep and loud, almost booming. The door behind her slammed close, causing her to jump instinctually. "Now, have a seat and let's begin."

After a long and draining hour and a half, May sold off some of her clubs for a pretty decent price. She half expected Elio to completely low ball her, but he was surprisingly reasonable with his requests. Even though the negotiations were all going in her favor, she knew better than to let her guard down, especially when there was still the unknown he wanted to discuss. Her mind raced, trying to think of what he might want besides her properties, but it came up blank.

"You're still in contact with all of your girls, aren't you?" His question came out of nowhere. "Mostly, yes." She answered truthfully, though she still felt confused. If he wanted any of her workers, why didn't he bring it up in the negotiations? "Good, I need you to get me in contact with a specific girl. I'll be happy to pay whatever price you want for her contract." While his tone seemed calm and relaxed, his eyes held a sinister look on them. "What's her name? I'm sure we can work something out." May answered politely. "I'm not sure... I can't seem to find anything on her besides a photo I had taken." He seemed angry at that fact, which only made her feel more on edge.

"Well, can I see the photo? I'm sure I can identify her easily." As worried as she felt, she was also curious about the mystery woman. She only knew of one person who didn't have any socials and was pretty difficult to track, but that woman definitely wasn't any of her employees. He tossed her over a phone that had a single photo on it. Fumbling the device for a second, May looked down and felt her blood run cold.

'Fuck.' She thought to herself, seeing Faye sitting in a nice restaurant, a look of resentment clear on her face. "Of course it's her. Why wouldn't it be her?" She mumbled bitterly to herself in her native tone. "Well? Who is she and how much does she cost?" Elio sneered impatiently. "About that... She's not actually for sale." May responded sheepishly. "What the fuck do you mean she's not for sale?" His hand inched closer to the gun that was strapped to his waist. "I mean, she's not mine. She doesn't work for me."

He narrowed his eyes, glaring menacingly at her. "Bullshit. I saw her out with that asshole Tommy Ladner and was told she was there at your request. If she doesn't work for you, then who the fuck does she work for?" A wave a realization struck her like a lightning bolt. "You were there?" She asked, dumbfounded. "Does it matter? Give me this girl or I'll break every bone in your fucking body and leave you out to die in the desert." May took a step back, no longer able to contain her terror.

"Look, like I said before, she doesn't work for me. This girl isn't a prostitute, she's just a friend who was doing me a favor!" She insisted, struggling to choose between her life and the fate of her young friend. "You really expect me to believe any of that? She ain't a whore, but she did you a favor by whoring herself out? Are you fucking serious?" He was only holding back because he desperately wanted this girl.

"She didn't whore herself out. She went on a single date with him under strict rules of no touching. She was under no obligation to actually be there and was free to leave at any time. No money was exchanged and she most certainly did not sleep with him." May felt as though she would faint at any moment.

"Fine. Let's say I believe you. Who is she then, and what does she do if she's not a whore?" He finally resigned, knowing this argument was only wasting his time. She took a deep breath, realizing that he would find out either way, so she might as well save everyone the trouble. "Her name is Faye Merci. She works at an animal hospital and has no actual connections to sex trafficking. I know it looks like she's some regular whore but…"

"I never said she was some regular whore." He suddenly interrupted her, no longer looking angry. "She sounds… interesting." He mumbled to himself, lost in thought. "I need you to get me in contact with her."

She looked shocked by the request, wondering if she heard him correctly. "Excuse me?" She asked before she could stop herself. "Get.. Me.. In.. Contact.. With.. Her…" He emphasized each word, glaring daggers into her. "I don't know if now is a good time. She's at work and…" "Now!" May quickly pulled out her phone, shakily dialing Faye's number. 'If Elio doesn't kill me, Faye sure as hell will.' She thought to herself, listening to the phone ring. After six rings, it went straight to voicemail. His hand went back to his gun, causing her to flinch. "Hold on. I told you she's at work. She's probably stuck in a rush." May frantically explained, dialing Faye's number again.

Much to her relief, the pharmacy tech picked up after two rings. "I've got thirty prescriptions to fill, a large shipment to put away, my work phone won't stop fucking ringing, and the manager is on my ass right now. What the hell do you want?" May felt a pang of guilt knowing she was just about to make Faye's obviously terrible day worse. "I'm sorry you're having a bad day, but this is kind of important. I have this guy here…"

"Nope!" She was quick with the answer. "You didn't even let me finish." May retorted. "Don't need to. My answer is no! I already stuck out one bad date for you. There is no way in hell I'm going through with another one." She said pointedly, with her hand on her hip. "Look, I'm not asking you to do me a favor. I thought you might want to talk to him." She insisted, knowing it would be fruitless. "Why? So you can set me up with some other douchebag? May I thought I told you to stay the hell out of my dating life. Don't you have something better to do?"

Faye was not having any of it. She was stressed out, extremely exhausted from the lack of sleep, and wanted nothing more than to go home, crawl into bed and not exist for a few hours. As well intentioned as she believed May was in trying to set her up with someone, she just wasn't in the mood. "I'm sure whoever you're trying to set me up with is a very nice guy, but I'm just not interested. Okay?"

"Awe, you're not?" A low, husky voice echoed through the phone, captivating the young woman. Elio had snatched the phone out of the red-head's hand, ready to put an end to this little game. "I… Well…" she stuttered out, not expecting him to take over. "I understand that it's so sudden, but I really want to meet you, maybe take you out somewhere nice." His voice was so hot it could melt butter.

"That'd be a little difficult at the moment, seeing as I'm at work." She attempted to joke, her face bright red. "I heard, and it sounds like you're having such a rough day. Maybe we could talk about it over dinner." He was really upping his game trying to persuade her. "I mean, I guess there's no harm in it. If I end up burning this place to the ground, though, we might have to take a rain check on it." "You ain't burning shit to the ground. I already hid the lighter!" One of her coworkers shouted at her from afar. "Dammit." She grumbled.

Elio's scowl turned into a smirk, realizing he caught her. "Well, in that case, I'll get your number from May and we can discuss when we should meet up." He purred. "Damn, you're good." Faye said, looking rather impressed. "Alright I guess. Dinner sounds nice." She finally agreed, much to May's shock and horror. "Good, I'll be looking forward to meeting you." He said. "You as well… Um… What did you say your name was again?" May wanted to slam her head against a wall, listening to this insanity. "Elio." He chuckled. "Well Elio, I'll see you tonight. Now, if you don't mind, I got a lighter to find." She hung up the phone, leaving the dangerous man to face May once again.

He threw the phone back to her, no longer looking at her with a smug expression. "It was great doing business with you, but I really must leave. I got a date to prepare for, after all." He snickered, snapping his fingers to signal for his men to escort her out. She was in so much shock she couldn't react properly and instead followed without a single complaint. Once outside, May quickly shot Faye a text message.

'Are you fucking insane? Why in the hell did you agree to go out with him?' 'I don't know, I panicked.' 'Panicked? Really?' 'Yeah. I told you I'm stressed the fuck out and he seemed cool. Why would you bother to ask me if you didn't want me saying yes?' 'Maybe because I'm used to you saying no. Are you really that stupid?' 'Probably. Besides, it's just one date. What's the big deal?' 'You've just shortened your own life.' 'I'm here for a good time, not a long time.'

This message chain was getting her nowhere, and it was far too late. *'Can you at least promise that you won't do anything to piss this guy off tonight?' 'Don't tell me how to live my life.'* Yep, she was doomed. May had already started planning out a funeral for her dear friend. As much as she wanted to stop this encounter from happening, it would be impossible at this point. The moment Elio laid his eyes on Faye, her fate was sealed. She could only pray for her friend's safety.

After her little text exchange with May, Faye skipped off back to her desk, unable to contain her excitement. Normally, she hated going on blind dates, but this guy seemed interesting and fun. Plus, if May was against him, that had to be a bonus. Her phone went off once again, this time coming from an unknown number. *'Hello doll, I can't wait to see you tonight.'*

Doll? She wasn't the biggest fan of pet names, but there was something about this guy that made it okay. *'Me neither.'* She quickly logged his number, trying her hardest not to smile. *'If you want, I can come grab you now. That way, we don't have to wait any longer.'* She giggled quietly to herself, thinking he was just trying to be funny. *'Very tempting, but I'm going to have to politely decline the offer. I still got bills to pay.'* After sending the message, she turned on some music, set her phone down on the countertop, and got back to work.

Chapter: 3

A few hours had passed by and Faye was on the brink of a mental breakdown. Her scrubs were covered in pill dust, dog hair, and chicken flavored suspensions. She had tangles in her hair, and the last couple of phone calls she took were really taking their toll on her. "I'm going on a break." She announced to the receptionists. "I might not come back." Normally, that was a joke, but it sounded really tempting at that moment.

Faye made her way into the breakroom, shutting the door so the sound of constant barking wouldn't disturb her. Slumping into a chair, she let out a frustrated groan. All she wanted to do now was go home and pass out. She no longer held any interest in going out later that night with some stranger, so she figured she'd shoot him a text asking for a rain check. *'Hey today is seriously kicking my ass. Is there any way we can go out another night?'* He had to be understanding about the situation. It was a Monday after all, so it made little sense to stay out all night when she had work in the morning.

The phone rang, Elio's name lighting up the screen. "Hello?" She answered nervously, not expecting him to call her. "Is everything alright doll?" His deep, sultry voice melted through the phone, nearly sending her into a trance. "Yeah, everything's fine… Just your typical Monday, you know." She attempted to laugh it off. "Are you sure? You sound stressed out." He stated, acting concerned. "Yeah, but I'm always stressed. No need to worry." She reassured him, surprised he wasn't trying to convince her to go out.

"What's got you so stressed? If you don't mind me asking." He seemed really worried about her mental state. It was kind of sweet. "Just work stuff. Dealing with medicine is pretty tough. These doctors are needy and the receptionists and techs won't stop bugging me with dumb questions. It's okay though, I'm used to it."

As nice as Elio seemed, she really didn't want to bother him with her problems. "A beautiful and smart girl like yourself shouldn't be used to that type of treatment." He was really digging his claws into her. "Beautiful and smart, ha! That's a good one. I look like a hot mess right now." She laughed. "Besides, if I was actually smart, I would have continued in human medicine instead of taking a long break to go into animal medicine." Why was she telling a stranger all this? Was she really this desperate for someone to vent to?

He hummed in disapproval at her words, pulling her out of her self-doubt. "When you get off, why don't you take a nice long shower to unwind and rest for a bit? I can come over to your place to pick you up. That way, you don't have to rush to get ready. Okay?" He offered. "Yeah, I guess that would work." She said with a soft smile, absolutely entranced by his words.

"Good, for a moment there, I thought I was going to have to come and kidnap you and force you to spend the evening with me." He said it in a playful manner, though he was completely serious. "Does being kidnapped come with a doctor's note? Cause that's the only way they'd ever let me miss work." She joked, feeling much less overwhelmed. Elio let out a low, hearty laugh that made her heart flutter. "Well, I suppose I'll let you go for now, but please don't be afraid to tell me when you're feeling overwhelmed. You're fun to talk to and I don't mind letting you vent to me." He had a soft smile that could be felt through his words. "Okay, I promise I will. See you tonight." She said cheerfully before ending the call.

Faye felt so giddy and excited to meet Elio. She was practically skipping out of the breakroom without a care in the world. "What got you so worked up? Did you finally get dicked down?" A kennel attendant asked crudely, causing her smile to drop to a frown as a look of disgust fell on her face. "Don't you have dogshit to be cleaning?" She retorted, flipping him the bird before stomping off back to the pharmacy. Funnily enough, she was so love-struck and bubbly that it didn't cross her mind that Elio hadn't even asked for her address.

The moment 5:00 hit, she fled from the building without so much as giving a single goodbye to any of her coworkers. Jumping into her car, Faye started driving without a single care in the world, making it home with no problems at all. She skipped into her house, humming a light tune, when the sudden reality of her situation hit. Not only was she about to go out with a complete stranger, but she also allowed him to come and pick her up from her house. What the hell was wrong with her? "I should start sending all my loved ones nice photos of me so they can submit them to the news when my body gets found in a ditch." She laughed to herself as she walked towards her bedroom, throwing her bag on the couch.

"Banshee! Caligula!" She called out as she entered her room where her two fuzzy felines laid curled up on her bed, waiting for their master's return. Her two cats stood up, chittering and purring as they greeted their master. The older of the two, a seven-year-old black and white Manx, was the first to actually greet her. She wobbled her way over towards the woman, demanding attention. "Hey Banshee." Faye giggled, carefully picking up the old lady and placing a kiss on her forehead. The younger cat, a giant orange Maine coon, followed the elder's lead, jumping down effortlessly before sauntering over to rub up against her legs, earning himself a good scratch on his head.

"Alright you two." Faye spoke to them in a strict, motherly tone. "I am going to be out tonight, so I want you two on your best behavior." The cats both sat still in front of her, as if they were actually listening to the strange woman. "I have the catnip locked up in the cabinets, so don't even try to get into it. Also, you are absolutely forbidden from having any friends over. Okay? Now let's get you silly little creatures fed." They followed her into the kitchen, where she quickly prepared their food and sat it out for them. "What do we say?" She asked, causing both cats to stare at her blankly before diving into their meals. "Yeah, okay, I'll just go fuck myself then." She mumbled as she walked to the bathroom.

Elio was right. She really needed a long, relaxing shower after the hell of a day she had. The warm water fell on her nude form, helping to loosen up her aching muscles. The scent of vanilla and honey milk encompassed her in the steam as she worked the tangles out of her hair. Once her hair was clean and manageable, she got to work on scrubbing all the dirt and grime off of her skin, leaving her looking refreshed and rejuvenated. While Elio was practically a stranger to her and normally she could not care less what people think, she had the strangest urge to impress him. "It's one date. It's not like I'm planning to marry him or anything." She told herself to settle her nerves. "Besides, just because he's got a great voice, is very charismatic, and actually seems caring, it means nothing."

She shook her head, trying hard to clear her thoughts of anything and everything. "Just go with the flow." She repeated to herself as she stepped out of the shower, wrapping an old tan towel around her body. She took out her bottle of cherry almond lotion and rubbed it into her skin, figuring she was probably going to say plenty of stupid things to make him feel uncomfortable, so the least she could do was look pretty for him.

As she went through her closet, trying to find a halfway decent outfit, she couldn't help but wonder what her date would be like and who he was. "He's obviously suave, has to be well put together." She said out loud as she pulled out her favorite dress, a knee-length black dress decorated with golden stars. "May says he's the devil, but so far he's been the nicest guy to ever ask me out… That's sad, isn't it?" She was talking to her cats again, mostly to calm herself down. "I don't know if her not wanting me to go out with this man is a good thing or not. I mean, have you seen the dumpster fires she's set me up with?" She pulled the dress over her head, happy that it still fit her perfectly.

"What do you think?" She asked, doing a little spin for her cats. The skirt flowed around her waist like a flower in full bloom. The dress showed off every curve on her body without causing her any discomfort. Rarely did she have an excuse to wear this outfit, so she couldn't help but feel excited. Banshee gave a little chitter as she lightly swatted at the skirt in approval. "Why thank you Ban-Ban, I also think I look good in this." She smiled proudly before walking back to the bathroom to brush her hair and teeth.

She pushed one side of her hair behind her ear, pinning it back with a decorative golden hairpin that had a sparkling blue flower at the end. Rummaging through her make-up box, she pulled out some lip gloss, eyeliner, and mascara. "You know Caligula, eventually I'll learn how to actually do make-up, and when I do, this world better watch it's fucking back." She joked with her orange baby, who sat in the bathtub, lapping up water from the leaky faucet. "Just watch. I'm putting all this time and effort into looking my best and he's going to show up in torn up cargo shorts and an old t-shirt."

Her nerves were seriously getting to her, and it was almost tempting to call and cancel the whole thing. "I can tell him I suddenly started running a fever, or maybe say my best friend just ended up in the hospital." She rubbed her arms, trying to shake off the anxiousness she felt. "This whole thing is weird, right? We're moving way too fast. He's got to understand." She awkwardly laughed as she looked in the mirror. "What to do you think, baby boy? You're right, maybe I should just call and cancel. I mean, I don't know this man after all. For all I know, he could be a serial killer or a mob boss. Or worse… He could be extremely allergic to cats. I don't even know what this man looks like, or how he knows what I look like. Okay, he obviously knows what I look like because of fucking May. But still…"

A loud knock sounded at the door, pulling her out of her psyched out rambling. "Welp, it's too late now." She sighed, throwing on a pair of black flats that had pretty little golden bows on top. She grabbed her purse off the couch along with her house keys. "Deep breath…" she mumbled to herself. "Just go with the flow." With one final pep talk, she breathed in and put on a smile as she opened the door.

Her soft blue irises met fiery orange eyes that seemed to hold hypnotic powers over her. The blood rushed to her face as she stood frozen, unable to speak or move. "I'm glad I can finally meet you, doll." He spoke in a seductive manner, with a sly smirk on his face. "Damn you're handsome." She muttered without thinking. He let out a low chuckle at her boldness, taking her hand in his as he bent down to press a gentle kiss to her wrist.

"I'm happy to not disappoint." He purred, causing her to giggle at the display. "I mean, the night's still young, there's still plenty of time." She said playfully, causing him to look at her in a bit of shock. "I suppose you're right, but I'm hoping to avoid committing such an unforgivable crime." A shiver ran up her spine as he spoke. If he kept this up, she might not survive the night. 'May could have given me a heads up he was hot.' She thought to herself as she followed him down the steps of her porch, not realizing there was so much more May should have warned her about.

He led her towards a huge and luxurious SUV that didn't match the white trash aesthetic her neighborhood was going for. It looked like it was worth more than her yearly salary and made her feel even more anxious than she was before. As out of place as she felt being anywhere near it, she still didn't want to give any hints to her date that she was uncomfortable with stepping into such a nice car.

"Is this not up to your expectations?" Elio teased, opening the back door for her. "On the contrary, I was expecting a windowless white van, so this is pretty… Nice." She remarked, stepping in and sitting down in the leather seat, noting how much leg room it had. They could comfortably fit a horse back there if they wanted to, which might be what they were going for, seeing as her date was pretty large. "Sorry doll, my windowless white van is in the shop today, so I guess we're stuck with this." He smirked as he crawled in next to her, slithering his long arm around her waist.

She let out a surprised squeak at the sudden physical contact, attempting to move away from him on instinct. "What's wrong doll? Am I making you uncomfortable?" While his tone made it sound like he was genuinely worried for her, his face showed he was enjoying her skittishness. "What? No, never!" She lied stubbornly. "I'm just worried about you, is all." He looked at her in confusion. "Why are you worried about me?" He asked.

"I've been known to collect hands. Got a pile of them sitting in my guest room." She retorted, trying to sound serious. "You're going to cut off my hands?" He questioned her, shock written all over his face. "I mean, I don't want to, but it is the rules." She said matter-of-factly. "The rules of what?" He was trying his hardest not to laugh at her goofiness. "The rules of blind dates. One of us has to be the killer." She declared proudly.

Elio could no longer contain his laughter at how ridiculous she sounded. "And how do you know I'm not the killer? I could easily be planning to drive you out into the middle of the desert, fuck you, and then shoot you." His grip on her tightened as he pulled her closer to him. "Why waste the gas? Just do it right here." If only Faye knew whose bluff she was calling, well, it still wouldn't make a difference to her.

"As tempting as that is, I'd rather buy you dinner first." He purred, tilting her chin up so that her eyes could meet with his. "You're the nicest killer I've ever met." She said, her cheeks bright red. "And how many killers have you met before me?" He squished her cheeks as he moved her face around to examine her properly. "I'm not sure, but most people I talk to are assholes, so with that percentage in mind, it's only natural to assume the people I talk to who happen to be killers are assholes."

This girl was an absolute riot and he couldn't believe it took him this long to meet her. Normally, he wouldn't let anyone talk to him in this manner, but there was something about her that captivated him. At first he thought he was simply curious, wondering what kind of crazy dame would call out Tommy Ladner like that, but she had been plaguing his mind for so long it had to be something more.

Maybe he felt the need to control her? That could be it. This outspoken, beautiful girl walked around his city acting like she could say and do anything she wanted with no consequences, so maybe he felt the need to reel her in. But if that were true, then why was he taking her out to dinner? And why did he continue to let her speak out of turn?

His eyes were glued to her lips, watching them move as she continued to talk, wondering what she would taste like. Before he could stop himself, he leaned in, pressing his mouth to hers, forcing her into a soft kiss. Her eyes widened with a look of uncertainty as he savored her flavor. She had a cherry taste to her mixed in with a hint of cinnamon that melded well with her sweet scent, which seemed to wrap around him like a silk scarf. Her skin was so soft and warm, he just wanted to pull her close and hug her tight like a favored stuffed animal.

He pulled away with a satisfied smirk, leaving her both speechless and breathless. "I'm sorry, I just couldn't resist." He apologized, giving her a little more space to gather her bearings. "I-it's fine…" she stuttered out. "You just caught me off guard." She ended up scooting closer to the large man, questioning her own sanity. Did she actually enjoy being kissed like that by some random guy she just met? "So you did like it?" He teased, draping his arm over her shoulder. "Because if that's the case, I have no problem taking it further." He stuck his tongue out to emphasize his point.

Faye couldn't help but laugh at this display, finding his demeanor silly and strange. "Knock it off." She giggled, gently pushing his chest away. He sat frozen in place, never having heard such a beautiful sound come out of anyone before. Her soft, sincere laughter was the perfect melody for him, something he wanted to burn into his mind and listen to over and over. How was it fair that the rest of the world got to experience her before him?

"Never. Not when I have such an adorable little dame sitting next to me." He cooed, nuzzling her cheek. "You know how tempting it is to take you home with me?" He wanted to have her right there and then, thinking that if he could just get it out of his system, then maybe he could wipe his hands clean of her. But after that kiss, he was having doubts about that theory, wondering if he might have felt something deeper than lust.

"Maybe some other day, but sadly, I got work in the morning that I can't miss. Unless you're planning to pull over and blow my brains out in some back alley." She remarked, half joking. "I would never waste such a beautiful girl." He retorted slyly. "Such a gentleman." She giggled, rolling her eyes. He swore if she kept giggling like that, he would take her back to his base and never let her leave.

"So, where are we going?" She asked after they had been traveling for half an hour. He got her to lay her head against his chest as his arm sat wrapped around her. "It's a surprise." He retorted, stroking her side lightly. "You know, the last time someone told me that, I ended up in the desert half-naked with nothing but a bottle of ketchup and a ruler." He gave her a strange look, unsure of how to respond to that comment.

"I feel like I should worry about you." He said, concern in his voice. She shrugged her shoulders as she leaned in closer to him. "Nah… I'm fine. I've made it this far." He chuckled, finding her more and more tempting. Did she even consider how close she was to being kidnapped?

By the time they made it to their destination, Faye was completely relaxed and comfortable, finding Elio rather easy to talk to and joke with. He was non-judgmental and had a great sense of humor, both major green flags to the woman. "Well, we're finally here, doll." He announced, gently kissing her temple. God was this man affectionate, almost to the point of being slightly creepy, and yet she was loving every ounce of it.

She couldn't help but wonder if he was like this with every girl he met. That thought bothered her a lot, but she quickly put on a smile, trying not to look too down. It's not like she'd ever see him again after this, so she should just relax and enjoy the date without worrying too much about his history.

He was the first to step out, offering his hand to her so she could safely exit the vehicle. Faye gave him a grateful smile, which fell down the moment she saw where he had brought her. Large black trees surrounded them with long branches covered in bright pink flowers that gently floated to the ground like snowflakes. In between the trees were vibrant bushes covered in blooming moonflowers that seemed to light up the walkway, which was made of a black stone that had small flakes of gold in it. The entrance to the beautifully lit building had a large arch made of the same material as the path and a lit up sign hanging down that read 'Crescent Waves.' Looking past all the vegetation, she noticed two small rivers running on either side of the path flowing towards a waterfall sitting near the entrance.

She couldn't help but notice that all the guests coming in and out were in formal attire and looked high class and fancy. Faye felt pretty insignificant in appearance compared to the gorgeous evening gowns and expensive suits surrounding her. Looking up at Elio, she couldn't help but wonder if he brought her to the right place.

"Well? What do you think? You seem like the type that can appreciate a nice seafood restaurant." He said, amused by her worried expression. "It's lovely, but… Ain't it a little too much? This place seems… Above my level." She admitted sheepishly, feeling eyes all over her as he pulled her against him, leading her inside. "Not at all. I'd say you're on a higher level than anyone here." He remarked with a look of pride on his face, as if he were holding a trophy.

Because she was already there, she found no use in arguing over it with him, figuring it would be futile, anyway. "Just relax and have fun. I'm sure after the shit day you had, you deserve it." He said gently, shooting warning looks to any nosy eyes that stared for a little too long. He could feel her relax the moment they entered the restaurant, her eyes sparkling with amazement.

It felt as though she had stepped out of a submarine to explore an ocean cave. The walls and ceiling were made of a strong glass which held a vast number of sea creatures behind them, bathed in blue lighting that lit up the surrounding area. Large statues designed to look like coral crept up to the ceiling with different colored plants decorating them. The music they played was soft and chill, a mix of techno and hip hop that didn't overwhelm the atmosphere, making it easier for the guests to chat with each other.

"Hello, how may I help you?" The hostess asked with a polite but nervous smile as she greeted the couple. "I have a reservation for two under Elio Eclisse." He answered, his tone less jovial and more monotone than he had been with Faye. "O-of course, sir! F-follow me!" She stuttered out quickly, ushering them further into the building where she led them to a private room.

Faye was completely mesmerized, barely even paying attention to anything. She let Elio control her movements, guiding her to sit down in the large silver booth that wrapped around a table. "Y-your server will be with you in a moment!" The hostess squeaked out before running out of the room, leaving them all alone.

Elio's expression softened the moment his eyes landed back on the young woman who looked to be in absolute bliss, her head moving back and forth, watching as a boxfish swam around to avoid the other fish. "You seem to be enjoying yourself." He hummed, running his fingers through her soft golden locks. "Huh? Oh… Sorry. Yeah, it's a beautiful place." She laughed out of embarrassment. "Sorry if I'm being rude." He gave a hearty chuckle at her flustered expression. "It's okay, you're not being rude. I'm just happy you're having a good time." He said in a warm tone.

There was something endearing about the way she could go from being confident and playful to shy and flustered in a matter of seconds. It made him want to take full advantage and steal her away from the world, keeping her all to himself. He was feeling confused about how he felt about Faye and what he actually wanted from her. He'd spent the last few weeks obsessing over her, putting her on a pedestal that she'd surely collapse on and yet here she was, exceeding every expectation for him.

He found it infuriating that he couldn't come up with a single reason to hate her like he did everyone else. Every little thing she did that he would see in others as annoying was done in such a way that made her lovable. How dare she come off that way. Didn't she know who he was? What he's done? He spent the whole day stalking her and yet, here she was, cuddled up against him without a single care in the world.

"So, how was your day?" Faye asked, pulling him out of his thoughts. "It was pretty good, had a few meetings to attend, and only needed to snuff out a few fires." He spoke nonchalantly, not giving her too many details of his job. "What about you?" He asked, already knowing the answer. "Like I said before, it's a typical Monday. Lost my lighter privileges, and my sharp object privileges, but it wasn't the worst day ever." She shrugged, which made him laugh. "I'm glad you're doing better. I would have burned that place down myself if they kept you from being here with me." She giggled, once again not realizing just how serious he was.

"Anything in particular you want to drink?" He asked, opening up the wine menu. "Oh, I'm not really a drinker." She replied with a hand wave. "Not much of a drinker, or can't drink at all?" He asked, attempting to clarify her situation. "Not much of a drinker. I drink occasionally, but tonight's not a good night. It's a weekday and I have to get up early in the morning." She explained. "I get it, but it would be nice to share a single drink with you. One glass of wine won't cause you too many problems, besides you won't be driving so you could just relax in the car ride home." He very much insisted.

"I'm not sure…" she retorted nervously. "I promise it will be fine. Worst-case scenario, I could get you a doctor's note to excuse your absence." She thought about it before resigning. "Okay, I guess one drink won't kill me." She sighed. "Good girl." He praised, squeezing her shoulders lightly. "Now what type of drink do you like?" He asked. "I'm good with anything, as long as it's sweet." She answered honestly.

After a few minutes, the server finally came in wearing a nervous smile. "Hello and thank you for your patience. My name is Marco and I'll be your server. Can I get you started with any drinks today?" He asked politely, avoiding eye contact. "We'll take a bottle of 2019 Inniskillin Ice Wine Cabernet Franc and two wineglasses. Does that sound good to you, doll?" He turned to her, wanting to make sure she was okay with the drink of choice. "Oh, sure." She held back a nervous chuckle. "To be honest, I have no idea what you just said." The server looked as though he was about to laugh at her ignorance, but, with one warning look from Elio, he somehow kept it all together long enough to flee the room with a simple nod.

Once the server was out of the room, Elio turned his attention back to Faye, pulling her face up close to his. "You're adorable, you know that, right?" He cooed, lightly kissing her lips. "Am I now?" She retorted with a heavy blush. "Very." He mumbled against her, wanting so desperately to deepen the kiss. He finally pulled away, allowing her to move back to her spot so she could look at the menu.

Her face went pale white the second her eyes landed on the prices. While she knew this was a high-end restaurant and everything would be a bit more costly, she didn't expect for them to be this high. Some of the cheapest things on there could buy her a week's worth of meals, plus some, which made justifying eating there difficult. Elio took her hand in his and rubbed small circles into her knuckles to soothe her. "Order what you want, doll. Dinner is on me." He promised to make her feel less anxious. As much as she appreciated his attempt, it only made her feel worse knowing he'd be paying. She figured the cheapest dish on the menu looked pretty good and didn't cost an arm and a leg, though the price was still outrageous in her opinion.

The server came back carrying two wine glasses and a fancy-looking bottle that she was almost certain she'd never find at any grocery store. "C-can I take your order or do you two need a minute?" How was it the server was more nervous about her date with Elio than she was? "We're good." Elio said. "We'll both start off with the lobster bisque. I'll have the dry-aged New York with seared scallops and a side of roasted Brussels sprouts." He spoke with no hesitation, as if he's eaten here plenty of times before to know what he likes.

"And what about you, ma'am?" He turned his attention towards her, happy to not be focusing on the intimidating man in front of him. "Oh, I'll have the shrimp scampi." She said far too quickly. "And for your main?" He asked. "My main?" She questioned. "Yes, we have different seared steaks, lobsters, whole crabs…" the server trailed off, feeling Elio's intense stare on him.

'Wait, the shrimp scampi is a side dish? What the fuck?' She acted calm and collected, mentally panicking over it. "Oh, my bad. In that case, I'll have the um… The roasted chicken?" She said wearily. "And last, what other side do you want with it?" 'Oh for fuck's sake.' She was getting frustrated. "You should try the Sautéed mushrooms." Elio suggested thoughtfully. "Okay, I'll have that." She took him up on his suggestion, slightly embarrassed over the whole thing.

Feeling the awkward mood shift, the server quickly excused himself to log their orders into the system. "Hey doll, do you mind sitting tight for me for one second? I have some business to take care of," Elio asked tenderly. "Sure, do what you need to do." She smiled at him as he leaned down to kiss her forehead before standing up out of his seat.

He followed the server out into the main lobby, snatching him by his shirt collar and pulling him into a nearby storage closet. "Don't you ever embarrass my girl like that again or I'll make your last days fucking painful. Do I make myself clear?" He sneered, keeping his voice down so no one outside could hear them. "Y-yes s-sir." The server squeaked out with a horrified expression. He scanned over the man's face, making sure his point was made clear before letting him go to get back to work.

Normally he'd be livid with his companion instead of the staff for not understanding how the restaurant worked, but he couldn't bring himself to feel any anger towards the woman, especially when she obviously had never been to a restaurant like this before. He also didn't appreciate the server standing there, allowing her to struggle as he added more choices she was uncomfortable with. It felt as though he was deliberately trying to make Faye look foolish.

After Elio took a moment to calm down, he re-entered the room, offering Faye a huge grin, which she returned gracefully. "Sorry about that again, just needed to address something really important." He once again apologized. "It's fine. I get it." She brushed it off, leaning back into his chest the moment he sat down. "Good, because I worked so hard to impress you. I'd hate to screw it up so late into our date." He popped the cork on the bottle and filled both glasses full. "At this point, you'd have to murder a puppy in front of me to ruin it." She joked, accepting the glass from him. "Damn, there goes my plans for our second date." He teased, taking a sip from his own glass.

Faye savored the sweet flavor of the wine, enjoying every little sip she took. Elio sat there, admiring her every expression with a gentle smile. He noticed the small noises she made showing how much she liked the drink, and he couldn't help but imagine what other noises he could get her to make. His feelings for her were becoming much more clear. He, of course, wanted her physically. There was no doubt about that, but he also wanted her mentally and emotionally as well. He felt the need to protect and spoil her, and he was ready to kill for her.

Elio snaked his arm back around her waist, pulling her closer and closer to him without her noticing. His movements faltered when she looked up at him with beautiful blue jewels that could put the finest gemstones to shame. "How are you liking your drink?" He asked, hoping for her approval. "It's really nice. Thank you." She said, appreciative of him. He could feel himself melt at her sincerity. "No need for thanks. I'm just glad you're enjoying it." He said bashfully. "If you want, I can send you a few bottles." Her eyes widened at this offer. "Oh, no! No need! I don't drink nearly enough for it to be worth going through the trouble and expense." She frantically explained, not wanting him to waste money on her. "Seeing you smile is worth every cent." He purred as he grabbed her wrists, pulling her onto his lap.

She set her glass down in surprise at his sudden boldness. "I… Um… There won't be much smiling done when I just feel super guilty for having you waste money." She mumbled out, feeling extremely flustered. "It wouldn't be a waste." He smirked, leaning in closer to her face. "But it would. I hardly drink, so it'll mostly just sit there gathering dust, which will make me feel bad." She insisted, hoping he wasn't actually serious. "If that's the case, then I guess I'll just have to bring you other gifts."

He pressed light kisses against her lips to stop her protests. "I'll spoil you fucking rotten." He mumbled against her, causing her to whimper. Her reactions to his teasing were both too much and not enough for the greedy man. His fingers danced up her thigh as he drank in every little moan from her. They inched further up her skirt, stopping right at the elastic of her panties. "Please stop." She cried out, barely pulling away from the kiss.

Elio quickly pulled away from her, moving his hand out from under her skirt. "Sorry, I got a little too carried away." He apologized, setting her back down next to him. "It's okay, just… Not tonight…" she breathed out. "Don't worry, doll, I'll never pressure you into anything you ain't comfortable with." He promised her, offering a reassuring smile. The tension she felt a moment ago completely disappeared from her body, allowing her to relax against him as he draped his arm over her shoulder. He decided he'd be patient with her for now. Of course, by their next date he'll have her on her back crying his name, but until then he'll just have to be a bit more subtle.

The server finally came back in with their soups, now completely avoiding eye contact with them. He set them down and started rushing out the door. "Thank you very much!" Faye called out to him, causing him to freeze. He wasn't sure if he should acknowledge her or not, but figured it was in his best interest not to be rude to the blonde woman. "You're welcome." He said with a nod before running out of the room.

"It must be busy tonight if he's having to rush. Poor guy probably should take a break." She remarked sympathetically. "Yeah, probably." He hummed in agreement, moving his arm so she could eat comfortably. He thought for a moment that perhaps he went a little too hard on the server, but then remembered the look Faye had on her face when he attempted to humiliate her in front of the large man. Although, if he would have known she would show sympathy for this waste of air, he might not have gone after the man like that. Oh well, he would just note it for next time and cool his temper a little.

Noticing her glass was getting a little low, he grabbed the bottle and began pouring it for her. "Oh, no thank you, I don't need any more to drink." She tried to decline the wine. "Another glass ain't going to hurt you." He insisted, offering it to her. "I'm a major lightweight.

Trust me, you don't want to see me drunk." She argued lightheartedly. "I would love to see you drunk. That way I can bring you home and take care of you." He smirked, pressing the glass up to her lips.

She laughed as she took the wine glass away from him, setting it down next to her. "Sorry, but you'll have to wait until our third or fourth date before you get to see me drunk." She crossed her arms and let out a playful humph. "I see you're already planning our future dates. Does that mean I managed to not disappoint you tonight?" He teased, pulling her face back over to his. "I'm just as surprised as you." She retorted, sticking her tongue out at him.

As their main dishes came out, Elio started feeling much more relaxed and jovial. There was something about this girl that made him feel so at ease. She would often go on a rant about either a hobby or a show she found interesting and describe it with such passion and excitement, he couldn't help but admire her. He constantly got lost in her eyes, clinging on to her every word as though it were gospel.

"Damn. I'm rambling again, ain't I? You know you could tell me to shut up, right?" She laughed nervously. "Nah, I enjoy listening to you talk. It's kind of cute." He retorted as he leaned on his arm, a soft smile on his face as he admired her. Her eyes darted away, opting to look at the fish while she attempted to control the dark red stains on her cheeks.

After an hour of conversing and eating, Faye noted the time. "It's getting pretty late." She sighed, realizing this wonderful night was ending. The smile on Elio's face slowly fell to the news. "I suppose you want to go home, right?" He asked, not even attempting to mask his disappointment. "I have to." She corrected him. "I still need to go to work in the morning and I can't just leave my cats alone for the rest of the night." She retorted sadly. "But I would love to meet up with you again. Maybe sometime this weekend if you're okay with it." He seemed to perk up at this proposal. "Of course I'm okay with it. Hell, I was planning on holding you hostage until you agreed to a second date with me."

Faye fell into a fit of laughter as she stood up from the booth, following Elio out. He reached down and picked her up, bridal style, causing her to squeal in surprise. "You jerk!" She exclaimed, smacking his chest lightly. "Awe, come on doll, I'm just making sure you get back safely." He snickered, kissing her forehead as he made his way out of the room and back into the lobby area. She could once again feel judgmental eyes all over her, though it didn't bother her as much as it did when she first arrived. As much as Faye hated being picked up and carried around, there was something about how Elio held her that made her feel safe.

He got them both out to the vehicle and lowered her back down to the ground so that she could enter first. Just as she made it to the other side of the car, he had her pulled back to him, settling her on his lap. "And where do you think you're going, my pretty little doll?" He purred against her neck, his sharp teeth pressing against her sensitive flesh. "I was just… Mph…" Before she could finish her sentence, he carefully bit down on her, forcing out a loud moan. He pulled away, leaving a large mark on the side of her neck. With a devilish smirk, he dove right back in, peppering kisses under her jawline as she clung desperately to his shoulders. "I… Ah… Please…" Every little nip drove her wild, leaving her wanting more.

Finally, much to her relief, he pulled away with a satisfied smile. Just as she got her thoughts in order, he smashed his lips against hers as he squeezed her body so tightly to his, she could feel his warmth engulfing her. She ended up lost in the moment, allowing her eyes to flutter shut as she gave him full control. He was more than happy and willing to take advantage, running his long wet tongue over her bottom lip, beckoning for entrance. Faye, having little experience in anything past a chaste kiss, kept her lips closed.

Elio let out a low growl, refusing to accept that he had been denied access to her. Moving one hand under her skirt, he squeezed her bottom, causing her to yelp in surprise. He shoved his tongue into her mouth, nearly gagging her. He half expected her to show resistance and anger towards him at the sudden intrusion, but she held a look of curiosity and confusion, as if she wasn't sure on what to do next. Could it be she had never done something like this before? If that was the case, then this was going to be much more fun and interesting than he thought.

He pushed down on her backside, forcing her to grind against him while he explored her mouth, drinking up her little mewls and whimpers. He tasted of whiskey and tobacco, two flavors she wasn't too fond of and yet she couldn't get enough. It was all so intoxicating to where she felt extremely light-headed and drunk on his affection. His lips melded so well to hers, and he was just so warm, like a large weighted blanket, it all just pushed her past cloud nine.

After what felt like an eternity, he pulled away, allowing her much needed air as he stared at her with a large grin and lust in his eyes. He licked his lips, savoring her sweet taste as he watched her reaction. She sat frozen, unsure of whether she should say something or move away from him. "You know, if you want to continue, I have no problem taking you back to my place." He purred, slowly moving her so that she was lying on her back against the seat. His face hovered over her as he took both her wrists in one hand. "What do you say?"

As tempting as his proposition was, she couldn't find it in herself to actually say yes. Faye already knew she was playing with fire by allowing this stranger to come to her house and drive her to god knows where. She might as well sign her own death certificate. "I… I still need to get home." She whimpered, wanting so badly to just say yes. For a brief second, his eyes flashed with a look of disappointment, but returned to normal as soon as he noticed her hesitation. He knew he couldn't keep her tonight. Too many questions would be asked and too many people would come sticking their nose in his business. "Alright fine. I'll let you go home, but you owe me another date." He gave a sharp toothed grin before pulling her into another heated kiss as if to seal the deal with her.

She squirmed the moment she felt his hand crawl up her skirt, inching closer to her clothed heat. Her legs kicked up as she struggled to pull out of his grasp, but her efforts showed to be futile. He had no problem at all keeping her pinned under him, using her as he pleased. He pulled away from the kiss to move his face back into the crook of her neck. "You smell amazing." He groaned, sliding his tongue up her neck. "Taste amazing as well." Faye's body was completely on fire, and it became almost too much for her. Confusion and panic set in and she was struggling between wanting him to go further and needing him to stop.

"Please… Ah… Stop…" she begged, listening to the more logical side of her brain. Upon hearing her pleas and seeing the tears that stained her eyes, he complied with her wishes, moving his hands away from her body and lifting himself off her. He helped her sit up, moving her back to his lap where he held her close, stroking her hair carefully. "It's okay. I will not force you to do it." He whispered in her ear, feeling her relax against him. "You've been so good for me all night doll, I just want you to relax." She nuzzled into his chest, inhaling his wonderful scent, as her eyes slowly fluttered shut and her body went limp in his arms. "You really had a long day, didn't you?" He chuckled, moving his jacket so that it would cover her.

Just as he started getting comfortable, Faye's phone rang, catching his attention. He nonchalantly pulled it from her purse, having no care at all for her privacy as he checked to see who could be trying to call her at this time. Narrowing his eyes, he scowled at the screen as it read May's name. What could she possibly want? Hitting answer, he held it up to his ear, waiting for her to speak. "Faye? Is everything okay? He didn't hurt you, did he?" Her voice was laced with worry and guilt as she spoke, her thick accent coming out in full force. "She's fine." Elio sneered, keeping his voice low, so he didn't wake the tired woman up. He could feel her terror through the phone the moment he spoke.

"Elio? Where's Faye? What are you doing with her phone?" She sputtered out. "She's right here, completely knocked out." Faye seemed to snuggle closer to him as he said that. "Please, just let her go. She has done nothing wrong." May begged, terrified for her friend's safety. "No, I don't think I will. She's way too interesting and entertaining for me to give her up. I ought to say thank you for handing her over to me." He smirked as he hung up, not giving her another chance to speak.

His face softened as he looked back down at the woman completely passed out in his lap. "She's trying to save you, but you don't look like you have any intention of being saved." He said teasingly, pecking her lips gently. "Even if you did, it's far too late for that. You belong to me now, doll." She mumbled a few incoherent words against his chest, completely oblivious to the world around her.

Elio started nudging her awake as they grew closer to her house. Her blue irises slowly blinked open, attempting to adjust to the light. "Sorry to wake you, doll, but I believe this is your stop." He said gently, nuzzling her head. She rubbed her eyes, trying to gather her bearings as she felt the vehicle come to a stop. It took her a second to process where she was, but when she did, she couldn't help but groan in protest of having to leave his warm and comfortable lap.

Once she was fully awake again, he opened the door and helped her out, keeping a tight grip on her waist as they went up the porch steps. "Thank you again for dinner. I had so much fun tonight." She said in gratitude. "So did I, and I can't wait to do it again." He cooed as he leaned over, stealing another kiss from her. "Me neither." She breathed out, her heart fluttering as he pulled away, making his way back over to the car. She stood there watching him leave with a big goofy grin on her face. Faye slowly walked into the house and collapsed on the couch, feeling nothing but excitement and giddiness as she touched her lips. "I hope we end up meeting again." She said to herself before preparing for bed.

It had been a few days since Faye went on that wonderful date with Elio, yet she still got butterflies thinking about how incredible the night was. The love bites he left on her neck didn't seem to help at all, especially when they were placed in spots that were difficult to hide. She found herself stuck wearing either a sweater or a scarf while she worked in order to maintain a level of privacy and professionalism. But working in an office full of nosy gossipers didn't help make that goal achievable.

"What's with the scarf?" One of the techs commented. "I mean, if you're that cold, you could just turn up the temperature." She pointed out. "You touch that thermostat and I'll kick your ass. I'm not cold, I'm just wearing this for… Different reasons." Faye retorted, adjusting the cloth. "She's trying to hide a bunch of hickeys she got from some guy she hooked up with the other night." A receptionist remarked while scanning in some paperwork. "Shit really? Damn, I didn't think you had it in you, Faye." The tech said in amazement. "No! We didn't hook up, we just went on a date! He just got a little… You know what, fuck you, I ain't got time to explain myself." Faye sputtered out.

"You went on a date? On a weekday?" The tech pressed on, practically eating up the juicy gossip. "Yeah, it's no big deal." She waved her off. "Where did you go?" The receptionist spoke up again. "He just took me to some nice little seafood restaurant called Crescent Moon." She shrugged. "Crescent Moon!?" This time a doctor chimed in, coming out of the treatment area. "Who the hell did you go out with that could afford to take you there?"

Faye rolled her eyes, irritated by this conversation. "It is literally not a big deal. He took me out. We had a wonderful time, that's it." She insisted. "I bet it's super crowded there. Heard that place takes months to book." The tech stated. "It was fine. I mean, once we got into our room, it was just us." She shrugged. "Your room?" "Yeah, our room. The place separates rooms so people have more privacy." She explained. "He got you a fucking private room? Jesus Christ Faye! Are you dating Tony fucking Stark?"

"Hey, I need you guys to keep it down in the pharmacy area. The clients do not need to hear your private conversations." The manager snapped, sticking her head out of the office doorway. "Hey Rachel, Faye's quitting!" The receptionist told her. "What the hell are you on about?" Faye asked. "You got a rich man now. You don't need this job anymore." She teased. The pharmacy tech let out an annoyed groan before telling the receptionist to get the hell out of her pharmacy so she could get back to work.

Since their date, Elio had been texting and calling Faye nonstop, attempting to persuade her to go out with him right away, but she completely shot the idea down. While she had a lot of fun, it left her feeling sore and tired, which nearly caused her to oversleep and show up late. As much as she liked the gentle giant, she still had bills to pay and mouths to feed, so she stayed adamant about not meeting until the weekend, eventually coming to a compromise that they could go out on Friday night after she got off. He begrudgingly agreed to it, realizing she would not back down with him.

While he found it rather adorable that she was putting her foot down over the matter, he couldn't help but feel extremely frustrated. Not only did he wait weeks to meet her, due to him only having a single photo to go off of, but he even allowed May to approach him instead of him approaching her. He could have easily taken the redhead captive and beat her until she gave up Faye's name and location, but he didn't. What's even worse was the one date he convinced her to go on hadn't been nearly enough to satiate his craving for the young woman.

Elio couldn't stop thinking about her, her beautiful laugh, her intoxicating smell, her soft, supple skin, her addictingly sweet flavor. Everything about Faye was an incredible experience. His desire for her was overflowing and yet, he remained patient, showing far more self-control than he had ever used in his life. A large part of him wanted to show up to her house, bash her door in, and snatch her up before she could even register what was happening, but he needed to keep that part of him under control. The last thing Elio wanted to do was give her a reason to run away from him and, unfortunately, abducting her would do just that. His only option now was to take out his pent up frustration on his work.

Recently, a rat had been discovered among his men giving out information to a rival gang that had been on his ass lately. While the man had put in some effort to hide his deception, it wasn't enough to keep him off Elio's radar, and soon he would find himself on the floor, tied up and squirming around like a pathetic little worm. Unfortunately for him, the mob boss wasn't feeling merciful that day. After yet another failed attempt at persuading Faye to spend the night with him, he really needed to blow off some steam before he accidentally said something cruel to his precious little doll.

"So you think you can stab me in the fucking back and get away with it, huh?" While his tone seemed calm, there was an edge to it that warned the man of his fate. "Ain't got nothing to say? What? Did you use up your last words on those bastards?" As he spoke, he pressed the heel of his shoe against the man's chest, slowly pushing down and squeezing every last breath of air out of him. Just before he could pass out, Elio lifted his foot off of him, allowing the man to gasp. "You're a fucking waste of oxygen, you know that?" He sneered in disgust.

"I... I..." the man attempted to say, but was quickly silenced by a smack to the face, causing his head to hit the concrete floor below him. "Fucking pathetic. Get the fuck up." Elio ordered, roughly kicking the man's body. Slowly, he lifted himself off the ground, only to be met with a harsh punch to the face, breaking his nose. "I said get up!" the mob boss snapped as he grabbed the man by his neck, dragging him back up to his feet. "For someone who talks too fucking much, you sure as hell don't know how to listen, do you?" He threw another punch that shattered the man's jaw, nearly destroying all his teeth.

The man fell back to his knees, fading in and out of consciousness. "Wake the fuck up. You ain't fucking dying until I tell you, you can." He snapped his fingers, signaling for one of his men to step forward. The gangster was holding a small syringe filled with a clear liquid. Its needle was the largest and thickest size available, insuring he felt every part piercing his skin. The gangster didn't wait for his boss to say anything before plunging the needle into the side of the man's neck, causing his eyes to shoot open as an unbearable pain rushed through his body like liquid magma flowing through his veins.

"Please…" He begged, but was stopped by another punch right to his stomach. "There you go again, running your fucking mouth." Elio taunted him with a malicious grin. "We're going to have to fix that." Two more of his men stepped forward, holding a box filled with various tools inside.

Just as the gangsters closed in on him, Elio's phone rang, the tone echoing off the walls. A murderous look fell on his face, which quickly softened up the moment he saw who was calling. "Hello doll. What's up?" He greeted the woman happily. "Oh, nothing much. I'm just at lunch right now and really wanted to talk to you." She answered, speaking the last part a little quieter. "Awe, you want to talk to me, do you? How cute." He cooed, smirking at the thought of her turning bright red from his words. She started sputtering off a retort when a loud yell sounded from the man, muffling up her words. "Hang on one second doll." He muted the phone before turning his attention to the dying rat. "How many times do I have to tell you to shut the fuck up?" He sneered, slamming the man's head against the wall, nearly killing him. "Leave, I'll finish him up." He dismissed the gangsters, who left without hesitation, not wanting to anger the mob boss more.

Taking the phone off mute, he began speaking to Faye again, keeping his foot planted on the rat's face. "Sorry about that doll. I was in the middle of something." He said in a far more lighthearted tone. "Oh, no it's fine. If this is a bad time, I can just call you back later." She felt guilty for interrupting him from his work. "Doll, for you, it ain't ever going to be a bad time." He purred, stomping down harshly on the man's skull, silencing him for good. "So, what do you want to talk about?" He discovered that no matter how angry and bloodthirsty he was feeling, talking to Faye seemed to always put him in a good mood.

"I wanted to see what you're up to." She sounded so adorable he just wanted to squeeze her tight and never let go. "Nothing really, just taking care of a rat." He replied, kind of telling the truth. "Got a rat problem? I'm sorry, that must really suck." She said sympathetically, unaware of what he actually meant. "It's not so much a problem anymore. I already killed it." He reassured her, trying not to laugh at how oblivious she was. "If you say so, but you should really put up some traps. Usually if there's one, there's a whole colony of them." She advised, which only made him chuckle. "You have a point. I might do that." He found himself agreeing with her judgment on the matter.

"When you catch them, make sure you release them far away from your house, otherwise they'll just come back." It was endearing of her to think he'd be merciful enough to actually let the rats live. "Is that what you do with the pests at your place?" He asked teasingly. "No, I rarely deal with them. That's what I have cats for. Though lately, Caligula has been making it a habit of leaving their corpses lying around the house." She laughed. "He's probably just sending a message to the other pests not to cross him. Got to respect that." He shrugged. "While you make a very valid point, it's still disgusting. I swear if I find one more decapitated water bug on my couch, I'm going to lose my mind." She gagged at the very thought of the little pests running around her house, getting ripped to pieces by her psychopathic cat.

"Shoot, my lunch is almost over." She sighed, wishing she had more time to chat with him. "Awe, really? But I was having so much fun chatting about dismemberment and pests." While he sounded playful, there was sincerity to his words. "It's unfortunate, but I really have to go. I'll talk to you later, though." She promised, wanting so badly to continue conversing with him. "Okay, I'll let you go, but call me on your next break. You know I love hearing your voice. It always brightens up my day." He purred, smirking at how flustered she sounded because of his insistent flirting.

They both said their goodbyes before ending the call, leaving Elio all alone with the dead corpse of a former gangster. His lips curled up into a sinister grin as he lifted the body off the ground. "My beautiful doll and her little pets have some interesting ideas, don't they?" He spoke out loud to himself, thinking that just like her cat, he had his own message to send out to the world, and maybe this disgusting little rat would be the perfect messenger.

The moment Faye ended the call with Elio, her phone rang again with her best friend's name popping up on the screen. "What's up?" She said into the speaker with a somewhat agitated tone. "Hey, bitch." He answered back, his voice aggressive yet playful. "Just calling to let you know that you, me, and Luca are going out Friday night. We want to take you bar hopping." Faye smiled, rolling her eyes at his demand. "Sorry Atlas, but I can't go. I have plans Friday night." She explained. "Fucking liar." He said accusatory. "Binging movies with your cats does not count as plans."

"First, yes it fucking does." She snorted out. "Second, how dare you. I have a life outside of work and you guys." "Bullshit." He retorted. "But seriously, are you really not able to make it?" His voice sounded more sincere. "No, sorry man. Believe it or not, I have a date."

A loud squeal that sounded from the background caused her to pull the phone away from her ear for a second. "Like a real date?" Atlas said in disbelief. "Not one of those fake ones that May finds for you? Cause you know those men are all a bunch of scumbags, right?" He had an underlying serious tone in his voice. "Relax, it's not like that," Faye reassured him. "Yes, May did technically introduce us, but I was the one who wanted to date him. She was absolutely against us dating." Somehow, that didn't make him feel any better about her going out with one of the mistress's acquaintances.

After a moment of silence, Atlas let out a resigned sigh, knowing that arguing with her was completely futile. "Look, I will not tell you who you can and can't date, but please be careful. If this guy makes you feel uncomfortable, text me immediately and I'll come up with an excuse to get you away from him, okay?" He wanted her to understand that no matter what, she could rely on him to help her out. "Dude, I'll be fine, I promise. So far, this guy has been super respectful of my boundaries. If anything, I'll probably make him feel uncomfortable." She retorted lightheartedly.

He couldn't help but roll his eyes, knowing how airheaded his best friend could be. "Just try not to get fucking kidnapped. Getting you back would be too much of a pain in the ass." He lightly teased, not wanting to be overly preachy with her. She was a grown woman, after all, and knew her own boundaries. "Don't bother. If I end up dead in a ditch, then maybe I won't have to come in on Monday." She shrugged. "You say that like those assholes, don't have a Ouija board on hand so they can summon your dumbass." She snickered at his comment. "Speaking of summoning me, I need to get back to work." She said, giving a quick goodbye before hanging up so she could carry on her day.

Chapter: 5

Faye counted down the days, hours, and even minutes until she got to see Elio again, which led to his constant teasing to break her down so she'd give in. As tempting as it was to just say screw it and let him pick her up, especially after some particularly stressful days, she just couldn't afford to give in to him. That didn't stop him from trying to convince her, though. In fact, it only caused him to get more creative with persuading her.

"This isn't very fair, you know." He commented during one of their casual conversations while she was on break. "What isn't fair?" She asked with one eyebrow raised and a soft smile on her face. "The fact that your coworkers get to have you every day and yet all I get is one short evening with you."

He sounded so sad and disappointed, it practically broke her heart. He had a point, after all. She did like him a lot, more than most people, especially her coworkers, so why was she only willing to spare a few hours for him? While she couldn't give up any of her workdays, as much as she really wanted to, perhaps there was more she could do so that they could spend time together. "I mean, I'm free all weekend, so it doesn't have to be one evening." She countered with a small giggle. "All weekend?" He repeated with a devilish smirk. "I think I can work with that. I'll just book us a hotel room to stay in."

She nearly choked on air after he said that, unsure if he was just joking around with her or if he was actually serious. "Isn't spending three nights alone with each other moving things along a bit too quickly?" She asked nervously. "No, of course not. It's actually a great opportunity for us to see how compatible we are with each other." He reassured her with his silver tongue, almost fully persuading her it was the best idea ever.

Faye went silent, weighing all the pros and cons of staying with him the whole weekend. As fun as it sounded, she still felt skeptical about his intentions. "This ain't going to end up like one of those true crime podcasts, is it?" She asked, half joking. "Why? Are you planning to butcher me the first chance you get?" He asked, easily playing along with her dark humor. "Nooo?" She trailed off, her voice going into a much higher pitch, which made him chuckle. "In that case, I'll pick you up Friday night and maybe, if I feel like it, I'll bring you back Sunday." Again she brushed it off as him just teasing her, unaware of just how serious he actually was.

"Fine, you win. I'll just have to find someone to watch my cats for the weekend. That way, they aren't left to fend for themselves." She gave in relatively easily to his request. "If you want, I can call up one of my *employees* and have them watch your cats," He offered, putting an emphasis on the word 'employees' that seemed to go unnoticed by her. "No, thank you. As much as I appreciate the thought, I'm a little picky about who interacts with them. They are pretty much my everything right now." After a few seconds of no response, she was worried she might have offended him. "Not that I think your employees are terrible people. I just need to know who they are before I can trust them." She attempted to backtrack.

He let out a hearty laugh, catching her off guard. She truly didn't know how right she was to be cautious of his men. "It's okay, doll, I totally get it. If I had someone that special to me, I'd do everything in my power to protect them. I wouldn't allow anyone I couldn't trust around them." He assured her he took no offense at her words, hoping to gain even more of her trust. "Thank you for understanding, and I seriously can't wait to see you again on Friday." She said happily before ending the phone call, leaving him feeling much more satisfied with the plans.

He, of course, would love to have more than the three nights, but he will compromise for the time being. Right now, he had a few phone calls that needed to be made, and a few men to send out so they could watch over his little doll. He too had someone special to him that needed to be protected after all.

Between dealing with difficult clients, issues with her order not coming in, and the overall demand for her to go beyond her job title, Faye felt absolutely drained. By Friday, she had somehow successfully scared most of her coworkers into completely backing off of her. They more than likely did not want to push the pharmacy tech into a severe mental breakdown.

Unfortunately, there were some who hadn't quite got the message yet, specifically three individuals in particular. The first one being her manager, who had been hounding her nonstop. It seemed every day that week there was some sort of complaint against her, not from any clients, but in the manager's twisted mind, that fact didn't matter. Being the only person in her area, she understood how everything fell on her when it came to medications, but it didn't mean they should blame her for every little thing that happened.

It was especially frustrating when the tasks she was being blamed for not getting done were supposed to be completed by a specific tech who had a tendency to leave it all up to the overworked woman to do. "Why are the syringes still sitting there?" The tech who had been second on her *eat shit and die* list asked in a demanding tone. "Because it's not in my job description to put your things away," Faye shot back, trying to concentrate on filling sixty capsules of benzonatate. "Wow, she's got a lot of attitude today, doesn't she?" And there goes the last and debatably worst individual on the list, trying to start drama as usual.

This recently hired kennel attendant had been causing her a lot of problems lately. For whatever reason she'd find him anywhere but kennel, which normally wouldn't bug her, not her section, not her problem, but he's proven to be an absolute menace. Every corner she turned, he was there, standing with the most obnoxious smirk she's ever seen. He'd usually make disgusting, bordering on sexually harassing, comments towards her which seemed to go completely unnoticed by management. She had attempted to report him a few times, but that only seemed to make things worse for her. Apparently, this place doesn't believe in the anti-retaliation laws and completely encourages harassment. A part of her wondered if the reason he has yet to see any consequences was because he's sleeping with the manager.

"Faye, you were told to do something by a lead. Now do it!" The manager sneered at her, causing her to lose count of the slippery golden capsules for the third time. In frustration, she poured the pills back in the bottle and threw her counting tray on the ground before storming off to the break room. "Where are you going?" The tech called out, still not getting the hint. "On a break! And you'll be lucky if I come back!" She snapped, slamming the door shut.

She started pacing back and forth, mumbling profanities as she tried to calm herself down. This whole week had been terrible for sure, and she was on the verge of a panic attack. It wasn't just the three stooges that were causing her grief, either. Outside of work, she felt completely on edge, having the strange sense that she was constantly being watched. No matter where she went, she'd notice some old car following her around. While they never got too close to her, nor did they make a bunch of risky turns to keep up, it was consistent enough for her to notice their presence.

What made things worse for her was all the body parts that started turning up around her area. While she was almost certain it had to do with the active gang wars going on, which she only knew about through friends, it didn't make it any less unsettling for her to pull up to her grocery store only for it to be surrounded by cops after a body had been discovered inside a dumpster. She actually got a glimpse of the corpse, and it looked absolutely wrecked. The whole thing was mangled up like a semi had run it over, and there seemed to be obvious parts of the body missing. As far as she could tell from news broadcasts, the police could not identify the corpse. It went without saying they had no suspects or leads of any kind.

That was only the beginning. A part of a finger was found at the park near her house. She did not know whether it was related to the body, but it seemed a little too close in events for it to just be a coincidence. That wasn't even the worst thing found, either.

They had found a human heart on a table at some restaurant near her work. It started feeling way more personal at that point, especially after only two days, and her paranoia was going through the roof. A part of her wanted to call in for the rest of the week and stay home, where she felt the safest, but she had far too much pride. If she hid away from every little inconvenience, she'd never come out. Besides, she had bills to pay and mouths to feed, so she really couldn't afford to be scared. There was also her date with Elio to look forward to that kept her pushing forward.

Just as she got her heart rate down and pushed past the tears, her phone rang. "Hello?" She answered, cringing at the way her voice cracked. "Doll? Is everything okay?" Elio asked with concern in his voice. "Yes, I'm just a little stressed out, but it's fine." She attempted to reassure him, but the break in her voice gave away just how terrible she was doing. "You don't have to pretend with me. If you're having problems, you can tell me. I don't mind listening." He promised her, practically begging her to tell him what's wrong. "It's honestly no big deal. Just some petty coworker drama."

As much as she really needed someone to vent to, it didn't seem right to overwhelm him with her problems. "Doll, if you don't tell me what's wrong, I'm going to come down to your work and steal you away from them." He threatened, which made her laugh. He could feel himself heating up at the sound, falling for her even deeper. Now he really needed to know who's been causing her problems.

"There's been a lot of harassment this week and it's just been a bit too much." She finally admitted what her problems were while he silently listened, keeping a mental note of everything. "Who's been harassing you?" He asked, trying to hide the growl in his voice. "My manager and one of the lead techs are on some power tripping bullshit, which is normal, but now I have this kennel attendant up my ass constantly, and he's only gotten worse since I reported him." She sighed as she leaned against the door. "Why did you report him?" He asked both out of curiosity and also to justify a reason to go after this man.

"He grabbed my ass. They tried to write me up for slapping him, but that didn't go over too well when I wrote on my report the number to my lawyer. He hasn't physically harassed me since, but that doesn't stop him from going after me any chance he can get. I wish he would just drop dead already, you know?"

What she didn't realize was just how much Elio was holding back. He didn't know this guy, and yet he already hated everything about him. Unfortunately, there wasn't a lot he could do right then without causing serious problems for Faye. She's already put in complaints and used self-defense, so if something were to happen to him, she would be the first person the cops questioned. He didn't want to have any unwanted attention thrown her way.

"If you want, I could put a hit on him." He jokingly offered, hoping that would cheer her up. "That is very tempting, but I'll have to say no. My lawyer would lose his mind if he found out I accidentally put another hit out on someone." She giggled, sounding much calmer and happier than before. "Damn, guess I better call off my men," He teased earning another giggle from her. Her laugh was so euphoric, he could just listen to it all day.

"So, what did you want to talk about?" She asked, taking a small breath to stop her giggles. "I just wanted to talk about tonight and how excited I am to spend the *whole* weekend with you." He purred, wishing he could see just how flustered she looked. "You know, I was thinking, since you're having such a rough day, maybe I can take some of that stress away and pick you up straight from work, that way you don't have to worry about driving all the way home." He was trying to be sly with her, allowing his impatience to take the lead. "Elio, as much as I want to see you as soon as possible, I can't." She declined his proposal in the nicest way she could.

His smile fell upon hearing her rejection, but he was not ready to take no for an answer. "And why not?" He asked, hiding his irritation. "Well, for starters, I have nothing to wear. All my things are still at my house and I'm kind of a hot mess right now. I would prefer to freshen myself up before we meet." She argued, pointing out the obvious.

It sounded like his little doll wanted to play hard to get, well he didn't mind playing along. "No need to worry about any of that. I already have a few outfits picked out for you to wear, plus we'll be heading straight over to the hotel so you can get cleaned up there. Though, being a hot mess isn't necessarily a bad thing. I find it rather cute." He cooed, causing her to blush.

"What about my car? I can't leave it parked here for three days. Plus, I'll need it to get to work on Monday." If he had it his way, she wouldn't be returning to work Monday, but he'd worry about that later. "I can have someone come pick it up and drop it off at your place. That way, you don't have to think about it. It would also save you gas." He added the last part to sweeten the deal. She thought about it for a moment. "And what about my cats?" She asked. "Didn't you say you have someone coming by to watch them? I can have my employee stick around until she shows up just to make sure everything is all good. I promise he won't hurt them."

Faye thought about all his retorts, realizing it wasn't a terrible idea. It probably wouldn't kill her to let him pick her up from work, and it might even give her a chance to rest up on the car ride to the hotel. When weighing the pros and cons, there were hardly any reasons to say no to his request. "I guess when you put it like that, there isn't really any harm in letting you pick me up." She relented, smiling at the soft cheer he gave at her acceptance. "Good, I can't wait to see you soon." He responded happily, ending the call before she could change her mind.

Faye stood there for a couple of minutes, attempting to process what had just happened. Did she really just agree to let him pick her up from work? What the hell was wrong with her? 'Just go with it.' She thought to herself. 'It might be better in the long run if I don't have to worry about traffic or anything.' With that, she left the break room and got back to work.

Chapter: 6

Time ticked by slowly as she continued on with her long and frustrating day waiting for the magical time that is 5:00 to finally hit. After spilling half a bottle of liquid enrofloxacin onto herself, she made a trip over to the bathroom to scrub the disgusting suspension off of her. The smell was positively horrendous, comprising the flavor combo of artificial chicken and marshmallow. 'Whoever created this flavoring is a complete sadist.' She thought bitterly to herself as she ran her scrub top under some hot water, covering it in some watered down hand soap.

There was a washing machine in the building, but it was primarily used to wash the blankets and towels that the animals slept on in their kennels. That didn't mean it was off limits to use for this situation. It would only mean she'd have to put it in with whatever laundry was being washed. The thought of throwing her clothes in with whatever the blankets were covered in made her want to throw up.

While she wasn't all too happy with how her scrub top looked, she felt it was manageable enough for her to wear the rest of her shift. Before slipping it back on, she sprayed it down with some air freshener in order to get rid of the lingering smell and threw it over her office chair to let it air dry for a few minutes. Luckily she had on an undershirt, giving her the luxury of going topless for a little while, though it was an oversized graphic t-shirt that seemed a little too unprofessional. The manager would have to get over herself. It was this, or she wore nothing, and she didn't think her coworkers really wanted to see her naked.

She went to work on cleaning up the suspension, grumbling angrily to herself about wasted material. A pair of eyes burned straight into her head, causing her to feel even more annoyed. "Don't you have something better to do than watch me clean?" She sneered, not even bothering to face the obnoxious kennel attendant. "Nope. Walks aren't until 5, so I have plenty of time to watch you shake that little ass of yours." He smirked, pretending to get some water. "Leave me the fuck alone, Chuck!" she snapped, doing her best to keep herself from throwing the dirty rag at his disgusting, perverted face.

"Watch your language!" The manager shouted from her office. "And get back to work, Chuck!" Finally, she said something to the jerk. Not wanting to take any chances, the kennel attendant fled the pharmacy to go back to his corner of the hospital. 'That's what I thought. Take your creepy uncle looking ass back to the kennel and leave me alone.' She thought to herself, not wanting to risk her job by saying it out loud.

The day was long and seemingly unending, but finally it was time for her to leave. Faye felt exhausted and gross, thinking there was no way she actually looked even remotely put together for her date. It was very tempting for her to call Elio and try to convince him to let her go home to shower but judging by her last experience with trying to get a raincheck from him; she knew she had better chances of winning the lottery than changing his mind. Instead, she did the next best thing and made a trip back to the bathroom so she could at least attempt to freshen herself up.

The moment she stepped in front of the mirror, Faye wanted to scream. Hot mess was the biggest understatement of the year. Her clothes were covered in pill dust and animal fur, along with a bit of blood that came from who knows where. She had dark bags under her eyes and her face was unusually pale because of her lack of sleep, honestly, she wouldn't have been surprised if she found rats living in her hair with how tangled up and frizzy it had become due to her constantly pulling on it. If she had a rope, she would have hung herself right then and there so that she wouldn't have to face the sweet and loving man that was waiting for her outside.

Sighing in defeat, she opened up her purse, pulling out a small travel size brush that she now felt grateful her mother insisted she carry everywhere. Faye figured if anything, she could at the very least straighten out this terrible mess of tangled yarn that she called hair. There wasn't much she could do for her face aside from washing it with cold water, but she figured she could spray herself with more air freshener just so Elio wouldn't have to suffer whatever smells lingered around her due to her job. At least she didn't work directly with any of the animals, otherwise she knew it would be ten times worse.

It took a few minutes, but she finally got herself to a place where she was somewhat decent looking, though she still wasn't satisfied with her looks. Unfortunately, she would need a hot shower, shampoo, body soap, and a lot more time to meet that level of expectation. For now, this would have to be enough. Besides, it was extremely rude of her to keep her date waiting. Oh well, at least he seemed patient enough.

Elio paced around in the parking lot outside of his SUV as he waited for the pharmacy tech to finally come out of the hospital. He was more than tempted to stomp into the building and pull her out by her feet kicking and screaming, but he silenced his impatient thoughts, knowing that going through with a stunt like that would only cost him his progress with Faye. Luckily, she was smart enough to send him a text warning that she'd be a little late. She was such a sweet and thoughtful girl, making sure he didn't think for a second she was going to ghost him. It's not like she could, even if she wanted to. He'd do everything in his power to stop her from running away.

After what felt like an eternity, he finally spotted the pharmacy tech dragging her feet through the back door with her head hung low. She looked absolutely exhausted, as though she were on the verge of passing out. Worried that she might just drop dead against the sharp rocks, he quickly made his way over to her, opening his arms so that she could fall into his embrace.

Her eyes lit up with joy at the sight of the large man as she wasted no time jumping into his arms, allowing him to hug her tightly. "I take it you missed me just as much as I missed you." He teased, kissing the top of her head. "Very much…" she mumbled into his chest. "You know how tempting it was to just say screw it and stomp out of that building?" He couldn't help but chuckle at her question. "I assume it was about as tempting as it was to drag you out of there." He retorted, slowly dragging her into the parking lot where his vehicle was parked.

He let go of Faye with hesitation so he could open the door for her. Just as she was about to enter, she felt something run straight into her legs. Looking down, a miniature golden doodle was clinging on to her leg, crying its little head off. "Miss Choco!" Faye exclaimed, astonished to see the young pup in the middle of the street. "What are you doing out of your kennel?" She quickly scooped Choco up into her arms, scared that the poor sweet pooch would run further out into the road.

As Faye slipped away from Elio with the dog cradled gently against her chest, she made her way back to the hospital so she could figure out what happened. The man's face darkened as she walked away from him, glaring menacingly at the annoying pest that dared to steal his doll away from him. He followed her back to the building, knowing that he would upset her if he took out his frustrations on the small dog, so he instead wanted to find out who was responsible for this annoying distraction.

Faye stopped abruptly, her eyes narrowed and her nose scrunched up as she glared daggers at what had been the bane of her existence the last few days. There stood that useless kennel attendant wearing a cocky smirk on his face as he held up an empty slip lead. "What the fuck happened?" She asked, trying her hardest not to scream at the arrogant man. "She got out." He shrugged nonchalantly. "Accidents happen." She wanted so badly to slap the smirk off his face, but with her holding Choco and Elio standing right next to her, she had to keep her cool. "She got out, and you did not try to get her back?" She retorted in exasperation. "Like I'd run out into the middle of the fucking street to catch some dumb dog. Are you actually that stupid?"

The longer this exchange went on, the more patience Elio lost. He already knew taking his anger out on the dog was completely out of the question, but this little punk was another story. This man seemed to take great pleasure in egging Faye on, probably knowing there wasn't anything she could actually do to him without creating problems for herself. Now that he thought about it, this guy seemed to match the exact description Faye gave of the man who had been harassing her. That would make complete sense, given her reaction and the way she held back when she wanted to say and do more. This man clearly thought of himself as being untouchable. Elio kept note of that, thinking of all the ways he could show him how unrealistic that idea truly was.

"Well, give me the fucking mutt back then, you dumb bitch!" He snapped, reaching out to the angry woman. Before he could even get close enough to grab her, Elio quickly pulled Faye away from the terrible man, pushing himself in-between the two. She turned bright red in embarrassment at the realization that her date had watched the whole argument go down.

"I'm sorry…" she apologized quietly to the large man, though he hardly heard her as his attention and anger were fully directed towards the man standing in front of him, who looked much less confident in himself. "Do you want to repeat yourself?" Elio asked in a calm yet threatening tone. He knew he really shouldn't interfere with her business, but he couldn't help himself. Especially not after this asshole dared to insult her in front of him.

"W-well I… Um… I'll just take the dog back so you two can get back to your…" "I'll give her to one of the techs." Faye interrupted, not wanting to humor the jerk. "And I'll make sure they file a report against you… Jackass." She grumbled the last part under her breath as she marched back into the building, leaving the kennel attendant and Elio alone.

"Look, whatever you think is going on, that's just how we banter. It's all in good fun." The attendant attempted to backtrack, feeling nothing but dread under the stoic gaze of the larger man. "Is it now? So much fun. She had to file a complaint against you?" He sneered, containing his rage as best as he could, knowing this wasn't the time and place for it. "Complaint? Oh, come on, she only did that because she was upset I rejected her."

As much as he tried to sound genuine, Elio could easily tell the man was talking out of his ass. This worthless pile of garbage more than likely used something similar to this defense to charm Faye's boss. If that's the case, he was a bigger problem than he initially thought. "You will leave her alone." He warned the pathetic man, silencing his nonsense. "Or else what?" Chuck retorted, once again feeling cocky. "This isn't a request or a threat. I'm telling you what will happen. You ain't ever going to bother *my* girl again. I'll make damn sure of it." He inched closer to the man with a deadly aura surrounding him.

Before the kennel attendant could stutter out a response, Faye came back from dropping off Choco. "Since you can't even be bothered to do your damn job properly, I gave her to a vet tech. They said they'll help you finish the walks so you're not *overwhelmed.*" She told him with bitterness in her voice, once again feeling as though her concerns were just going to be swept under the rug. Elio made a quick phone call before wrapping his arm around Faye's waist, guiding her away from the creepy kennel attendant.

They walked back out into the parking lot, making their way towards the large vehicle. Elio opened the door, practically pushing her in so there wouldn't be another chance for her to be pulled away from him. He followed her into the car with a soft look on his face. "Is everything good?" He asked, concerned over her wellbeing. "Yeah." She replied, a little quieter than normal. "Luckily, she wasn't injured." He felt bothered by the girl's demeanor, knowing it was completely out of character for her to act so meek.

"That's good." He spoke with a calm voice as he pulled her into his lap. "What about you? Are you okay?" Faye shook her head and took a deep breath. "I'll be fine. Just angry right now." She sighed. Elio stroked her hair, being mindful of the tangles in it. She couldn't see it, but he had a cold, murderous look in his eyes. He was going to make this pile of garbage suffer for ruining his doll's mood.

She found it difficult to keep her eyes opened as she sat nuzzled against him, nodding off while attempting to keep up a conversation. Elio didn't mind at all as he was content with simply holding her close, allowing her to fall asleep on him. Faye did exactly that, finding that his lap, strangely enough, felt safe and secure, as though it was okay to relax. He was just so warm and his scent, a mix of tobacco and nice, mild smelling cologne, was just so intoxicating. It didn't take long for her to give into temptation and allow herself to go into a deep sleep, practically wrapped in his large jacket.

Elio enjoyed watching Faye, who clung tightly to his dress-shirt, sleep peacefully. "How much sleep do you get, doll? You shouldn't go around passing out in random places." He teased, while kissing the top of her head gently. She mumbled into his shirt, complete gibberish, though he could swear he heard her say something about strawberry lemon gum. He was absolutely delighted with how cute the young woman acted around him. She showed no worry or fear and didn't ask questions, which he'd normally be suspicious of, but there was something about her that made him feel as though he could trust her.

He'd never tell her this, but the reason he demanded that they meet up right when she got off was so he could see her at her worst. Eight hours of work and stress would surely make her look and act horrendously unattractive, and he would undoubtedly lose interest in the woman instantly moving on with his life. But for some strange reason, seeing her in this state did the exact opposite for him. He wanted to remove her tattered and stained scrubs along with her worn down shoes that were at the end of their lifespan and decorate her in the finest fabrics.

He desired nothing more than to set her unconscious body onto a large, soft bed and pull her close so that she could have some of the best sleep ever. Seeing this beautiful, angelic woman at her lowest gave him the yearning to take her away from all her stress so that she could thrive at his side. Every time he attempted to topple that pedestal he placed her on, it only grew in size and strength, making it almost impossible for him to even dent it.

A low ringing sound ruined the moment of tranquility he drifted off into, thinking about all the wonderful things he'd do to his doll. Faye's face twitched a bit, but otherwise, she remained undisturbed by the sudden noise. He dug his phone out of his pocket, hitting answer with more force than necessary. "What?" He growled quietly into the phone. "Sir… We have a bit of an issue." A pathetic voice squeaked out from the other end. "A bit? Deal with it, I'm busy." He snapped. He could hear the young gangster trembling on the other end. "It's Mike Ladner, Sir. He wants to meet with you immediately." 'That bastard.' Elio thought, gritting his teeth. "What the fuck does he want?" He kept his volume in check so as not to awaken the young woman sound asleep in his lap. "It's about the weapons deal. He wants to negotiate a contract, but is only willing to do it with you."

He had to think about it for a moment, not wanting to put off his time spent with Faye. As much as he wanted nothing more than to spend the rest of the day with her, this deal, unfortunately, needed to take priority. "Fine, tell the old bastard I'll be over there in three hours and that he better not waste my fucking time." He sneered before ending the call so that he could turn his attention back to Faye. "Sorry, doll." He mumbled into her hair. "I was looking forward to spending the whole night alone with you, but our plans will just have to wait." She mumbled out a 'tis okay' not understanding a single thing he said to her. "Don't worry though, I'll be bringing you with me, so you're not all by yourself in a strange room." He whispered in her ear, wondering if she could actually hear him in her state.

Chapter: 7

As they approached their destination, Faye's eyes fluttered open, her body stiff from the position she was in. Gaining awareness, she looked up to meet Elio's eyes, embarrassment flashing through her own. "Ah beans, did I fall asleep again?" She felt mortified at how quickly she fell asleep on him, but wanted to play it cool. "I'm sorry. That must have been uncomfortable for you." She said sincerely. "It's alright, doll. I was just enjoying the view, anyway." He gave her a sharp toothed grin. "Oh, I guess the city can be weirdly beautiful." She commented, oblivious to his attempt at flirting. "Especially at night when all the lights are on." He raised an eyebrow, smiling genuinely at her cluelessness.

The vehicle came to a sudden stop, causing Faye to fall back into Elio's chest. He wrapped his arms around her, keeping her pressed against him as he nuzzled the top of her head. She pushed herself away from him, much to his dismay, so she could take in her surroundings. Her jaw nearly dropped when she saw where he brought her. The hotel they were planning to stay in was grand and extremely luxurious. From the checkerboard tiles leading up to the front entrance to the large pond with a powerful fountain system which created a gorgeous water show, she was absolutely awestruck.

Upon realization that she was refusing to move out of pure shock, Elio slipped one arm under her legs and wrapped the other around her waist, easily picking her up and sliding her out of the SUV. She let out a small squeak at the sudden movement, clinging on to his shoulders for dear life. "Are you sure we're in the right place? I mean, you got to know by now I don't do well at these fancy places, right? I'm kind of like a bull in a China shop." She attempted to joke, but her voice gave away her uncertainty. "It's okay, doll, you'll be just fine." He reassured her with a peck to her lips before carrying her into the building bridal style.

Once they made it into the lobby, Elio gently sat Faye on the ground, making sure she was fine. As he brushed her off, she pulled him down by the collar of his shirt and smashed her lips against his, pulling him into a heated embrace. His face burned bright red as he sputtered a bit, caught completely off guard by her sudden boldness. She gave a cheeky smile, mentally celebrating her victory at finally making him flustered for once. Her victory was short-lived, however, as he didn't seem to take her actions too lightly.

Elio grabbed her chin and pulled her close to his face with a predatory gleam in his eyes. "When I get you all alone, I'm going to fucking break you so bad you'll only crave my touch." He growled, his sharp teeth nicking her lips, turning them slightly red from her blood. He swiped his tongue over the beads of blood, savoring her sweet and metallic taste. She took in a shaky breath, her face bright red at his words. 'Okay, he won this round.' She thought to herself, ignoring all the strange looks from the surrounding guests. He wrapped his arm

36

around her waist, pulling her along while he wore a satisfied smirk on his face, leading her over to the front desk.

An exhausted-looking woman sat at the desk, typing away at the computer when the couple approached her, Faye offering a sincere smile while Elio held a neutral look on his face. The receptionist seemed to completely ignore the young woman in lieu of giving her full attention to the large, handsome man. She made no effort in attempting to hide her obvious flirting as she gave Faye constant side eye glances. Elio, in all his respect for his date, did not even bother to humor her attempts. He was far more interested in getting his blue-eyed beauty all alone so he could finally have her. All he wanted was for this broad to just hurry already and give him the room key.

Elio put on a little show so as not to scare his date by making very light conversation with the woman at the desk, but his patience started running thin. Faye only halfway listened to the small talk, noting that whenever she made a pass at him, he'd politely reject her. 'Shameless.' She thought. 'Hitting on a man who's clearly taken.' Though she wouldn't blame him if he ended up ditching her for a woman like that.

The receptionist was just so beautiful and put together, the exact opposite of her, but he was clearly not interested in her. Still, that bitter look she kept shooting her was starting to really get to her. 'Time to put on my people pleaser face.' Faye thought, deciding it was best to douse the hostility before it got out of hand.

"Your hair is absolutely beautiful." She spoke up, grabbing the attention of both the receptionist and Elio. "Oh, thank you…" the girl mumbled, blushing a bit at the compliment. "Where did you get it done? The colors are just so vibrant." She held a sincere smile as she asked, causing the woman's heart to flutter. "I did it myself, actually." She smiled proudly, loving the attention. "Really?" Faye exclaimed. "That's incredible. I wish I had that type of talent. Half the time I struggle to even brush out my hair."

The girl gave a lighthearted laugh. "I'm actually planning to go back to school next semester so I can become a hair stylist, maybe even open my own salon one day. I'm just saving up money right now. You know how it is." She shrugged nonchalantly. "Oh, I understand the struggle. But you should totally go for it. I would love to have you do my hair someday." Faye smiled, happy to ease the tension a bit. "You have pretty nice hair, honestly. Kind of like a doll's hair. It would be fun to work on." She pointed out, eyeing the messy blonde locks. "Well, good, because I'll be expecting perfection from you," Faye teased, sending the receptionist into a fit of giggles before she finally handed Elio the key card and waved goodbye to them.

"What was that about?" Elio asked as they stepped into an elevator. He pushed a button, allowing the doors to shut as he kept his gaze on her. "She seemed upset. I figured I'd try to cheer her up." Faye responded with a goofy smile, which made him chuckle quietly. "Did she? I didn't notice." He hummed, wrapping his arm back around her waist. "Woman's intuition." She shrugged, leaning her head against his side. "That makes absolutely no sense." He commented, wanting her to clarify her statement. "There was something about her vibe that felt off. She looked kind of broken, so I figured I'd say something to cheer her up." He gave her a strange look but dropped the topic.

Faye stood next to Elio, wearing a nervous expression on her face as she watched the floors go by. He kept his eyes on her the whole ride, acting as though if he looked away for even a second, she would disappear. It made her feel a little insecure about her looks, realizing she was still wearing her old stained up scrubs. She still didn't understand why he was so determined to pick her up straight from work instead of letting her go home and get changed. Was it really necessary for him to see her in such a disastrous state? Everything about this whole date was strange, and yet she continued to go along with it even though she hardly knew the man standing next to her. At least he was cute and funny.

Finally, after what felt like an eternity, the elevator came to a stop. The moment the silver doors slid open, Elio wasted no time escorting her out into the long hallway, pulling her along excitedly. There was something about his giddiness that unlocked a level of joy in her, reminding her of when she was a little girl going to her friend's house for the first time.

She always felt extremely nervous in those moments, not wanting to upset her friend or any of their relatives and yet they were always excited to show her their house as if she were the missing piece to the puzzle that was their happiness. It brought a level of satisfaction in her to be the one that made others happy.

They stopped in front of a door near the end of the hallway. Elio pulled out the key card and quickly swiped it over the reader, waiting for the clicking noise. The moment it opened, he ushered her inside, closing the door, leaving them all alone together. Faye stood there, taking in everything with eyes as wide as saucers. The room was huge, way bigger than any place she's ever stayed in, and judging by the area they were in and the hotel he chose, this couldn't have been cheap.

The room itself was separated into three sections. The first section was the bed area where a large king-sized mattress sat on top of a beautiful golden frame. The mattress had on top a large white comforter with a silver trim going around it. The head held four big fluffy pillows neatly tucked inside black pillow cases, while the foot of the bed had a black bed scarf going across it, with the same silver trim as the comforter.

She couldn't help but blush at the realization that she would share a bed with Elio during their stay, which shouldn't have come as a surprise. 'I mean, we're technically a couple, of course we'd be sharing a bed.' She rationalized with herself, knowing it was such a small thing to get flustered over. She spent the whole car ride passed out in his lap after all, so she should really be used to 'sleeping' with him by now.

Shaking the perverse thoughts out of her head, she focused on the other aspects of the room. Past the bed there was a lounge area separated by a small, cute black gate. A small gray loveseat sat next to a couple of plush chairs, surrounding a mini bar area. A large window sat near them with two giant grey curtains decorated with an elegant floral pattern which lined the bottom. A golden handle sat on one side, allowing them to open it up into a large balcony that oversaw the city. She walked towards it, her curiosity controlling her movements.

She stepped closer and closer, reaching her hand out to the curtain when she felt a weight on her shoulder, stopping her in her place. Looking up, she saw Elio had grabbed on to her, slowly guiding her away from the balcony. "Sorry, doll, but we got some things to do that are pretty time sensitive." He said apologetically, pulling her into a tight hug. "And as beautiful as you are, I'm sure you probably want to get out of your work clothes. Blood stained scrubs ain't in style yet." He joked, giving her a wink. "Ah man." She snapped her fingers in disappointment. "Someone clearly misinformed me. I better call up my stylist then I got words for them." She teased. "Don't be a smartass." He warned, caressing her sides.

Shaking off the strange yet pleasant feeling, she pulled away from his embrace. "But that's my favorite thing." She whined with a cute smile. He couldn't help but laugh, feeling completely relaxed around her. "Doll, I swear if you don't keep that pretty mouth shut and behave, I'm going to have to punish you." His voice grew deeper as he made his way towards the bed, pulling out a bright red bag that sat next to it. He tossed it over to her carelessly, giving her a lighthearted chuckle as she fumbled the bag. She stuck her tongue out at him with a childish pout. "I said behave," He growled, playfully. "Make me!" She retorted before quickly running off to the bathroom the moment she saw him move. "That's what I thought!" He called out to her with a smirk. Oh, the things he wanted to do with that pretty little smart mouth of hers, but he would control himself for now.

Faye made her way into the bathroom, unable to contain her large smile as her heart raced. She had fallen so hard for him that every minute she spent with the man felt like she was closer to melting into a puddle of mush. There was no way she could handle a whole weekend dealing with his constant teasing and flirting.

Wasting no time at all, she stripped out of her work attire so she could make her way into the shower, shivering as the cold air hit her nude form. This was so strange, being naked in a hotel bathroom with some guy she's barely known for a week, and yet it felt so incredibly exciting. Faye was no fool and understood the end goal for him was more than likely to sleep with her, but it was the small chance he wanted something more that kept it interesting.

As she stepped into the shower, Faye looked around at her surroundings. There were different shampoos and soaps laid out neatly on the surrounding shelves, obviously brought to the hotel for her personal use. She couldn't recognize any of the brands, but they looked both exotic and expensive, items she'd never even dream of owning. It felt almost wrong for her to use such pricey products, but it wasn't as though she had any choice in the matter. After all, Elio refused to let her go home and grab her own things, so using them was her only option. Besides, if he didn't want her touching them, why would he bother to bring them?

Turning on the water, she let the hot steam caress her aching muscles, relieving some of the tension from earlier in the day. She poured a dollop of shampoo in her hand, running it through her tangled locks to help loosen them up. A look of disgust made its way to her face as she felt a hardened piece of hair that more than likely had some dried up medication stuck in it. She carefully worked her fingers through the thick sludge, removing it completely, leaving her hair feeling slick and soft.

Faye let out a content sigh, basking in the wonderful aroma that was her body wash. The smell of rose and vanilla surrounded her like a comfortable blanket, staining her skin with the scent. She thought for a moment about how vulnerable she was standing in the shower with nothing but the steam to cover her up. If Elio wanted to, he could easily take advantage of her, and yet she completely trusted him not to.

After thoroughly washing her body off, she slipped out of the shower, wrapping herself up in a fluffy white towel. She looked at herself in the mirror and rolled her eyes in annoyance at the dark circles that were forming. "I really need to get better sleeping habits." She mumbled to herself while reaching over to the ruby colored brush that sat next to the sink. Faye figured she'd deal with whatever horrors awaited her in the strange bag after she dealt with her hair and face.

"Doll, are you almost done in there?" Elio called out, trying not to sound too irritated. "Yeah, just trying to make myself look pretty right now!" she shouted back, applying some eyeliner and mascara to her eyes. "Why is it taking so long, then? You're already beautiful!" He argued, which made her laugh, as she finished up her makeup that she was so grateful she remembered to bring. 'God forbid he sees me looking natural.' She thought to herself sarcastically.

Finally, it was time for her to open the bag and see what this man brought for her to wear out with him. "Oh, what the hell is this?" She asked as she pulled out a red lacey bra with matching underwear. Her nose scrunched up as her face went bright red, unsure if he seriously thought it appropriate to buy her lingerie on the second date. "There is no way this actually fits." She said skeptically, figuring it was best not to ask too many questions. Slowly, she slipped on the underwear, feeling absolutely shocked that it actually fit. "Nope. Not going to ask. Just going with it." She shook her head, figuring she'd deal with this problem later.

Looking back in the mirror, she adjusted the straps, noting how nicely the bra shaped her breasts. She still didn't understand how he got her size after only meeting once, but then again, she didn't really want to know. "Don't make me come in there!" Elio once again teased her. "Patience is a virtue, you know!" she stated with her hands on her hips. "It ain't a virtue I carry!" He retorted, earning another giggle from her. "I'm almost done, I swear!"

Faye turned back to the bag, looking to see what other surprises lay hidden for her. The next thing she pulled out was a very elegant wine red dress. While it went down to her ankles, the front of the skirt was cut shorter than the back, allowing her legs to be seen. The top had a heart-shaped cut, and two straps connected the back to the front of the top, keeping the dress secure. She noticed it hit every curve just right, showing off her body better than anything she had ever worn before. Faye was so impressed that he got her dress size without asking. She was even willing to wear her rose-tinted shades so she wouldn't see any of the clear red flags. 'He's good at this. I should ask him to pick out all my outfits.' She giggled to herself.

Finally she got to the very last piece of her outfit, and what terrified her the most, the shoes. As funny as it would be to slip on her old, worn out sneakers and wear them out on their date, she wasn't too sure Elio would appreciate the humor in it. Taking a deep breath, she reached back into the bag one last time, pulling out the most beautiful pair of flats she's ever seen. She sighed in relief seeing that they did not have heels on them, meaning no unwarranted trips to the hospital that night. Slipping them on, Faye once again felt impressed. He got her shoe size correct. She'd, of course, ask him about it later, but for now all she could think about was how incredible this weekend would be.

She placed her old work clothes into the bag neatly and made her way out of the bathroom with a skip to her step. Elio sat on one of the lounge chairs with his feet propped up on the coffee table near him. As nervous as she felt, she couldn't help the giddiness that beckoned her over to the large man, and before she could even think, she was already standing in his line of vision. "Well?" She asked, doing a little spin for him.

He looked her up and down with that same predatory gleam he held earlier, as if he were ready to pounce on her. Without uttering a single word, Elio rose from his spot and reached out to grab her. She let out a squeal of surprise as she found herself in his arms once again, clinging on to his shoulders for dear life. Finally he released her, dropping her onto the bed where she nearly bounced off it. She looked up at him with sparkling blue jewels, waiting in confusion for him to make his next move.

"Elio..? Mph!?" Before she could ask what he was doing, his lips were over hers in a matter of seconds, completely silencing her words. He had his hands planted on both sides of her head, completely caging her in while he forced his legs in between hers, slowly grinding against her. She felt his tongue swipe against her bottom lip, begging her to open up. Having been surprised and feeling lightheaded, Faye parted her lips, taking in his long, slick tongue.

"To answer your question…" He started, barely pulling away before going back in for more. "I think you look perfect… So perfect. In fact, I almost want to call off all our plans just so I can have you." She was so focused on his mouth and the feeling of his tongue exploring her, she hadn't even noticed his hand creeping down her side, making its way to the bottom of her dress. By the time she figured out what was happening, he had already taken both of her hands in his and pinned them above her head so she couldn't stop him.

He pulled away from the kiss, giving her a moment to catch her breath before diving back in, drinking up all of her mewls and moans. "Such a pretty little present. I can't wait to unwrap you later." He purred, his hand inching further up her leg until it reached the elastic of her panties. With the way he had her trapped underneath him, unable to speak or move, she was left with no other option but to submit to him, allowing him to do as he pleased. Even if she could do something, she was far too drunk with desire to even attempt to put up a fight. In this moment of vulnerability, Elio could do whatever he wanted to her, and she'd consent.

Her body relaxed as she wrapped her legs around him, pulling him even closer to her so that he laid completely on top of her, pressing her body into the bed. He moved his face away. Their lips remained connected by a single strand of saliva, as he stared at her with a lust filled gaze. Nuzzling into the crook of her neck, he nipped at her soft spot, leaving little bite marks littered across her flesh.

"I bet you want me to go further, don't you?" He mused, enjoying just how quickly he could turn her into such a needy mess. She nodded her head obediently. Her breath hitched at the feeling of his fingers dancing across her clothed heat, clearly avoiding the one spot she needed them to be.

"Yeah, I know you want it, deserve it too for being such a good girl." She let out a soft whimper at his words, attempting to buck her hips up against him to gain some friction. With a low growl, he sunk his sharp teeth into the side of her neck, causing her to cry out in both pain and ecstasy as tears flowed down her cheeks. "It seems my sweet little doll enjoys a bit of pain. How cute." He chuckled, lapping up the beads of blood that formed. "Please!" She begged, unsure of what she actually wanted. "Please what?" He asked with his tongue hanging out. "Please, just take… Ah!" Before she could finish her statement, he dipped his head into her neck again, his lips placed right under her chin.

"Mph… Yes… Ah… Please… Oh… Elio, I… Ah…" She was an absolute mess underneath him, moaning out gibberish as he continued his attack, letting go of her hands so he could stroke her hair. Without thinking, she moved her hands down, looking for anything they could grip on to for stability. They made their way onto his face, moving up towards his hair, where she got a good grip on some locks. He let out a low animalistic growl against her skin as he thrusted against her roughly, causing her to lose her grip.

"I swear to God if we didn't have somewhere to be right now, I'd screw your fucking brains out." He spoke in a deep, husky voice, dripping with lust. She let out a soft whimper, begging him to do just that. "Don't worry, doll, I promise the next time we step foot in this room, I'll have you on your back screaming my name." He had his lips against hers, forcing her into another heated battle. "I'll make it impossible for you to walk. That way, you'll never be able to get away from me." After one final peck to the lips, he pulled himself off of her, helping her up. He took a moment to fix his tie before offering his arm out to her, which she mindlessly took, far too flustered to even think properly. "Well, we better get going, doll. Wouldn't want to be late." He smirked, ushering her out of the room. She sucked in a shaky breath, following him without a single word. All she could think as they moved along was that if he kept it up, this was going to be a long weekend.

42

Chapter: 8

Elio led Faye out to the car wearing a proud smirk as she clung to his arm with her face beet red. She still felt extremely lightheaded after their little *moment* and certainly wasn't in any position to talk, as her words would most likely come out as absolute gibberish. He didn't seem to mind her silence at all, especially after seeing her so flustered. Though, as much fun as it was for him to tease her, he really didn't want to push her past her boundaries just yet, so he decided it was in his best interest to monitor her overall reaction.

He opened up the door, allowing Faye to enter first before crawling in after her. Without prompting, she moved to sit in his lap, resting her head against his chest. "Such a good girl." He whispered in her ear as he gave her thigh a light squeeze. She craned her neck so that she could shoot the large man with a halfhearted glare, which only caused him to chuckle as he nuzzled her head. "You're lucky you have a comfortable lap." She huffed, crossing her arms childishly.

Unbothered by her playful pouting, Elio grabbed her chin, tilting her head up to meet his eyes as he gave her a devilish smirk. "I'm glad you think so, cause you'll be doing so much more in my lap than just sitting." He purred, leaning down to plant a kiss on her lips. She giggled against his mouth, enjoying every ounce of his affection as he started peppering kisses down her neck, stopping right above her collarbone.

"Oh, no…" she whispered, feeling his tongue slide across her skin, tasting every inch of her neck. "Not again." She bit down on her bottom lip to quell her moans as she felt his sharp teeth ghost over her flesh, threatening to take another bite. "Come on, doll, just one more." He begged teasingly, laying soft kisses against her, causing her to clench her fists to hold back her moans. "P-please… Mercy…" she whined, face bright red. "Don't worry, doll. I only want to show these assholes who you belong to." His voice was deep and possessive, causing shivers to run up her spine.

She could feel his nails digging into her sides, forcing her to remain still as his lips moved down to her collarbone, sampling her sweet, addicting taste. "I.. Ah… I belong to… Mph… You." she softly moaned. "Obviously." He smirked, feeling the way she was grinding against him, her movements automatic. "You're acting like a puppy in heat." He playfully chided her, moving his own hips in time with hers.

Sharp teeth pierced through her skin, causing her to let out a startled yelp which turned into a quiet moan that she attempted to muffle up. "You know I can't help but notice how messy and inexperienced you've been acting." He said nonchalantly, as if they were having a normal conversation. His lips trailed back up to meet her own, not giving her a single moment to respond. "You'll talk all sorts of shit and act all cool about things until I start touching you. Suddenly you're this whimpering, flustered mess who doesn't seem to have a single clue… Hmm… I wonder why that is, doll." The close proximity and unrelenting passion was causing her to overheat, making everything almost unbearable.

"Please…" she whined against his lips, though her pleads were fruitless, as he was far too focused on his own pondering to humor her. "Now that I really think about it, you kind of act like a virgin." He pointed out, causing her to freeze up, her face bright red. Finally, he seemed to acknowledge her reactions, observing how she desperately attempted to pull away from the kiss.

Elio stopped all his teasing and took her chin in his hand, forcing her to look him in the eyes. "Seriously?" He couldn't help but ask. She nodded her head hesitantly, feeling extremely embarrassed about the situation. His face softened as he offered her a warm, tender smile, kissing her gently. "You're so amazing, you know that?" He placed his hand against her back and began rubbing it, using his fingers to massage circles into her tense flesh.

A soft, angelic sigh fell from her lips as she watched him with beautiful blue jewels that seemed to shine brighter than any diamond he'd ever seen. Faye was so precious and fragile, like a delicate flower that needed to be guarded. "I'll never hurt you." He whispered, dipping his head back in for another kiss. Faye couldn't help her look of amusement at what sounded like a promise. "You won't?" She retorted with a slight giggle. "No. Never. I'll take good care of you." He swore, with a sharp toothed grin. "Oh? And how are you planning to do that?" A playful gleam sparkled in her eyes as she waited for his response.

He tilted his head and tapped the bottom of his chin as though he was putting thought into his answer. "Hmm, I could just tie you up and take you back to my home." He answered with a smirk. "I'll keep you locked in my room, where you'll never see the light of day again." She could no longer control her laughter, blissfully unaware of just how serious he was. "You sound like you're about to turn my skin into a suit." Tears fell from her eyes as she laughed. "Your skin is pretty soft." He remarked, stroking her leg as if to emphasize his point. "Oh, my god I'm going to get murdered." She shook her head with a large grin on her face. "Okay, fine, just don't throw me in a hole. If I die Buffalo Bill style, I lose a bet."

Elio let out a sincere chuckle, loving just how unpredictable the strange woman could be. "I thought *you* were planning to be the serial killer." He teased, kissing her temple. "You're the one talking about kidnapping me and wearing my skin." She pointed out. "I promise I won't wear your skin." He crossed his heart. "What about kidnapping?" She wondered with her arms crossed. "Come now, doll, let's not take the fun out of everything." His arms slunk around her once again, tightening their grip on her.

For a moment, she struggled against him, trying to break out of his tight grip, but she soon relaxed against him, her face smashed against his chest. "I suppose being kidnapped by you wouldn't be too bad." She muttered into his shirt. "Oh?" He retorted, daring her to continue. "I mean, you're warm and you smell good…" Her voice drifted off, embarrassment taking control of her once again. "Well, in that case, we better make a quick stop by the store. I got to get some rope for you, after all." She rolled her eyes at this comment and shook her head. "Are you planning to tie me to the bed or hang me from the ceiling?" She asked with a raised eyebrow. "I think hanging you would be a little counterproductive." He smirked, his eyes glued to her lips. "I ain't one to kink shame." She shrugged with a cheeky smile, earning a small chuckle from the man.

Leaning in close to her ear, he whispered in a deep, sensual voice, "You do not know what I'm into, but I promise you'll find out." Another shiver ran down her spine as he spoke, his rough and gravelly voice becoming her weakness. "I can't wait." She breathed out, leaning in closer to his face as though he beckoned her to do so. Before she could even process what was happening, he already had her pulled into another heated kiss, her mind going completely blank of anything and everything that didn't involve the large, handsome man who held her tightly. Slowly, her eyes fluttered closed as her fists knotted into his shirt. She parted her lips and allowed him entrance, putting up very little fight for control.

There was something about Elio that she just couldn't place, something dangerous and yet so alluring, drawing her to him. Realization hit her she needed to breathe, so carefully, Faye pulled away from her date, panting heavily as she attempted to catch her breath. "You're a pretty quick learner, you know that?" Elio stated as he leaned back into the seat, settling her on his lap. "I'll have you well trained in no time." Faye shot him a glare, not appreciating his comment. "Talk to me like I'm a dog one more time and I'll bite you." She sneered, feeling slightly offended.

He tilted his head, staring at her strangely. Normally, he'd never let anyone speak to him with such an attitude, and yet she did it in such a way that left him feeling almost guilty. How could the sheer thought of upsetting her make him feel bad? Sure, the young woman intrigued him, but that didn't give her the right to snap at him, especially after everything he did for her. Of course, he'd talk to her like that. He owned her.

The moment he felt her shift in his lap, as though she was attempting to move off of him, panic fell on his face. "I'm sorry." The sincere words left his mouth before he could even register saying them. She stopped her moving and instead looked at him curiously. "I shouldn't talk to you like some stray mutt. You far exceed anything close to that degree. What I see is someone above everyone, a beautiful goddess that I wish to tame. I know now that it was a mistake, and I'm willing to take whatever punishment you wish to strike me with so long as I gain your forgiveness." He kept a sincere tone as he spoke, watching for her reaction.

That's when he heard it, her angelic laughter that he found positively enchanting. "Oh my God, you sound like a jackass." She laughed in amusement. "I'm not mad. Just don't talk down to me." She shook her head, not realizing how much danger she was putting herself in. Leaning her head in, she planted a small, sweet kiss on the tip of his nose. Oddly enough, even her insults didn't seem to irk him, instead he felt relief knowing she wasn't angry with him. "Alright, I guess I'll talk to you like a person." He teased, to keep the mood light. "Jeez, it's almost like you have boundaries or something." She nearly fell off his lap with how hard she laughed, no longer feeling even an ounce of irritation towards him. "Yeah, I'm a pain in the ass, so what?" Faye shot back, blowing him a raspberry. "That's it. When I tie you to my bed, remind me to duck-tape your mouth shut."

The air no longer felt tense and instead it was filled with their playful banter as they chatted about their lives. "You were actually right about there being more rats." Elio stated, being very careful about how much he shared with her. "I caught two more of the little pests." For some strange reason, he felt comfortable enough to share this information with her. "I told you so." She responded. "So did you end up releasing them or did you just, you know…" She made the throat motion with her thumb, which made him laugh. "I did, in fact, put them out of their misery. Taught them a lesson first, though." He answered, stroking her hair. "What did you do? Torture them?" She stifled her giggles, wanting to know exactly what he did to a couple of rats.

"Well…" Elio answered with a large grin. "I did a little waterboarding, some electrocution, then I started cutting off body parts, as one normally does." He stated as though it was the most normal thing ever. "Oh yeah, totally. I read that in the exterminator handbook." Faye shot back, shaking with laughter. As far as she could tell, he was completely joking with her, which was exactly how he wanted things to be for right now.

"So, where are we going this time?" Faye asked, her eyes drifting over to the window, wanting to check out her surroundings. Neon signs and brightly lit buildings zoomed past them along with interesting looking people who were out living their lives. As loud and crowded as the city was, she enjoyed its mysterious beauty that could only be experienced during the darkest hours of the night. It often brought her to a state of relaxation, which could only be deepened by the sound of classic rock.

Elio grabbed her shoulders and pulled her back to his chest, resting his chin on the top of her head. "We got to head over to Slim Pickings really quick. Then after that, I wanted to take you some place special." He answered her question after a minute of silence. "Slim Pickings? Ain't that a strip club?" She inquired, not sure what business he could have with an old, rundown place like that. "Yeah, I had a last-minute meeting come up for work." He responded quickly, not giving too many details.

"Hmm… That sucks… Who are you meeting with? Anyone I know?" Faye, for the life of her, did not know why she even bothered to ask. Chances were, she'd have no clue who the person was. Perhaps a part of her wondered if it was someone May had introduced her to. That would at least be entertaining, especially knowing most of the red-head's old associates had some kind of image in mind for her.

Long fingers combed through soft locks as Elio's eyes stayed focus on Faye, refusing to let up on her. "Funny enough, you probably do know him. We're meeting with Mike Ladner tonight to see what bullshit he's trying to sell me." A low growl sounded from him as he spoke the name, disgusted at the thought of dealing with the man. Faye tilted her head in confusion, trying her hardest to think if she remembered the name.

"Who?" she wondered. "Mike Ladner…" Elio repeated. "The father of Tommy Ladner…" He figured if he gave the son's name, it would click for her and yet, she still held an oblivious look on her face. "Okay..? And who's Tommy?" He raised more questions than answers for her. "Seriously..? You don't know who Tommy is?" He couldn't tell if she was messing with him or not.

"Should I?" She definitely wasn't messing with him. "Doll…" He shook his head, trying to contain his own laughter. "Tommy Ladner is the man you went out with weeks ago." Her eyes still held a hint of confusion as she attempted to register this information. "Was he? Hmm… I could have sworn his name was Jimmy… Wait, how do *you* know who I went out with?" It suddenly clicked with her that Elio seemed to know an awful lot of things about her and her personal life.

He went silent for a moment, his face stoic and unreadable. "Well… I was there…" He answered as truthfully as he could. She eyed him suspiciously, waiting for him to give her an actual explanation. "And how did you know it was me?" She pressed on, realizing she would get nothing else out of him. "I just asked around. Looked to see if anyone knew who the tiny, angry woman was, and they pointed me toward May." That made sense, and also explained the random phone call she received on Monday. "Alright, I'll believe it… But you're on thin ice." She said with a playful glare.

"Now it's my turn. How do you not know the name of the man you went out with?" He turned the questioning around on her. "Fair question… And to answer it, I just never bothered to learn it." She shrugged as though it was the most rational explanation ever. "Never bothered to learn it?" Elio repeated, completely dumbfounded. "Yeah, why would I bother with something so pointless when I'm pretty sure he didn't even bother to learn mine. This is honestly the first time he's even crossed my mind since that night." He looked at her, feeling rather impressed at how cold she sounded.

"Wow, not even bothering to learn the client's name. You are the worst escort ever." Elio teased, nuzzling her neck affectionately. "Oh, shut the hell up." She retorted, lightly smacking his chest. "And here I thought you were May's *top girl*." Faye made a gagging noise at the statement. "I swear to God… Sometimes I wish she never went into that business. Pain in my ass…" she muttered as she pressed her face against him.

"Oh, well… At least I got to meet you." She suddenly said, her soft voice so muffled by his shirt, he almost didn't hear her. "Once again, I'm happy I haven't disappointed you." He smiled down at her with a warm, tender look in his eyes. Strong, thick arms held her close as he continued to stroke her soft, luscious locks. It took a lot of thinking, but Elio was finally beginning to come to terms with his feelings and what he wanted from her. He adored her in every way and wanted nothing more than to be her one and only. The very thought of Faye being with anyone else made him feel a rage like no other.

After a few minutes of her silence, Elio looked down to see she had fallen asleep. He couldn't help the smirk that crept on his face as he felt the blonde girl slowly drift off, her light snores filling the silence wonderfully. "Sleep now while you can, doll." He spoke as he kissed the top of her head. "Cause I guarantee you ain't going to be getting much sleep later tonight." He gave her inner thigh a light squeeze, as if to show just what he had in mind.

The light moan that escaped her parted lips brought out a nearly feral reflex that almost caused him to wake her. "Keep it up and I won't be gentle." He warned with a growl to his voice. He was so close to having the driver turn around and take them back to the hotel, but decided it would be far more beneficial for him to wait.

Chapter: 9

Not too much time had passed before they finally made it to their destination. "Doll." Elio whispered, kissing her lips tenderly. "We're here." Her blue irises slowly fluttered open as she lifted her head, attempting to see where they were. His large frame completely blocked her vision as he carefully moved her out of his lap and into the middle seat. "Where are we again?" She yawned, attempting to stretch out her arms and legs. He made his way out, offering a hand out to her, which she graciously accepted. "Slim Pickings." He reminded her, gently pulling her out of the vehicle so he could hold her close to his chest.

Faye looked around, taking in all of her surroundings. The building was so old and decrepit, it barely registered as operational. Wooden planks covered a few of the windows, and the walls were sprayed with various tags. There was a large neon sign that sat on top of the entrance which read *Slim Pickings* in bright pink lettering that had the lighting on the 'M' and 'P' fade in and out with a constant buzzing. The many brightly lit businesses that surrounded it overshadowed the small building, giving it the perfect cover.

It seemed strangely quiet for a strip club on a Friday night, especially when the city was normally so lively around this time. Faye felt a nervous pit grow inside as she continued to look around, attempted to ignore the horrendous odor that seemed to close in around her, nearly suffocating her. It was a sour smell, one that could only be described as wet garbage doused in vinegar. She scrunched up her nose in disgust and buried her face in Elio's jacket to escape the smell.

"I know it's not ideal, but I promise I'll make this quick." Elio assured her, feeling her discomfort. "It's fine. Do what you need to do." She said as she lifted her head to meet his eyes. "Are you sure it's fine? I understand if this is a little frustrating, especially since I promised a great weekend." He sounded completely unsure of himself as though he was rethinking whether he should have brought her along, fearing that it would upset her. "I'll be just fine. I honestly don't care where you take me as long as I get to spend time with you." Faye gave the sweetest smile as she spoke, straining her neck up so she could give him a small kiss on his chin.

Elio looked at her with an inquisitive expression, attempting to determine the sincerity of her words. He watched as she swayed side to side, using his arms as an anchor in order to prevent her from falling over. Faye seemed genuinely content to be in a strip club with him, acting as though he were taking her out to the most extravagant place in the city. Was she truly happy just being with him?

It didn't take long for Faye to notice the revolving door of men coming and going as they pleased. That was all the evidence she needed for her to be at least eighty percent sure the strip club was still opened. It brought her some level of comfort to know her date wasn't planning to drag her into some abandoned building in the middle of the night, but she could do without the feeling of eyes all over her. It felt a little violating to be ogled at like some piece of meat. One man watched her unblinking, with a lascivious smirk on his face, as though he were a starved beast looking for his next meal.

"Disgusting." Faye's nose scrunched up as she sneered, turning back to the large man so that she could distract herself from the predatory gazes. "Let me know if anyone makes you uncomfortable, okay?" Elio stated with a cold look on his face, ready to shoot the first man that gave them trouble. He certainly didn't see this place as the perfect spot for a second date, but unfortunately, business had to come first. All he could do was keep her close in case some low life tried to do anything. "I will." She responded, hugging him tightly, which he reciprocated with as much enthusiasm.

Glancing back at the vehicle, she saw two men hop out of the front seat, both wearing red button ups and black slacks. A thought crossed her mind, causing her face to heat up in embarrassment; those two men definitely heard everything she and Elio had done in the back seat. While they didn't seem at all fazed by the couple, she couldn't help but feel a bit of shame over how needy and sinful she acted in the heat of the moment. Elio didn't seem to look at all embarrassed by his flirting and teasing, though why would he? These were his employees, after all, so they should at the very least be used to his antics.

He reluctantly let go of his doe eyed date, taking large strides over to the two men while he wore a stoic expression. Faye watched, her eyes brimming with curiosity, as he leaned down to whisper something to them. She couldn't help but giggle at how silly he looked talking to his men. "What's so funny?" He asked as he made his way back over to the amused woman who held her hand over her mouth the stifle her laughter. "Oh, nothing." She retorted in a singsong voice, trying hard to contain herself. She let out a small squeak at the feeling of his arms wrapping around her tightly, pushing her back against his chest. "Don't lie to me, doll." He growled quietly in her ear, causing goosebumps to run up her arm. "Lie? To you? I'd never." She playfully huffed, crossing her arms for dramatic effect. Elio let out a deep chuckle and gently ruffled her hair. "Don't act like a brat either." He teased. "Fine. Just take all the fun away." Faye lightly swatted his hand away so she could fix her hair. The strange, almost terrified, looks the two men held went completely unnoticed by her.

Elio walked through the entrance with Faye held firmly against his chest, her feet barely touching the ground as he moved. Both of his 'employees' followed close behind, taking large steps in order to keep up with the large man. "I'm gonna need you to stay close to me, no wandering off, okay?" He stated with a serious look on his face. "Who knows what these pieces of shit would try to do with a pretty little thing like you." The very thought of *his* Faye being touched by one of these drunken assholes rubbed him the wrong way. "And to think this place looked so safe and cozy…" she retorted sarcastically with a giggle. "But seriously, I think I'll just stick with you tonight. Not feeling too adventurous today." As she spoke, she relaxed into his chest, which seemed to calm his nerves, though he still stayed on high alert.

The moment they stepped inside the strip club, Faye was hit with the nauseating smell of cigarette smoke, alcohol, cheap perfume, and body odor, forcing her to cover her nose and hold her breath to escape the stench. The lighting inside the room was so dim, she had to strain her eyes to see. The temperature and humidity rose to an extremely high level, amplifying her discomfort. The club was just as trashy on the inside as it was on the out. "At least the book matches the cover." Faye mumbled quietly to herself, attempting to ignore the feeling of her shoes sticking to the floor.

She couldn't help but wonder when the last time the building had been thoroughly cleaned. 'This can't be even remotely legal.' She thought to herself, though there seemed to be a lack of concern coming from the overly intoxicated patrons and the irritated staff just trying to make a quick buck. "I wonder how many OSHA training videos they had to do." She joked, this time catching Elio's attention. "OSHA ain't a problem when they ain't a legit business." He retorted with a smirk.

Just as Faye was about to respond, she felt something scurry across her foot, causing her to freeze up completely. "Was that a roach?" She dared to ask, refusing to look down at the ground. Luckily, the large bug quickly fled from the creeped out girl, more than likely sensing her hostility. 'Just breathe.' She told herself, taking in a shaky breath as they continued their journey through the revolting, pest infested lobby. "If it gets to be too much for you, let me know and I'll carry you." Elio offered, worried she might turn around and leave. "I'm fine. The roach just scared me a bit." She waved him off, not wanting to seem too prissy. He stared at her for a moment, wondering how genuine she was actually being over everything, but figured she'd voice her complaints if she had any.

There were eyes everywhere, watching her every move carefully, as though they were waiting for an opportunity to approach her. Faye kept her guard up, not willing to take a single chance with those around her. Not that she was afraid of the loud drunken men that couldn't keep their eyes to themselves, but she really didn't want to create problems for Elio and whatever business he had with this place. Because of that sentiment, she held her tongue and played nice.

Elio hugged her tightly, resting his head on her shoulder as he whispered in her ear. "Don't worry, doll, none of these assholes would ever dare lay a finger on you." She gave a soft laugh at his reassurance, realizing he thought she was worried for her own safety. "I know." Faye said nonchalantly. "I'd probably beat them to death with a fire extinguisher if they tried." Elio gave a devious smirk at her very blunt statement. "Fair enough." He retorted as he rubbed her shoulders, beckoning her to move forward.

Her shoes squelched as they hit the old, damp carpet, causing her to cringe with each footstep. His offer to carry her was growing more tempting, but she really didn't want to give anyone the impression that she couldn't handle being in a rundown strip club. For some odd reason, Faye chose this as her hill to die on.

Because of her friendship with May, she was no stranger to strip clubs and would often visit the red-haired woman at her businesses to hang out, but this place was completely unhinged. There were no bouncers around to protect the employees, and the bartenders were serving alcohol to guests who were near the brink of being blackout drunk. The stage was littered with trash which the strippers clumsily danced around, using the pole with extreme caution and hesitation. She noticed how it moved, as though it had a few screws out of place. One wrong move and it could easily collapse, bringing the stripper down with it.

In order to keep her mind off of all the clear violations surrounding her, Faye focused on something far more amusing, May's reaction to being inside a club like this. Maybe that could be her form of payback for the terrible date she had to endure. That woman would freak out, and possibly light herself on fire, if she had to even stand here for more than a few seconds.

"What's got you all smiley?" Elio asked playfully. "Oh, nothing much, just thinking of ways to torture May," Faye responded in an overly cheerful tone. "Makes sense. I also find the thought of torture relaxing." He retorted teasingly, nuzzling into her neck. Unbeknownst to her, the two men following close behind faltered for a moment, terror written on their faces.

Elio guided them towards the back of the club where a lone booth sat, hidden away from everything else. As they approached it, the two men had stopped following them and, instead, took a position to stand guard over the couple. 'Weird.' Faye thought to herself, curious to find out what type of deal her date was doing to need security. If the father was anything like his son, then he shouldn't be too dangerous, but she figured her date wanted to be extra careful. One can't be too cautious when doing their business in a strip club.

As they approached the worn out leather sofa that lined the booth, Faye checked out their company for the evening. The moment her eyes landed on the man they were supposed to meet, she had to do everything in her power to keep herself from laughing. The man, Mike Ladner, was almost an exact copy of his son, from the short, chubby stature to his beady black eyes. It was almost uncanny. The more she studied him, the more amazed she was at how powerful this man's genetics were. 'They even share the same yellow, crooked teeth.' She thought to herself, watching him flirt with the two disinterested strippers who clung to his arms begrudgingly.

"Elio! My old friend," Mike greeted after finally noticing their presence. He stood from his spot, shooing off the two girls who were more than happy to abandon the gross old man. As he approached them, offering his hand out to shake Elio's, Faye couldn't help but crinkle her nose in absolute disgust. His cologne was far too pungent in smell, as though he dowsed himself with it instead of showering.

Interestingly enough, she recognized the scent as the same one his son used on their 'date.' With the clear lack of a wife and mother figure in their lives, she couldn't help but wonder if Mike reproduced asexually. 'That would explain how he created an exact clone of himself.' She thought to herself, stifling another giggle. This man and his son were an anomaly that she almost wished she could study further.

"How have you been?" Mike continued, paying no mind to the young woman snuggled up against the large man. "Cut the shit, Ladner, and tell me why we're here." Elio's tone held a level of resentment to it that went over the old man's head. Instead, he gave a hearty laugh, acting as though the irked man told the funniest joke ever. "Still as threatening as ever, I see. Oh, and what's this? Did you finally swallow your pride, take my advice, and get yourself a cute little escort?"

Mike had finally turned his attention to Faye, much to her dismay. She could feel his beady eyes burning right through her with the same perverted desire his son had held all those weeks ago. Elio gritted his teeth as he strengthened his grip and dug his nails into her sides. "She looks familiar as well... Wait a minute. You're one of May's girls, ain't you? I can't believe she let you buy this one. I had to seriously convince that red-headed bitch to let me rent this one out for my son, and even then, he wasn't allowed to have any real fun with her."

He spoke in an overly cheerful tone that made Faye feel sick to her stomach. It felt like he was trying to dehumanize her, to make her feel small and feeble. This attitude was completely unacceptable, and there was no way she would ever let his comments slide. Her date be damned.

"Did you just call my girlfriend a fucking whore?!" Elio snarled before Faye could say anything. His bright orange eyes glared holes into the man's head as he moved to stand in front of the woman, blocking her from Mike. "I swear to God I'm ten seconds away from hanging you by your own intestines." The old man's face went pale as his blood ran cold. "L- look Elio, I m-mean no h-harm from it. She just looked like May's top…"

"She doesn't work for May, so get that thought out of your fucking head before I bash your brains in." Elio cut him off in the middle of his stuttering. "Oh yes, yes, of course. I only said it as a joke! Not to be taken seriously." Mike attempted to backtrack.

So much for keeping Faye ignorant about everything. She is surely going to know about his violent tendencies now. She was probably terrified after that little outburst and was more than likely trying to think up an escape plan to distance herself from the scary man. Why couldn't Ladner just keep his mouth shut and keep it strictly professional? Instead, he just has to keep talking and now Faye was behind him thinking up an excuse on why she needed to leave.

"You know, jokes are supposed to be funny." Faye deadpanned, catching everyone off guard. Her fingers entangled with Elio's as she took a step forward, wearing an annoyed expression. "That wasn't funny at all. Maybe try a knock-knock joke next time." She sounded completely unbothered by the conversation, allowing her date to lead her over to her seat. Elio took off his coat and placed it on the sofa before guiding her to sit down on it.

"I'll…. Keep that in mind." Mike mumbled softly, relieved that the young woman had calmed the angry man down. Faye simply ignored him and focused all her attention on her lover instead.

What she didn't realize was that Elio was just as relieved, knowing he didn't completely blow it in the heat of the moment. It was strange, really, how calm and unimpressed she seemed to be after he threatened to murder a man. At the very least, he expected her to flinch away from him, but she simply cuddled up closer, finding some level of amusement in playing with the buttons on his cufflinks. She even offered him a heartwarming smile the moment she noticed him staring down at her.

It felt as though her very presence held a mysterious aura to it that seemed to keep him level-headed. Even after such a blatant insult by some lowlife slime ball, he kept his temper in check. Elio realized it might be in his best interest to keep her around, especially for these high stakes meetings.

Mike and Elio got right into their meeting, using different code words so as not to attract any unwanted attention. Faye, finding the whole discussion somewhat boring, allowed her mind to drift off as she focused on what she believed to be far more interesting things. For instance, the stain that sat on the wall right behind Mike kind of looked like a male betta fish. It held an oval shape for the body, with the large tail spread out around it as the creature floated mindlessly through the water. Now that she thought about it, the creature looked more like a jellyfish than a betta fish. Its long stingers stretched out far, daring someone to touch them. So dangerous and yet so beautiful, like a firework that went off a little too close to a house… Wait, did they just say something about the mafia?

Just as Faye was tuning back into the conversation, the meeting had drawn to an end, leaving her feeling confused over the whole thing. "So we agree, then?" Mike asked, hopeful that he persuaded the intimidating man. "Fine, it's a deal. But if anything goes wrong, it'll be your fucking head. Okay?" Was it weird that she found him even more attractive when he threatened people? A part of her wanted him to talk in that aggressive, authoritative tone more often, but she knew deep down that her heart wouldn't be able to handle it. Especially if he used it on her.

Elio rose from his spot, offering his hand out to Faye, which she graciously took. As he pulled her up to her feet, his expression softened with a look of adoration in his warm orange eyes. That look alone melted any tension she felt moments ago, allowing her to feel completely safe and secure regardless of their surroundings. "Are you ready to go?" He asked in a soothing voice that was much more pleasant than the one he had while addressing Mike. "Yeah, I'm not really feeling the vibe here." She retorted with a goofy smile as she breathed in his smell. He grabbed his large jacket off of the sofa and swung it over his shoulder before ushering her towards the exit, keeping a tight hold on her. They left Mike sitting there with a look of shock and horror frozen on his face as he attempted to process everything that had happened.

Apparently, Faye wasn't moving nearly fast enough for him. Within seconds, he already had her scooped up off the ground and rushed out to the vehicle as though their very lives would be in danger if they stayed in that club any longer. The moment the backdoor opened up, he had her pinned to the backseat. He slowly ran his nails through her hair, entangling his fingers into her soft golden locks as he pushed her further into the seat.

"I absolutely adore you." He spoke those words as though they were facts, allowing her no room to argue with him. "So sweet yet so feisty. I've never met anyone like you before." He continued to murmur against her lips, moving his arms so that he had her caged underneath him. "I can't help but wonder though… What do I need to do to keep a woman like you by my side?" He slid his tongue into her mouth, muzzling her with his own face. "Because I promise I'm willing to do anything. I'll burn this whole damn city to the ground for you if you want, so long as you agree to be mine."

He pulled back from the kiss, giving her a moment to catch her breath before he continued. "Now doll, why don't you tell me what I can do to get you to say yes?" He stared at her expectantly, waiting for her answer. "I…" she started, carefully thinking about what to say. "I think I just want to be with you, and not worry about you getting bored with me. Can you do that?" She stared at him with beautiful, innocent jewels.

Elio stayed silent, attempting to process her request, which caused her to feel nervous. "Sor…" Before she could finish her unwarranted apology, he pulled her into another heated kiss, forcing her to remain quiet. "I adore you so much, with every bone in my body. I promise I'll never get bored with you." The kiss softened to something much more tender and loving, allowing him to show just how honest his words were. He knew no matter what, he'd keep her by his side, never to throw her away. Slowly, he pulled away, leaving her bright red and flustered as he crawled off of her to exit the vehicle. Faye sat up and adjusted herself so that she looked at least halfway put together while waiting for her date's return.

Looking out the window, she watched as he approached the two men who traveled with them. He appeared to be having some kind of serious talk with them, his face stoic and clear of all emotions. The men weren't too bothered by his demeanor and seemed to nod along, possibly agreeing to whatever directions he was giving them. It more than likely had something to do with the meeting they just attended, which left her wondering; what did Elio do for a living?

Obviously, he held some pretty high level position for his company, possibly president or executive. His employees seemed to hold him in high regards and were willing to do just about anything for the man. It was no wonder either, as he seemed like the type to have no problem with doing the dirty work. But what exactly was the dirty work? Perhaps he was in the sex trade industry like May. That would explain how they knew each other and why she seemed a little hesitant to introduce them to one another. But then why had he been acting so shady about his career?

As she sat there thinking of other jobs he could have, she zoned out, becoming completely oblivious to her surroundings. It was then that Elio quietly crept into the seat next to hers, wearing a mischievous smile on his face. "Whatcha thinking about, doll?" He whispered in her ear, causing the now startled woman to jump in her seat, nearly hitting her head on the ceiling. "Jesus Christ! Are you trying to give me a heart attack? Don't do that." She reprimanded him, trying her hardest to sound angry. "Awe, I'm sorry." He said in a playful tone, pulling her back onto his lap. "You're just so cute when you're scared." She let out a little laugh and laid back against his chest, completely giving up on her attempts to scold him.

Elio peppered kisses up and down her neck, taking in her intoxicating scent and incredible flavors. There was just something so enchanting about her that kept him craving every little piece of her. No matter what he did, he could never get enough of her. It got to where he was almost certain he had an addiction for the adorable woman. And yet here she sat, feeding into his addiction like the enabler she was, allowing him to use her as he pleased. "I want you." He mumbled quietly to himself as he focused his attention on her plump lips, savoring the taste of her cherry lip gloss that seemed to mesh so well with the rest of her.

Faye was so immersed in all of his light, feather touches and gentle kisses, his words went completely over her head. The world around her seemed to disappear, leaving her all alone with Elio. That was fine by her seeing as the large man had her completely under his spell, keeping her in a state of hypnosis. It wasn't until she felt his hand creep under her skirt that she finally snapped out of her fantasy.

"Please. Not in the car." She requested in a soft, timid voice, trying her hardest to cover up her moans. "Rejected again, I see," He said playfully, though he still moved his hand away so as not to upset her. "Sorry, I know it's cruel not to let you screw me out in public. I just have this really annoying thing called boundaries." She retorted sarcastically. "Boundaries? What are those? Are they some kind of STD I haven't heard of?" He asked teasingly, burying his face into her neck. "Yeah, they are the worst ones you might get. They keep me safe and comfortable." He let out a low, genuine chuckle at her response.

Chapter: 10

"So, where are we going now?" Faye asked, stifling a yawn. "It's a surprise." He retorted, decidedly keeping it at that. "But I'm sure you'll love this one." As confident as he sounded with that statement, deep down, he felt a little nervous about what she might think. There wasn't any guarantee that she would actually enjoy the place he was taking her to, and yet, when he looked down at her, watching as she absentmindedly played with his tie, tracing the patterns that seemingly only existed to her, even if she truly hated his plans, she'd still go along with them wearing a smile on her face. He could only hope that her smile was genuine.

Elio ran his fingers through her soft locks, basking in her content sighs. His hands slowly made their way down to her shoulders, feeling just how soft and delicate her skin was. His smile dropped when he felt the knots in her back. "You're very tense." He mumbled with a worried look on his face. "Has work really been this stressful?" Faye gave an airy laugh at his question, brushing off his concern. "Life's stressful. It's fine though. I'm not in any actual pain." She shrugged to reassure him. It didn't seem to work at all as he still held a look of skepticism, but that look went unnoticed by the woman, who was far too distracted to even be bothered to care.

Ideas invaded his mind about what to do about the situation. He found it completely unacceptable that his beautiful girlfriend was in pain and yet refused help. She even went as far as to lie about the severity of it, which seemed to really bother him. What did she have to gain from acting so nonchalant? Perhaps he was overreacting to something as small as her needing a massage, but he couldn't help it.

Never in his life did he care so much for someone and yet, all he could think about was how much he needed to love and protect her. "If you say so, doll. But when we get back to the hotel, I will work out these awful knots for you." He whispered against her lips. "Looking forward to it." She mumbled back, attempting to meet his eyes as he pulled her into another kiss, this one far less heated.

Elio didn't need to take her anywhere else. He could bring her back to the hotel and she would happily comply with whatever he wanted to do to her. For whatever reason, that just wasn't good enough for him. It was absolutely important to him that she truly enjoyed their date. Oh, how badly he wanted to spoil her, give the world to her. If only she would accept it. Faye was so sweet, so cunning, and absolutely gorgeous. She was perfection incarnated, and he found himself lucky to have such an opportunity to take her out.

Their next destination came quicker than expected. As the car screeched to a halt, Faye looked out the window, her eyes lit up with childish excitement. The establishment held a cylinder shape to it, covered in blue glass panels that made up the walls. A giant statue of a tiger shark stood tall at the entrance, towering over everything around it. Absolute glee

55

washed over her as she clung to Elio's arm with a python like grip. "I figured you might enjoy the aquarium." He explained with a smug smile, knowing that he did well in picking the location. As he opened the door for her, she quickly hopped out of the car and bounced up and down, waiting for him to exit.

Elio made a beeline towards the driver's side, leaving Faye to wait just a little longer. "Go, get the body and bury it deep in the desert. This bastard better not ever be found, or it's your fucking head." The gangster snapped at the driver, his voice quiet yet intimidating. "Yes, sir." The terrified man responded quickly before driving off, leaving no room for conversation. He turned his attention back to the young woman, who seemed to be in a daze.

A soft smile highlighted her face as she rocked back and forth on her heels. He made his way to her at a swift pace, pulling her close to him. "You ready to go, doll?" He purred in her ear. "Yes!" She squeaked in excitement. Without a moment wasted, they walked into the aquarium, smiles covering both their faces.

Cool air drifted across her skin, causing goosebumps to form as she took in the sweet yet salty air that felt so refreshing. The aquarium was so quiet and serene allowing her watched all the sea creatures swim around without a single care in the world. The blue lighting that surrounded them was very nice and welcoming, like a cool lake on a hot, sunny day. "So beautiful." She mindlessly whispered, watching as a few seahorses danced around some kelp. "Yes, you are," Elio muttered under his breath, refusing to look away from the entranced girl. He wanted so desperately to burn the image of her childlike joy into his mind, watching as she practically skipped towards the large tank.

As she got closer to the tank, a large gray reef shark suddenly appeared in front of her, bonking its face against the glass. She let out a little giggle at the large predator's silliness as it bonked its head again, far softer this time. "Aren't you the cutest little killer?" She cooed at the beast, stroking the glass in an attempt to pet it. The shark paid no mind to her words and eventually left, seeing as there was no food around for it. She gave it a little wave, wishing it a safe journey, before she turned her attention back to her date.

"Having fun?" He asked in a sincere voice, unable to contain his delight in seeing her so happy and carefree. "This place is amazing." She responded as she wrapped her arms around his waist. "Thank you for bringing me here." Her large, sparkling blue eyes looked up at him through long lashes as she spoke with such gratitude it nearly caused his body to freeze up. "Anything for you, doll." His voice came out shaky and uncertain, worried he'd say the wrong thing to her. This sudden nervousness went unnoticed by the enthusiastically adorable girl who threaded her fingers in between his so that she could pull him along.

Faye leaned her head against his side, allowing him to lead her deeper into the aquarium, past the entrance desk and towards an escalator. Elio had her step on it first while he stood directly behind her with his arms wrapped around her waist. The stairs were extremely steep, which would normally terrify her, but she felt completely safe having the large man behind her. His heavy build made it easy for her to rest against him, giving her the opportunity to look out the windows that lined the stairway.

Peering outside, she spotted the large courtyard where the giant statue stood in all its glory, surrounded by vegetation and various types of lighting. Now having a clear view of the facility, she noticed there was something off about the building they were in. "It's quiet in here." She pointed out with a confused expression. "Are we alone?" Elio nuzzled the back of her neck, wearing a proud grin as he answered. "Of course we are, doll. I figured you'd have way more fun if you weren't stuck in a large crowd, so I rented the place out for tonight."

She stared at him in disbelief, trying to gage his reason for going to such extremes for her own comfort. "You really didn't have to go through all this trouble for me." She spoke but quickly got cut off. "I swear, it wasn't any trouble at all. In fact, I wish I had done more, but I wanted to start off small, you know?" He gave her side a light squeeze as he spoke, guiding her off the escalator. She gave a quiet laugh at the word small, wondering what exactly his definition of small was because this seemed way over the top. But, as she looked up to meet his eyes, she could only see sincerity painting his face while he held a soft smile.

Thinking about it for a moment, she finally let out a conceded sigh, realizing just how fruitless this conversation would be. "Well, I absolutely love it. Thank you so much." She declared as she kissed him on the cheek. The moment she pulled away, Elio placed his hand where she kissed, relishing in how soft and gentle her lips were. "Thank god. I was worried for a moment that I messed up." He sounded so relieved by this that is caused her to giggle. "You're so sweet, you know that?" She remarked with the biggest smile. For a moment, his expression fell as a feeling of guilt hit him hard, but he quickly pushed it aside, figuring it was for the best that she continued to believe that sentiment.

The two of them moved forward, stopping at the beginning of a beautifully lit tunnel that seemed to beckon them to enter. The large tank that arched over her head absolutely mesmerized Faye, allowing her the ability to see the fish from multiple angles. Fish of all shapes and sizes seemed to fly over them without a single care in the world. A large shark swam next to them, carefully following the couple as they slowly made their way through. Elio kept an arm wrapped around her, maintaining a slow, steady pace so that she could properly observe the surrounding creatures.

He almost wanted to say something, perhaps strike up a conversation, but he was worried doing so would ruin the moment. "Wouldn't it be fun to swim with them?" Faye suddenly pondered, breaking the silence. "The sharks?" Elio asked in amusement. "Yeah, I mean when you think about it, they're constantly fed, were probably raised in captivity and have no natural enemies here. I bet they act like huge water puppies to their caretakers." While she made decent points, the idea of her trapped in a tank full of sharks rubbed him the wrong way.

The look of unease that he held surprisingly did not go over her head. "But I wouldn't want to cause any harm to the sharks. I mean, jumping in their tank could disrupt their routine, cause them stress and it might make them seriously sick. For their safety, it would be beneficial for me just to watch and dream." She felt the need to reassure Elio that she held no intention of actually swimming with the sharks.

He kept his eyes locked on her while they continued through the tunnel, watching as her face lit up at each new creature that appeared. Faye looked so adorable with the way she gushed over a large stingray that swam past them. A part of him wanted to move her along so that they could get through the aquarium faster, but another part wanted to stay here for as long as possible, cuddled up next to her as she pointed out the fish that came by.

Resting his face against her neck, he gave her a soft kiss before whispering in her ear. "Come on, doll, there's still a whole aquarium to be seen." Too entranced to speak, she simply nodded her head before continuing forward until they finally exited the tunnel, moving on to the next exhibit.

Faye clung to Elio's arm, skipping like a giddy child towards the next tank. She noted how quickly the lighting changed alongside the atmosphere of the building. It grew darker the further down they went, showcasing the stranger and much more light sensitive sea creatures.

Without thinking, Faye dashed off towards a large tank near the entrance of the next room, eyes drawn to the many unique looking fish that swam around without a single care in the world. Fearing that he might lose her in the room's darkness, Elio quickly marched over to Faye, pulling her back into his chest. Even though he kept a tight grip on her, refusing to let up even for a moment, she didn't seem to mind as she was far too focused on a tiny little pufferfish to even notice.

The tiny creature puffed up at the sight of the large man, making itself twice the size it once was to intimidate him. "Awe! You scared it." Faye teased, playfully chiding him. "Did I now?" Elio hummed, barely acknowledging the small creature, instead focusing all of his attention on the adorable woman that was pressed against his chest. He listened closely as she made various noises in order to entice the fish, knowing full well that it probably couldn't hear her.

"Caligula would absolutely love this place." She said quietly as she moved on to the next tank. "He loves watching birds and fish. He also loves chasing things, especially me." Faye continued on while she stared at a jellyfish tank that lit up in different colors. "He chases you?" Elio asked with a hint of worry in his voice. "Yeah, for fun, not to cause me any harm. He'll stalk me around the house and then grab my leg before running off." She explained with the biggest smile, which he found incredibly contagious as he too started smiling just as big while listening to her talk. "I'm just happy he's going after me and not my poor old lady. Could you imagine how miserable Banshee would be if that crackhead chased her around every morning instead of me?"

Faye continued to tell him stories about her two cats, which he found pretty amusing, not realizing just how entertaining felines could truly be. Perhaps it wasn't her stories, but simply the way she told them that made him more interested in owning a cat, something he had never considered in his life. "You really love those two, don't you?" He said as more of a statement than a question. "Yeah, with all my heart." She agreed. "Half the time they're my only reason to wake up in the morning. Especially Banshee. I don't think I could continue without her."

Elio gave her a curious look, not expecting her to say something like that with such dark implications for it. "That's dramatic, ain't it?" He sincerely hoped she was just exaggerating her feelings about her pets. "No, not really." She shook her head sadly. "I've gone into some pretty dark places in my mind..." she trailed off, not wanting to continue that sentence as she looked away from him, feeling somewhat shameful for sharing such personal information. Her date was far more concerned for her mental wellbeing to think anything less of her.

It was such a strange feeling for him to care so deeply for someone that he could feel their pain. Sure, in his line of work, he's dealt with plenty of people who were on a downward spiral mentally, but it's never affected him negatively like this. The last thing he wanted to hear was that his Faye was struggling with her mental health. He couldn't help but wonder if outside forces caused her problems. If that was the case, then he needed to intervene as quickly as possible, taking her away from everything that was causing her pain. Of course, he'd need to also plan on taking her cats in as well, seeing as they've done a pretty decent job of supporting her so far.

Nuzzling his face against her neck, he stroked her soft, blonde locks. "I don't even know these cats yet and I'm already starting to like them." He mumbled into her shoulder blade, tickling her lightly. "I'm glad you feel that way, and I'm sure with time, they'll tolerate your existence." She giggled cutely. "Only tolerate? Damn, that cuts deep." He joked with a sly smirk. "Be proud to be tolerated. Few get that honor from them. Caligula loathes strangers and Banshee gets super jealous when I have my attention on anything that isn't her." She retorted honestly. "So me and her already have something in common then." Faye rolled her eyes.

"Are you planning to scream every time you're in a room and can't find me?" She asked as they walked past the various fish tanks. "No, I suppose not, but I am planning to have you on your back screaming in every room we go in." His smirk deepened as he said this, noting the way her face turned bright red. He much preferred her flushed and stuttering over hurt and melancholy any day. "I don't know if I can do all that screaming." She tried to cover up her flustered expression with humor, hoping he wouldn't push any further.

He tilted her chin up with a single finger as he placed his lips against hers, wearing a devilish smirk. "I'm sure after a little practice, you'll be more than capable of doing it." He purred, causing her heart to skip a beat. "Better watch out Elio, people might think you're trying to seduce me." She really couldn't help but try to tell dumb jokes just to ease the tension. "Don't worry, doll, I'm trying to make them think way more than that." She felt his other hand wonder around her body, making its way towards her lower half as he pulled her back into a deep, passionate kiss.

It wasn't until they made it to the next area that Faye even realized they were walking. Finally he pulled away, turning her body so that she could look at the display in front of her, and boy was she blown away by it. The tank took up the entire wall and held hundreds of different aquatic species, all so unique in appearance and size. With the way it was set up, it almost made her feel as though she were down in the bottom of the ocean, trapped in a small glass room.

"This is so freaking amazing!" She exclaimed in excitement before pressing her face to the glass. "You think so?" Elio asked, feeling rather smug about how much she loved the date so far. "I've never seen so many species of shark before. And just look at all those rays! Holy crap! Is that a manta ray? Those things are huge!" She continued to ramble on and on about the different fish that pass by, occasionally looking up to gage her date's reaction. He seemed perfectly content just standing there, watching her explain the large ecosystem that stood before them while he kept his hands in his pockets.

Unbeknownst to Faye, Elio began rummaging through his pocket as though he were looking for something important. "You know, doll, there's something I've been meaning to discuss with you." He said in a gentle tone as he slowly approached her. "Oh? What about?" She asked, keeping her eyes glued to the tank." I want to discuss our future together and what my long-term plans are with you." That sentence alone caused a wave of anxiety to wash over her as a worried look fell on her face. She attempted to turn around but was stopped by the weight of his body, pinning her to the glass.

"The first time I saw you, I thought you were cute and interesting. Figured you'd at least keep me entertained for a few hours. But the longer I spent with you, the less I was willing to part. You have got to be the greatest woman I've ever met. You're funny, beautiful, charming, not to mention extremely witty. I know a guy like me doesn't deserve a woman like you and you've been more than generous with obliging me this whole time, but..." He stopped midway, noticing a tear run down her soft, pale face.

"Please don't cry doll, seeing you so sad absolutely destroys me. I just want to know if you're willing to be my girl..." "Yes!" Faye exclaimed, finally turning around to hug him in a tight embrace. That awful feeling in her gut completely went away the moment he asked the question. "Really?" He wondered, confused by her blunt answer. "Not even going to think about it?" He knew better than to question it, but curiosity got the best of him. "I don't need to. I already thought about it long enough and I just can't see myself moving on without you. You say you are sure you don't deserve a woman like me, but I don't understand why. I think you are absolutely perfect in every way. So, if you're willing to have me, I want nothing more than to be yours."

It took every nerve in Faye's body to muster up the courage to respond to him like that, but, by the looks of it, it was worth saying. Elio stood there for a moment, looking completely baffled by the response before his face completely softened. "Well doll, if that's what you want, then so be it." He chuckled warmly, pulling her into a passionate kiss. "From here on out, you're my girl, and I'll kill anyone who tries to change that." He muttered it so calmly it almost sounded normal. So caught up in the kiss's intensity, his words barely registered in her head, leaving alarms left untouched.

As she pulled away, she felt something light and cold wrap around her neck. Looking down, Elio had placed a necklace around her, clasping it in the back for her. "Much better." He stated, admiring his work. The chain was thin yet durable, carefully crafted out of yellow gold. It sat beautifully against her collar, with a small pendant that hit the top of her chest. The small piece was shaped like a sun, with the rays being a mix of yellow and rose gold. In the middle sat a beautifully cut ruby that complimented the rest of the necklace.

She looked up at him with bright blue jewels, wearing a look of bewilderment on her face. "Well? What do you think?" Elio asked, though by the way she smiled, it was quite obvious he knew the answer to that question. "It's so beautiful. Are you sure you want to give it to me?" She couldn't help but ask, worried he'd end up regretting his decision. "Of course, I had it made special just for you, after all." He said earnestly, lifting her head back up so she could look at him. "You belong to me now, after all." She felt her heart flutter at his words, a mix of emotions stirred up inside of her.

Before she could say anything else, Elio had her scooped up with her legs wrapped around his midsection and her arms wrapped around his neck. He held her up by her bottom with her back pressed flush against the glass. "Eli... Mph!" Before she could actually speak, he, once again, captured her lips, forcing her into silence. "Relax." He cooed as he nibbled on her bottom lip, beckoning her to open up. "Just one more taste before I have the real thing." Her heart beat so fast it sounded like a snare drum pounding in her ears. "You won't... Ah... In public... Mph... Will you?" The question made more sense in her head, and yet it came out as a jumbled mess. "No, I promise I won't, so long as you willingly come back with me." He answered with a low, sensual purr.

With wandering fingers inching closer to unexplored territories and experienced lips that seemed to keep her drunk and craving more, it would have been damn near impossible to refuse him at this point. "Please..." she begged, ready to give in to her desires. "Please what? Little doll." Elio teased as he flipped her so that she lay bridal style in his arms. "I want to go back with you..." Her words trailed off near the end, embarrassed by how needy she sounded.

"Anything for you, my dear." His words were a wonderful spell that kept her still as he quickly strolled through the aquarium, holding her carefully in his arms.

He decidedly took the stairs instead of the escalator, not in any mood to show even an ounce of patience for the slow-moving staircase. He needed her and wasn't afraid to show it. By the look of how bright red she turned, Faye obviously needed him as well. "Don't worry, we're almost to the car." He promised, racing out the front entrance and towards the vehicle in question.

Faye was practically thrown into the backseat with Elio following in after, slamming the door shut as he laid on top of her, caging her underneath him. "Are we.." "Yes, we're going back to the hotel." He interrupted the question with a sly look on his face. "It's getting late after all, and I think we both need to be alone with each other." She nodded her head in agreement, knowing if she tried to speak, it would only come out as a soft moan. Planting her hands firmly against his chest, she pushed up, attempting to keep him an arm's length away, knowing that if she didn't, there was no way she'd be able to keep him from having her right there in the seat. Hopefully, they'd reach the hotel before he lost the rest of his patience.

It felt as though an eternity had passed before they finally made it back, but luckily Faye held him off her. The second the vehicle stopped, the door flew open as Elio dragged her out of the back seat, throwing her over his shoulder before marching into the building. "Elio!" She whined as she bounced around. "You're going too fast!" He was far too focused on getting up to the room to pay any mind to her complaints, though he adjusted her slightly so that she wouldn't continuously smack into his back as he walked. It wasn't until they reached the elevator that he finally set her down while still keeping a tight grip on her waist.

A loud ding sounded, signaling that they reached their floor. As the doors slowly opened up, Elio pulled Faye along towards the long hallway, stopping in front of their room. He quickly got the door opened, allowing her to enter first before following right after, picking her back up and slamming her down on the bed as he used his body to trap her underneath him.

He captured her gaze with his own, allowing his hands to do all the work as he watched her expression, making sure she was completely okay with everything he did. Slowly, his hands trailed down her sides, moving underneath her dress. She felt the cool air hit her skin as he carefully pulled the skirt upwards until the dress sat at her neckline, leaving her undergarments exposed to him. "Lift your head." He ordered, helping her sit up slightly so that he could finish pulling her dress off of her.

"Now doll." He purred, trailing kisses down her neck towards her bosom. "This is going to hurt a little, but I promise I'll be real gentle with you." She looked at him with half-lidded eyes, her face bright red. Not a single thought went through her brain as she allowed herself to be lost in the pleasure...

Faye shuffled in the bed, attempting to sit up, but found that she was far too worn out to actually move. "Stay put," Elio ordered her, knowing that she had little choice in the matter. It would be a miracle if she could even sit up on her own, let alone stand by herself. Still, she couldn't help but try, wincing in pain as she lifted her head up. He rushed over to her side, gently coaxing her back down until her head reached the soft pillows. "Just give me a minute and I'll help you, I promise." He pleaded with her, worried that she'd seriously injure herself.

She let out a cute little huff but did as she was told, waiting for her lover to finish cleaning himself up. Soon he made his way back over to her, placing his hand on her back to help her sit up. Pulling out a cold bottle of water he grabbed from the mini fridge, he held it up to her lips, prompting her to take small sips from it.

Satisfied that she was now hydrated, Elio went to work on cleaning her up. "Did you have fun?" He asked, while patching up the light scratches that littered her otherwise perfect skin. "Yeah. I did." She replied in a bit of a daze. She felt so overly tired, it grew difficult to keep her eyes open. "That's good." He smiled as he reached down and picked up his red button-up shirt. Knowing that she had nothing to sleep in, he figured this would be comfortable enough for her to wear.

Once he got the shirt on her, he took a step back to admire how adorable she looked in his clothing. It practically swallowed most of her body, causing her to look smaller than she actually was. "Elio?" She said softly with a yawn. "Yes, doll?" He responded, moving back over so that he could crawl into bed with her. "You meant it, right? That I belong to you?" Her eyelids grew heavy as she snuggled close to his side. "Yes, I do. You're mine from now on." He declared, feeling her beginning to fade into a deep sleep. "Good... You're mine too..." she mumbled before she completely blacked out. "I know." He whispered, kissing her temple lightly. "I... Love you. 'Lio." Her words were muffled against his chest, and yet he could still hear them loud and clear. "I love you too, Faye."

Chapter: 11

Sunlight leaked in past the thick curtains that were open just a crack, bathing the slumbering woman in its golden rays as she lay curled up against the large man whose arms were wrapped snuggly around her. Faye nuzzled deeper into his bare, well-toned chest, fighting hard to remain asleep, knowing that she'd have to deal with the aches and pains of the previous night's activities the moment she opened her eyes. While she enjoyed every part of the evening she spent with Elio, she still had to mentally prepare herself to face the consequences of her actions.

Elio, who was normally impatient with his sexual partners, felt oddly calm while holding his lover close to him. The sound of her slow, steady breathing mixed in with the rhythm of her heartbeat was strangely relaxing for him. Her body felt so nice pressed up against his, as though she were created specifically for him.

As he grew lost in thought, fantasizing about the adorable little dame that lay sound asleep in his arms, he hardly noticed the way she began to toss and turn. It wasn't until her eyes slowly fluttered open that he realized she was finally awake. "Good morning doll, how are you feeling?" Elio purred, stroking her exposed leg. He held a devilish smirk at the feeling of her flinching from the contact, her body more than likely still sensitive from their late night fun.

"Sore." She mumbled, only half awake, trying to find a comfortable position to get in so that she could fall back asleep. "That's good, means I did my job right." He responded nonchalantly, combing his fingers through her hair, allowing her to snuggle closer to him.

She mumbled out a string of curses, her words completely muffled by his smooth chest. By the end of the small, unintelligible ramble, her breathing slowed down, back into the soft, steady pace that it once was. Soon enough, Elio could hear the light snores that left her plump lips. "Falling asleep on me again? How predictable." He teased before giving her temple a gentle kiss. "You know, normally I ain't the type of man you want to let your guard down around. Some say I'm pretty dangerous. Do you know how many hits I've carried out on people who were in less vulnerable positions than you? I mean, you have no sense of self preservation, do you?"

As he spoke, he danced his fingers across her smooth skin, remembering the way it felt underneath him as he had his way with her, pleasuring her in ways she'd never experience with anyone else. He could spend all day listening to her cries and whimpers as she begged him for more. She sounded like a pretty little songbird, *his* pretty little songbird, so desperate and ready to be used. "It's okay, little doll. Pretty soon, you won't have to worry about being taken advantage of. I'll make sure you never leave my side." His voice was full of reassurance, speaking as though this was her biggest worry.

In Elio's mind, that should be her biggest concern. After all, she was a fragile soul who needed his help, his guaranteed safety. Of course, he was more than happy to give her that, only asking for her love and loyalty in return. It was such a small price to pay, he couldn't see any reason for her to reject it at all. Faye had already agreed to be his. The beautiful golden pendant that hung from her neck was proof of that. But he still wanted to take things even further. He'd have every piece of her, mind, body, and soul, keeping her safe and innocent, untouched by the cruel world that faced them. As long as she continued to give him the chance, he'd love her in every way that she deserved.

It took a few minutes, but he finally worked up the nerve to move her off of him. Moving carefully, he untangled her limbs, lifting her off of his large frame and slowly lowering her back down onto the large, plush bed. Faye curled up into herself, hugging a large pillow that originally sat on what was supposed to be Elio's side of the bed. His eyes scanned over her unconscious body, watching as her chest rose and fell with every little breath. "So beautiful." He mumbled, using every bit of willpower he had to not crawl on top of her, spread her long, pretty legs, and absolutely wreck her.

Oh, was it a difficult battle, almost impossible to win the more he watched her. She looked so gorgeous wearing his red button-up shirt, especially when it was thrown onto her body so haphazardly, with the buttons out of place. The bottom of the shirt rose up around her waist, exposing her midriff for him to drink in. Her silky locks, which seemed to glitter in the sunlight, flowed around her head like a halo.

He shook his head, attempting to rid his mind of all his dark, lustful thoughts pertaining to the sweet, vulnerable woman resting peacefully. As tempting as she was, the last thing he wanted to do was take advantage of her while she was unconscious. It took a lot of hard work on his part to gain and maintain her trust, so he'd be damned if he destroyed it for a moment of weakness.

"I'll just have to learn patience." He said to himself, a phrase he's repeated anytime he was with Faye. He gave her one last look, his eyes drawn towards her collarbone, which was littered with bruises and hickeys, showcasing every bit of his love for her. He took pride in marking her as his own, relishing in the fact that she enjoyed every little nip he left on her flesh.

Quickly he turned away, moving over to his suitcase, which was neatly placed next to the nightstand. Rummaging through the bag, he pulled out some clothes for himself before making his way into the bathroom so that he could properly clean himself up. As he started up the shower, he couldn't help but think about how perfect this weekend had gone so far. In fact, the whole week worked in his favor. Not only had he convinced Faye to go out with him, but she has clearly fallen head over heels in love with him, something he honestly wasn't expecting her to do. It was quite the welcoming surprise though, especially given how stubborn and closed off she appeared to be. He thought it would take a lot more work and time for him to get her to sleep with him, but she proved to be very submissive towards him.

A strange feeling crept over him as he boasted to himself about how easy it was to get Faye's attention. It was a feeling of guilt that slowly crawled into his chest, nearly suffocating him. There was something wrong with thinking about her as easy, especially after hearing her confess her love for him. "She's not easy." He mumbled to himself in mild irritation. "If she was, then she would have let every man use her like I did. She's only easy for me because she knows who she belongs to." He smiled at the thought of having the cute woman all to himself, knowing that she'd never feel the same way about anyone else.

Elio was becoming extremely possessive of her, needing to have every last drop of her attention. He knew he had feelings for the girl, which were completely obvious as he had never treated any person with as much love and care as he had for her, but he wasn't sure of what steps he should take next in dealing with those feelings. While he did the obvious thing and make her his girlfriend, he wasn't sure how satisfied he'd be with just that title. Sure, they were exclusive now, something he'd never thought he'd be with anyone, but that didn't mean he'd get to have her all the time.

Thinking about it now, he already has to give up forty hours a week with her because of her pointless job, not to mention the fifty-six hours a week she needed to get a proper rest. While he was okay with her sleeping long hours, seeing as he can still keep her close, Elio really didn't see any reason for her to work. It made no sense that she'd go to some low-paying job, work her ass off, and then come home too exhausted to even hold a conversation over the phone, much less spend the night with him. He had plenty of disposable income and practically owned the city, so there was no need for her to work.

"She's just going to have to quit." He said out loud to himself as he cut the water off and stepped out of the shower. "There's no other way around it." He decided he'd discuss it with her later, figuring it would damper the mood of their date if he brought it up this early in the day. He wasn't planning on giving her a choice in the matter either, especially after she had already agreed to be his. He was merely informing her of what was going to happen.

Making his way back into the room, he took a seat at the edge of the bed, admiring his beautiful girlfriend while he got dressed, putting on his usual attire alongside his giant, heavy jacket. Once finished, he leaned over the bed and lightly pressed his lips against hers, giving her a gentle peck. "You know what would be even better than just quitting your job? Agreeing to live with me." Faye, being completely unconscious and unable to register his words, was relaxed and unbothered as she remained curled up in the blankets, hugging a pillow close to her chest.

Just as he was about to pull her back over to him, allowing her to sleep on his chest, a muffled ringing filled the room, catching his attention. He moved off the bed, making his way over to the stand where Faye's purse sat undisturbed. Reaching in, he took out her cellphone, not even feeling an ounce of remorse in invading her privacy. Without thinking, he quickly hit answer, putting the device up to his ear so that he could hear the fool who had the audacity to interrupt his and Faye's time together.

"Hello? Faye?" A deep, gentle voice laced with caution and worry sounded over the phone as the speaker called out to the slumbering woman. Elio felt himself shake in anger at hearing a male voice speak his doll's name. "Who the hell are you?" He snarled quietly, his voice dripping with venom. Besides her siblings and her father, Faye never told him about any other men in her life and for someone to call her so casually in the early morning on a weekend, they had to have been close. Looking at the caller ID, the name that popped up didn't look like any name that was previously mentioned before.

"Excuse me?" The man asked in a shocked tone. "*Who* are you? And why do you have Faye's phone?" He threw the question back in Elio's face, not realizing what kind of mistake he just made. His rage nearly boiled over hearing this moron question him. Oh, how he wanted to yell at this man, threaten him and possibly carry out his threats, and yet he held back, not wanting to wake up his sweet little girlfriend. While he knew there was no way his doll was two-timing him, she all but confessed her love for the man after all. He couldn't help the feeling of jealousy that wrapped its tight coils around him.

Elio took a moment to gather his bearings, figuring he should play along for now until he got the full story. "My name is Elio." He growled through gritted teeth, hoping this man wasn't nearly as oblivious as his beloved. There was a pause on the phone as he heard the gears turning in the man's head. "Elio?" He repeated, his voice trembling with uncertainly. "Like the…" "Yes, yes. Now answer the damn question." He interrupted his thought process, satisfied, knowing that the man recognized him.

Atlas felt his mouth dry up and his face turn pale the second he heard the name. All he wanted to do was call and check in on his best friend. Never in a million years did he think she'd get taken by the mafia. What did she even do to provoke their wrath, anyway? 'I know she can be very blunt and her humor can be dry sometimes, but that doesn't mean she deserves whatever they're planning to do to her.' He thought to himself, trying to figure out what she did and how he can get her out of it.

"Well?" Elio asked impatiently, trying to keep his voice down. "Sorry sir, my name is Atlas, Atlas Heflin." He answered quickly, not wanting to irk the terrifying gangster more than he already has. "And who are you in relation to Faye?" Elio wasted no time in trying to figure him out. 'Oh no, he's already trying to track down her friends and family. She must have done something terrible. Shit, I'll need to tread carefully so I don't get us killed.' Atlas took a deep breath, attempting to relax his nerves. "I'm her friend and lawyer, so if she's in any trouble, I'm sure we can discuss it civilly." He used his best professional voice, hoping to reason with him.

'Trouble?' Elio thought in confusion. 'Why would my precious doll be in any trouble?' He looked over at the bed, seeing Faye still curled up sleeping peacefully. "What the fuck are you talking about?" He asked in irritation, still not happy that some asshole had interrupted his morning. "Look, I get it. She probably said or did something that offended you and I'm not trying to downplay her actions, but I promise she didn't mean any harm by it. Faye was only trying to get you to laugh. She's weird like that." He frantically explained his friend's personality.

Atlas paused for a moment, taking in another shaky breath as he thought out his next words carefully. "Please, sir, don't hurt her. I'm sure we can work out paying off whatever retribution you ask for. Just let her go." Elio balled up his hand into a tight fist, feeling nothing but anger towards this man. "Let her go? You really want me to let her go?" His voice echoed his malice towards Atlas. A part of him wanted to wake Faye up, put her on the phone and have her tell this man who she belonged to and that he was no longer welcome in her life ever again, but because of the mystery and uncertainty of this man's identity, it might cause more problems for him.

"Yes. Please just let her go," Atlas begged, hoping the terrifying gangster was feeling somewhat merciful. "We'll pay whatever price you ask for, just don't hurt her." Elio was getting rather irritated by the assumption that he was planning to harm his Faye. "What do you mean by we?" He asked. "I mean me and my aunt May. I'm sure you've heard of her and her business. She'll gladly help pay to keep Faye safe. She's like a little sister to her." He carelessly explained, not realizing Elio had been taking mental notes of everything he said.

"Interesting…" Elio mumbled to himself, hanging up the phone before Atlas could get another word in. While he didn't receive a satisfying answer about who this man was, he was handed a tool to help figure it all out. Of course, he could just wake Faye up and ask her, but what was the fun in that? Besides, if he didn't like the answer he got, the plan was to encourage Faye into cutting Atlas off completely, and that would be much harder to do if she was the one vouching for him.

Scrolling through her contacts, he finally found the number he was looking for. Hitting dial, he held the phone back up to his ear listening for the ringing. It took four rings before he heard the familiar voice on the other end. "Hallo? Faye?" May sounded confused and unsure why her young friend was calling her. "Hello May," Elio answered back, his voice low and dangerous, a warning for her to speak with caution.

May could feel her heart drumming in her chest as she heard the very voice that haunted her dreams. "E-Elio?" She stuttered out, clearly not expecting the terrifying man to be the one to speak. "Why do you have…" "Who is Atlas Hefflin?" He interrupted before she could finish her question. "Huh?" Was all she could say in reply, the question coming completely out of nowhere. "Who.. Is.. Atlas.. Hefflin..?" He repeated much slower, grinding his teeth at every word. "He's my nephew." She responded, wondering why he wanted to know.

Elio rolled his eyes, annoyed by the answer. "No shit, I wouldn't be calling you if I didn't already know that. Who the hell is he to Faye?" He couldn't stop the jealousy that leaked out with every word. Luckily, May was smart enough not to call attention to it. "They're really close friends. Like sibling close." She answered, quickly adding on the last bit in order to soothe the giant mob boss. "What do you mean by sibling close?" He needed clarification before he could be satisfied with an answer. "I mean, they're pretty protective of each other and hang out all the time, but most of their conversations involve insults and arguments. No romantic feelings at all."

"No romantic feelings? Are you sure about that?" He sounded skeptical of her words. "Yes, I'm sure. Atlas is happily married and holds no interest in women, while Faye is single and holds no interest in dating." May retorted, trying to sound calm and confident. 'Not anymore.' Elio thought with a proud smirk. "Well good. It better remain that way, otherwise I'll have no other choice but to end his life." He all but threatened, allowing his voice to lower into a growl.

May swallowed back a lump, knowing he was only trying to establish dominance. "Why the sudden interest in their friendship?" She asked before she could stop herself. "I'm just making sure everyone knows their place here." He answered with arrogance in his tone, his grin widening at how obviously confused the redhead seemed to be. "I'm sorry, but I still don't understand." She really needed to stop talking. "Well, now that Faye belongs to me, I need to make sure there aren't any pests following her around." He sounded so suave, as though he practiced those words relentlessly. Before she had even a moment to process what he said, he had already hung up on her, leaving the red-headed mistress to drown in her fears.

No longer plagued with jealousy and doubt, Elio could finally crawl back into the bed and cuddle up with his Faye. Any leftover anger he felt quickly melted away at the sight of the adorable young woman quietly snoring as she shifted closer to him, allowing him to pull her into his chest. His eyes scanned over her delicate form, lighting up at the sight of each little mark that covered her body. "I'm completely serious when I say I own you now. Body, mind, soul, it all belongs to me to use however I please." His tone sounded so loving, it almost didn't match the words that came out.

Faye proved it true by curling up into his embrace while she mumbled about how much she loved him. He found it interesting that she had already professed her love for him after barely a week of dating. It was even more interesting that both times had been while she was asleep and therefore not influenced by any outside force. Those words came straight from her heart, which made it even more wonderful to hear. It wasn't as though they weren't reciprocated either, especially after he spent weeks trying to find her.

She struggled against him, her fragile form pushing away from his grip as her light snoring ended. "Hello again, beautiful." Elio purred, watching as her eyes slowly fluttered open. "Morning 'Lio." She mumbled as she gave a soft yawn, attempting to stretch out her sore muscles. He moved off of her, allowing her some space to sit up as she stretched. He placed his hands on her shoulders, rubbing gentle circles into her tense flesh. She let out a sigh of relief as she leaned into his touch and rested her head against his chest.

"I'm guessing you're still feeling sore." He stated it more like a fact than a question. "Yeah, you were just so rough last night." She mumbled with her eyes closed, feeling him slide the red shirt off of her so he could have better access to her body. "You were the one that begged me to be rough." He reminded her, pressing his thumbs into a tense muscle, slowly rubbing out the tissue. Faye let out a shaky moan as the feeling of relief washed over her. "I know, and it felt amazing." She breathed out, focusing her attention on his magical fingers that seemed to dance across her skin. "I just like to complain." She admitted, causing him to laugh.

He moved his hands down into the small of her back, guiding her to lie down on her stomach. "I know, but that's alright, I still find you pretty cute." He added pressure towards her back, using his knuckles to really dig into her. "Really? I couldn't tell." She remarked sarcastically before pausing to take a deep breath as he pushed into her spine. He bent over her, placing his face next to her ear.

"Don't act surprised. You're one adorable comment away from being taken to my home and tied to my bed." His voice went down an octave, giving it a deep gravelly sound which turned her face bright red. "Elio, I got to say, you are far too tempting. I mean, if it weren't for my friends and family, I would happily disappear with you in a flash." She retorted, attempting to look back at him, but he kept her still as he continued to massage her. "So what you're saying is I should kill your friends and family and then kidnap you. Right?" He teased while he took a bottle of massage oil and poured a generous amount on his hands, rubbing them together.

"You could just kidnap me. No need to bring my friends and family into this." She giggled, drinking up the wonderful aroma of vanilla and sandalwood that surrounded her. "But you're the one who said they're the only ones keeping you from being with me." He reminded her as he continued to work out the knots in her back.

Faye let out soft little mewls and moans at the sensation, feeling relief as the stress quickly left her body. "No, I said they are keeping me from running away with you willingly. If you're gonna kidnap me, then what's the point of harming them? You already got me. Just make sure you pick up my cats on the way there."

"Will do." He whispered against her ear, placing a soft, sweet kiss against her temple before moving to get off her. As Faye rose from her spot on the bed, she notice just how incredible she felt after having her whole body massaged by the large man. It felt as though he had made every pain in her body magically disappear, leaving her feeling completely relaxed. "Oh, my god that feels amazing. Thanks for doing that." She gushed, pulling him into a tight hug. Elio's expression softened as his lips rose to a genuine smile at how grateful she sounded. "Anytime doll." He mumbled sheepishly, carefully hugging her back.

Pulling away from the embrace, Faye bent down to pick up the discarded shirt, slipping it back over her head. "What time is it, anyway?" She asked, plopping back down on the bed. "10:45." Elio responded, sitting next to her, allowing her to lean against his shoulder. She crinkled her nose in disapproval at that answer, groaning quietly to herself. "Jeez, it's already that late? I better call Atlas before he has a panic attack over me being MIA for so long." She grumbled in irritation, knowing how pushy and overly protective her friend can be when she goes out on dates.

Elio's eyes widened slightly at the mention of the name. Questions raced through his mind. "Who *is* Atlas?" He asked, bitterness and jealousy leaking through in his voice. "He's my best friend, of course. Haven't I told you that before?" She answered with a raised eyebrow, certain she had mentioned the man in question to him before. "No, you haven't." He retorted through gritted teeth. "He's not an old lover or crush, is he?" Faye couldn't help but laugh at the absurdity of his question. "No, of course not! He's both my best friend and also the third ugliest thing on this planet next to my two brothers." She giggled, nuzzling into his arm.

He relaxed a little after her explanation, realizing there was no way his Faye could have ever been attracted to this man. "Are you sure he isn't secretly in love with you?" Elio asked, wanting a complete guarantee there was nothing to worry about with Atlas. "Ewe gross, no, of course not. He has no romantic feelings for me at all. He isn't even attracted to women." She made a gagging noise as she spoke, emphasizing how disgusted she was with the very thought of dating him.

That was all he needed to hear to know her little friend could be trusted to keep his hands to himself. "Why the sudden interest?" She asked with a raised eyebrow and a cheeky grin. "He called earlier while you were asleep. I just wanted to make sure my little doll wasn't cheating on me with Mr. best friend over there." He shrugged, not feeling any reason to lie to her. She gave him a strange look before she burst out into laughter. "Cheating? Oh, honey, I would never. Pursuing two men at the same time takes far too much time and energy, totally not worth it." She stated through giggles.

"Glad to know the reason you won't cheat on me is because you're lazy." He playfully huffed, folding his arms to emphasize the point. "Hey! Just because I'm lazy doesn't mean I'm not loyal. You were the one to ask me out and now I'm your problem. No turning back. I'm sticking by your side until the bloody end." She said bluntly, pulling his face down to meet her eye to eye.

Try as he might, Elio couldn't keep a straight face after seeing her look at him with a goofy expression. He doubled over into laughter, bending his form to mold around hers as he pressed her into the bed. "You are too fucking cute for your own good. You know that?" He asked, nearly suffocating her with his body. "I really want to keep you trapped here with me." Maybe it was the way he spoke, or maybe it was the lack of oxygen, but for a moment, Faye wanted the same thing.

After gently smacking his arm to signal her need to breathe, he finally pushed himself off of her, only to pick her up and set her on his lap, pulling her into a tight embrace. "I guess I should probably let you call your friend back. He's probably scared shitless after the conversation we had." Elio shrugged, handing Faye back her phone. "Why? What did you do? Threaten to fill his house with spiders?" She lightly joked, earning a low chuckle from the man.

Faye quickly unlocked her phone, completely oblivious to her lover's nosy gaze, easily memorizing her passcode. The phone barely rung once before she heard the frantic tone of her best friend's voice. "Please tell me you thought about it! I promise me and May will pay you whatever amount you ask for if you let her go. Just give me a number." He pleaded, sounding completely desperate. "How about 3.50?" She answered playfully while rocking back and forth in Elio's lap.

There was a brief pause as Atlas processed the familiar voice. "Faye?" He asked with both hesitation and hopefulness. "The one and only!" She proclaimed happily, stifling a small giggle. He let out a sigh of relief, realizing his goofy friend was safe for the time being. "Oh, thank God. Where are you?" He asked with concern in his voice. "I'm in a hotel room." She responded nonchalantly. She could feel Elio tighten his grip around her waist, keeping her still and urging her to lean all the way back against him.

"Why?" Atlas asked, sounding both curious and exasperated by her answer. "Elio brought me here so we can spend the weekend together." Her words only brought more confusion to the man. "Elaborate." He said, putting emphasizes on the 't.' "What's there to elaborate on? I told you earlier this week I was going on a date. We spent the whole weekend together." She made it sound so simple, as though it were completely normal to *want* to spend the whole weekend with Elio. "I know you told me you were going out with someone you met through May…" He trailed off, questioning his friend's sanity.

Faye looked up at Elio in confusion, wondering why her friend was acting so weary of the large, kind-hearted man she was dating. The man in question gave her sides a light, reassuring squeeze as he kissed the top of her head. "Everything alright, doll?" He purred loud enough for Atlas to hear. "Yeah, everything is fine. My friend is just being his usual paranoid self." She answered jokingly, snickering at the sound of her best friend groaning on the other end.

Atlas flinched at the sound of Elio's voice, not realizing he was listening to their whole conversation. "Faye, do you think I can talk to you in a more *private* setting?" He pleaded, hoping he could warn her about the man she was dating. Elio's eyes narrowed at this request, knowing just what this man was about to pull. "Sorry, no can do." She said apologetically, blissfully unaware of the daggers her boyfriend was staring into the phone. "Please?" He begged, desperate to warn his dear friend of who she was with.

Elio felt a subtle rage course through his body as he wondered who the hell the man thought he was asking *his* girl to talk to him privately. To add salt to the wound, he obviously wanted to warn her about who Elio was, something that she really shouldn't be concerned with right now. Atlas should consider himself lucky they weren't speaking face to face, otherwise he'd end up with his skull bashed in.

As he sat, fermenting in his anger, it wasn't until he felt Faye lift up that panic really set in. "I'd really hate to interrupt, but you might want to start getting dressed. We have *plans,* after all." He said, tightening his grip and pulling her back down to remain seated in his lap. "Oh yeah… Sorry, I totally forgot." She admitted sheepishly. "Sorry Atlas, I really need to go." Before he could say another word in protest, Faye had already hung up the phone, leaving him more worried than before.

"It's alright doll, I get you're pretty excited and want to show off to all your friends, right?" He mumbled into her neck, taking in every bit of her scent. "Not really, just want to make sure he doesn't call for a wellness check. Again." She added the last part, clearly annoyed. "How often does he call for a wellness check?" Elio asked curiously. "Atlas? Not too often, but most of my friends and family do it all the time when they don't hear from me for a few days or I go off on my own. It's super fucking annoying that none of them can trust me to do things by myself." She huffed with her arms crossed. "Especially when it's usually their fault bad things happen to me." She whispered the last part so quietly he barely heard her.

Elio's gaze softened as he tilted her chin up to meet his eyes. "I promise you won't have to worry about any of that when you're with me, doll." He reassured her, his voice laced with sincerity. 'Because you won't be going anywhere without me.' He thought to himself with a devilish grin. "Thank you. I truly appreciate the fact that there is at least one person out there that believes in me." She responded with a soft smile. Leaning down, he pressed his lips against hers, coercing her into a heated exchanging in which she happily obliged.

She slung her arms around his neck, allowing herself more stability as he pushed her body flushed against his so that he could deepen the kiss. He didn't bother to ask permission and instead forced his tongue into her mouth so that he could explore the familiar territory. "Mph..." she moaned out, unable to speak as he had her gagged. "Such a brave and beautiful girl. It's no wonder everyone is so obsessed with you." He mumbled thoughtfully against her lips. "They must all want to keep you for themselves, the selfish bastards." 'They even went through the trouble of keeping you hid from me,' He added in his mind.

She felt herself growing lightheaded from the lack of oxygen while he kept her in this tight embrace. He seemed so lost in thought he nearly forgot she needed to breathe. It wasn't until she shook his arm desperately that he finally snapped out of the trance he was in. He quickly pulled away, offering a sincere apology for nearly suffocating her. "It's fine, really. A little brain damage from a lack of oxygen hurt no one." She joked, running her hand over his cheek. "Fair enough. It might do you some good to be brain dead. Apparently, you get into a lot of trouble when you're capable." He teased as he pressed his lips against her neck so that he could nibble on her soft spot.

"Ah! Elio!" she cried out, her face bright red. He swiped his tongue across her neck, tasting every inch of her as he rocked her hips against him. Her hands made their way up to his head, reaching out to grab onto his hair, but before her hands even made it close to his locks, he had her flipped over and pinned to the bed, thwarting her plans. "Better watch what you grab, little doll, or you'll be leaving this room with a terrible limp." He growled against her neck, smirking at the sound of her heartbeat racing. "S-sorry..." she stuttered out, too lost in bliss to actually care about what he said. "Are you though? Are you really?" He continued to tease, placing his knee in between her legs to separate them. "Y-yes?" It came out as more of a question than an answer. Her body felt like it was completely on fire.

"Oh? Well, if you're truly sorry, then surely you're planning to make up for it, right?" His featherlike touches grew heavier and far more adventurous as he slowly, yet carefully, drug his nails across her sensitive flesh. All she could do was obediently nod as she helplessly watched his every move through love drunk eyes. "So, little doll, what are you planning to do?" He purred with his face mere inches away from hers and both hands placed on either side of her head, caging her in.

"Boop." She spoke the word in an adorable high pitched tone, gently tapping the center of his nose with her index finger. The room went silent as Elio sat there on top of her, wearing a look of bewilderment. "Did... Did you just poke my face?" He asked, completely baffled by her actions. "Yep!" She responded in a cheerful voice. "And if you don't move, I'll do it again." She playfully threatened, bending her finger to show she wasn't bluffing.

Faye was about to poke him again when, suddenly, he went completely limp on her, costing her the use of her arms and legs. She wiggled and squirmed in an attempt to shake him off of her, but try as she might, he wasn't budging. Soon, though, she felt his body vibrate as a low chuckling sound came out. Lifting his head, he offered her a toothy smile as he placed his hand on top of her head, ruffling up her hair.

"You're so fucking cute, you know that?" He stated it as a fact, quickly rolling off of her so that she could catch her breath. "Am I?" Faye asked, taking deep breaths before moving to sit up. "Yes. So cute, in fact, that I'm thinking about just tying you up and carrying you everywhere with me." He stated with a sly smirk on his face, acting as though the very idea was absolutely genius. "Why does your answer to everything involve kidnapping me?" She giggled, leaning her head against his shoulder. "Because kidnapping you would solve all of my problems." He shrugged nonchalantly, pulling her body as close to him as possible.

Faye looked up at him with bright blue jewels, wearing the softest, most loving smile he'd ever seen. "Wouldn't it be easier if I just stayed by your side willingly? That way, my friends and family don't act all crazy to get me back?" Elio couldn't help but chuckle at this idea, finding it somewhat ironic that she was joking about the very thing he wanted more than anything. "You're right, that would be so much easier." He responded, hypnotized by her captivating eyes and beckoning lips. He shook his head, trying to snap out of the trance he was placed in.

"Of course, this will be an actual discussion later." He stated, moving her off of him. "But for now, we have plans for today, so you might want to get dressed." Faye looked slightly disappointed by the lack of physical contact but quickly got over it, instead putting on a massive grin as she stood up from the plush bed. "What do we have planned today?" She asked, stretching her arms out to relieve some of the strain sleeping placed on her limbs. "You'll see." He promised as he bent over to grab another bag that looked similar to the one she received the night before.

Faye rolled her eyes, acting annoyed by how mysterious he was trying to be. "Fine, keep your secrets." She jokingly pouted, sticking her tongue out at the large man. "Keep it up and I'll gag you when I kidnap you." He shot back, gently handing her the bag. "Jokes on you. I'm into that shit." She retorted, quickly regretting her words when she saw the look on her lover's face. She wasted no time in fleeing for the bathroom, knowing that if she stuck around any longer, Elio very well might follow through with his threats.

"That's right doll, you better run!" He teased with a goofy grin on his face. His heart raced with absolute joy as he laid back down on the bed, thinking about how incredible this weekend had been. Not only had Faye agreed to be his girlfriend, but she even confessed her love for him, albeit she was completely unconscious. It still didn't matter. Faye was his now, and he could do whatever he wanted with her. Hold her, kiss her, please her, keep her. He could do it all, and if she tried to complain, he'd just remind her this was what she agreed to.

There was one issue, though, that weighed heavily on his mind. Come Sunday evening, he'd have to send her back. That thought alone brought him complete dread, as he knew there was very little he could do to assure her safety and wellbeing. Anything could happen to her after he dropped her off. She could be kidnapped, murdered, tortured, or even...

No! He shook his head of the terrible thoughts, trying to weigh his options on how to keep his precious doll safe.

'I could just take her now.' He thought to himself. 'She loves me, so it shouldn't be too much of a fight to get her to agree.' It seemed like a reasonable enough request. Plenty of women in his past would have jumped at the opportunity to live with him, leaving behind their old life without a second thought, so there was no reason for Faye to act any different. He had everything she could possibly want, a secure home, a generous allowance, constant stimulation, and never again having to worry about bills or food, not to mention all the love and attention he was willing to give her. What more could she possibly ask for?

His smile faltered as his eyebrow twitched in irritation. While normally his points would apply to most women who seek his company, none of them stood true with his little doll. She had her own home, made her own money, had plenty of loving and trusted friends and family in her inner circle and didn't seem too pressed for cash. As far as he could tell, Faye wasn't running from anything in her past, and she most certainly did not have any kind of tragic upbringing. She had no reason or desire to uproot her whole life, and forcing her to do so would only create resentment.

The more he thought about it, the more stressed he became. While yes, theoretically he could just drug her and carry her back to the base, what then? He'd have to keep her doped up for who knows how long, just to make sure she doesn't escape. Best-case scenario, she gets Stockholm syndrome and eventually falls in love with him, but there is always that chance of her loved one's coming after them, risking everyone's life.

Currently, they were on incredible terms, moving the relationship along at an amazing speed, so he wanted to be extra careful not to completely ruin the progress. So long as she continued to comply with him, he would continue to act patient, and eventually she'll come around to the idea of depending completely on him. "I can't wait to spend the rest of my life with you." He spoke quietly to himself, wearing a devilish grin.

So deep in his thoughts, he almost didn't hear his own phone ringing an annoyingly cheerful tune. The number that appeared on the screen wasn't one that he was familiar with, so he showed a bit of hesitation before eventually answering it. "What do you want?" He sneered angrily, upset that someone once again had the sheer audacity to call him while he was out on a date. "Hello *brother*." A low voice echoed through the phone, greeting the mobster as though he were an old friend.

Elio narrowed his eyes and barred his teeth at the familiar-sounding voice. "Hello *Cosimo.*" He answered back sarcastically, venom lacing every syllable. "So much for pleasantries." The speaker retorted with a hint of disappointment in his voice. "You can shove those pleasantries up your ass, you piece of shit!" He couldn't help but snap, cringing at how loud his own voice got. "Look Elio, there's no need for the hostility, I only wanted to talk." Cosimo attempted to reason, but Elio was having none of that.

"Cut the shit and tell me why you're bothering me." He demanded, keeping his volume down so that Faye didn't accidentally overhear him. "Okay…" Cosimo sighed, hesitating to actually say his reason. It took Elio a little more probing before he actually told him. "I…" He started, but quickly cut himself off. "We want you to turn yourself in." It took the mobster a moment to process what he said, but when he did, he couldn't help but to let out a loud, hardy laugh.

"Turn myself in? Seriously? Are you fucking dense? Why the fuck would I do that?" He asked in disbelief of the request. "I know it seems ridiculous, but hear me out. If you turn yourself in, we can get your sentence down to only four years, which is pretty fucking amazing considering everything you did." He attempted to reason with Elio, who was not impressed by the offer. "Or I could not turn myself in and serve no time in prison. That seems like a more beneficial deal to me." He shrugged, somewhat amused by the audacious statement.

"I know there's bad blood between us, but me and Luciano really want to help you out. Taking this deal would be like resetting your life. All your crimes would be paid for with very little time wasted. Four years is nothing compared to the rest of your life and after that, we can start all over again." Cosimo said to convince him. His words only further angered Elio, causing him to grit his teeth in frustration. "Start over? You want to start over? After everything you two assholes did to me, you think we can fucking start over and play happy family again? Are you out of your fucking mind!?" He had to step out onto the balcony, knowing he could no longer control his volume.

Cosimo winced at his spiteful words, knowing his brother's anger was completely justified. "Okay, yes, we fucked up! I know but…" "But what!? You two assholes left me for dead in that fire without a second thought! Didn't bother to even look for me until it was too late! And now you think you can call me up and demand I throw away a life I worked hard to achieve!? I finally find some fucking happiness and peace and here you come to rip it away from me! Give me one good reason I should turn myself in and don't give me any of that family bullshit!" He couldn't contain the burning rage he felt towards this man, ready to hang up the call out of frustration.

"We know about the girl!" Cosimo blurted out before he could stop himself, panic taking over at the thought of Elio hanging up and becoming unreachable. "What the fuck did you just say?" Elio's voice went dark and quiet, daring him to repeat himself. "We were given a tip about you and some girl leaving *Cresent Waves* together and that there is you two are allegedly a couple." He further explained, hoping to keep his attention. "We did our research and know who she is and what she does. Faye seems like a really sweet girl and it wouldn't be right for her to get caught up in your shady lifestyle. It would be a shame if something terrible happened to her because you refuse to comply."

"Are you threatening me?" He growled through gritted teeth with a rage bubbling inside of him. "Because if you are, I promise I'll make your last days fucking miserable." Cosimo felt a cold chill at his warning, a part of him wanting to tread carefully with his next words. "Brother, I promise you it's not a threat. If you continue down the path you're on, and she chooses to stay with you, regardless if she knows or not, we will have no other choice but to treat her as an accomplice." He warned, swallowing down his worry.

Elio's eyes glowed red with fury upon hearing these words as a bloodlust overtook him. "If you lay so much as a finger on her, I'll rip out every vessel from your body and bleed you dry as I tear your ugly fucking head off and mount it to my wall. Don't fuck with me!" With that final warning, he ended the call, nearly breaking his phone. His body trembled in anger as he attempted to calm himself down before going back inside.

Thoughts raced through his mind, wondering if his brothers were really that cruel to go after his beloved Faye just to get under his skin. The very idea of her being taken away from him chilled him to his core. After all that time and effort in trying to get her, there was no way in hell he'd let them get close enough to take her. After everything, he refused to be alone again. If Elio had to burn this whole city to the ground just to keep his Faye safe, he'd gladly do it without a second thought.

As he walked back into the hotel room, still steaming with anger, he stopped frozen in his tracks the moment he spotted Faye sitting on the bed, her long, smooth legs lazily swaying back and forth as she waited for the man's return. He almost tripped over himself at the sight of her in the outfit he picked out. She had on a white laced blouse that shaped her chest beautifully, allowing her golden necklace to rest proudly in the center, showing off who owned her. The sleeves were long and puffy cuffing around her wrists, with red ribbons wrapped on each end. She wore a flowy red skirt that stopped at her ankles and almost looked like a flower with the way it moved around her.

The more he stared at her, the more he appreciated every little detail that went into her outfit. She had on pretty white sandals that had white flowers that covered the straps and accented her adorable petite feet perfectly. His eyes traveled up her legs, drinking in every inch of exposed skin until he landed on her face. Her silky blonde locks were styled into a half ponytail decorated with her flower hair clip. Everything about her appearance was just so perfect it almost made him forget about his anger.

"Is everything okay?" She asked in her sweet, melodic voice. "Yeah, don't worry about it, doll." He answered, sounding far calmer than he did a few minutes ago. He slowly made his way towards her, eyes not leaving her face. Before Faye could utter another word, he was already on top of her, pinning her to the bed. Something felt different about his embrace this time, almost desperate and protective, seeming as though if he let go she would disappear forever.

She allowed herself to relax into his touch, feeling his body melt around her. While she closed her eyes. With her ear pressed up against his chest, she could hear the soft beating of his heartbeat, which further soothed her. "Elio…" she mumbled, trying her hardest to stay awake. "Shh.. I know… I know… Just bear with me for a few minutes." He retorted in a soft, loving voice, taking in every part of her. While he knew they needed to get up, Elio wanted to stay in this position as long as possible.

They had remained cuddled up with Faye laying underneath him for a good fifteen minutes, nearly causing her to fall back asleep. It wasn't until her stomach let out a low growl that they finally untangled from one another. Faye's face blushed bright red in embarrassment at the noise, praying that Elio didn't hear it. Unfortunately, his sudden shift and light chuckle were clear indications that he definitely heard her. "Hungry?" He asked in a playful tone. "A little…" she admitted with her head hung down in shame.

Pulling himself up with one arm, he offered her a kind, gentle smile while he helped her off the bed. "Any cravings?" He asked, attempting to make her feel less embarrassed over something so small. "I'm fine with whatever." She said in a sweet voice, swaying back and forth on the heels of her feet. "I figured you would be, but still there has to be something in particular you want." He insisted, wanting so badly to treat her to a nice brunch.

Faye thought about it for a moment, unsure if she should really decide, especially since Elio was the one paying for it, but she figured he wouldn't ask if he truly didn't want her to pick. "Well… I could go for a good omelet." She suggested, fully expecting him to shut her down. "Hmm… That sounds pretty good." He nodded in approval. "I think I know a place to get a decent one." He responded, offering his arm for her to take. Faye, without a second thought, accepted his arm, hugging it tight to her chest.

Chapter: 12

He led her out of the hotel room, making sure the door was locked behind them before leading her down the hall towards the elevator. As excited as Faye was to spend another day with her boyfriend, she couldn't help but notice something was off about him. "Everything okay?" She asked, concerned by his sudden aloofness. "Oh, yeah… Everything's just fine. Why?" He responded quickly, causing her some suspicion. "It's just… You seem troubled. Like someone just told you, the world is going to explode." She said, attempting to throw in a joke in case he wasn't in the mood to fully open up.

He tilted his head in curiosity, wondering how she picked up on his distress so easily. "Yeah, I guess I am, but don't worry, everything will be fine." He retorted, kissing the top of her head gently. "If you say so, but you know you can talk to me about anything, right? I am your girlfriend, after all." She reminded him with a sweet smile. Elio couldn't help but perk up at that, wishing he had recorded her saying she was his girlfriend, so he could hear it repeatedly. "Yes, you are," He stated proudly, pulling her into a tight hug. "And not a damn thing could change that." 'Except a wedding ring.' He thought to himself with a devilish grin. "Good, glad you understand." She mumbled against his chest, waiting for the elevator to transport them back down to the lobby.

Once they finally made it down, Elio swept Faye off her feet, carrying her bridal style through the hotel. Breathing in his intoxication smell, she allowed herself to relax, trusting he wouldn't drop her as he practically skipped out the door. "There is something I want to confess to you," Elio whispered quietly to her. "What is that?" Faye replied in an equally quiet voice. "We won't be returning to this hotel tonight."

Her smile drooped down into a disheartened frown upon hearing those words. "Oh…" she breathed out, trying her hardest not to sound too dejected. "I understand." Faye sounded so heartbroken, it nearly broke Elio. "What's wrong doll?" He asked, confused by the sudden mood shift. "Nothing's wrong. I mean, I'm sad to cut the date short, but like I said, I understand. I'm sure we can always meet up later." It took him a moment to process what she was saying, but when he did, he couldn't help but laugh.

"Doll, I ain't cutting our date short. You are still spending the rest of the weekend with me. We are just staying somewhere different." He explained in between chuckles. Faye's face held an 'O' expression as she realized her own mistake. "Oh, thank God." She sighed in relief, excited that their weekend get-away was still ongoing. "That's so cute. You were sad about going home early." He cooed, nuzzling his face against her cheek. "Of course I was sad. I've been looking forward to spending time with you all week." She retorted in a soft tone, sounding like a kicked puppy.

Elio's expression softened at her tone, his eyes shining with a look of adoration for the girl. "You're such a sweet girl, you know that?" She beamed up at him, nuzzling happily into his chest. "Only to you." She admitted with a loving smile. 'I wish.' He thought to himself. 'If you were a bitch to everyone else, then it would be far easier to kidnap you.' He pushed those thoughts towards the back of his mind, knowing soon enough she'd be his and his alone.

They finally made it outside into the hotel's courtyard, where Elio sat Faye down on a wall near the fountain. "Stay here." He told her, giving her no other options but to listen. The outfit he had her wearing wasn't really suitable for climbing after all, so she could only nod in acknowledgement as she sat there, watching the fountain rain down. He took one final glance at her before turning around and walking towards the parking lot.

He made his way over to the SUV that had been chauffeuring him and Faye around, walking straight up to the driver's side. The driver rolled down his window, awaiting orders from the large, intimidating man. "Our location has been compromised. I need you to head up to the hotel room and pack it all up to bring back to the base." He ordered, holding a stoic expression. "What about the girl?" The driver asked, motioning towards Faye, who seemed completely oblivious to her surroundings as she sat comfortably on the wall, humming a jolly tune. "She'll be coming with us." He stated it as though it were obvious.

After giving the order, Elio turned back towards the cheerful girl who seemed to be in a deep level conversation with a dove that landed next to her. He couldn't help but laugh at how silly she looked, attempting to give the brainless bird an existential crisis while she waited patiently. "And after having your stomach pumped, you have to go on a strict diet while also taking medications that should kill off the worms. It's honestly a traumatic experience with lifelong effects." He did not know what the hell she was talking about, but she looked adorable talking to the bird.

"Ready to go, doll?" Elio asked, helping her off of the wall. "Ready as I'll ever be." She responded cheerfully. He placed her on the ground, helping her dust off the dirt that collected on her skirt before wrapping his arm around her, guiding her towards a pathway that led to the sidewalk.

"What a lovely day." Faye observed with a look of tranquility on her face. "Yeah, it really is. Figured it was too lovely to pass up on a nice stroll." He responded awkwardly, rubbing the back of his head. Elio was not one for pointless small talk, but he knew walking in silence wasn't a better alternative. "Fair enough. I'm always down for a nice walk and light chatter." She giggled, loving how bashful he was acting. "Oh? Anything in particular you want to talk about?" He asked, hoping to get past the cumbersome conversation.

Faye stopped for a moment, looking up at the sky in thought before turning to look back at a curious-looking Elio. "Let's see… Hmm… Well… Did you know you have freckles?" She asked with an adorable smile. "Freckles?" He repeated, wondering if he heard her right. "Yeah, freckles. You have these cute little brown specks all over your cheeks. It's pretty hard to see unless someone gets up close and personal with you." She explained enthusiastically, nearly causing him to fall to his knees in laughter. Out of all the things she might talk about with him, the last thing he was expecting was a discussion on his features.

"Up close and personal, eh?" He said with a mischievous smirk as he bent down to her height. Before she could say anything, he had her up in the air, clinging to his shoulders as he continued to march forward. "See any freckles?" He asked teasingly. "Maybe. It's hard to tell. I better get closer." She retorted with just as much mischief. He was about to respond but was cut off by her smashing her lips to his, catching him completely off guard. "You really like playing with fire, don't you?" He chuckled as he sat her down. "If it means I get to catch you by surprise, yes. I love playing with fire." She shot back, sticking her tongue out.

Elio was practically drinking up this banter, enjoying every second he spent talking to her. She had this aura of comfort that surrounded her, making her feel like a safe space for him. The way she smiled so warmly at him, the soft, sweet giggle she'd do when he said something that amused her, every part of her, was what he imagined heaven to be. "You would be the type to like it hot." He responded with a sly smirk as he reached down to grab her bottom, giving it a light squeeze.

"Actually, I prefer cooler weather." She said playfully. "Then why the hell do you live out here in the desert?" Elio's question was pretty valid, though he did not know how they went back to talking about the weather. "I have no idea." She shrugged, leaning her head against his arm as they continued to walk. "For a while now, I've been considering moving to a colder and quieter place." This off handed comment really bothered him, though he attempted to play it off cool. "It's pretty quiet up where I live, and a lot cooler, too. Closer to the mountains, you know?" He said, keeping a straight face. Faye looked at him for a moment before snorting at his comment. "Is this your way of asking me to move in with you?" She giggled, feeling his arm tighten its grip on her. "Maybe." He retorted with a cheeky smile. "But we can always discuss it later. For now, why don't we get some food?"

Before Faye could respond, Elio had already pulled her into a nice, high-end restaurant, rendering her speechless. "Is this really necessary?" She asked, completely shocked by her surroundings. "Absolutely." He nodded with a smirk, loving how nervous she was acting. "I only want the best for you, after all." He winked, kissing the top of her head. "Well, I... Really appreciate it. This is such a lovely place." She said nervously, trying not to appear an ungrateful brat.

Elio gently grabbed her chin, pulling her face up to meet his. "You are an amazing woman who deserves the world. Please let me give it to you." His tone was so soft and gentle and his eyes shined bright with affection. He was begging her to let him spoil her, and yet she still hesitated, unsure if his actions were to show her kindness and generosity or to hold power over her. The more she stared into his beautifully hypnotic optics, the more she felt obligated to give in and enjoy the date. There was something about him that felt safe and sincere, allowing her to relax as he pulled her along through the restaurant, barely acknowledging the hostess as he led her near the back.

"Aren't we supposed to wait to be seated?" She asked, while trying to catch her breath. "Nah, I come here often enough that they keep a seat reserved for me." He answered with a proud smile as he motioned for her to crawl into the booth as he followed her. "Dang, this place must be good, then." She retorted, stifling a giggle at the thought of Elio showing up every morning to this restaurant and the staff all but rolling their eyes before pointing to the back of the building.

"Something wrong?" Elio asked, concern in his voice, noticing that his girlfriend had been sitting in silence for a good minute. "Yep, all's good." She responded, giving him a thumbs up as she leaned her head against his shoulder. "Just making sure it worries me when you stop talking." He mumbled, wrapping his arm around her waist so he could pull her in even closer to him.

Faye looked up at him with a skeptical look etched on her face. "You really like when I talk?" She asked in disbelief. Most people would prefer if she talked less, so hearing something like this from the handsome man was almost too good to be true. "Yeah, of course I do." He answered without hesitation. "You have a very soothing voice, and your laugh is contagious. You also show such an incredible passion for every topic you discuss. I could honestly listen to you talk about Viking torture techniques all day. That's how mesmerizing you are."

Her eyes softened as a look of awe adorned her face. He was making it far too easy to fall deeper in love with him. "You make it sound like Viking torture techniques aren't already interesting." She playfully huffed while crossing her arms, which earned a laugh from the large man. "Not really. As fun as the bloody eagle sounds, nothing beats good old fashion flaying. Nothing like slowly peeling off your enemy's skin." He stated rather matter-of-factly. "Flaying is a good one, but what about impalement? The fact that it takes days for the person to die is pretty brutal. Plus, imagine the victim struggling desperately to get off the pike while they slowly slide down it." She retorted, going into detail about the process.

Elio wasn't lying when he said he loved hearing her talk. She always had some sort of retort for him, which was usually followed up with a fun fact about the topic they were invested in. It helped that her quirky brutality gave him pretty good ideas on how to face his enemies, but that wasn't something he'd tell her, at least not right now. Maybe when he had her moved in and fully dependent on him, he'd tell her the truth, but only if he was certain she could handle it. Staring at her now, cuddled up next to him as they waited for their food, he couldn't help but hope she'd never find out.

After knowing each other for barely a week, he still couldn't believe she was with him as his girlfriend. He felt so giddy, like a child spending time with their crush on the playground. Every date he took her on created a deeper bond, one that almost felt inevitable, as though they were made for each other. Elio absolutely loved her in every way possible. He both desired and was willing to do anything for her if only she'd allow him the chance to do so.

"So, where are we going to next?" Faye asked, pulling Elio out of his thoughts. She held a look of excitement on her face as she waited patiently for him to explain their plans. He offered her a sly smirk and a wink, nearly gushing when she covered her mouth as she stifled a giggle. "Well doll, I figured we could go on a small walk, look at the city and check out some shops around here." He purred, nuzzling into her neck. "After that, I want to take you back to my place so we could unwind a little, maybe cuddle a bit." She felt a pleasant shiver run up her spine at the mention of cuddling. "That sounds wonderful." She breathed out, completely flustered by his plans.

She rested her head against his arm as he stroked her hair affectionately. They took a moment to enjoy each other's company, letting the atmosphere fall into a comfortable silence while they cuddled together. Bystanders passed by the couple's table, looking on with utter disbelief at the sight of the terrifying man acting so gentle and loving towards the sweet yet oblivious young woman. Those whose gazes lingered a few minutes too long received a threating glare from Elio, warning them to mind their own.

"Ready to go?" He asked in a soft voice as he gave her side a light squeeze. "Yep!" She chirped happily, slipping out of the booth quicker than Elio would have liked. His eyes flashed with a look of longing and disappointment at the lack of warmth from her soft body. "Excited?" He said, amused by her enthusiasm. "Of course I am. I get to do more things with you." She retorted cutely. He let out a hearty chuckle, lazily moving up from his spot to stand next to her. He pulled her into him, pressing her close to his body as he moved his long legs forward towards the exit.

Faye clung onto his torso, trying her hardest to keep up with his fast pace. He was practically dragging her out of the restaurant, excited to show her the city in a way that she had never seen before. "Elio! Slow down!" She whined, completely out of breath. "Sorry doll." He apologized, slowing his pace down to a simple stroll, allowing the small woman to comfortably walk next to him.

"So, doll, have you ever thought about marriage?" Elio asked, guiding her down a path against the city streets that were lined with brush and desert marigolds. "Not really. I always figured I'd just rescue fifty cats and grow old as a crazy cat lady." She joked with a slight shrug, wearing a goofy smile. "You're already a crazy cat lady, so that ain't much of a deal breaker. I can see you marrying some big shot and forcing the poor bastard to take in those fifty cats of yours." He teased, ruffling her head. Secretly, he hoped that poor bastard ended up being him.

"What about you?" Faye asked, leaning her head against his side. "Is there potential for a Mrs. Eclissi in your future?" Elio gave the woman a soft squeeze before offering her a sly smile. "Maybe. Why? Are you putting in your application?" He remarked with a low purr, causing her to blush. "Perhaps one day, this relationship is still too new. Who knows how far it will go." She answered honestly, causing him to laugh. "Damn you're brutal. Keep acting like that and you won't have a say in marrying me. I'll just force you to." Faye, ignorant of the dark glint in Elio's eyes, giggled at his statement.

They continued to chat as they walked. Occasionally, Elio would steal a kiss from her, causing her heart to flutter. This felt like a wonderful dream for her, walking around the city with the handsome and protective giant as he hugged and kissed her while whispering words of endearment into her ears. Everything just seemed so perfect. There wasn't a single thing that could ruin the day for them.

Suddenly, Elio stopped walking and pulled Faye in close to him, practically hiding her in his jacket. His eyes narrowed as he bared his sharp teeth. "I'm going to pick you up." He warned in a serious tone. "When I do, I need you to keep your face hidden until I say everything is clear." Faye looked up at him, confused by his sudden shift in tone. "What's going on?" She asked worriedly. "Don't worry about it doll, I promise everything will be fine. I just need you to do what I say, okay?" He leaned down, giving her the sincerest look he could muster up. She nodded in response, allowing him to scoop her up bridal style. Quickly, she pressed her face into his neck, hoping that would be enough to cover her from whatever threat was present.

What Faye failed to notice was the black van that slowly crept down the road, following them for the last two blocks. Elio caught on immediately, guiding her in weird directions just to be sure they were being followed. After the last random turn, his suspicions were confirmed that the van had to have been one that belonged to his rivals, the Black Spades. While he already knew exactly what they wanted from him, there was one thing he couldn't quite figure out. How did they cross over into his territory without being detected? Surely one of the men he assigned to guard the area had to have seen them, unless one of them was secretly a traitor.

He shook his head to clear his mind of those thoughts, knowing it wouldn't do him any good. Elio was planning to punish those men either way, so there wasn't any point in stressing out about it too much, especially when he had Faye with him. Last thing he wanted was to cause her any unnecessary worry.

With Faye comfortably settled into his arms, he started walking at a quicker pace, attempting to not draw too much attention to himself. He moved away from the road, making it impossible to follow by car, as he pulled out his phone and dialed a number. "They're here. I'm heading back to the parking lot now." He spoke in a cold, menacing tone, hoping his girlfriend didn't pick up on it. Luckily, she seemed so busy trying to stay hidden she didn't even notice the tone change.

"You're doing good, doll." He praised in a sweeter and gentler voice than he had held seconds ago. Shifting Faye in his arms, he settled her in one arm while he placed his other hand on his gun, gripping the handle for dear life. If it came down to it, Elio was prepared to have a full on shoot out with the rival gang members, risking the lives of many innocent bystanders possibly sending them to their graves. If that's what it took to protect his precious Faye, then so be it. Her life outweighed the lives of every man, woman, and child in this city, so a few worthless casualties meant nothing to him.

Heavy footsteps sounded behind them, moving closer with each step. Nervousness had crept its moist, bony hands around Faye's body, causing her to tense up in anticipation. "Cover your ears," Elio whispered, feeling just as nervous. Without a second thought, she did as she was told, blocking her ears so that the world around her was muffled out.

A loud bang rang around them. The smell of smoke invaded her nostrils as she remained hidden against his chest. The temptation to ask questions grew more intense the longer they walked, and hearing what could very well be a gunshot only watered the seed of curiosity, but Faye once again swallowed down the urge. Surely Elio wouldn't keep her in the dark for too long.

Finally, after an eternity of walking, they safely made it back to the parking lot where their vehicle sat waiting for their return. Elio sat her inside before crawling in after her, signaling for the driver to go. "You can open your eyes again, but I need you to look at me and nothing else, okay?" He said gently, taking her small, soft hands in his much larger and rougher ones. Slowly she opened her eyes, obediently doing as she was told, while giving him a warm, comforting smile. "Okay." She nodded without complaint.

In the distance, she could hear more loud bangs followed by police sirens, which almost prompted her to look out the window. Instead, she focused all of her attention on Elio, who seemed completely on edge. "Is everything okay?" She asked, worried about his stress levels. "Yes, everything's fine. It's just…" He let out a frustrated sigh, a look of guilt flashed into his eyes. "Something has just come up, so I don't think it's safe for us to linger in the city any longer. I know it's not ideal, but I think it would be best if we spend the rest of the weekend at my place."

The vehicle went quiet for a moment as Faye processed what he said. Elio couldn't help but worry about how she was planning to react to the news. He was almost certain she would be upset over having to change plans, and he wouldn't blame her for reacting that way. Who wants to be locked in their significant other's bedroom all day as a form of a date?

Despite his irrational fear, she proved him wrong by offering a sincere smile as she wrapped her arms around his waist, nuzzling her face into his chest. "That's totally fine. As long as I get to spend the weekend with you, the location doesn't matter." She promised, just happy to be with him. "So you're really not going to ask any questions?" He wondered, flabbergasted by her understanding. "Nope, not right now." She shook her head, still smiling. "Good. That's why I like you so much. You're willing to do things, no questions asked." He chuckled, petting her hair.

"Oh no, I'm still going to ask those questions. It'll just be at the most random time when you least expect it." She playfully retorted with a mischievous glint in her eyes. "Fair enough." He chuckled before placing a soft kiss on her temple. "No, seriously, you will not see it coming. It'll be like forty years from now when we're lying together on our deathbed, about to take our last breaths. That's when I'll hit you with the questions." She giggled, cuddling up close to him. "Why does that actually sound nice?" He wondered, his features softening as he felt her body relax against him. As irritating as the situation was, at least he had his Faye to help pull him through it.

Chapter: 13

After an hour and a half of driving, they made it past the city, leaving whatever nonsense disrupted their date behind them. Elio was on his phone most of the drive, quietly yelling at whatever poor sap was on the receiving end. Faye, who had her whole face smothered into his chest, found entertainment in messing with his jacket while she patiently waited for him to finish up.

She tried with all her might to stay awake, but found it difficult because his body was extremely warm and comfortable. 'It's no wonder I keep falling asleep.' She thought to herself, letting out a soft yawn. "Oh, I'm sorry doll, am I boring you?" Elio asked with a smirk as he ended his phone call. "Yeah, kind of," Faye retorted bluntly, looking up at him with sleepy eyes. "Damn, cold as ice." He chuckled with a sharp toothed grin. "I wasn't raised to be a liar." She shrugged nonchalantly, earning another laugh from the large man.

"So, where are you taking me again?" She asked, attempted to look out the window. He quickly grabbed her chin, forcing her eyes to remain on him. "My place. But I can't tell you where it is, at least not yet," He explained calmly. "No fair. You know where I live." She pouted cutely, crossing her arms. "Life ain't fair, doll." He retorted as he attempted to distract her with his lips. "Why not?" She playfully whined, moving her head so that he could have more access to her neck. "Because it's not. Not everyone should be allowed to have what they want." He mumbled, his lips practically glued to her skin.

Faye bit her lip, holding back a loud moan as she gripped onto his shoulders for stability. "So I'm not one of the people whose allowed to have what they want?" She asked through half-lidded eyes, feeling his wandering hands move up her skirt. "I never said that. Obviously, you'll have everything you want soon enough. You just have to do one thing to get it all." He smirked, pulling away from her neck to admire his work. "And what's that?" She wondered, curious about his condition for her. "You'll find out later." He teased, tapping her on the nose. "Ugh…" she groaned, smashing her face back into his chest. "Why are you so difficult?" As much as she tried to sound annoyed, she couldn't help her little giggle that gave away how much she enjoyed this little game.

"If you insist on not letting me see, wouldn't it be easier to blindfold me?" She asked, bringing logic into their conversation. "Yeah, it would be easier, but forcing you to look at me is far more entertaining." He retorted, tightening his grip around her waist. "You know this is the exact reason I keep falling asleep on you, right? You're too damn warm and comfortable." She grumbled, breathing in his heavenly aroma. "Really? I figured the real reason is because you stay up all-night binge watching dumb shows." He jokingly chided, kissing the top of her head affectionately. "Be honest, that's the case, right?"

Faye gave him a look of fake astonishment before going back into a more stubborn stance. "You know what? I know my rights and I'm not answering that without a lawyer present." She huffed while crossing her arms. "I ain't no cop and you have no rights." He responded quick as lightning before capturing her lips again, silencing her protests once and for all. What a strange woman she was, having her only questions and concerns act as playful banter. He could get used to this life with his new found girlfriend.

Once the vehicle slowed down, coming to a stop, Elio reached into his pocket, pulling out a long, thick piece of fabric before grasping Faye's face in his other hand. "Actually… I need to blindfold you for this part." He informed her, his tone sincere and apologetic. She shrugged her shoulders with a soft smile and a look filled with understanding. "I figured you would. It's alright." She beamed up at him, feeling him relax at her words. Holding the blindfold up to her face, he gently tied it around her eyes, being extra cautious not to pull on her hair.

"How are you feeling? It's not too tight, is it?" He asked, concerned that she might be uncomfortable. "I'm fine…" she started, her voice quiet and distant. "It's just…" He looked at her, worry etched on his face. "Did you purposely give me the see-through blindfold?" She sounded so serious that it caught him completely off guard. "What?" He asked, shocked by her sudden question. Faye burst out in to laughter, wishing she could see the look on his face. "I'm just kidding! It's fine." She exclaimed in-between giggles. "You dork." He grumbled, flicking her forehead. "You're lucky you're cute, otherwise I'd have you dumped in the nearest lake." While this was his attempt at sounding threatening to her, it was not received as a threat at all. "It is a lovely day for a swim." She jested, earning herself another flick to the forehead.

The moment the vehicle came to a stop, Elio wasted no time in throwing the door open before quickly jumping out, slinging a blindfolded Faye over his back. To an outsider, it looked as though the enraged man had kidnapped the poor girl and was holding her hostage, but that couldn't be further from the truth. In reality, Elio, while still miffed about everything, was more concerned with his lover's safety, worried that if he allowed her to wander the base by herself, his men might not contain themselves around her. The very thought of them dirtying his precious doll nearly sent him into a rampage.

Upon noticing all the quiet whispers and curious stares that surrounded them, Elio harshly slammed his fist into the wall, creating a decent sized hole. Consequentially, it made Faye flinch from the sound, but his show of anger was indeed affective towards his men, who all moved along, making as little eye contact as possible. If she asked about the sudden bang, he'd just have to make something up to ease her mind. "I want Flako's clique in the red room now!" He demanded; his request directed at a nearby capo who was attempting to walk beside him. "Right away, boss!" The gangster responded in affirmation before quickly darting off in another direction.

He kept a stoic, almost terrifying expression as he continued to march forward, with Faye still dangling helplessly from his shoulder. "Elio…" she whimpered quietly. "Please slow down. I think you're bruising my ribcage." The large man stopped in his tracks and moved her back into his arms so that she could be comfortable. "Sorry doll." He apologized, his voice much softer than when he was addressing his men. "It's okay." She replied sweetly, reaching her hand up to touch his face.

His lips twitched up into a small smile as he leaned over to kiss her on her cheek. She was such an adorable dame, so loving and forgiving, he just wanted to throw her on a bed and keep her trapped underneath him. Someone as precious as Faye needed to be kept locked up, safe and happy, hidden away from the trash that covered this disgustingly cruel world.

Quickly making his way down the long, wide hallway that was littered with doors, he finally came to the end. There he stood, with Faye in arms, in front of a large, ten foot tall door made of reddish-brown mahogany wood. He shifted her into one arm and used his now freed hand to pull out a set of keys. After a moment of struggling, he finally found the right key and quickly slid it into the lock on the golden doorknob. The moment a click sounded, he threw open the door before kicking it shut, locking him and Faye inside alone together.

"Alright, I'm going to put you down now and take off the blindfold, but only if you promise to behave." He told her in a playful tone, slowly lowering her to the ground. "I promise." She retorted, just as playfully, with a mischievous smile gracing her face. The second her feet touched the ground, and she felt the fabric slip off her face, she sped towards the door, reaching for the handle as she snickered wickedly to herself.

Just as her hand touched the cool metal, she felt a pair of arms slip around her waist, pulling her back against a large chest. "What the hell did I just say?" Elio spoke in a stern voice as he squeezed her tightly. "Let's play tag, I'll be it?" She answered sheepishly, her face bright red and heart beating out of her chest. "No, I told you to behave." He chided, carrying her over to a huge bed that was three feet tall and had a mattress that seemed to be ten inches thick.

The bed was a king sized bed that sat in the middle of the room, decorated with beautiful ruby colored silk sheets and a large red and black checkered pattern quilt. At the head of it sat six huge, fluffy pillows adorned with pillow cases mirroring the same fabric and color as the sheets. Neatly placed in front of the large pillows were three smaller, decorative pillows made of sheep skin dyed wine red.

Faye felt herself being slammed against the large plush mattress, causing her body to bounce slightly. Just as she was about to sit up, Elio had her pinned to the bed with a look of determination etched onto his face. Before she could speak, he had his lips over hers, kissing her with an intense amount of hunger and desperation while trying to force his way into her mouth. His hands made their way up her skirt, lifting it towards her stomach.

In a desperate attempt to push him off of her, she thrusted up against his crotch, causing him to let out a low groan. "I am going to fucking break you." He growled against plump lips, loving the way she turned into a submissive whimpering mess before his very eyes. As he pulled away, he still kept his body pressed on top of her, keeping her pinned to the bed. "Anything to say?" He smirked, eyeing her up and down as though she was a delicious steak and he was a starved wolf. "I'm starting to think you're not joking when you say you're going to kidnap me."

Tilting his head to the side, he looked down at her, his eyes filled with curiosity. "How do you manage to remain a smartass through all that?" He asked in amazement. "I'm just built different." She shrugged nonchalantly. "I mean, you should have seen some of the shit I said while being waterboarded." Elio could only shake his head, amused by her dumb comment. In response, Faye lifted her head up so that she could plant a small, tender kiss on his lips, pulling away quickly before he could react.

He looked down at her with adoration, silently wondering how he got so lucky. "This is pretty unfortunate." He spoke solemnly, hanging his head low to give the illusion of melancholy. "What's wrong?" She asked with a worried expression. "I finally have you all to myself and we get caught up in petty bullshit." He sounded so dejected when he spoke, as though he were truly disappointed at the turn of events.

Reaching her hand up, she took Elio by his tie, pulling him back down to her face. "We're together now. That's all that matters." She quickly replied before pressing another kiss onto his lips. He relaxed into the kiss, slowly taking control of the moment. Feeling a soft nibble on her bottom lip, she opened her mouth up, allowing him access without too much of a fight. Heavy eyelids fluttered shut as slender arms slithered around his neck, locking him in place.

Faye couldn't get enough of him; his deep, husky voice, his handsome, well-proportioned features, his dark, unapologetic sense of humor, all of it was everything she wanted in a man plus more. He was such a sweet and caring lover, making sure she was always satisfied with their activities. She's only known him for a week and yet she felt so comfortable around him, as though they've been together for years.

Many times she had to bite her tongue, terrified she'd accidentally tell him she loved him. She knew a relationship that was moving along as quickly as this one was extremely fragile, and placing any amount of pressure on it would shatter it completely. With this mindset, she treaded lightly, keeping her feelings sealed up so as not to push him away.

It took every ounce of willpower for Elio to pull away from her, but he finally pushed off the bed, leaving her a flushed and panting mess. As he stood up, he adjusted his tie before taking a glance over in Faye's direction. She looked at him with the brightest doe eyes he's ever seen. "Leaving already?" She asked, sounding a little disappointed. "Yeah, sorry about this doll, but I got business I need to take care of." He explained apologetically, offering a soft smile. "I promise I'll be back in an hour. Just hang tight."

Faye sighed quietly as she laid back down, waving her hand to shoo him off. "Fine, leave me then." She playfully pouted. "I'll just lie here all alone and cold, possibly naked." Elio seemed to perk up at that word, which she noticed immediately. "If you're going to be naked, I'll try to get back here a lot sooner." He joked while attempting to control the sudden urge to jump on her again.

Pushing herself up, she jumped off the bed and slowly saunter over to him. "Please don't rush your work for me. I promise I'll be fine for an hour." She said, concerned by the slight chance he wasn't joking. "I won't, but trust me when I say this meeting won't take too long." It was a simple punishment after all, no need to draw it out. "Good." She smiled, leaning over to pull him into a tight hug. "That would be both hilarious and upsetting if you brought me here just to abandon me." He gave a soft chuckle as he gently stroked her hair, loving how needy she acted with him.

"For someone so insistent on only going out during the weekend, you really seem to hate being away from me," He remarked in amusement, trying to work up the willpower to separate. "I only recently decided I enjoy spending time with you, so now you're stuck with me." She retorted, sticking her tongue out at him. "Oh no, I'm stuck with you? Whatever will I do?" He asked in a monotone, sarcastic voice, still refusing to let go of her. "Guess I'll just have to tie you to the bed, then."

Before Faye could react, he scooped her up and tossed her back on the bed, applying just an ounce of pressure to keep her down. "You don't want to go back home anyway, do you?" He towered over her with a predatory look shadowing his face. Her face turned beet red as she watched him with large blue jewels, trying to think up a response for him before things go too far. Suddenly, her lips twisted into a mischievous smile.

"I mean, if that's what you have to do, rules are rules, but there are a few demands. First, I need both of my cats because I ain't leaving them for dead. Second, I need to send out a mass text to all my friends and family letting them know I'm not dead, I've just been kidnapped. Third, do not tie me up with some cheap, itchy ass rope. I prefer leather or silk." She ended her rant with a playful huff, crossing her arms for good measures.

Elio looked at her with a confused expression, scanning over her face to see if she was actually being serious. The moment he realized she was only joking, he broke out into a hearty laugh, pulling her into a tight hug. "Okay, fine, I'll agree to your conditions, but you're not allowed to wear clothes." He retorted pointedly, giving her an equally playful smile.

Faye tilted her head, the playful glint no longer in her eyes and instead being replaced with one of curiosity. While most people enjoyed her sense of humor and nonchalant attitude, they usually got sick of it after spending a certain amount of time with her. Not only had Elio laughed at every one of her jokes, he also kept up with her banter, throwing in a couple of jabs for good measure. Every second she spent with him made her fall more and more in love. "Why are you every bit perfect for me?" She mumbled quietly to herself, her eyes half-lidded as she stared at him, completely lost in his eyes.

He couldn't help but smile at her question, knowing full well what the answer was. "We were designed for each other." He retorted, moving his hand down to brush some of her soft locks of hair out of her face. Nuzzling into the palm of his hand, she completely relaxed against the plush mattress, almost relieved by his answer. In truth, she was genuinely relieved, especially knowing that he clearly felt the same way about her. His answer had to be true. There was no other way around it. The fact that she could build a whole bond and trust with him in less than a week when it took years to build with people she's known for well over a decade really said a lot.

"Of course we are, and I'm happy we finally get to be together after all this time of existing without each other." She remarked, wishing so desperately for him to crawl back down into bed with her and cuddle. "Me too doll." He said sincerely, slowly moving away from her, much to her dismay. "But seriously, I need to go." His expression held a lot of guilt at abandoning her, though he hoped she truly understood his predicament. "I understand. You got a job to do. I'll be here when you get back." She reminded him. "I know that. I just hope you don't get too bored waiting for me." He retorted while adjusting his tie, so he looked more put together. "Don't worry, I mastered the art of keeping myself entertained. I was a middle child, after all."

She was just so forgiving and understanding. He couldn't help but feel more love towards the sweet woman. 'I'll just have to make this meeting fast, so I don't end up disappointing her.' He thought to himself, determined to get back to the date as soon as possible.

"Alright, as long as you're fine, I promise I won't take too long. Just stay in here and keep the door locked." He sighed, still feeling guilty over the whole thing. "Darn, there goes my weekend plans of getting lost in a strange building surrounded by strange men. That sucks." She retorted sarcastically. "Smart ass." He mumbled with an amused smirk. "But seriously, I'll wait right here for you to come back." Her voice held reassurance as she offered a lazy smile. "Thank you." He sighed in relief, happy that she, in a way, understood the importance of her not wandering around. He made his way over to the door, giving Faye one last longing look before leaving, slowly shutting the door.

Chapter: 14

She stretched out her limbs and yawned deeply before crawling off the bed so she could make her way to the door. As instructed, she locked the door, hopefully preventing any unwanted guests from entering. She slipped off the sandals, freeing her feet from their prisons so that she could feel just how soft and plush the rug underneath her was. Now that Elio was gone, she could really examine his bedroom and possibly tease him for anything found out of place. She wasn't really going to tease him, but the thought of it amused her.

The first thing she noticed was the wooden flooring, a deep red made of the same type of mahogany wood as the door. It felt so cool and sleek under her feet, way nicer than the old lament tiles she was used to in her house. The large area rug she stood on was soft and almost felt like stepping on bunnies with how plush it was. The fur had been dyed the same shade of red as the throw pillows and didn't show any wear to it, almost as though it was new and hadn't been used yet. The floor itself was completely spotless, not even a speck of dust could be seen.

Her focus switched towards the overall size of the room. "Damn, this place is huge!" She exclaimed, holding her arms out as she spun around a few times before falling back on the bed, further examining the room. The walls were a darker, more crimson shade of red and they had golden accents near the floor and ceiling. She couldn't help but notice the color theme that seemed present in all aspects of the room. Red painted the walls, ceilings, and all the décor. Even his clothes were red, something she hadn't even noticed until now. Everything either had touches of the color or were flat out painted a shade of red.

"Welp, he had a theme, and he stuck to it. Got to say I'm proud of the big guy. Not many people can show this level of dedication." She said out loud to herself with an amused smile on her face. Faye found his preference for the color endearing, seeing it as another reason to love him. Red was obviously his favorite color, so the fact that every outfit he picked for her had some form of that color added to it made her heart flutter with joy.

Crawling towards the top of the bed, she made it to a side that held a cute little nightstand next to it. She snatched the remote that sat in the center of the table and crawled under the heavy quilt, laying her head against the fluffy pillows. As fun as exploring Elio's bedroom was, she felt extremely uncomfortable with digging through his belongings. That was far too invasive for her taste and almost seemed like a breach in his trust.

"I doubt he'd care if I watch tv and take a nap." She shrugged, flipping on the large television mounted to the wall. She figured if he really didn't want her in his bed, he wouldn't have pinned her to it twice. "I kind of wish I brought something sexy to wear for when he gets back." Faye muttered to herself. "Like a cute lingerie set, or even… Hmm… Let's think what else is sexy… Oh I know!" She continued to talk to herself, lost in thought. "What about a

89

nice hospital gown? Nothing says sexy like an unflattering piece of paper that barely ties up in the back. I might even be able to find one with a floral pattern that makes it look like an old lady's nightgown."

Faye found great joy in thinking up ways she could seduce her boyfriend, or perhaps traumatize him. She let her imagine flow free as she flipped through channels hoping to find something halfway decent to watch. Normally she'd just pull out her phone and watch random videos or play some game, but her phone was in her purse, which she left back at the hotel. While she knew that was something to be worried about, she bottled up that nervousness and trusted that Elio already had that figured out.

In the end, she settled on some old sitcom that halfway caught her attention. She decided she'd just set the volume low to give her some background noise as she slowly shut her eyes. Elio said he'd be back in an hour, so that was plenty of time for a quick nap. She had a feeling she'd want to get as much rest as possible for when he comes back, if the previous night was anything to go off of.

Pulling one of the throw pillows up to her chest, she hugged it tightly, burying her face in the soft fur. While the scent was mild, she could smell a hint of Elio on the pillow. It was enough to put her at ease, knowing his presence surrounded her. Her breathing gradually slowed down and her eyes fell shut as she curled up into a ball. Soft snores fell from her parted lips as her face completely relaxed. The tv still played, though it was so quiet only the laugh track could be heard.

The moment Elio stepped out of the bedroom, his face twisted into a terrifying sneer as his eyes grew ice cold. A wave of malice surrounded him, knocking over any poor gangster that dared cross his path as he quickly made his way through the long, seemingly unending hallway. He had been done wrong by his own men, punished with their incompetence, as he nearly lost a precious life at the hands of his enemies. If those thirteen men held even an ounce of intelligence, they would know to take themselves out before being confronted by the deadly mobster.

How the hell did the Black Spades invade his territory? With as many men as he had watching over the area, it should have been near impossible, and yet there they were. Either he had rats in that group or they were just that stupid. Either way, he was planning to snuff them out. Their cooperation would only help lessen the pain they'll suffer through before the final blow as he cut out the weakest link in his organization.

He stood tall in front of a large metal door, grinding his teeth and clenching his fists as he allowed the rage he was feeling to possess his movements. Without warning, he slammed the heavy door open, revealing thirteen men sitting in the room, tied up and frightened. They stared at him with large, terrified eyes, shaking in their shoes as they waited for him to make his first move.

"Why the fuck were the Black Spades in my territory?" He demanded, his tone calm yet threatening. No one spoke up, knowing the first man to talk would be the first to die. "Well!?" His voice echoed as he grew impatient. "T-they snuck past u…" "Bullshit!" Before the brave soul could finish his sentence, Elio grabbed him by his scalp, digging his sharp nails into his skull.

Dangling the man a few inches into the air, he quickly dropped him, slamming his body in to the cold, hard concrete. Blood splattered across the floor as Elio repeatedly smashed his face into the stone, leaving him an unrecognizable mess. For a moment, he worried about his Faye seeing him covered in the man's blood, but figured he'd just slip into the shower before she could even notice.

As quickly as he ended the life of the first gangster, he made his way through every one of them, their punishments growing more and more sinister. Unfortunately, he had to limit his torture to only a few minutes per person, so he wouldn't run past the time he gave his Faye, but that didn't bother him too much, as he was determined to get his point across to them. Whether it was a betrayal or negligence, they still screwed up big time, and he would never let that level of disrespect slip by him.

Blood pooled around his feet from the litter of crushed bones and smashed brains. As he stood there still wearing the terrifying expression, he entered the room with; he turned his attention to the final man who sat there still bound by the old itchy ropes that the other men once wore. Unlike the other gang members in this group, Elio held no particular interest in culling him. He was young and had been recently initiated into the mafia, so he still had plenty of time to show his potential and use.

Elio could also acknowledge the fact that this man had the unfortunate luck of being placed in Flako's group this very day, right before everything went to shit so there was no way possible he had anything to do with the gang war that broke out in his territory. While he was a cruel and sadistic mob boss, he wasn't completely unreasonable, especially when he had more to gain from showing an ounce of mercy. Of course, just because he used mercy this time, it didn't mean he wasn't a monster. The reason he kept this gang member in the room when he did nothing wrong was so that Elio could show him what will become of him if he were to ever step out of line.

He stepped closer to the trembling man, taking absolute pleasure in the gangster's terror as he leaned down, still towering over him. Reaching his large hand down, he use a switchblade he just pulled out of his pocket to quickly tear through the ropes, freeing him from his tight bounds. "Stand up." Elio ordered, his voice booming through the metallic room. Without a second thought, the young gangster stood up from his spot, not wanting to disobey the mob boss. "I want this room scrubbed top to bottom, and the bodies disposed of before the end of the day, or I swear to God you'll be joining them." He didn't even bother to give the man a chance to respond before quickly fleeing the room, leaving the poor gangster to mop up fresh blood.

Blood dripped down from his fingertips, staining the carpet as he fell into a steady stride back towards his bedroom. He quickly wiped it off onto his pants, soaking them in even more of the thick, sticky bodily fluid. Cringing at the damp feeling, he shook his head, wanting nothing more than to take a nice shower so that he could wash off the grime that had collected on him from his job. After a relaxing dip in the shower, he would cuddle up with his amazing girlfriend, who he could only hope was currently taking a nap.

He made it back to the room much quicker than when he left, obviously excited to spend the rest of the weekend with Faye. Without hesitation, Elio reached for the doorknob, twisting it slightly only to find that it had been locked. He couldn't help the soft smile that covered his face as he thought about how she actually listened to his warning and locked the door. 'Of course she listened. My doll is so obedient, I bet she'd follow me anywhere if I told her to.' He thought to himself in amusement before shuffling through his keys.

After a moment of struggling, he finally found the right key, pushing it into the lock. Slowly, the door creaked open, allowing him to peer inside. Nothing on this planet could have prepared him for the sight that befell him as he scanned the room, searching for the young woman. There she lay in the middle of the bed, the blanket curled up around her as she nuzzled into his pillows. She looked so peaceful and beautiful, like an innocent angel who was completely oblivious to the devil that stood in front of her. While he had watched her sleep plenty of times already, seeing her lay defenseless in his own bed was on a whole other level.

He shook his head, clearing his thoughts of all the things he could do to her in this position. He, of course, was planning to follow through with those perverted thoughts, but he certainly would not so much as touch her in his current state. The idea of her being touched by him while his hands were covered in filth disgusted him. Faye deserved him at his best, so he refused to give her anything less than perfection. "I'll be right back, doll." He whispered before cautiously creeping towards the bathroom, not wanting to wake her up. He chuckled at the sound of her mumbling something in her sleep, clearly trying to respond to him.

Stripping out of all of his clothes so that he could get in the shower, Elio couldn't help but let his mind drift back to Faye. A part of him wondered how she would have reacted had she been awake. Chances were she would have begged him to cuddle with her and he might have given in, doing everything in his power to not get blood on her. The task would be extremely tedious and near impossible, especially when it came to his desire for the beautiful woman. He shook his head, not wanting to think about his lover covered in the blood of the men he slaughtered. The very idea of his perfect and pure Faye being tainted by another man's bodily fluids could easily send him into a murderous fury.

"I got to get this damn filth off me, for Faye's sake." He mumbled, scrubbing away at every piece of flesh, hoping to wash the red substance off him. As much pleasure as he usually took in the process of beating a man to death, the gore was becoming too much of a burden. He no longer just held the title of a terrifying and ruthless mafia boss, he was now Faye's boyfriend and so he had to carry himself in a much cleaner, less physically violent manner. That meant he had to keep his torture methods limited to psychological.

After he thoroughly scrubbed himself clean, Elio stepped out of the shower and made his way back into the bedroom. Opening his closet, he searched for a new outfit to wear. "Almost a waste, honestly. I'll just be taking it all off again." He chuckled to himself, shooting the slumbering girl a lust filled look. "Oh well, I'm sure you'll appreciate the show, won't you, doll?"

Just as he finished tying his tie, he suddenly realized the television was turned on, playing some local news channel. Faye must have turned it on before she fell asleep, probably to use as background noise. He strode over to the side of the bed she was sleeping on and reached for the remote that lay abandoned on the side table. "You really shouldn't be watching the news, doll; it could taint your beautiful brain." He mumbled, his finger hovering over the off button.

Before he could press it, a familiar face appeared on the screen, causing him to falter. A tall man, around Elio's height, spoke. He was well built, with beautifully tanned skin that looked similar to the mobsters. His black hair had a gray streak in it, making him look far more mature and handsome. The outfit the man wore fit him pretty well. He had on a light blue dress shirt that was cuffed at his elbows and dark blue slacks. The tie around his neck was also dark blue with small, golden stars decorating it. To tie his whole outfit together, on top of his perfectly styled hair, sat a blue trilby hat.

Chestnut brown eyes seemed to stare right through the camera as though they were looking directly at Elio as the detective spoke. "We are currently investigating the shoot out that allegedly happened between the Crimson Kings and the Black Spades. As of 2PM today, the downtown entertainment district is closed off for the investigation." He explained his thoughts on what happened, attempting to paint Elio in a bad light. Of course, the detective was smart enough to not outright name the mobster, but he all but accused Elio of being the mastermind behind the whole event.

"That's just like him, quick to point fingers." He muttered in irritation as the detective continued. "You know he used to be my brother? Back in the day, we were pretty close. Now the fucker is dead to me." He felt comfortable in confessing his past to Faye while she was asleep. It was as though her unconscious body was a haven for him to talk to. "If him or the other bastard ever goes near you, please tell me and I'll wipe them from existence. Got it?" His request was only met by quiet groans and soft rambles.

Just as he was about to say more to her, a picture appeared on the screen. "If anybody has any information on the whereabouts of this woman, please contact me at..." *Click...* He quickly hit the off button, not wanting to see any more of that news story. "That piece of shit." He growled quietly to himself. "He can say whatever the fuck he wants about me, but he has no right... No right at all to bring Faye into this."

Before he turned the television off, the screen showed what appeared to be a traffic cam photo of Faye and Elio. The photo was set at an awkward angle, making it difficult to see the couple clearly, but it picked up on enough details for him to recognize himself and his lover, who hid her face in his coat. While he had no clue what his brother was up to, there was no doubt in his mind that the detective was trying to hurt Faye to get to him. "What a sick bastard." Elio scoffed, running his fingers through her soft blonde locks. "Don't worry, doll. I promise I won't let him get to you."

He moved his hand away when he was suddenly stopped by the girl. She gripped his wrist tightly, pulling it back down to her chest, attempting to curl up with it. "Miss me that much, eh?" He chuckled, making no attempt to gain control of his arm back. Instead, he moved his other arm under her back, carefully lifting her up so he could crawl in next to her. The whole time she held onto his arm, treating it like her favorite stuffed animal.

"You know you can stay here if you want, right doll? I mean, I can take good care of you and love you the way you deserve. I can take you out to nice dinners and take you on luxurious vacations. You'll never have to want for anything. I'll give it all to you. In fact, I'll even let your cats live here. All you need to do is say yes." He meant every word, practically pleading with her to stay with him. "I know it'll be weird for you at first. Large scary men with guns'll always surround you, but I promise you'll get used to it. They'll only be there to protect you."

He wasn't sure why he felt the need to plead his case with her while she was unconscious. Maybe it was practice for when she woke up, or maybe he hoped she'd hear him in her dreams and wake up convinced she needed to be with him. Regardless of the reason, he still desired more than anything to have Faye by his side at all times. He was no longer afraid to admit that he loved her to the point that the thought of her leaving Sunday night tore him up inside.

"I love you, doll, so fucking much. I know it's strange to say, especially since you just met me a few days ago, but it's true." He pulled her into a tight hug, nuzzling into her neck while he spoke. "Mph… Elio…" she mumbled in her sleep, lulling her head to the side. He smirked against her skin as a devilish idea popped into his head. Slender fingers slid down her side, slowly making their way to her exposed thigh. He began to steadily knead into the fat, feeling her thrust up into his hand in time with his movements.

"P-please… Mph…" she quietly begged, still very much asleep. Her face turned bright red as she panted, clearly flustered by his actions. "What's wrong doll?" He whispered in her ear as he carefully crawled on top of her, trying his hardest not to wake her up. He moved his hand up her skirt, resting it on the elastic band of her panties. He used his other hand to grope at her chest, gently squeezing the soft mounds as he pulled adorably soft moans out of her. "E-Elio… Harder…" She mewled out.

"Glad to know I'm invading your mind just as much as you're invading mine." He said with a smirk before dipping his face back into her neck, allowing his long, slick tongue to slip past his lips and slide against her supple flesh, tasting every inch of her skin. "I want you so bad, doll, can't you tell?" He groaned out, moving his lips down her collarbone and towards her chest, leaving a trail of kisses in his wake.

"Doll, I need you to wake up." He gently purred, his face once again hovering over hers. She let out a soft snore in response, completely unaware of the world around her. Before he could stop himself, he plunged his face back down, smashing his lips against her, forcing her into a heated kiss. He forced his tongue into her mouth, shoving it down her throat.

Blue jewels shot open in surprise as she grabbed his face, attempting to push him away from her so she could breathe. Finally, he pulled away, licking his lips hungrily, as he gave her a predatory smirk. "Hello doll." He purred, happy to see she finally woke up. "Hi?" She greeted in confusion, extremely groggy from her nap. "W-what's going on?" She asked nervously, noticing a dark, lustful glint in his eyes.

"Oh nothing, I just suddenly decided I want you to stay in my room forever." He purred in a deep, husky tone, pulling her back in for another kiss. Slowly grinding against her. "I-is… Ah… Forever negotiable? I… Mph… Still have work on m-m… Oh… Monday." She attempted to say.

Elio suddenly stopped all movement; a dark look fell over his face as he moved his face so his lips were next to her ear. "Quit your job." He growled aggressively, not willing to humor her excuses. A chill went up her spine and her eyes went wide with shock at his boldness. "Wha..?" Before she could finish her retort, he pressed his lips against hers, once again silencing her. 'He can't be serious.' She thought to herself, allowing her lover to have complete control of her body.

After an hour, the two finally came to their end, both exhausted. He gently held her, using his large hand to rub soothing circles into her back, messaging out any knots that formed during their fun. In this moment, he wanted to say something, anything, to break the silence, but he couldn't bring himself to ruin her peace.

Slowly, he rose from his spot, shifting Faye in his arms so that she rested bridal style against him. She watched him blankly, attempting to stay awake after using up so much of her energy. With a fuzzy mind, she focused all of her attention on her lover's face, taking the time to count his beautiful freckles. He couldn't help but smile down at her, finding her sudden interest in his face absolutely adorable.

The moment they entered the bathroom, Faye's eyes left Elio's, instead taking in the sight of the grand and very spacious room, her mouth dropped in disbelief of just how huge it was. 'Holy shit! This room is bigger than my house.' She thought to herself in utter shock. It was gorgeous, of course, with the sleek black and red marble tiles that decorated the floor and the huge bathtub, which almost looked like a large jacuzzi, that sat near a large window that was shut closed, she almost felt out of place in there.

Elio sat Faye down on one step that led up to the tub as he started up the water, carefully checking to make sure the temperature was perfect. Satisfied, he pushed down the stopper before reaching into a cupboard that sat near the tub, trying to find something hidden within. With a triumphant grin, he pulled out a fancy-looking glass bottle containing some type of red liquid inside.

She watched unblinkingly with extreme curiosity as he opened up the spherical looking cap. Her senses were greeted with a wonderful aroma of forest fruits and sultry florals alongside warming spices. With a tilt of the wrist, he poured the strange elixir into the tub, allowing it to foam up and amplify the smells. Once he was satisfied with the level the tub reached, he turned his attention back towards the naked woman, moving to lift her from her spot on the steps.

"I can move on my own, you know." She gently chided him, feeling her muscles instantly relax the moment she touched the water. "I know, but I really want to take care of you." He retorted, kissing her forehead softly. The moment the warm, soapy water surrounded her, she let out a satisfied sigh in relief, knowing this was exactly what she needed after their little activity.

"You know, I'm not against it." She said quietly, as though she were telling him a secret. He tilted his head, confused by her random statement. "What aren't you against?" He prompted, wanting her to continue her thought. "Living with you. You've been hinting about it all day, and I honestly wouldn't mind at all." She pawed at the suds, swishing them around as she spoke in an attempt to look calm.

Elio couldn't help but perk up in excitement at her words as his smile grew wide. "So your answer is yes, then? You'll come live with me? Because if that's the case, I'll call some people up to have your whole house packed up and moved out by tonight." He sounded so giddy, like a little kid being given a new toy to play with.

Blue eyes widened in surprise at his sudden proposition, not quite expecting him to want it done right away. The very thought made her feel a pit of nervousness in her stomach. "I don't think I could do a large, sudden move like that tonight." She stated, attempting to bring him back down to reality. "Oh... I see," He responded, lowering his head in disappointment. That nervous pit turned into one of guilt the moment he spoke. The last thing she wanted to do was disappoint him, but she couldn't find it in herself to give in to such an insane demand.

"If not tonight, then when?" He asked in a more hopeful tone. Faye looked up thoughtfully, attempting to rationalize a reasonable moving date. "I could maybe make the move in a month." She responding hesitantly. "One month?" He muttered bitterly, his expression darkening for a moment. "Yeah… Sorry, there's just so much to do, and I would like a chance to really get to know you before we jump right into something so permanent."

She started rambling off reasons she couldn't live with him so early, worried she might offend her lover. The reality was they were moving faster than she could process, as though there was a deadline quickly approaching for their relationship's endgame. That thought terrified her as the pressure grew to be too much.

Upon seeing his lover's worried look, his expression softened to a much tender, more loving gaze. "I suppose that is fair, considering what I'm asking." He finally spoke up as he grabbed a loofah hanging from a hook right under the window. Pouring a generous amount of body wash on it, he leaned over Faye's body and began lathering her up.

"But, if you must wait a month, then I have one more ask of you." He hummed nonchalantly. "What is it?" She asked, curious about his request. Leaning his face closer to hers, his lips brushed across her own. "Quit your job." He whispered against her, smirking at the sight of her flustered form. "Quit my job?" She repeated, unsure if she actually heard him correctly. "Yeah, quit it. Once you move in with me, it'll be pointless for you to remain employed there." He shrugged as he reached into the tub to release the drain.

Faye lowered her head, watching as a whirlpool formed to suck all the water down the pipes, leaving the sweet-smelling bubbles in its wake. She let the large man lift her out of the tub, wrapping a giant, fluffy red towel around her body as he led her towards the bedroom. If the idea of moving in with him right away was terrifying, the thought of quitting her job and being completely financially reliant on her lover sounded down right horrific. While he had a point that she didn't need to work, as he was obviously well off financially, it still seemed all too sketchy. She couldn't help but wonder in the what if scenario of if they were to break up, what would happen to her? Where would she go? How would she get by with no income?

Elio, noticing her weary expression, offered her a reassuring smile. "This house is nowhere near the city and takes an hour to drive to. No job would be worth the commute for you." He explained, hoping she would understand. "I get it, it's just… I'm worried I'll be a bit of a burden to you while I'm unemployed." She stated, allowing him to see her point of view. "Don't worry about that, love. Don't think about it as unemployment, but simply a new job opportunity." He smiled, pecking her lips lightly. "Huh? How would this be a new job opportunity?" She asked in confusion.

"Well, my dear, I've been thinking about last night and how you reacted to Mike's bullshit. You didn't hesitate to put him in his place and kept me calm and rational throughout it. Usually negotiations like that are tedious and painful, but with you at my side, it went a lot better than usual. So, I figured maybe it'll be more beneficial if I brought you to all my meetings." He sounded almost nervous and embarrassed for asking, but swallowed it all down as he explained.

Her eyes seemed to light up at his explanation. The thought of being needed by her boyfriend brought immense joy. "Oh, when you put it that way, it makes sense for me to quit." She agreed enthusiastically, causing his own face to brighten. "So you'll do it?" He prodded, wanting a guaranteed answer. "Yes. I'll quit my job." She stated affirmatively, determined to do her best as his partner. "Thank God. That makes it so much easier." He sighed in relief, pulling her in for a tight hug.

She felt him lift her up off her feet, causing her to cling onto him for dear life. Suddenly, he turned to fall down on the bed, with Faye landing on his chest. She let out a small squeak in surprise before relaxing against his body, snuggling into him. "I'm so happy you're going to be living with me." He purred, running his fingers through her hair. "You just make things so much easier and better."

Faye took in a deep breath before moving her face up to meet his, her blue jewels shining brightly with affection. "I'm happy too. I get to live with the kindest, most incredible man ever. Just kind of dreading the conversation I'm going to have with my boss on Monday." She gave a little giggle as she spoke, stretching her neck out to kiss him on the lips. "Just walk in and tell her to get fucked. What else is there to dread?" He teased, nuzzling her nose.

Rolling her eyes, she gave a light huff before peppering kisses all over his face. "I still have to deal with her for a month." She reminded him, "and I ain't the type to leave bad blood, so I'll have to leave that *get fucked* for my last day of work." He let out a deep chuckle at her statement before carefully moving her off of him. "I still think your last day should have been yesterday." He shrugged as he bent down to gather all of his clothes so that he could get dressed again.

"One month isn't that long." She chided him, moving to sit up on the bed. "It's only four weeks." Elio shook his head with an amused smile at her rationalization. "Yes, my love, but four weeks translates to thirty days, which turns into 720 hours. When you think about it, that turns into 43,000 minutes, which is 2,592,000 seconds, that you're not living with me. Do you see how long that is?" He whined, smoothing out his shirt before neatly tucking it into his pants. "Oh my God, you're so dramatic. You'll still see me on the weekends." She retorted in exasperation, falling back onto the plush bed.

Elio made his way over to the closet, pulling out one of his large, red button-ups before turning back to the naked woman. "Doll, with you, I'm allowed to be dramatic." He smirked, reaching into a bag to pull out a pair of red panties decorated in floral lace. Making his way back over to the bed, he handed the clothing to Faye, giving her an expectant look. Without hesitation, she quickly slipped on the underwear before fumbling with the button up.

"Sorry, I don't have any nightgowns for you." He apologized, taking a seat next to her on the bed. "It's no big deal. I usually sleep naked anyway." She shrugged calmly, still trying to undo the buttons. Just as she got the last button open, she noticed his eyes burning into her head. "What?" She asked absentmindedly. "Hurry and put on the damn shirt before I fuck you again." He warned, flicking her forehead lightly. As much as Faye wanted to call that bluff, she knew her body was in no shape to go another round with him.

Once the shirt was on, swallowing her body whole, she leaned her head against his shoulder, shutting her eyes lazily. "Already trying to fall asleep on me again?" He joked, lightly petting her side. "Maybe… You took all my energy…" she mumbled, feeling herself beginning to drift off. "My poor little doll… Well, I'm sorry to say I can't let you fall asleep just yet." As playful as he sounded, he truly was apologetic.

Faye lifted one eye open to look at him. "I don't think I can go another round tonight." She stated bluntly, causing him to roar with laughter. "No. No. Not like that. I have a meeting to attend and I would love if you could accompany me. So long as your body is ready for that." He said the last part with a wink, making her giggle. "I might be, but only if we get to do something after." She retorted cheekily. "Oh, and what's that?" He asked, curious about her demand. "I want to cuddle with you."

Elio practically melted at her words, knowing she was completely serious and not trying to be funny and cute. Hugging her tightly against his chest, he nuzzled into her neck, taking in her sweet scent. "If that's what you want, then of course we'll cuddle after. I'll never say no to holding you." He purred, wearing a content smile.

"You know… I've never thought I'd fall in love with someone so quickly." She suddenly said after a few minutes of silence. "Oh, really?" He responded with an amused tone. "Yeah, I keep waiting for you to disappoint me, but you never do… I'm worried, though." She continued, her voice quiet and muffled. "About?" He prompted, feeling his own concern bubble up. "I wonder if everything is moving too fast. What if you really love me right now but in a month or two, you end up sick of me?"

Elio's lips fell down into a frown at her words, knowing that was a legit concern. "I don't think I will." He shrugged, hoping to reassure her. "I mean, I'm a pretty dedicated man. Anything I find interest in, I'll stick with it for as long as I'm allowed to." Faye couldn't help but relax at the comment, feeling as though it put her mind at ease.

"Why *did* you find interest in me?" She wondered, having the question stuck on the tip of her tongue for a while. "Hmm… Well, to start with the more superficial shit, you're very beautiful. Even after a long day of work, you still look good in your scrubs, which was something I never thought would be attractive." He looked her up and down as he spoke, drinking in every bit of her appearance. "But getting past your good looks, you got a great personality to go with it. You're so sharp and clever, always having a witty comeback of some kind. Like I said before, you can make any subject interesting."

He took her chin in his hand, tilting her face up to place a soft kiss against her lips. "I love a woman who can hold a conversation. You also come off as kind and passionate, something that's rare to find in a person. I mean, hell, in terms of romantic partners, I just hit the lottery." Faye could feel her heart flutter at his words, not expecting him to speak so fondly of her. They've only known each other for a week and yet he made it sound like they've been together for ages, long enough for him to assess her.

"Good enough reason?" He teased, pecking her lips again. "I suppose…" she mumbled, melting into his embrace. "Excellent, now we better get going. Don't want to leave these men waiting. They get a little antsy when they're trapped inside a room for too long." While he meant for it to come off as a joke, Faye felt a little bad for keeping her boyfriend's employees waiting. "Okay." She muttered softly, rising from her spot on the bed as Elio followed closely, wrapping his arm around her.

Chapter: 15

He took large steps down the hall, making it nearly impossible for the shorter girl to keep up. "Make sure you stay by my side," He chided the moment he noticed her falling slightly behind. Faye shot him an irritated glare as she went into a jog just to remain next to him. "Slow… Down." She whined in-between deep breaths of air, feeling as though her lungs were about to explode. "We're almost there." He reassured her, amused by her annoyance at him. "You… Suck…" she stated bluntly, still attempting to catch her breath. "Quit complaining." He chuckled, stopping in front of a large door.

As they stood there, mentally preparing themselves to enter, Faye couldn't help the feeling of nervousness that plagued her. "So doll, I want to let you know once we get in this room I need you to…" "I know. I know. Don't speak, don't react, don't show emotions of any kind. I need to act like I just had a lobotomy." She grumbled, attempting to swallow down the nervous pit. "Lobotomy?" He asked, curious about her word choice. "I don't know. It's what my mother always told me to do."

Suddenly, Elio pulled her up against him, as though he could sense her feelings of discomfort. "It'll be okay, my love. Nothing will happen to you, I promise." He said gently, pulling her into a deep, passionate kiss. 'I'd kill them if they tried anything.' He thought to himself with a darkened expression that seemed to go unnoticed by the woman, who was absolutely loving every second of the kiss. She wasn't sure what to expect inside the room, but as long as Elio was with her, she felt safe.

As they stepped into the room, dozens of eyes fell on the two, watching, unblinking, as they made their way through the cramped space. Faye couldn't help but feel underdressed with her outfit after seeing everyone wearing neatly pressed business attire. 'At least I'm wearing a button up.' She thought to herself jokingly, knowing she was practically ready for bed at this point.

Looking up at her lover, she noticed he held a cold, stoic expression contradicting his normally kind and lighthearted demeanor. He had a similar look when they met up with Mike Ladner, so cold, so calculated, so dominating… For some strange reason, it caused her heart to flutter in excitement. She decided it would be in her best interest to not speak during this meeting and keep her eyes completely focused on her boyfriend, not that it was too difficult for her to stare at him regardless of the situation.

Elio pulled Faye along, guiding her towards a large chair placed at the front of the room. He took a seat, forcing her to sit awkwardly on his lap. She rested her cheek against his chest, feeling his fingers dig into her highly sensitive and recently abused thigh meat. It felt as though she were sitting on the lap of a king as he addressed his subjects, causing her to question her role throughout all of this.

What exactly was her purpose in attending this meeting? What was he discussing while it was supposed to be his day off? Would there be a point where she was required to speak? These questions and more ran freely throughout her mind, overcrowding it and causing the poor woman more confusion than she could handle. Looking up, she observed Elio's cold, unreadable face, trying to find even a semblance of instruction.

With a soft sigh, she leaned back, laying her head against his chest as she attempted to listen into the conversation. Something about a weapons shipment that's coming up soon. She barely focused on every other sentence, not in any real mood to listen as her boyfriend spoke to his employees, but the parts she picked up on sounded really shady. While a part of her was curious to know more about what type of business he ran, he had completely worn her out to the point she could hardly keep up with the conversation.

Blue eyes stared blankly at her lover, wondering how long this meeting was going to last. She couldn't help but notice that he hadn't even smiled once since they got in there. It almost felt as though he was trying to hide his emotions completely, though with one glance at the room, she didn't blame him. The men in this room looked plenty intimidating, almost appearing as the evil henchmen types. All of them looked as though they could easily snap someone's neck and hold no remorse afterwards.

Gently, his fingers stroked her leg to soothe her of her obvious anxiety. So badly did he want to kiss her and whisper in her ear that everything would be okay, but unfortunately, he had to continue with this meeting. As risky as it was to drag her along with him and have her listen in, he felt it would be a greater risk to allow his beloved the chance to wander around the base unsupervised. He got lucky that she took a nap, especially when she had the news playing, broadcasting every bit of his business. He could only imagine what would happen if she got bored and decided to explore.

A menacing shadow fell over his face as he continued to speak, his brain playing what if scenarios. If she were to wander around, she'd run into some of his men. As terrified as they were of the gang leader, there was only so much he could do when he wasn't around. He doubted any of them knew who Faye was and probably assumed she was some unlucky whore that caught his fancy. Being trapped in a building filled with pent up men who held no morals was a recipe for disaster. 'I should get her a bodyguard.' He thought to himself as he continued on with his orders.

Luckily, he had complete control over everything being discussed so he could easily manipulate the meeting so that nothing sounded too shady. Faye looked far too preoccupied with his tie to even bother listening in anyway. Every so often, he noticed sets of eyes lingering too long on his girlfriend, so he'd shoot them down with a warning glare. It wasn't until the end that everyone in the room seemed to get the hint, but that still wasn't satisfying enough for him.

As he got closer to the end, there was one final point he needed to make. "In case ya'll haven't noticed the pretty little dame sitting in my lap…" He started, calling attention to Faye, who moved on from messing with his tie so that she could play with his buttons. "This woman belongs to me and no one else! If I so much as catch one of you bastards ogling my girl, I'll make sure you're buried six feet under! Do I make myself clear?" All the men seemed to give a slight nod, too terrified to actually speak. His lips twitched upward into a sadistic smirk, loving the way they all cowered before him.

With one final reiteration of all the topics discussed, he finally dismissed all the men who fled the room without a single ounce of hesitation. For a moment, Faye thought she saw one of them giving her a look of pity, but figured she was imagining things. She couldn't think of one reason any of them should feel sorry for her, especially during a meeting where she got to sit in her boyfriend's lap and cuddle with him while he lectured a bunch of grown ass men on the importance of keeping their areas '*locked up.*' Honestly, it was all pretty fun and entertaining for her, though that didn't make her any less tired.

The moment the door closed, Elio completely relaxed in his seat before pressing his face into Faye's hair, taking in her wonderful scent. The sensation caused her to let out a little giggle, which only made him smile triumphantly. "You know that look suits you way more." She stated matter-of-factly. "What look?" He asked, confused by her comment. "The smile. It looks way better on you than that grumpy face you had this whole time." As she spoke, she lightly poked his cheek, causing him the chuckle.

"Sorry about the grumpy look doll, but it can't be helped. I ain't in the type of business where a friendly smile gets you far." He explained, lightly pecking her forehead. "So I'm guessing you don't work in customer service?" She joked, relishing in their moment of peace. "Never, though I doubt a friendly smile goes far in that profession, either." Elio teased, making a decent point as he peppered kisses along her face. "Fair enough… Now that I think about it, a friendly smile doesn't get you jack shit."

Elio tilted her head up to meet his soft gaze, allowing him to place a gentle kiss on her lips. "Normally no, it doesn't, but I promise yours will get you anything you want," Faye gushed at his statement, loving just how sweet he could be. "Oh? Anything?" She gave him a mischievous smile. "Of course. Money, jewelry, fancy dinners, luxury getaways. Say the word and it's yours." He insisted, excited to hear her request. "Can we go back to your room to cuddle?" She said it in such an adorable manner, it was completely impossible to say no. "If that's what my doll wants." He purred, rising from his spot with Faye settled into his arms. "Now, let's get back to *our* room."

Chapter: 16

Letting out a quiet yawn, Faye stretched out her sore limbs as she woke from her deep slumber after a long night spent cuddling and fooling around with Elio. Speaking of which, he was nowhere to be seen, instead a large dent in the bed sat in his absents. Pushing herself up to a sitting position, she lazily scanned over the room searching for her lover, but was left disappointed.

"Really?" she huffed out, crossing her arms in mild irritation. "Did he really blindfold me, bring me to some strange building in God knows where, fuck me, then leave me all alone?" As much as she didn't want to admit it, she was a little hurt that he had abandoned her. "Elio!" She called out to him, hoping he was somewhere close by. "You can't just vanish like this!" A hint of sadness sounded in her voice. "I swear you have ten seconds to come out, otherwise I'm turning all your socks into puppets!" It was unclear if that threat was empty or not, though a small part of her was aiming for it to not be.

After a few minutes of waiting for a response, she finally gave up with another huff, crawling out of bed with her bare feet hovering over the cold floor. The moment her feet touched the icy wood, she winced at the feeling, like a dozen tiny needles piercing her sensitive feet. "He really needs to consider moving that rug closer to the bed." She mumbled in mild annoyance, mostly just upset that she still had no clue where her boyfriend was.

Just as she began to walk, the tip of her toes brushed over a large bag, nearly causing her to trip and fall. Mumbling a few choice words under her breath, she picked up the bag with one hand and placed it on the edge of the bed. An envelope sat neatly inside, barely poking out with the words, *To my beautiful Faye.'* Butterflies fluttered around in her stomach as she ripped into the letter, desperate to see what her lover wrote. 'I'm so sorry to leave you, doll, but something came up for work. I promise I'll try to make it back as quickly as possible, but for the time being, please stay in the room. There's a change of clothes in the bag and I left your purse in the bathroom. I love you so much and I'll see you real soon. Love, Elio.'

Her heart pounded in her chest while her face turned bright red. She couldn't help the goofy smile that adorned her face as she read the note repeatedly, etching each word into her memory. The young woman felt so light and giddy, as though she could easily float away if given the chance. "Calm down." She told herself, trying to pull her own brain back down into reality. "You're really starting to act like a little puppy with attachment issues." As much as she tried to reprimand herself, she couldn't help the excitement she felt upon seeing his words.

Shaking her head of all her lovesick thoughts, Faye opened up the bag, peaking inside so that she could see what outfit Elio wanted her in. The first thing she noticed was the vibrant red color that seemed to beam brightly, like a flashlight in a dark room. Clearly her lover had a fondness for this color, which she was totally okay with her. Red was her favorite color, after all, and he used the color tastefully.

She reached in the bag, her long, well-manicured fingertips lightly brushing over the delicate fabric. It had a lacey and smooth feel to it, making it soft to the touch. With one swift motion, she pulled the article of clothing out of the bag, revealing yet another dress for her to wear. This one was much simpler than the others, with no intricate designs or details to it. It had a heart-shaped neckline, along with flowy sleeves that stopped at the elbows. The skirt, like all the others, flowed out, allowing its wearer to have an hourglass shape.

"I'm really starting to think he has some sort of kink for dresses." She said to herself, giggling at her own joke. She didn't mind, especially when he went through all the trouble of picking out her clothes for her. She still didn't understand how he got her size down perfectly, but that was one of many questions she chose not to ask in fear that she might not like the answer. She had already let him have his way with her, so there was no need to be prudish over clothing.

Without another thought, Faye took the dress, along with some underwear, and quickly skipped towards the bathroom to take a much needed shower. It took a moment for her to figure out how the levers worked, but once she did, she slowly relaxed in the warm water. The steady stream hit her in all the right spots, soothing her aching muscles after an intense night of fun.

It was strange really, how rough he had been with her during their activities when the previous night he acted so gentle with her. It was as though he was actively trying to leave marks all over her body. Actually, now that she thought about it, he seemed far more possessive of her. As much as she pretended not to notice, she knew of the looks he gave other men whenever their eyes lingered on her form a bit too long. Honestly, Faye found it quite sexy how territorial he acted regarding her.

As she got lost in thought about her lover, her fingers wandered off on their own, brushing over some light bruises he left on her otherwise flawless skin. Each mark she touched left her with a soft smile, knowing every last one of them was caused by the large man who only wanted to have his way with her. She remembered every squeeze and thrust of his movements, how he looked so intimidating and yet spoke so sweetly to her. Every part of him was simply perfect.

"Elio…" she whispered with a soft smile, her hands slowly trailing up her body towards her neck. "My Elio…" Mindlessly, she grabbed the pendant that rested against her chest, stroking the beautiful metal while she let his words echo throughout her head. She still couldn't believe he wanted her to quit her job so that she could live with him, and it only made matters worse that she was considering it.

After a good half an hour of letting the warm water rain down on her, soaking her soft, silky, blonde locks and hydrating her well-loved pale skin, she finally decided it was time to leave the shower. Turning off the water, she hesitatingly stepped out onto the cold, hard tile, causing a shiver to run up her spine. Grabbing the nearest towel, she quickly wrapped it around her body, drying herself off before she started dressing herself.

"Man, he is too good at picking out my clothes." Faye stated as she admired herself in the mirror, loving how the dress hugged her perfectly. "Maybe he works in fashion." She couldn't help but giggle at the thought of her lover secretly being some fashion icon. That could explain why he seemed so picture perfect, almost as though he practically invented vogue.

"Designers can be pretty damn aggressive." She shrugged, willing to run with the funny narrative she made up.

With a quiet laugh, she made her way back into the bathroom, grabbing her purse off the countertop. Quickly she opened it up and took her cellphone out, figuring she could kill some time by playing a few games on it. Just as she unlocked it, a notification appeared on the screen, showing one new text message. *'Free to talk?'* The message read with May's name appearing above it. *'Probably.'* She texted back, attempting to act mysterious. Just then, her phone started ringing with the familiar cheery, yet inappropriate tone she set for the beloved red-headed woman.

"Hello?" Faye answered with an amused smile. "Faye? Are you okay?" May asked, concern lacing her voice. "Are we talking mentally or physically?" She retorted, snickering at the aggravated huff she received from her dear friend. "I'm being serious!" She snapped, already frustrated with the conversation. "Are you? Really? It's hard to tell." The younger woman fell back against the bed as she continued to taunt May, who grew more frantic.

"Faye! Please! I need you to answer me honestly! Has he hurt you at all?" She was practically begging her, needing complete reassurance that her friend was safe. "May what the fuck are you even talking about? Are you drunk?" Faye's playfulness slowly slipped into confusion as she spoke. "Oh, my God!" May snapped in exacerbation mumbling a few choice words in her native tongue. "You are going to lead me to alcoholism. Elio! He hasn't hurt you?"

Puzzled by the strange question, Faye paused for a moment, putting thought into the question. "No? Why would he hurt me?" She decidedly asked, wondering why her friend was so worried. "Why? Because he's Elio! That's what he does." May responded, her normally loud voice turning into a whisper near the end as though she were telling a secret. As much as the redhead didn't want to add any more stress and unease to an already difficult situation, she had no other choice but to rip the band-aid off.

It took Faye a good thirty seconds to process what May said, but when she did, she couldn't help but laugh. "Elio would hurt me? Seriously? You expect me to believe that the man who just spent a whole evening letting me drag him around an aquarium and talk his ear off is dangerous? Good one May!" She had already fallen so hard for the man that there was no use in convincing her that he was in any shape, evil and dangerous.

The silence on the other end was nearly deafening as the red-headed mistress attempted to process what exactly her idiot friend had just said. "Are..?" she started, trying to form the question she desperately needed to ask. "Are you actually dating Elio?" May finally spat out. "Yeah, no duh," Faye retorted with a playful attitude to her voice. "jealous?" She couldn't help but add into her taunt, knowing that, if anything, her friend was definitely not.

"Why?" May asked, still finding it hard to process the news. "Because he's really sweet and fun to be around. I think I love him." She confessed, wearing a soft smile. "You shouldn't love him." She retorted bluntly, fear and anger bleeding out in her tone. This was a dangerous game Faye was playing, involving herself with Elio, one that May never thought her young friend would ever play. "I do, though, very much. In fact, I'm planning to move in with him." While every word she spoke was the truth, she was only telling the red head this information to cause mild annoyance.

May's right eye twitched as her lips fell into a rather irritated frown once again, feeling as though the younger woman wasn't taking her situation serious enough. "Why the hell would you move in with him!? You don't even know him!" She was practically shouting, her temper getting the better of her. "Don't I? May, we spent the last two nights together, getting to know each other really well. I mean, he's got my *whole* body memorized at this..." "Okay, stop!" She interrupted before any more details could be spared. "I really don't want to hear what you and that *monster* did last night." Her voice held a lot of disdain at the thought of Faye and Elio fooling around with each other.

"Monster? What do you mean by that?" A confused look fell on the young woman's face as she prompted for more answers. May was taken aback by her question, unsure of how to respond. "You really don't know?" She hesitantly asked, wondering how much the younger woman actually knew about the man she was dating. "Know what? May, what are you talking about?" A hint of irritation could be heard in Faye's voice. "Who Elio is..." she replied softly, almost in a whisper.

Faye thought about it, realizing she really didn't know her boyfriend all that well. His interests, his hobbies, hell, even his career were all a mystery to her. In a way, that was a little unsettling for her to not know the real him. "Well, no, I don't... But I will know in due time. I mean, isn't that the point of dating, anyway? To get to know my partner before we marry each other?" Faye reasoned, figuring her mentor would see the logic in her words.

A long, aggravated groan sounded over the speaker, causing Faye to quickly pull her ear away from the phone. "While yes, that is normally true, you should at least know the very basics of your partner. I mean, what if you're dating a serial killer?" She went into full-blown lecture mode, making it very tempting for the young woman to just hang up. "You've known Elio longer than me." Faye pointed out. "Did you set me up with a serial killer?"

The phone went dead silent as the red head processed her friend's words. "Well, no... Of course I didn't, but that doesn't mean Elio is safe to hang around. Look, we really shouldn't be having this conversation over the phone. Why don't I just pick you up? Where are you, anyway?" She wanted to break the news to her in a more private area where she could guarantee they'll be alone. "I'm at Elio's house." Faye responded with a nervous laugh, realizing May might be a little upset by that news.

May's blood ran cold as her hands trembled. Quickly she pressed the end call button, terrified of the repercussions that would come her way for daring to speak poorly of the dangerous mobster. It might have been a cowardly move to hang up on the young woman mid conversation but there was no way in hell she would risk her and Faye's life like that just to give out a warning. The thought of her dear friend and *"little sister"* remaining attached to that monster made her feel all sorts of way.

'I have to be careful.' She thought to herself, staring down at the blank screen. 'One wrong move and Elio could have us both killed.' It seemed oddly out of character for the Faye to speak so fondly of someone, almost as though she was pleading her case on why she should stay with him. Is there a chance Elio had a bit of a soft spot for her young friend and truly wanted to treat her right? Shaking her head, she snapped herself out of such a ridiculous thought. "He is a cold-blooded killer. Of course, he's not catching feelings for her." She grumbled to herself as guilt and regret quickly flooded her mind. "I need to save her, and fast." She finally said with determination in her eyes.

Faye stared blankly at her phone, feeling both amused and confused about the phone call. While she took some pleasure in hearing the normally proud and confident mistress tremble and panic, she felt a little concerned that her boyfriend was the reason for her friend's distress.

Atlas also seemed bothered by Faye's company as well, which might not be a good sign. "Oh well, Elio is good to me and that's all that matters." She shrugged as she fell back onto the bed, figuring whatever issues her friends had could wait another day. For now, she wanted to enjoy her final day off without drama.

Chapter: 17

Elio wore a scowl as his large boots stomped across the cold, concrete path, making his way towards his next destination. His movements held haste as his impatience and irritation grew to consume his whole being. Just as he was relaxing and really basking in the young woman's company, he received an update on a casino he'd been having ongoing issues with. For weeks he'd noticed the revenue it brings in did not match up with its actual profits. A lot of cash had gone missing and now he has an answer to who the culprit was.

He made his way around to the back entrance, not wanting to give the hustler a single chance to escape his punishment. Four large, intimidating men walked behind, following closely as they pushed through the swinging doors. A look of determination fell on his face, causing him to pick up speed as he had one thought that bounced through his head. He needed to hurry and snuff out this bastard so that he could get back to his Faye.

While he could have easily had his men deal with this situation instead of him, he made the tough decision to give up part of his date to make a statement. Elio wanted this man's execution to be semi-public, a grave reminder of what would happen if anyone so much as stepped out of line. It appeared a few too many were getting a little too arrogant and brave. They needed a quick reminder of who was really in charge. Unfortunately, Faye would have to wait for a little while, seeing as this was important for his work.

They entered a dimly lit room in the back of a casino where a sharply dressed man sat tied up and blindfolded. A gag had been shoved in his mouth, preventing any speech from leaving his trembling lips. His tan skin dripped with sweat and his once sleeked back hair fell down into a shaggy mess. The smell of cheap cologne and old tobacco filled the air with its rancid scent. Elio could picture Faye scrunching up her nose in disgust at the smell. The thought made him want to chuckle, though he pushed past the feeling in order to keep his menacing expression.

The sad, pathetic man sitting in front of him was one of the gaming managers whose job it was to oversee the day-to-day operations, while also making sure everyone stayed in line. He was such a highly trusted and well-respected man, and yet here he was, tied up and groveling in front of the mob boss like a filthy, dumb animal. Elio couldn't help but sneer in disgust, feeling no remorse for what he was about to do.

"So you thought you could fucking steal from me, eh?" His voice was deep and emotionless as fire burned through his eyes. "Didn't think I would notice? Do you take me for a fucking idiot? Huh?" Either the man sitting on the ground thought he could outsmart the mafia or he figured they'd let it slide. Whatever his reasoning was, Elio didn't want to hear it.

Enough of his time had already been wasted, and he really needed to get home to Faye, so without a second thought, he drew his gun on the man. The other gangsters stood behind him, quiet and still, knowing how this whole scene would play out. The manager, who looked downright terrified, continued to whimper and beg through the gag, leaving his words muffled and pointless.

As Elio's finger rest on the trigger, his mind drifted back to his beloved Faye. He couldn't help but wonder how she would react to this situation. Obviously, he wouldn't bring her along to one of his jobs until he was certain she was fully ready to accept the monster he was, but it didn't stop him from fantasizing about it.

The gun went off; the noise causing the room to shake as smoke filled the air. He pictured her face as she stared at the sight before them, her adorable nose scrunched up in disgust at the smell. "Ow! That hurt my ears." He imagined her whining. "Can't you kill people quieter?" Perhaps she'd tighten her grip around him and snuggle her head against his chest. She might crack a joke about blood getting in her mouth, which he'd respond with a quick, 'close your mouth then.' There would be banter between the two as he slowly picked her up, carrying the sweet woman out bridal style.

'What the fuck is wrong with you!' Suddenly his image of her distorted, her normally cheerful and loving expression changed to one of pure terror. He saw her pounding against his chest, tears streaming down her face as she attempted to escape his embrace. No matter how hard he tried to explain himself, she wouldn't listen. *'Leave me alone, you monster!'* He could feel her body trembling as he tightened his grip around her. Harder and harder he would hug her, hoping she'd be able to feel his love for her and understand that she'd be safe with him. The tighter his embrace got, the more she'd struggled against him until finally. *Snap!*

Elio shook his head, ridding his mind of all negative thoughts as he stared at the scene before him. There the man lay, half his face missing as his blood and brains leaked all over the floor. No longer could the man speak. His one intact eye sat lifeless and gray, staring blankly at the mafia leader that stood over his fresh corpse.

Slipping the gun back into his pocket, Elio calmly turned on his heels, moving towards the door as he waved his hand up in the air. "Clean this mess up." He ordered nonchalantly, as if he were asking his men to take care of basic chores. The sound of tearing flesh and clinking metal sounded as the gangsters moved quickly, butchering the body for easier disposal. Satisfied in his men's obedience, Elio turned on his heels, making his way out of the room, ready to return to his home.

The cold tile floor turned to plush carpet as he made his way into the game room, ready to make his escape through the front door. As the smell of cigarette smoke and hard liquor flooded his senses, his mind drifted off to his beloved Faye. This didn't seem like the proper place to bring a girl like her to, though knowing his beautiful doll, she more than likely wouldn't mind so long as she got to spend time with him. He couldn't help but wonder what her true reaction would be towards his work. Would she look past such a small problem in order to be with him, or would she leave him without a second thought?

Shaking his head to rid himself of all these terrible thoughts, he stared on ahead at the large, automatic door, his face completely void of all emotions. *'She'll love me no matter what.'* He told himself, not willing to accept any other option. He'll either ease her into the life of a gang or keep her completely in the dark. Either way, there was no way she could ever see him as anything less than her sweet and loving boyfriend. He wouldn't allow it.

"Hello Elio!" a familiar and overly cheerful voice greeted him, forcibly pulling him from his thoughts. His fierce and fiery orange eyes narrowed to a murderous glare as he stared at the man that dared to stand before him. Rage flooded his body, his fingers twitched in irritation as a desire to strangle this asshole grew stronger by the second.

In front of Elio stood a man that took on an eerily similar appearance to him minus the color scheme. The man's skin was a shade lighter than Elio's and even Cosimo. His blue eyes held a glint of playfulness in them that matched his large, goofy smile. He had on an orange button up dress shirt that was paired with a slick yellow and red striped tie. The perfectly smooth shirt had been tucked into a pair of gray slacks that pulled the whole outfit together. His shaggy blonde hair seemed to stick up in different directions, giving his put together look a chaotic edge to it.

While most people would turn and flee at the sight of the large mafia boss, especially when he looked less than pleased to see them, this one seemed to enjoy the man's anger. "How are you?" He asked in his disgustingly sweet voice, acting as though they were old friends. "What the fuck do you want, Luciano?" Elio spat, wanting to quickly move this conversation along. "Awe. Is that any way to greet your brother?" He asked, disappointment in his voice.

"You lost the right to call me your brother when you and that piece of shit abandoned me in that fire!" Elio snapped, venom leaking from every word. A look of guilt flashed over Luciano's eyes for a brief second before they went back to a more cheery expression. "Oh, come on 'Lio, can't we leave the past in the past?" He asked, trying to sound reasonable. "I'm trying to, but you assholes won't leave me alone." He shot back, causing the slightly shorter man to flinch. "Now either tell me what bullshit charges you want to throw on me or move out of my way so I can go home."

"I'm not here to cause problems. I only want to talk." He raised his hands in surrender, signaling he meant no harm. "Talk? We have nothing to talk about. As far as the law can prove, I have done nothing wrong." Elio sounded both smug and bitter about his statement. "Again, I'm not trying to cause problems, nor am I speaking to you as an officer of the law, just as a brother." Luciano insisted, causing the man to roll his eyes in anger.

As much as Elio wanted to ignore the annoyingly positive detective, he knew his brother was far too persistent to let him leave so easily. Unfortunately, the fastest way for him to get back to his home to continue his date with Faye is by humoring the man in front of him. "Fine, what the fuck do you want to talk about?" He asked, making it obvious he'd rather be anywhere but there.

Luciano tilted his head to the side as a large grin crept up onto his face. "Hmm... Let me think... What do *I* Want to talk about... Oh I know! Let's talk about that adorable new girl you've been exploiting." His voice dropped into a more serious tone as he spoke, causing a menacing aura to surround him. "What the fuck are you talking about?" Elio sneered, clenching his jaw in anger. "You know damn well what I'm talking about," Luciano snapped back, feeling absolutely no fear towards the man in front of him. "You had that poor girl in a chokehold, for crying out loud! She looks so sweet and innocent. What the hell could you possibly want with her?"

As he grew more and more angry with every word, Elio could only stand there and stare at him, completely confused over what the detective could be ranting about. It wasn't until he went into detail about the girl that it finally clicked for him. "Wait, are you talking about Faye?" He asked in a much calmer tone. "So you actually know her name, do you? I'm really fucking surprised you'd even bother learning that. She isn't some worthless little whore, you know? She's got friends, family, and a whole career in front of her."

For some strange reason, he sounded extremely livid when talking about Faye. Elio couldn't fathom why he cared at all. "What's it to you?" He growled through gritted teeth. "I've had plenty of women clinging to me in the past, and you've never been bothered before. Why do you give a shit now?" The detective's eyes widened in shock at this question, unsure of how to answer it. He didn't know why he suddenly felt the need to attack his brother's dating life.

"Look, I can't stop you from *'dating'* whoever the hell you want, but I just wish you would think before ruining this innocent young lady's life. She seems like a decent person." Luciano said, hoping to steer the conversation away from him. "Of course she's a decent person, that's why I'm dating her! I ain't planning to ruin her life, either. All I want is to make things easier for her." He snapped, feeling extremely offended the detective would imply he'd cause problems for Faye. "She ain't some pathetic little hostage and isn't doing anything against her will. If she asks to go home, I'll bring her home with no complaints, so why don't you fuck off?"

Luciano was taken aback by Elio's outburst, not expecting him to get so defensive about his relationship with the cute little blonde-haired girl. In a way, it was pretty endearing to hear the alleged crime lord act protective over someone. Of course, he was almost certain this was all for show just to get the detective off his back. "You've never acted this protective of anyone before. What's with the sudden change of heart?" He wondered thoughtfully. "She's different from anyone I've ever met. Perfect in every way that it makes me want to keep her by my side, safe and loved." He admitted, his face softening for a brief second.

Blue eyes filled with skepticism stared him down, doubting every little word. "Seriously? You think she'll be safe and loved with you? My dear brother, you are incapable of loving anyone but yourself." His comment cut deep, and yet Elio found a bit of humor in it. "You know, a few weeks ago, I would have agreed with you. Maybe I have been cold and cruel in the past, but this is different. *She's* different. I love her more than anything, and I want to make sure she knows it. I'll protect her from all the scum of this fucked up world no matter what."

Luciano stood silent, unable to utter a single word as he watched his brother's expression grow colder the more he spoke, as though he were issuing out a threat. While he attempted to gather his bearings, Elio wasted no time in moving past him, clipping his shoulder. Before the detective knew it, the mobster was gone, disappearing into a random car. He couldn't help but feel a sense of unease at his brother's words, imagining the lengths the man could go for someone he loved.

Chapter: 18

Laying near the edge of the bed with her head halfway off, Faye held her phone above her face, playing a simple game of block breaker to pass the time. Feeling bored, she couldn't help but check the time religiously, hoping that at any second her wonderful boyfriend would walk through the door. This was their final day together before she had to go back to work, so she really did not want to waste any time.

Just as she was about to beat the current level, a sound hit her eardrums, causing her to miss the ball costing her the game. That didn't bother her in the slightest, especially when she recognized that sound of the jingling of keys. Her heart raced with excitement as she attempted to move out of her position, only for her phone to slip out of her hands, smacking her in the face. From there, it all went downhill. She let out a string of quiet swears, trying to push herself off the bed. Unfortunately, that didn't seem to go as planned, either.

Because of her awkward position, she had to roll herself onto her stomach and push upward until she was on her knees. After that, she could easily crawl off the bed. In her haze, she rolled herself the wrong way, causing her body to tumble off the bed. A loud thump echoed across the room as her body smacked the ground. "Ouch." She mumbled, rubbing her aching body parts.

The noises on the other side stopped for a moment before the jingling started up again, sounding far more panicked. Before she knew it, the door flew open as a worried Elio stormed in, scooping her up in his arms. "Are you okay, my love? What happened?" He asked frantically, gently setting her back on the bed so he could inspect her body for any bruises.

Faye couldn't help but let out a soft giggle, amused by all of his fussing. "I'm fine. I just fell off the bed." She explained while she allowed him to move around her different body parts, making sure each one was okay. Rolling his fiery orange eyes, he tilted the clumsy girl's head up to peck her on the lips. "You need to be more careful doll, a pretty girl like you could seriously hurt herself in a place like this," He said ever so sternly, a glint of playfulness in his eyes. "Yeah, yeah." She retorted, waving his words off. "I'm sure I'll be fine. I have you here to protect me, after all." Faye meant this as a joke, but he seemed to take this comment to heart. 'Of course I'll protect you. You belong to me, after all.' He thought to himself, knowing that saying something so forward would only scare her away.

Elio sat next to her on the bed, pulling her into a tight embrace. "I'm so sorry I had to leave you." He mumbled into the side of her hair, taking in her intoxicating scent. "I really didn't want to. It was just unfortunate timing, but I promise I'm yours for the rest of the day." Faye felt her heart race hearing his words, causing her face to turn bright red. "It's okay, I'm just happy you're here now." She tried to sound nonchalant, but her voice grew higher with each word. A smile crept up onto the large man's face, noting how flushed his cute little girlfriend became at the constant contact.

Tilting her face up to meet his lips, he pulled her into a soft, gentle kiss, slowly moving her closer and closer to him until he had her straddling his lap. He leaned back against the bed, keeping her on top of him as he deepened the embrace. "I want you to know, every moment I spent away from you was pure torture. I'm not sure I'll be able to survive a whole week of not having you." His words held a hint of sorrow to them, causing the young woman to feel a tinge of guilt. "I really wish you didn't have to leave."

His words were a sharp blade piercing through her heart, making it impossible for her to breathe. She gently placed her hand on his cheek, looking into his fierce orange eyes lovingly. "I wish I didn't have to leave either. These past few days have been some of the best days of my life." She admitted, causing him to sit up in excitement. "You really feel that way?" He asked hopefully. "Because if that's the case, you really don't have to leave."

Faye couldn't help but shake her head in amusement, stifling a small giggle that threatened to come out at his childish antics. "Elio, my love, I have to go back. I still need to go to work tomorrow." She reminded him, nuzzling his nose cutely. "Doll... You don't *have* to do anything. If you don't show up tomorrow, what's the worst that could happen?" He argued as he gently kissed her forehead. "I could get fired, and that would kind of suck." She stated with a slight eye roll. "So?" He retorted, unaffected by her argument. "If I lose my job, then I won't be able to pay rent, so I'll either end up on the street or forced to move back in with my parents. Either way, it would suck." She explained calmly.

Elio's whole body vibrated as he let out a hearty laugh, clearly amused by her words. "Doll, I can assure you neither of those things would happen to you. If you lose your job, you'll simple just move in with me, which is a win-win situation. I get to have you full time and you don't have to worry about paying bills ever again." He sounded so casual, as if it were set in stone, that she would move in the very next day.

"Please stop. I already promised I'll move in by the end of the month." She whined against his chest. "I just have a lot of loose ends to tie up first." Long, sharp nails stroked through her soft, silky locks as he let out another sincere chuckle. "I wonder what loose ends an adorable little dame has to tie up so suddenly." He pondered quietly, continuing to pet her head delicately. "Just got some business and personal things I need to get done. Can't leave my job high and dry, plus I don't want to suddenly disappear on my friends and family, you know?"

She mumbled out a string of excuses on why she couldn't just randomly uproot her life, hoping he would move on from the subject. Unfortunately, he didn't seem to take the hint. "Doll, you realize you don't owe anyone, especially your job, anything at all, right? You are way too kind to people that don't deserve it." There was a slight edge to his tone that almost sounded serious. "Elio, please... Mph!" Before she could ask him to drop it, he pressed his lips against hers, completely silencing the flustered young woman. "You know I'm right. These people don't deserve such a sweet and caring woman. You're too good for them, my love."

Before Faye could react, Elio flipped her over onto the bed, pinning her to the mattress. She let out a loud squeak in surprise at the sudden movement, struggling for a moment to free her hands that he had pinned over her head. Moving his lips towards her collarbone, he nipped ever so lightly, causing her to stop her pointless struggling. She tilted her head to allow him further access to the sensitive flesh, her body now completely trained to obey his every move.

"Come on, doll, please? Just disappear with me. I promise I'll take good care of you." Why was he acting so persistent over this whole thing, treating it like it wasn't a big deal at all? "Elio... Mph... Please, just let me have a month." She pleaded, her skin burning from the constant stimulation. "After that, I... Ah... I promise I'll be all yours." Elio stopped his ministrations, giving her a curious yet predatory look. "What exactly do you mean when you say *I'll be all yours?*" He asked, allowing his perverted thoughts to plague his mind. "I mean whatever you want me to mean!" she panted out, feeling as though her brain would turn to mush at any moment. "I'll be yours to do anything you want with." She doubled down, nervous about the sudden glint in his eyes.

"Anything I want huh?" He said, his smirk growing wider with each word. "So you'll let me lock you in this room and tie you to the bed to be used whenever I please?" He had her wrists in one hand as he used the other to trace along her inner thighs, watching as she flinched at the contact. "Y-yes?" She stuttered, unsure of herself. "Oh, come on, doll, I need you to sound far more confident than that." He tsked, pecking her lips lightly. "Yes! Yes! I'll let you do that to me!" she finally cried out, loving every bit of his teasing.

Just as suddenly as he started, he quickly stopped, pulling away from the flustered girl so that she could catch her breath. "Fine, fine. It's a deal." He stated nonchalantly, slowly moving off of her only to pull her into a much gentler embrace. "You can have one month and that's it. After that, all those loose ends of yours better be tied up, otherwise we'll have to cut them." Faye truly believed her boyfriend was just being playful with her, but in her position, she couldn't see the dark look that fell onto his face. She didn't even bother to question why he suddenly acted so pushy with her all over again.

Faye snuggled deeper into Elio's chest, relishing in his warm embrace. There was a sense of comfort and peace that surrounded them as they lay together, quietly enjoying each other's company. This bedroom almost felt like a sanctuary, keeping her safe and secure. If only she had her two precious cats with her, then this would be absolutely perfect. She could picture herself spending the rest of her life in this room cuddled up to her boyfriend, watching television together, playing games, and even working on her art projects.

Glancing up, Faye was met with Elio's intense, unwavering stare. It held focus and passion, feeling as though he were afraid to look away for even a second. She couldn't help but stretch her neck up to give him a small peck on the side of his cheek. Her heart fluttered with joy at seeing his face soften as his lips turned upward into a smile. He returned her little gesture of affection by pulling her back into another kiss, this time far more tender and gentler than before. There was no heavy teasing or forced entry involved, instead he kept it more chaste so as not to put any more pressure on her.

Just as they pulled away from each other, Faye's phone rang, forcing her to move away from her irritated lover. A soft, unhappy sigh left her lips as she grabbed the offending device, looking to see who could be calling her this time. She took a quick glance at the screen before hitting answer with her brows furrowed in worry. "Hey what's up?" She spoke into the phone as she moved to sit on the edge of the bed. "I'll be home later tonight. Why?"

Elio watched carefully as Faye spoke on the phone, trying to figure out who she was talking to. "He did what?" She sounded a little frantic. "Well, are you okay? He didn't get you too bad, did he?" He kept note of her expression with each sentence, watching as she went from panicked to relieved. "Well, that's good. At least he didn't draw blood. Still, you need to make sure you clean up the wound... Pika, darling, it's okay... Calm down, you did nothing wrong. Caligula can be a little too rough when he's playing... It's fine... No he doesn't hate you... No!

I don't hate you… It's fine that you can't find him, he's probably just hiding in one of his spots…"

Faye's voice remained calm and collected with every word, trying her hardest not to freak out her friend. While Elio could see the obvious frustration on the blonde girl's face, she kept that hidden while she spoke. It was honestly pretty impressive for the man, though he knew it was probably a skill she learned over time working in customer service and healthcare. He could never dream of achieving the level of patience and care that she kept during this phone call. *'You are simply incredible.'* He thought to himself, feeling prideful that he found such an amazing girl.

"It's okay if you need to leave right now… I promise they'll be fine for a couple of hours… Pika, they do just fine while I'm at work… Four hours alone will not traumatize them… It's okay, I'm not upset. Just take care of yourself, okay?.. I'll talk to you later… Bye." Finally, after a long and grueling conversation, Faye finally ended the call. She turned towards Elio and offered him an apologetic smile.

"Sorry, that took so long." She said softly, leaning her head against his shoulder. "It's fine. I just hope everything is okay." He replied with worry in his tone. "Oh everything is okay, that was just my cat sitter. Apparently, Caligula got a little too excited and scratched the shit out of her. She's fine, though, no blood drawn." Faye shrugged nonchalantly, not the least bit worried. "I see… Does that mean you need to leave early?" A worried expression fell on his face as he spoke, anxious that she might request for the date to be cut short. "No, not unless you want me to. The cats are used to me being gone for eight hours each day. A few hours shouldn't be that much of an issue. Besides, they have plenty of dry food in their dishes, so they'll be fine."

Elio let out what sounded like a sigh of relief, his body completely relaxing at her words. For a moment he almost thought she was planning to ditch him for her pets, but luckily they were facing a non-problematic problem. Of course, he knew this time they were just lucky about the timing of everything. If this were to have happened the previous day or maybe even early morning, there might have been a huge chance she would have left right then and there. With all the future dates lined up for them, he really didn't want to risk having any of her attention taken away because of the incompetence of her own friends.

His eyes narrowed as frustration built inside him. The fact that Faye wasn't upset at all over the whole thing bothered him a little. He knew the reason this person had volunteered her time was because she owed his girlfriend a favor. It was obvious this woman held no intention of following through and wanted to take advantage of her kindness. His sweet, gentle Faye was none the wiser either, as she simply took this excuse without question.

No… This was completely unacceptable. His doll would not be taken advantage of so long as he stood by her. From here on out, any favor that was owed to Faye would be paid in full, and if they tried to weasel their way out, he'd destroy every part of them. In the meantime, he should probably insist on having one of his men watch her cats whenever they go out. At least then he could guarantee no interruptions would occur on future dates.

As he laid there, lost in thought of what to do in the future, Faye wrapped her arms around his neck, snuggling her face into his chest. She took a deep breath, inhaling his scent, allowing herself to get lost in the aroma. The smell of tobacco and cologne that she loved filled her senses, causing her heart to flutter with joy. Though underneath the welcoming smell was something strange, yet familiar. It smelt both coppery and sickeningly sweet, noticeable but easy to ignore. She thought back on what this smell reminded her of, bringing back a memory she had to shake to the back of her head.

"Hey doll." Elio's deep sultry voice cut through the thick silence, causing her to completely forget what she was thinking about. "Is there anything in particular you want to do for our last day together?" His slender fingers traced circles into her inner thigh as he grinned down at her expectantly. "No, not really…" she answered hesitantly, not sure if she had given him an acceptable answer. "Really? Are you sure?" He asked with a playful tone to his voice.

Faye mumbled a few incoherent words into his chest before lifting her head to look into his eyes. "Yes, I'm sure." She said in affirmation before smashing back into his body. "Oh, come on, there has to be something you want to do." He pressed on lightheartedly. "I'm doing exactly what I want to do." She mumbled defiantly.

A soft, earnest chuckle rumbled through Elio as he stroked her head. "What exactly are you doing, doll?" He couldn't help but ask. "Cuddling with the man I love." She retorted proudly, causing his heart to flutter. "Ah, I see. But is that really all you want to do? I mean we can go back in to the city, catch a show, go out to eat, maybe check out a museum. There's still plenty of time left." While it all sounded like loads of fun, she couldn't help but shake her head stubbornly. "I just want to cuddle with you."

She sounded so simple and childish, and yet her request was sincere. While she had truly enjoyed exploring the city with her lover, she needed a day where she could rest. This new found haven that came in the space of Elio's bedroom was almost the perfect place for her to do just that. He became a symbol of safety and comfort for her, making it clear as day she was free to do what she wanted with no worries.

Without a single word, Elio rose from his spot, lifting Faye. She let out a cry of protest, quickly grabbing on to his shoulders for support. Before she could actually question him, he fell back down at the head of the bed with her laying on top of him. Long, slender fingers reached for the hem of the blankets, pulling them on top of the two, trapping them under a layer of warmth and fluff.

A look of curiosity fell on the girl as she stared at her boyfriend, wondering what he could be planning. "If we're going to cuddle the rest of the day, we're going to be doing it right." He explained, brushing off her confused expression. Reaching for the remote, he quickly grabbed it before handing it over to the girl. "Here, find us something to watch. Just make sure it's not the news." The last part sounded almost threatening, though she could have misconstrued the intentions in his tone.

"Okay." She smiled happily, using the remote to flip through channels. Elio's eyes remained glued to the blonde girl, not willing to look away even for a second. Faye looked deep in thought, probably trying to find the perfect show for both of them. She was just so considerate, trying to keep him in mind when channel surfing. Of course, he didn't care what she put on so long as it was something she liked. He just wanted to see those bright blue eyes light up in joy at the sight of her favorite, whatever.

Cool lips fell against the drape of her neck, slowly moving against the soft, supple skin. "You know, doll, I'm really curious to see what a wonderful woman like you enjoys watching in her free time." His sultry voice sounded against her, causing a shiver to run up her spine. "Are you sure you want me to pick? It's your home after all, so I think it'd be more appropriate for you to choose the movie." She stuttered out nervously. "Nah, you should pick. I want to see your preferences. Besides, in a month, this'll be your home, too." He retorted as he dipped his head back into her neck, kissing and sucking the sensitive flesh.

Faye let out a shaky moan before turning her focus back towards the television, determined to make a decision. As she clicked through the channels, the screen landed on a movie that seemed to catch her interest. The film was an animation that had been made in the early 2000s and had a vast array of characters in it. The movie, in her mind, was a timeless classic that would forever hold a special place in her heart.

"So, this is the movie you've chosen?" Elio suddenly asked, causing her to jump in surprise. "Yes?" She replied hesitantly, hoping this choice was okay with him. "Hmm... Interesting. You seem like the type of person to appreciate a good animated movie." He nodded approvingly, causing her to relax completely. "So you know this movie?" Faye perked up at his approval. "No, sadly I don't. But if you like it, I'm sure it's worth the watch." He shrugged with a soft smile.

Faye was practically beaming with joy at his words as the nervous pit she once felt melted away. In the past, anytime someone asked her to pick something, whether it be a movie, activity or the next meal, she would be met with a look of disappointment at her choice, causing her to feel immense guilt. As tough as she liked to believe she was, deep down she's always been a people pleaser, so it bothered her to know her choices were the least favorable. It was comforting to know that Elio was true to his word, that she could pick whatever, and he'd still be happy with it.

A few hours had passed as the couple laid together, enjoying each other's company. They watched a couple of movies from the same genre as the original, comparing the similarities and differences of each animation style and plot. At one point, they got in to a heated argument over a main character's role and actions, which promptly ended in laughter after Faye did a playful reenactment of Elio's logic behind said character.

"You are such a dork." He teased, flicking her forehead lightly. "And yet you still love me." She retorted, sticking her tongue out at him. Reaching up, he placed his hands on her face, squishing her cheeks around softly. "Always and forever." He promised, pulling her down for a soft kiss. This moment felt so perfect and normal, like they were both a normal couple enjoying their time together. If Elio could have things his way, this moment would last forever.

Slowly but surely, Faye relaxed, her eyes slowly fluttering shut as she snuggled closer to Elio, burying her face into his chest as the TV turned into background noise. He nuzzled his face against her soft, silky hair, breathing in the lovely scent of her shampoo. As wonderful as this was, he knew this mini vacation was coming to a tragic end as his beloved needed to go home soon.

With a melancholic sigh, Elio nudged the sleepy girl back awake, causing her to lift her head so that she could meet his gaze. "It's getting late." His voice sounded so dejected. "Oh... I probably need to go back home soon." She responded, sounding equally disappointed. "I mean, you don't have to. You could always stay here." While he knew it was pointless rehashing this argument, a small piece of him still hoped she'd agree. "No, I need to get home. I have too many things I need to do." She reminded him, once again rejecting the offer. "You are such a stubborn woman." He grumbled, shuffling around before moving to get off the bed.

Faye felt Elio's arms wrap around her, lifting her up off the bed before setting her down. She rolled her eyes as she stretched out her limbs, feeling the satisfying pop of her joints.

Moving to one side of the room, she gathered her belongings, slipping on a pair of sandals before making her way back to her lover. "Ready to go?" He asked with a slightly pouty tone to his voice. "Yep." She chirped happily, wrapping her arms around his large biceps.

The moment they stepped out of the room, leaving what felt like a sanctuary for Faye, Elio's whole demeanor changed. He no longer acted jolly and cheerful, instead his expression hardened into something far more neutral. It felt creepy and unsettling, as though she were walking hand in hand with a stranger who wore the mask of her beloved. Swallowing down her nervousness, she kept a straight face to not gather any attention.

The further down they went, the more eyes she felt watching her. Strange men would pass them by, staring a little too long at Faye's form. As much as she tried to hide her emotions and act like none of it bothered her, she couldn't help but tighten her grip on Elio's arm, squeezing with all her might.

Upon noticing his girlfriend's sudden clinginess, Elio took a glance around at their surroundings, noting all the men that lingered around. The moment he realized the dark, longing looks they all gave his beloved, a shadow fell on his face as he clenched his teeth, seething with rage. He shot every one of them a warning look, causing them to cast their unwelcomed gazes elsewhere. 'This one's mine, you fucking mutts.' He thought to himself bitterly, knowing he'd have to keep a good eye on his Faye, otherwise his men might grow to become a little too brave.

Once she felt the perverse gazes vanish, Faye relaxed her grip and allow herself to enjoy the walk. Her eyes focused more on her surrounds, allowing Elio to take the lead, controlling her body completely. The hallways seemed long and unending, feeling almost like a maze. She couldn't help but feel slightly frustrated that she could only look for a few minutes at each painting that lined the walls. It was a subtle desire for her to stand and stare, treating her boyfriend's home like a museum.

Elio quickly moved her along, trying his hardest not to let her take in her surroundings. He knew any bit of lingering could alert the young woman that there was something off about him. The art pieces that lined the wall showcased his cruelties and crimes, each one despicable in context. He had them commissioned and hung to intimidate his men and remind them of what he could do. They were effective in their purpose, but it would be a cold day in hell before he explained any of them to his beloved.

Eyeing her up and down, he couldn't help but think that she would make a stunning model. He could picture her portrait hanging up in his office, brightening up the dull room with her beautiful smile. Maybe he would have one made of her, with her consent, of course. There was no way he'd ever force her to do something she was uncomfortable with.

Finally, they made it to the front door with no issues. Faye could feel her heart racing with excitement, waiting for her lover to open the door. She wanted so badly to see the area surrounding them, hoping to see what type of neighborhood a house like this would stand in. Unfortunately, her curiosity was not satisfied, instead it was doused out with help from the large man that loomed over her.

His hands covered her face, shielding her eyes from whatever sight awaited them. The look of disappointment was clear on her features, and Elio couldn't help but feel guilty because of it. "Sorry doll." He whispered in her ear. "But I can't let you see anything just yet. You'll just have to wait until you move in." Faye nodded in understanding, figuring it would be pointless to question his reasoning. It would only be a month after all, so there was no reason to be pushy on the subject.

Elio smiled approvingly at her obedience, relieved that she didn't try to fight him on the issue. Seeing past the fact that she already had an established life with friends and family that would miss her if she vanished, Faye would otherwise be the perfect partner. Not once has she seriously complained, nor did she ask a lot of questions. While that would normally raise suspicion to him, there was something about her that seemed completely trustworthy and genuine. She had a light innocence to her that compelled him to keep her close to him. That way, he could continue to protect her.

A silence fell on them, which was quickly broken by the sound of the large wooden doors creaking open. Faye felt a gust of wind rush past her, causing goosebumps to form along her exposed skin. Turning around in Elio's grip, she hid her face in his chest, taking cover from the elements. He found her odd behavior rather endearing, knowing it would be difficult to deny just how adorable she looked.

Without a second thought, Elio lifted the blonde girl up into his arms, keeping her face covered. He carried her out to the car, being extra mindful of placing her in the back seat. Faye felt him crawl on top of her, keeping her pinned to the seat as he shut the door behind him. She looked up at him with curious blue eyes, wondering if he planned to keep her in this position the whole trip.

She felt his lips brush against her skin, lightly peppering kisses around the soft flesh in order to distract her from her position. "This has been quite the experience." Elio spoke with a dreamy tone to his voice. "I could say the same." Faye breathed out, relishing in her lover's affection. "I love you so much. I can't wait for you to move in with me." She couldn't help but bite her lip, knowing that any response she gave might cause an argument to ensue.

He was very vocal about his desire to have her move in right away, treating it as a simple task. This was far from simple for the blonde girl. In order for her to move in, according to him, it would involve quitting her job and supposedly moving out to the middle of nowhere. She'd be sacrificing her independence and comfort, as well as allowing herself to be isolated from friends and family. This would be a difficult change for her, especially after she worked so hard to get her life back on track.

Awful memories flooded through her head, causing her to clench her fists. Taking in a shaky breath, she blinked away the terrible thoughts and instead focused on the man who still had her pinned. He stared at her expectantly, waiting for her response. "I love you too." She stated earnestly, leaving it at that. At the very least, she could be honest about her love for him. After all, he and his love weren't the issue.

Satisfied with her comment, he offered a sincere smile as he sat up in the seat, pulling her into his lap. He kept one hand on her face, grasping her chin with his large hand so she was forced to look at him. "I know this is a little uncomfortable for you, but I can't have you looking out the windows just yet. I'll let you know when it's safe to look," Elio said in a soft, compassionate tone, hoping Faye would understand his position. "Okay…" she mumbled, giving a soft yawn as she relaxed in his tight grip.

Faye held her head against his torso, listening to the pounding of his heart, allowing the soft, gentle thumping to lull her to sleep. But just before her eyes could fully shut, the car slowed down, stopping in front of a familiar-looking house. Her head peaked up from its resting spot, eyes lazily glancing at the sight before her.

Elio's gaze followed his beloved, his face darkening at the sight before him. In his excitement during their first date, he never gave himself time to properly exam her living conditions, but now in their final moments of the night, he couldn't help but grimace at how awful it was. The paint on the walls was peeling away, showcasing the layer of rust hidden away. The large, metal awning that hung over the front porch had a few panels missing and looked as though it would collapse at any moment. The wooden stairs rotted in some parts, creating an unstable flooring that could break with the slightest hint of pressure.

It was hard to believe Faye would even consider staying in a dump like this a minute longer, let alone a whole month. He's met crack whores with better living conditions than this. No, this was completely unacceptable. Elio wouldn't allow his wonderful girlfriend to step foot into something so rundown. Before he could voice his thoughts, she had already opened the door, jumping out of the car.

"Thank you again for the wonderful weekend." She beamed as she dug through her purse, searching for her keys. "Anytime, doll… It was my pleasure, after all." He replied as he crawled out of the car and pulled her into another hug. The embrace felt tighter and more desperate than usual, almost like he didn't want to let go of her.

"Would you like to come in?" She suddenly offered, her voice muffled by his broad chest. "Sure…" He replied, his voice stoic and unreadable, as though he were trying to hide his excitement. This was a great opportunity for him to spend more time with her, plus he needed to see how terrible the conditions of her house really were. "Great! Let's go." She chirped, practically dragging him over to the decaying staircase, seemingly oblivious to the destruction. Elio let out a soft chuckle, finding his girlfriend's enthusiasm absolutely adorable.

Making their way up the old porch steps, Elio started running estimates in his mind, thinking back on people he could hire to fix up her place. While she wouldn't be staying there for too much longer, that she'd still be there for thirty whole days was enough to make the repairs worth it. There was no way in hell he'd ever allow for his precious Faye to continue living in these conditions, not when he could easily do something about it.

"Doll, I don't mean to cause alarm, but I think your house is about to collapse." He said with concern in his voice. "I'm sure it'll be fine. It's just a little dented up." She attempted to wave off his worries, not wanting him to be bothered by her problems. Faye knew how bad her house was, being the run down trailer it was, but this was what she could afford with her salary. She was honestly proud of her home, grateful to have a place to herself after everything she had been through. Besides, she was slowly fixing the place up one room at a time.

He pressed his face into the back of her neck, nuzzling against her as she struggled to unlock the door. "It's more than a little dented, doll. It's falling apart." He pointed out, causing her to sigh. "Yeah, well, it is over fifty years old. Things do that after a while." She retorted, mildly irritated by his obvious comment. "You know I can't let you live like this, right?" A large hand wrapped over hers, helping her insert the key as he made his position on this clear.

A click sounded behind the door, allowing them to slowly push it open. "Oh, and what are you planning to do about it?" She asked with genuine curiosity. "Well, since you refuse to move in with me right away, I guess I'll just have to hire a crew to come over and fix it up." He shrugged, following her into the house. "That is completely unnecessary!" She sputtered, clearly not okay with that arrangement. "Sorry, doll, but that is the only way I'd ever allow you to live here." It almost sounded like Elio was talking to a child with the way he dismissed her feelings on the matter.

As she closed the door, she took in a deep breath before glancing up at him. "I know you're trying to make it more comfortable for me, but I am totally okay with the outside of it looking like a meth house." She realized snapping at him wouldn't work, so she decided she use gentle persuasion instead. Flashing her a toothy grin, he took her by the hand, spinning her around before pulling her close to him. Their lips met in a soft, sweet embrace as he slowly swayed her around the living room. Slowly, he pulled away, much to her dismay, and took her chin in his hand, forcing her to look up at him.

A dark expression flashed over his face for a moment as he stared down at her, his eyes filled with sinister intentions. "You can't live here like this. It'll make me look bad." His tone was harsh and strict, as if he were reprimanding the blonde girl for her choice of housing. Blue jewels blinked at him for a few seconds before an exasperated sigh left her lips. "Fine, do what you want." She said in a dismissive manner, finding it pointless to argue. "Just make sure whoever you hire doesn't disrupt my peace. I don't need to listen to constant banging when I'm trying to relax. Also, my cats don't deserve that type of stress."

His stoic, emotionless face softened at her words, a satisfied smile painting his lips. "Thank goodness you ain't planning to fight me." He spoke in relief. "Especially over something that could really put you in a lot of danger. I mean, look how fragile your door is. Someone could easily kick it in. Then what?" This wasn't the tone he'd use for playful banter, instead it sounded far more concerned. "I'd probably beat them with the baseball bat and call the cops." She shrugged as though it were the most obvious answer.

It took a moment for her words to register, but once they did, Elio gave an amused laugh. "Oh, come on, doll, you can call me instead of those pigs. The less law involved, the less hassle it is for you." Faye couldn't help but shake her head in disbelief at this sudden comment. "The cops aren't a hassle for me at all. In fact, I got a few friends in law enforcement who owe me big time." She said this like it was something to brag about.

As she stood there wearing a smug expression with her hands on her hips, she felt his arms wrap around her, lifting her off her feet. Cool lips pressed against her forehead as he carried her over to the old, torn up couch. "That's obnoxious of them to ask such a beautiful, sweet young thing like you to do their dirty work." He mumbled through gritted teeth. The idea that a cop, of all people, would try to take advantage of his perfect little doll rubbed him the wrong way.

She simply laughed away his concerns, dismissing them as weird jokes. Elio, not wanting for her to think his intentions were sinister, went along with her relaxed attitude. "Unfortunately, they'll never get the chance to repay your kindness. From here on out, I'll make sure you are completely protected." He declared with total confidence. Faye couldn't help but roll her eyes, completely amused by his semi-controlling personality.

"Don't make promises I can easily abuse." She chided, pecking his lips softly. "Abuse away, doll. Make me a hit list if you have to. I'll have it completed by morning." He half joked, secretly hoping she'd take him up on that. "Tempting." She mumbled, resting her head on his chest. Long fingers combed through soft, silky golden locks, carefully undoing every little knot and tangle. Every second they stayed cuddled up together made it even more difficult for them to depart.

Just as Faye relaxed, a slight movement from down the hall caught her attention. An unsettling howling noise sounded from beyond the darkness, growing louder and more distressed by the second. "I'm in here Ban-Ban!" She called out, sitting up slightly from the couch. Stomping soon filled the house, echoing down the hall as an old tailless tuxedo galloped down the hallway in search of her master.

Banshee's bright, loving eyes narrowed dangerously as she bared her teeth the moment she stepped foot into the living room. Pressing her ears back in warning, she let out a sharp hiss, attempting to scare the large man away from her precious master. "Really?" Faye sighed, rolling her eyes at the overly dramatic cat. "Awe, I think she likes me." Elio remarked sarcastically, earning himself a cute giggle from the girl.

Throughout their playful banter, Banshee hadn't eased up on her hissing for even a second. "Come on Ban-Ban, knock off all that fussing. This is your future dad you're screaming at," Faye joked, extending her hand out for the tuxedo manx to sniff. "Future dad?" Elio smirked as he nuzzled into her neck. "I think I like the sound of that." A low purr came from him as he spoke, causing her face to light up bright red.

His grip around her tightened as she struggled, attempting to get up off the couch. "Nope… No escape…" He mumbled, peppering kisses across her sensitive flesh. "Please, my child, she needs me." Faye gestured towards the confused cat, watching them intensely. "You should have thought about that before letting me snatch you. Now you're all mine and there's no escaping." His voice held a playful yet sinister edge to it, causing her to laugh gleefully.

She stretched her arm out further, trying to reach out towards the cat, who finally gave in and sniff her master's hand. The moment the blonde woman's scent filled the black and white cat's nostrils, her body instantly relaxed as she leaned into the touch. Banshee took a step closer, making it easier for Faye to pet her in her awkward position as Elio watched them with a look of amusement.

"I hope I'm not disrupting the peace around here." He said with a chuckle. "No, not at all." She replied as she pulled away from the old cat. Banshee made a disgruntled growling noise at the lack of affection. "She really doesn't like me, does she?" He mumbled in slight disappointment. "Don't take it personally. She's normally cold to strangers. Especially ones that steal my attention away. I'm sure she'll warm up to you quickly," Faye reassured him, cuddling up as close as possible to the dejected man. Her words seemed to ease his troubled mind, causing him to relax into the gentle embrace.

His large hand pressed against the back of her head, smashing her face into his chest, making it difficult for her to breathe. "You know, doll, she's not the only one who hates losing your attention." He purred against her neck as she struggled to break free of his grip. "I'd do anything to keep those pretty blue eyes on me." Finally, after what seemed like an eternity, he released her face, putting an end to her suffocation. "It's kind of hard to do that when I'm being squished by your damn chest." She huffed, poking him lightly. "Awe, you know you like it." He purred, rubbing his face against hers. Faye let out a defeated sigh, surrendering to his embrace as she allowed him to pepper her face with kisses.

In his feat of affection, he flipped her over, pinning the flustered woman to the couch. "So doll, where's the other one?" He asked, his sharp teeth barred as though they were threatening to take a bite. "Caligula? Oh, he's around somewhere. Probably went into a hiding spot the moment we stepped into the house. He hates strangers." She spoke, acting completely oblivious to Elio's intentions. "Really? You talk so highly of this tiny lion, I never thought he'd be a coward." The smirk present on his face only deepened as he teased her.

Wandering fingers slowly made their way up her long, smooth leg, inching closer to the hem of her dress. "Elio…" she whined, attempting to push him away. "I mean, for something that's so vicious he's willing to attack his own babysitter, I'd really expect him to be out here like the other, protecting his master at all costs." His lips gently pressed against the side of her neck, nibbling softly at the sensitive flesh. "P-please." Another attempt at escaping his affection was made, only to once again be ignored by the lust filled man.

Fiery orange optics glanced down at the flustered blonde girl, a look of amusement shining through in them. "What's wrong, my cute little doll? There's no way you're acting all shy because of a little groping." His voice was low and husky, causing a shiver to run up her back. Rough lips trailed up her neck, only to hover a few inches away from her mouth. "I mean, you already belong to me, so it's only natural that I get to play with my new toy whenever I feel like it."

Her heart practically drummed in her ears, the blood flowing so fast it almost burned. Normally she couldn't stand this type of flirting, as it was extremely dehumanizing, but there was something about the way he did it that made her want to submit. She knew he held the uttermost care and respect towards her and that he'd never force her to do anything she was uncomfortable with, so while he teased that he'd use her whenever he wanted, he didn't actually mean it. Regardless of how far into it they were, she held the power to say no, and he'd stop immediately with no hard feelings. He had already proven this on their very first date. Because of this reassurance, Faye knew she was completely safe in allowing her boyfriend to continue on with his fantasy.

Before she could respond, he had already pulled her into a deep, very passionate kiss, forcing his tongue into her mouth. Her arms moved on their own, slowly wrapping around his neck, keeping him locked in the embrace. Her quiet moans were swallowed up by her lover's lips, his long tongue sliding over the roof of her mouth, exploring the familiar territory. His fingers continued to trail upwards, making their way under her skirt while she remained distracted.

She could feel the large, lanky digits rubbed circles against her needy heat, attempting to draw out moans that could not be vocalized. There was no relief from this movement as it was far too light, like he was using a feather to tease her sweet spot. There was nothing more that she wanted than his full undivided attention on her core, but there was nothing she could do but wait for him to go deeper. Hell, she couldn't even beg for more because he had his whole tongue shoved down her throat like some makeshift gag.

In a pathetic attempt at gaining some friction, she rocked her hips up, pushing his fingers closer to her heat. "Awe, someone's frustrated." He chuckled, slowly pulling his tongue out of her mouth so that she could speak again. "Please… Mph… S-stop teasing me…" she begged in-between pants and desperate moans, wishing he'd hurry and take her already. "But you're just so cute when you're needy." He said playfully, moving one hand up to grope her chest.

"E-Elio…" she mumbled, being far too light-headed to say anything else. He stared down at her with a look of hunger and need, ready to tear her apart and devour her with an animalist ravenous. Her beautiful face so flustered and red; the sounds of her quiet, adorable moans; the feeling of her warm, soft skin; the taste of her sweet cherry flavored lips; and the wonderful aroma that seemed to follow her around, all of it overfilled his senses making him crave more and more of her like the strongest drug he could think of. *'More.'* He thought greedily. *'I need more of her. This just isn't enough.'* No matter how many times he took her, he'd never be satisfied. Eventually, there would come a time where she could never leave his side.

Being weak and powerless against the large male, Faye could only lie there and take it, allowing herself to enjoy every bit of his affection. She loved the feeling so much, wishing she could stay in this position forever. He was so gentle yet so forceful, applying just enough pressure to cause her pleasure, but not too much that she would feel any sort of pain. She wanted him, needed him, and could easily see that he felt the same. At this point, nothing could stop them from having one final round before the weekend ends.

A soft, fluffy orange paw landed on her forehead, causing her eyes to dart up to the sudden intruder. "Really?" She groaned, seeing the unbothered beast sit on the cushion above her, looking as smug as ever. "Meow." He replied in a cute, high-pitched tone, as though he didn't just put an end to his master's romantic escapade. "You are such an asshole." She pouted, sitting up from her spot as Elio moved to get off of her, trying his hardest to keep it together.

Normally, he would be absolutely livid about an interruption like this, but there was something so comedic about this orange cat's timing. "I'm guessing this is the other one." He said with an amused smirk. "Yep, this is the little asshole. Always walking in at the worst times." She huffed, reaching up to pet the menace in question. He let out a happy chitter, most likely proud of himself for acting as a fluffy little cock block.

A loud, hearty laugh erupted from the large man, causing the couch to shake. "Wow, I never thought I'd lose my girl to some cat." He exclaimed in-between chuckles. "This damn thing really is a menace to society." With his fur puffed up and his eyes narrowed, Caligula almost looked offended by that statement, which only made him laugh harder.

With a tiny shake of his butt, Caligula swiftly jumped from the couch cushion to Faye's shoulder, causing her to wince slightly. Digging his tiny little claws into her bare flesh, beads of blood formed. "Are you okay?" Elio asked, horror and worry clear in his voice. "Yeah, I'm just peachy. I think Liggy missed me." She attempted to joke, adjusting her clothing so that her beloved cat would claw into fabric and not her. "I see…" he was not amused by the position his girlfriend was in.

Noticing her lover's concern, Faye's face softened as she offered him a reassuring smile. "It's okay, he does this all the time… Owe… He just needs to adjust and… Sir! Can you please retract your claws? Get comfortable." As if on cue, Caligula settled down into a perfect orange loaf, nuzzled against her neck. "If you say so…" Elio said with a slight chuckle, finding the blonde girl absolutely adorable with her little orange menace. She seemed pretty happy with her cats around her so he'd need to get used to their strange antics, especially if all of them were going to be living together.

With slow and carefully calculated movements, Elio pulled Faye towards him without disturbing the cat on her shoulder. He pressed his lips against her forehead as he held her tightly, relishing in her warmth. "I love you so much." He mumbled sweetly. "More than anything on this planet." A strange statement to make, seeing as they've only known each other for a week. "I love you too." She retorted, letting her emotions control her words.

Just as her eyes fluttered shut and her body relaxed into his embrace, she felt her cat's tail twitch, smacking the wall behind them. "Don't..." she sighed, already foreseeing the trouble her furry child was about to cause. Elio looked down, giving her a curious look. Just as he was about to question her, Caligula's butt wiggled, signaling his desire for mischief. He gave one small leap, slightly scratching the girl's delicate skin before finding himself on the shoulders of the confused man.

A look of astonishment and fear fell on the orange cat as though he didn't fully plan out his next points of action properly. Elio, feeling rather amused by the situation, worsened it by standing up, raising the poor cat at least six feet in the air. In a panic, Caligula clung on for dear life as he cried in protest, demanding that the tall beast release him. "Having fun?" Faye giggled, absolutely loving the scene that played out in front of her. "Yeah... The little fluffy thing is pretty damn cool." He admitted as he shifted his body around, forcing the cat to constantly readjust on top of him.

Finally, after what felt like a lifetime for the poor creature, Elio finally bent down, granting Caligula his freedom. Without a second thought, the orange fluff ball booked it down the hall towards one of the bedrooms. Faye couldn't help but shake her head with a soft smile at her cat's strange behavior. Her boyfriend thought the cat was pretty amazing. "I can't wait to have that thing running up and down my house, terrorizing my men," He commented playfully as he pulled his gleeful lover back into his arms. "I give it a week before he has them all trained to obey him. The little asshole can be quite the dictator." She retorted, leaning her head against his chest.

As their laughter died down, they were left in a comfortable silence that was only slightly broken by the sound of the creaking floor as they swayed back and forth. "You know I'm going to worry about you, right?" Elio suddenly spoke up, ending their silence." You really don't have to." Faye hummed in reply. "I've kept myself alive for this long, haven't I?" He shook his head disapprovingly, his frustration clear on his face.

"That's not the point. Just because you have been fine for this long doesn't mean I don't need to worry about you. Anything could happen in a month." His tone held an edge to it that took Faye off guard. Elio's grip on her tightened to an almost painful level. "I know anything can happen, but so can nothing. There's no use worrying about possibilities..." She attempted to reason while holding back a wince from the pain.

Relief washed over her face as he loosened his grip, giving her a resigning sigh. "While that's a fair point, it doesn't make much of a difference to me." While he spoke, he slowly moved her back towards the couch, guiding her to sit on his lap. "You belong to me now, doll, so I got to worry and fuss over you. That's just part of the deal." Before Faye could respond, Elio had already captured her lips in a heated embrace. A large part of him wanted to tell her the real reason he worried so much about her, but he knew doing so would only cost him the whole relationship.

Faye felt herself completely relax underneath the man as her mind went completely blank. She was far too wrapped up in the passion to even attempt to argue with his logic. If Elio wanted to spend the next month worrying over her, then that was his choice. She just wouldn't get caught up in all his fretting.

"I got to leave soon." He mumbled absentmindedly as he nuzzled into her neck. "Kind of wish I didn't have to, but I got work in the morning." There was a hint of sorrow in his voice, as though the very idea of letting go of Faye would absolutely devastate him. "It's okay. We'll meet up again next weekend." She reassured him, offering a soft, sweet smile that practically melted his heart. "Oh doll, if you keep talking to me like that, I might never leave." He grinned, leaning his face in, giving her a kiss.

She couldn't help but giggle at how cute and clingy he sounded. A large part of her wanted to beg him to stay, but she knew that was a selfish ask, especially when she herself wasn't willing to stay with him. Elio was just so sweet and amazing that she considered him the greatest guy she's ever met. Who could have guessed she'd fall in love with him after only a week, and yet here she was willing to throw away everything she's ever built for herself just to be with him.

"I love you so much Elio…" she whispered against his lips as though she were telling him her darkest secret. "I love you too, Faye, regardless of how little time we've spent together." He replied sincerely, pecking her soft sweet tasting lips over and over as though he were trying to engrave the flavor into his tastebuds. "How the hell did I get so fucking lucky finding a woman like you? You're so funny and sweet with an incredible personality, and yet you're also so fucking beautiful it's unreal."

His gaze was practically glued to her facial expressions, drinking up every little reaction she gave to his words. He had her completely pinned to the couch, rendering her helpless and unable to move. "Not a damn person will ever touch you like I do. I'll never allow it." She could feel her head spinning while attempting to listen to his ramblings, but it was all in vain. "I'll fucking kill anyone that even thinks about it. And if you ever try to leave me, I'll tie you to the fucking bed." Even his threats sounded so appealing, she almost wanted to egg him on.

"Keep talking like that and I might tie my damn self to the bed." The words slipped out before she could stop herself. "Oh, really?" He purred, allowing his voice to lower into a deeper octave. A chill ran up her spine as her face burned bright red. "I didn't realize you were into that shit. I'll have to keep that in mind." His face hovered over hers, forcing her to maintain eye contact. Suddenly, the couch felt far too small for their bodies.

Elio slowly started rocking his hips against hers, his gaze never faltering as he wore a devilish smirk. Faye couldn't help but moan at the sensation as her body automatically moved in time with his. "So cute." He cooed, brushing her hair out of her face so that he could clearly see the red that tinted her skin. "Are you sure you don't just want to come home with me?" He asked, amused by her flustered form. "No? I'm not s-sure…" she whined pathetically. "Well, if you're not sure, why don't you just come back so we can figure it out together?" He teased, hoping if he was persistent enough, she'd just cave in. "Why don't you just move in with me?" Faye suddenly shot back, pushing through the pleasure he was causing.

All movements stopped as Elio gave her a strange look. "Move in with you? Doll, I live in a mansion…" He retorted in slight confusion at her random request. "And? What's your point? There's plenty of room in this old run-down shack. It's got two bedrooms, after all." She acted as though she were making a valid argument. "No… I don't even want you living in this death trap. There's no way in hell I'd be willing to live here." He sighed, moving off of her. "But Elio, why not? The water only gets shut off once a month because they don't know how to fix the pipes." It was extremely difficult for her to keep a straight face. "Faye, I swear to fucking God if you keep talking, I'm going to throw your ass back in the car and lock you in my damn house."

It was apparent that Elio had absolutely no desire spending the next four weeks trapped in the trailer with his beloved. His actual reason was anything but superficial, though he'd never tell her what it really was. Faye couldn't possibly understand that it would be far too dangerous for him to stick around in this area.

She didn't live in the same city that Elio secretly ruled, but lived in what was considered gray territory. This meant any rival gang could show up randomly, and he'd have little to no man power to scare them away, nor did he have the backings of any politician in this city. He'd be a sitting duck if he stayed here. Of course, he could never even come close to figuring out a way to explain these concerns with his sweet, innocent girlfriend.

"I need to get going now…" He sighed, desiring anything but that. Slowly, he made his way off the couch, pulling Faye up with him. "Please promise me you'll stay safe." He said with pleading eyes. She was about to argue that there was no need for concern, but one look at his worried expression was enough to silence her combativeness. "I will." Her voice held a sincerity that quelled his anxiety.

Long, thick arms pulled her smaller frame into a tight hug as he rested his face against her soft golden hair. "Thank you." He mumbled in relief that she was understanding of his problems. They began walking to the door, still holding each other in a tight embrace before finally, with a lot of hesitation, departing. "Alright doll, I'm off. Take care of yourself, okay? And if anyone gives you any troubles at all, call me immediately." As he spoke, he looked into her beautiful blue jewels, ensuring she had heard every word.

Faye stood there, playing with his collar as she stared at him with a goofy, dreamy smile, nodding along with every word he spoke. "Don't worry Elio. If anything happens to me, you'll be the first person I call." She promised, pecking him on the lips. "Good, I'm glad you're so understanding." He responded with tenderness in his voice. "I just got you. There's no way in hell I'm ever willing to lose you. I love you so much, doll." His words pulled hard on her heartstrings, causing her to blush bright red. "I love you too. Now drive safely, and call me when you get home, okay?" It was her turn to act as the worried partner. "I will." He promised before making his way out of her house, leaving it to feel a little too empty and quiet.

She watched as his car disappeared in to the distance before finally shutting the door and making sure it was properly locked. Walking back over to the couch, she collapsed on it without a care in the world as she let the memories of her wonderful weekend flash through her head. "How incredible!" She exclaimed out loud to herself. "And to think in one month, that will be every day for me." In her moment of pure bliss, Faye nearly forgot the meaning of their agreement. "Wait? Did I really just agree to move in with a man that I've only known for a week?" Suddenly, the realization of her actions started to really sink in, hitting her hard.

Grabbing the nearest couch cushion, she used it to smother her face, breathing deeply into it in order to calm her nerves. While this whole weekend was honestly a dream, she couldn't help but think that maybe they were moving too fast. Elio was incredibly pushy about the subject and gave her no room for objections, but even without that being an issue, she had allowed her heart to cloud her judgement. "Oh, well…" She shrugged, no longer bothered by her own choices. "I guess we're moving. I better tell my boss this… She'll probably be pissed."

Chapter: 19

Blue jewels lazily blinked open as Faye let out a long, dramatic yawn after a nearly sleepless night. While she only spent a weekend with her lover, she couldn't help but long for his warm and gentle embrace. The way he held her the last few nights made her fall asleep almost instantly, and yet she tossed and turning all night, unable to get comfortable.

Reaching her hand towards the old, worn down nightstand, she swiped her finger over the screen on her phone, silencing the loud, obnoxious alarm that blared across the room. "Ugh… Fucking hell…" she grumbled bitterly to herself, wishing she had more time to sleep in. Unfortunately, time was anything but on her side, because she had already slept through two of her alarms. "Shit." She cursed, looking at the time.

She gathered her clothing together frantically, worried about running late for work. While there was a huge chance of her moving in with Elio by the end of the month, (the guy was practically drooling at the idea of it,) she still needed to stay in good standing with her work, just in case it didn't pan out. This relationship was still too new, so anything could happen. Of course, that didn't mean the idea of living with him did not excite her. Elio was everything she could hope for in a partner. He was loving, caring, funny, handsome, intelligent, not to mention an extremely selfless lover. What more could she ask for?

"A better question is, what do I bring to the table?" She asked herself bitterly, realizing none of her qualities could ever compare to his. "The only thing I offer is a few huge favors owed to me by a federal agent and the undying loyalty of an ex-pimp." 'Not to mention a few favors owed by less than savory individuals…' Her eyes fell on the large journal that sat carelessly on her desk like a piece of junk she was too lazy to trash.

Slowly, she made her way over to the book, her eyes narrowed in annoyance as she snatched the object up in her arms. "This whole favors thing is becoming pointless and problematic. I mean, honestly, what are the chances that any of these assholes will ever follow up on their end of the deal? So far all this thing has brought me is years of trauma and a sexy, unstable boyfriend who wants to lock me up in his bedroom… I mean, the second thing sounds like a good time but the first, not so fun…"

Back and forth, the irritated woman paced, her eyebrows knitted together in frustration. "I don't even know if he's actually serious about moving in together or if he's just saying that as some form of pillow talk." As she continued to rant to herself, a message suddenly appeared on her phone. 'Morning doll. How did you sleep?' It was Elio, checking in on her. She couldn't help but smile, loving just how sweet and caring he was. 'Morning! I slept alright, just getting ready for work.' She texted back enthusiastically.

127

All the panic and negativity she felt moments ago had completely disappeared, leaving nothing but giddiness and butterflies in their wake. 'Awe. You only slept, alright? You slept amazing when I was around.' She could hear the smugness in his words. 'It's not my fault you're so damn comfortable.' She shot back, imagining the low, sensual chuckle he more than likely gave to her text. 'Well, if that's the case, maybe you should move in with me after all. Save us both the trouble.' Damn, was he persistent, never letting this topic go? 'Ha, ha, nice try. It's still going to be a month.' Hopefully, he'll hear the sarcasm in her words. 'Weird hill to die on, but okay.'

There was no way of telling if he was upset or not based on the texts alone, so she sent another one out, just in case. 'Sorry, but there's so much I need to get done before I'm ready to move in, but I promise I'll spend time with you at least once a week.' Faye held her breath in anticipation of what his next message would be. 'Fine, but I get you for the whole weekend.' A sigh of relief escaped her lips as the playful words appeared on the screen. 'Deal.' She typed back enthusiastically, not even taking a moment to process his words.

Just as the text was sent, she glanced down at the time, realizing just how late it had gotten. "Well, shit…" she muttered as she rushed towards her bathroom, attempting to keep her shower to just under five minutes. Wasting no time, she stripped out of the t-shirt and underwear she wore to bed and slipped into the tub, quickly changing the settings so that the water would come out of the showerhead instead of the spout.

Faye felt her body relax against the old, worn out wall, allowing the warm water to rain down on her. She reached over to grab the soap, using it to lather up her whole body. Long finger tips danced over the bruises and bite marks that decorated her skin like paint on a canvas. Each one showcased Elio's love for the girl, marking her so clearly there would be no mistake over who she belonged to.

Why did the thought of belonging to the handsome man cause her heart to skip a beat? It felt both exciting and terrifying, especially after she was gifted such a beautiful necklace that contained quite the abundance of meaning. Every little bite and handprint on her flesh told the story of his love and his many ways of expressing it. For any other person, they might have felt terrified for life, which would have been justifiable. Elio was a huge man with a strength that could put a gorilla to shame. If he wanted to hurt her, he very much could and there would be nothing she could do about it.

Surprisingly, this did very little to sway her, as she was far too love-struck to see logic. While most would see a dangerous being that needed to be avoided, she saw someone who chose not to use his strength on her. Elio had shown nothing but love and care for her, giving her the type of treatment that royalty would be envious of. As oblivious as Faye pretended to be, the truth was she could easily smell malicious intent a mile away. She knew when to put her guard up and when to lower it, and there were no negative vibes emitting from her lover.

Okay, there may have been something slightly off about her lover. People felt the need to do everything in their power to avoid him at all costs, to where she caught a few people crossing the street in heavy traffic to not walk near him. Some people, mostly those who seemed to be employed by him, looked absolutely terrified of the large man, their eyes holding a type of fear that could only come from witnessing true evil. A strange, almost dangerous aura surrounded him when a look was cast in his direction.

This is a pretty big red flag that no one in their right mind would choose to ignore and yet, here Faye stood with her rose-tinted glasses, acting as though it was never there. She found this issue completely unproblematic, and in some strange way, sort of useful. "I hate being around too many people, anyway." She giggled to herself, seeing the situation she was in as a win-win. Not only did she get to date a devilishly good looking and charismatic man, but he also acted as pest repellent too. She hit the jackpot with this one.

The water pressure slowed down, turning into the light, obnoxious, dripping noise that would often drive Faye insane. While she had done an outstanding amount of work to maintain her tiny property, something she felt an honest pride in, that didn't mean the place was absolutely perfect. There were still plenty of issues that reared their ugly heads by owning a fifty-year-old trailer, some of which involved old, rusty pipes.

Taking in a deep breath, she shook her head of all negative thoughts, allowing herself to exit the bathtub. She grabbed the old, large towel that hung on the wall next to the sink, wrapping it around her soaked form. While she was running short on time, it didn't stop her from dragging her feet along, as though the very idea of going to work was torture. It would take a lot of negotiating for her to actually find the mental strength to step into her car.

Evidently, it took a lot of energy and empty promises to herself for the young woman to actually get dressed and begin the long journey towards work. The drive was nice and relaxing, allowing her enough time to really think about everything going on in her life. "Am I really planning to move in with a total stranger just because he said a few nice things to me?" She suddenly asked herself, still in disbelief at how easily she caved to his demands. "A better question. Is he actually planning to let some random, mentally unstable woman come live at his house? I mean, the man is an absolute catch. Why the fuck would he want me?" The question wasn't meant to put herself down, she just lived in a constant state of disbelief.

While she continued to drive, thinking about all the reasons it was probably a bad idea for her to move in, she failed to realize a car following unusually close behind her. Every twist and turn she made, that strange vehicle made it with her, as though the two had an invisible rope connecting them. Faye, being the oblivious hot mess of a person she was, didn't stop to think for a second that this might be problematic for her.

She was so caught up in her own thoughts, she nearly missed her turn and almost ended up on two wheels maneuvering the vehicle towards the parking lot. The car came to a screeching stop, fitting perfectly in-between the lines. Stepping out of the vehicle, Faye let out a heavy sigh as she slammed the door shut, dragging her feet across the asphalt. She felt no sense of urgency, even though she was running ten minutes late. The moment her eyes fell on the small, dreary hospital, it felt as though her very life force was drained out of her.

"Another wonderful day." She grumbled to herself as she made her way towards the back entrance. Her hand barely touched the doorknob before it flung open, revealing a large, overly excited Akita running out with a small, exhausted looking kennel attendant attached to the other end of the leash. Faye's eyes instantly lit up at the sight of the large, fluffy pooch, finding him absolutely adorable.

"Baily!" she exclaimed, opening her arms to the dog, preparing herself to be jumped on. With no hesitation, he pounced on her, knocking the blonde girl to the ground as he nuzzled his face into her neck, whining happily as she scratched behind his ears. "Hey Alice." She said casually, as though she didn't have a 115 pound dog laying on top of her. "Hey Faye, how's it going?" The attendant responded, completely unfazed by the sight in front of her. This was a normal, everyday interaction between the two girls, where one would be completely crushed by another animal.

After a few minutes, the large dog finally released Faye from her furry prison. Alice, feeling slightly merciful, offered her hand to help the blonde girl up. She was no longer stressed for time, seeing as she had already clocked in from her cell phone the moment she reached the parking lot. Because of this small fact, she had plenty of time to catch up with the lead kennel attendant.

"So, did you hear what happened to Chuck?" Alice asked, already prepared to share juicy gossip as they walked around the little path leading behind the building. "No… I stay away from any drama related to him." Faye retorted, scrunching up her nose in annoyance at the mention of the crude and lazy kennel attendant. "They finally canned his ass!" She exclaimed, a little too excited. "What? Oh, no. that's terrible. What a tragedy…" Sarcasm dripped from her lips, causing her coworker to roll her eyes.

"Be nice." She chided lightly, though her slight grin gave away her amusement. "Why should I? He was a piece of shit and deserved to be canned." Faye retorted bitterly, with her arms crossed. "Fair point, but you still shouldn't say that out loud. He was only fired because of his back to back no shows, and you know the moment he comes back, they'll act like he didn't ditch us for the last two days." Alice's words held a disappointing level of sincerity to them that made her heart sink. "I hate how true that is…" she responded quietly, earning an empathetic nod.

Just as the mood dropped, a playful smile tugged at Alice's lips. "Hey, no need to be so down. There's a chance we'll never see Chuck again. I mean, maybe he crawled into a ditch and died like you've been telling him to do for months." Faye couldn't help but laugh at this statement. "Chuck actually listening to me for once? What? Has hell frozen over?" The two girls giggled together, fantasizing about how nice work life would be from here on out without the obnoxious pervert following them around.

After a brief conversation, Faye made her way back to the pharmacy while checking her phone every so often. *'Have a great day at work and don't forget to give your notice. I love you.'* Elio's text came through, causing her heart to flutter. A large grin took over her face as she practically skipped to her station. The moment her eyes fell on the pharmacy, her smile dropped.

To say that her workstation was a complete disaster was an understatement. The counter top was covered in empty bottles, pill dust, and unknown liquids that stained the smooth surface. Looking down, bird crap decorated the floors, giving her reason to believe the clinic bird was given free range of this area. Her once organized cabinets were completely out of order to where they made little sense. The alphabet meant nothing and there was carprofen in the eye drops. "You people are absolute monsters!" She exclaimed in frustration, careful not to use any foul language.

She took a moment to really look at the mess in front of her, second guessing her life choices. *'I wonder if that offer to move in today is still on the table.'* She thought half-jokingly as she began clearing off the counters. At this point, if anyone needed medications, they'd just have to wait. There was no way she could work under these conditions.

Just as Faye was about to grab a mop, Rachel decided this was the perfect moment to pop her obnoxious head out. "Hey Faye, I need to talk to you real quick." She stated, using a tone that could only be used by those who shouldn't have ever come to any power.

Her first reaction was to groan internally, but then a wicked thought popped through her as her lips curved into a devious smile. "Great timing, Rachel, because there was something I needed to talk to you about as well." Her voice held a false sweetness to it that nearly sent a cold chill up the manager's spine.

Wasting no time at all, Faye casually strolled into the office, allowing the door to slam shut behind her as she took her seat. Sucking in a deep breath, she looked the woman in the eye before calmly saying, "I'm resigning from my position here." Rachel stared at her with wide eyes, completely taken aback by her words. "And before you say anything about how unprofessional this is, I'm not leaving effective immediately. Just consider this my one month notice."

"Wait what? You're leaving us? Why?" she asked, flabbergasted. "Well, to start, did you see the pharmacy? I should quit today with how ridiculous my working conditions are," Faye responded bitterly, causing Rachel to roll her eyes. "Oh, quit being so dramatic. Did you really try to get out of our talk by faking your resignation?" She crossed her arms, acting as though she just called out a giant bluff.

With a raised eyebrow, Faye stood from her seat and circled around the arrogant manager. "I'm not faking my resignation. I'm really planning to leave by the end of the month. My boyfriend wants me to move in with him and he doesn't live in the city. The commute alone would cost more than my pay, so it isn't worth staying. I mean, some of you are alright and I absolutely adore the animals here, but let's be real. This whole place is a shit show. You and that head tech are not the easiest to work with. Ya'll practically run this clinic like a dictatorship."

Her tone held an edge of anger and resentment to it, not holding back at all on any of her criticisms. All Rachel could do was stand there wide eyed listening to the pharmacy tech's rant. "Also, the lead tech isn't even a real vet tech! She's an unlicensed vet assistant. Why didn't you give the promotion to a real vet tech? And why the hell does she have power over me? I don't answer to the lead receptionist or the lead kennel attendant. I shouldn't have to answer to her either. I'm here to help and make their jobs easier, not do their bidding. I'm sick of the disrespect, of the terrible pay, the piss poor management, so yes Rachel I'm really quitting. You're lucky I need time to pack my bags or I'd make today my last day."

The room went dead silent, as though the world around them was holding its breath. Faye, by some miracle, could keep herself composed as she stared at her manager, daring her to give a retort. "Well, then..." Rachel coughed out awkwardly. "I see the points you're making, and I suppose I have no other choice but to accept you resignation..." She had absolutely no words for the woman in front of her. Originally, she was planning to not only chastise Faye for being late, but also for the mess in the pharmacy. She made the wise decision to keep her mouth shut and allow the pharmacy tech to go back to work. Without another word, Faye left the office going back to her station so that she could clean it up and make sure all medications were filled properly.

The day dragged on, feeling unnecessarily long and strenuous. Finally, she made it to the final moments, wrapping up her closing duties as she cleaned up the small messes she made throughout the day. Just as she pulled out her phone, preparing to clock out, a message appeared on it. *'Off of work yet?'* Elio's name lit up above the text, causing her heart to flutter with joy. *'Just about, just wrapping up here. I'll call you when I get home.'* She messaged back with a large, goofy smile plastered on her face.

Saying goodbye to a few coworkers that passed her by, Faye made her way out the back exit. Her mind was so focused on digging through her purse, trying to find her car keys in the endless black hole, that she didn't notice the two large figures approaching her. It wasn't until she made it out to her car that she finally looked up to notice the two men standing in front of her.

"Hello Miss Merci. I'm detective Luciano and this is my partner, detective Cosimo. We would very much appreciate it if you came with us to answer some questions." The blond-haired detective had a very light and cheery tone to his voice, sounding as though he were discussing the weather. The young woman didn't buy his friendly demeanor at all and knew better than to answer questions brought on by two strangers claiming to be cops.

Faye stood with a raised eyebrow and one hand on her hip as she stared down at the two detectives, looking rather unimpressed by their sudden intrusion. "Questions about what?" She asked, her tone ice cold with a hint of irritation. "We can't disclose anything out in public. You'll need to come with us down to the station." Cosimo responded, matching her energy. "Oh, cool… I'll pass." She retorted, reaching for the door handle, only to be stopped by the black-haired detective.

"Listen here, you little brat. Either you come down to the station with us willingly or we come back with a warrant and some handcuffs." He hissed in a deep, threatening voice. Faye rolled her eyes, completely unbothered by his threat. "By all means, be my guest, but don't be too surprised when I get my lawyer involved. I'm sure he'll have a field day with this." She once again reached for the handle, but was again stopped, this time by Luciano.

"Come on, you two, what's with all this open hostility being thrown around? I mean lawyers, warrants? Are any of these really necessary?" He attempted to act as the voice of reason, causing the other two to groan in annoyance. "I wouldn't need to involve a lawyer if you would just let me leave." She pointed out, wanting so badly to be allowed into her car. It had been a long day, after all, and she still needed to call her boyfriend to let him know she made it back safely.

"Unless you have a valid reason for keeping me here, you cannot legally detain me, so leave me alone." Her voice remained steady, although she couldn't help the irritation that leaked out. "Not until you answer our damn questions!" Cosimo growled with a murderous glint in his eyes, banging his fist against her car. "Hey! Watch it! My car ain't a punching bag." She snapped back, wincing at the small dent he left on the side.

With narrowed eyes full of determination, she once again went to open the door, only for the two detectives to once again shut it. This time Luciano moved in front of the door handle, blocking her from it completely. She balled up her fists in anger, tears pricking at the corner of her eyes in pure frustration. "Move!" She yelled a little too loud, gaining the attention of some passersby. "How many times do we have to tell you? You can go after you answer some questions!" Cosimo shouted back, not caring how many people stare at them. "Keep yelling like that and I'll book you for disturbing the peace."

The frustration that Faye felt was almost unbearable, causing her to feel weak and helpless. On one hand, she knew her rights and knew they could not force her to talk to them no matter what, but she also knew rejecting them would only make her life worse. They could act so vindictive that they'd follow her around until they finally caught her doing something potentially illegal. This was so bothersome and unnecessary, not to mention cruel. What she needed right now was a good lawyer to give her ad…

Faye smacked her forehead, annoyed by her own stupidity. "You know what? I'll just call my lawyer. That way, I can at least go into this without having my rights stripped away." She said, wondering why she didn't think of this sooner. While she knew if she went with them to be interrogated, Atlas wouldn't be available to represent her. At least she figured the threat of having a lawyer would cause them to act carefully when questioning her.

Cosimo stared at her with an amused expression as Luciano looked in horror, knowing how screwed they'd be if she were actually serious. So many laws had been violated in the span of five minutes and he knew there was no coming out of it. "Call him then." Luciano shrugged, figuring the woman was just bluffing. She was a young woman with an old beat-up car that worked a low-paying job. There was no way in hell she actually had a lawyer on standby.

Rolling her eyes in irritation, Faye pulled out her cellphone and dialed her friend's work phone. "This is Atlas." Her friend answered quickly. "Hello, Mr. Hefflin, it's me, Faye Merci. I have a dilemma here, and I need some legal advice." Her tone was calm and professional, not wanting to give away her relationship with the lawyer. "Ah, Ms. Merci. What legal advice do you need?" He was in complete sync with her, following in her lead of remaining professional.

Faye sucked in a deep breath, feeling relief that her dearest friend knew her well enough to put on a show. "Well, to start, I have these two detectives here who think they can force me into questioning without a warrant and are refusing to let me go." She gave a side eye to Cosimo as she spoke, mostly just venting to her best friend. "Hmm, interesting, so you have stated that you show no interest in speaking to them?" He asked, just to be certain of what she was claiming. "Yes." Faye spoke in affirmation. "Do you know why they are questioning you?" He followed up with his question. "No." She responded simply. "Am I on speaker?" "Yes." "Good."

Atlas already knew what was going on and knew exactly why the cops were there bothering her. It obviously had something to do with her new boyfriend and his *'career'* choice. Of course, he didn't expect his dear friend to know these facts, especially if she didn't know them beforehand. Elio made it perfectly clear to him he was planning to keep her in the dark as long as possible, even if that meant cutting her off from everything.

A shiver ran up his spine at the thought of never speaking to his friend again because of some psychopathic man bent on destroying the city over some vendetta he has. Unfortunately, not talking to Faye ever again would be the least of his problems if he spilt the beans, especially if she had a negative reaction towards it. He really needed to be careful with what advice he gave her, as it could be the line between life and death for both of them.

"Well..." He started, tapping his chin thoughtfully. "You should demand that they explain what you're being questioned for. If they refuse to tell you, then there is no point in going with them." Faye nodded in agreement, finding it somewhat sound advice. It's not that she doesn't want to cooperate, it's just, she doesn't want to be completely blindsided by them.

Cosimo narrowed his eyes as a burning hatred was suddenly lit into them. "This line of questioning is completely confidential. We can't just go blabbing about it out in public." He retorted, acting completely stubborn. "If you can't tell her after publicly humiliating her like this, showing up to her job without a warrant and acting as though she did something wrong, then there is no reason she needs to stay. You'd do better finding someone else to answer your questions." While he knew that wouldn't get Faye completely off the hook, maybe it would do just enough to get them to leave her be.

"It's regarding the shooting that happened on Saturday and your involvement with Elio." Luciano answered quickly, much to his partner's annoyance. "Really Luciano? You did not need to tell her that." Cosimo pointed out, trying his hardest not to raise his voice. "It's either we tell her or she leaves." The blond-haired detective replied in a calm, informative voice. "Shooting? Elio? What are you talking about?" Faye's eyebrows knitted together in confusion. "Look Ms. Merci, this is truly all we can tell you right now. If you come with us, we'll explain everything to you." Luciano was practically begging her.

Atlas sat silently in his office chair with his phone up to his ear as he thought carefully about how he would advise his friend. On the one hand, the questions they were probably planning to ask had a high unlikelihood of incriminating her and she could refuse to answer questions that weren't yes or no, but then again, they would more than likely reveal Elio's identity. Doing so would definitely cause the oblivious woman to have a terrible reaction towards the mafia leader. But maybe he could prevent that from happening by coaching her on how to react towards everything. Technically, he wouldn't be the one telling her and the mafia wasn't on the best terms with the police force, so this might actually work out in everybody's favor. Well, everybody who matters.

"Ms. Merci, do you mind taking me off speaker for one moment so that I can speak to you privately?" He kept a light, well-mannered tone. "Of course." She responded, doing as he asked while the two detectives watched with bated breath. Without hesitation, she switched the phone out of speaker mode and put the device up to her ear.

"So, what's your verdict?" Faye asked quietly. "I doubt they'll let you leave so easily, so it might be in your best interest to get it over with." Atlas sighed, knowing this wasn't the answer she was looking for. "Oh." She couldn't help but sound disappointed. "I know, it's absolutely ridiculous, especially since you did nothing wrong, but it'll be for your peace of mind. Now, if you go with them, I need you to stay calm and keep a level head. Don't let any of their methods of questioning get to you. Don't give any personal details to them and only give answers to questions that were asked verbally. Also, remember you are not being detained so you can leave at any point."

He gave her as much legal advice as he could, preparing her really well for what might be a shit show. He really wished he could be there with her, guiding her through whatever line of questioning they did, but unfortunately he was already drowning in paperwork and couldn't afford to leave. The young lawyer could only trust that his friend could handle something like this. Of course, on the off chance that she continued having a relationship with a crime lord, she really needed to be prepared to do this all the time. Hopefully, it wouldn't come to this, but anything could happen.

As Faye hung up the phone, she took in a deep breath before exhaling a dissatisfied sigh. "Okay fine. I'll go with you." The resentment in her voice echoed throughout the parking lot, though it did nothing to unsettle the two detectives. A large grin broke out onto Luciano's features as he pulled her into a hug. "Oh, thank you so much!" He cheered, beaming with joy. Cosimo didn't look the least bit happy about her response. Instead, he dug through his pockets as he muttered to himself, complaining about difficult women.

They quickly lead the young woman back to their car, ushering her into the back seat. They got into their respective seats up front, giving her a small reminder to buckle up. Being the stubborn woman that she was, Faye refused to acknowledge them and instead crossed her arms while letting out a defiant huff. Was she acting childish? Probably, but it was well deserved, seeing as she was being taken against her will. These two cops were lucky all she did was pout, for Faye was capable of so much more.

"So, how was work today?" Luciano asked, hoping to break the tension. Unfortunately for him, Faye was in no mood for light conversation. The silence she gave them was terrifyingly loud, getting her point across. "You really aren't much of a talker, are you?" Cosimo grumbled in a condescending voice, causing her to roll her eyes. "You know we're going to be stuck with each other for the next hour. You might as well get used to us." She visibly cringed at the grumpy detective's words as the very idea of spending her evening in a police station being interrogated did not seem ideal at all.

"Please don't let this take too long. I still have a half hour drive back to my house." She stated in the most polite tone she could muster up. "Don't worry too much about it. Once we're done, we'll just drop you off at home." Luciano's cheery voice filled the car, causing her to feel nauseous. "What about my car?" She attempted to keep her voice calm, not wanting them to hear the clear panic. "I can't have it sitting there all night. I need it in the morning to get back to work."

A loud, obnoxious giggle bounced off the walls of the car, causing her to cringe. "No need to worry about that. We'll just have your car towed back to your house!" Luciano replied in an overly jolly tone. "Tow my car? Seriously!? Do you know the potential damage that could be done to it? The thing is barely hanging on by life support as it is." Her blood boiled with rage at the very thought of it. "Quit acting so fucking dramatic. It's either we have your car towed and drive you home or you can spend your night at the police station and we'll have one of our officers take you back to work in the morning." Cosimo retorted, showing no empathy towards her. "Or, if the police station doesn't sound comfy at all, you could always stay with us." The brighter detective added as though he was offering her the deal of the century.

"Fuck no!" Faye and Cosimo yelled in unison, causing Luciano to wince. None of their suggestions made any sense to her seeing how they could easily just drive her back to her car and let her drive home, but apparently, that option wasn't available. Why did she agree to this again? Oh yeah, Atlas suggested it. What a bastard.

After a long, extremely uncomfortable drive filled with awkward silence and unbearably thick tension, they finally made it to the police station. Faye still didn't have a single clue on why they needed to speak to her, especially if it was something involving her boyfriend. If they actually had questions about the man, then shouldn't he be the one being brought in for questioning? She knew better than to waste her breath asking though as it was made pretty clear the two detectives wanted to give her the least amount of information as possible.

Luciano was the first to exit the car, quickly moving towards the back door, opening it up for Faye. Cosimo simply rolled his eyes at the display, not in any mood to deal with his partner's chivalrous act. They both stood on either side of her, treating her as though she'd run away the second they let their guard down. It was beyond infuriating that they would openly treat her this way after she agreed to being questioned.

She let out an annoyed huff as she followed the two detectives into the building, letting them guide her through the police station. The noises that sounded around her were both far too quiet and far too overwhelming for her. The constant laughter and idle chatter set her on edge, causing her anxiety to boil her alive. There was something about being in a police station for any other reason than to visit a friend that set her nerves on fire.

Familiar faces passed her by, acting completely neutral towards the anxious woman. It was infuriating for those particular officers to act this nonchalant given everything she did for them. The least they could do was speak up and vouch for her. 'Cowards.' She thought to herself, her scowl deepening the further she walked. Was it too much to ask for a bit of compassion from those who owed her favors?

They made it through dispatch, passing by a few offices and jail cells until they finally reached one of the interview rooms. Anxiety really crept up on Faye, wrapping her up in a tight embrace as she attempted to keep it all together. There was something about being pulled into a room like this that felt completely wrong. She was not a troublemaker and had done all she could to keep her hands clean, so why was she being treated like a criminal? None of this made any sense to her.

Time seemed to move slowly as Cosimo took out a set of keys, digging through them to find the right one to unlock the door. Luciano, strangely enough, looked just as nervous as Faye felt. He kept rubbing his arms and swaying from side to side, looking like a kid who stole a cookie. Swallowing her nervousness, she crossed her arms and put on a bored face, trying her hardest to act completely neutral. She knew they were only drawing this out to amplify her nerves and cause her to slip up. There was no way she'd allow for these cheap tricks to best her.

Faye still didn't know what the detectives wanted with her and what information they needed to know about Elio, but she wasn't about to tell them anything. No matter what they tell her, she'll play completely stupid, hoping to frustrate them. Eventually, the two detectives would give up and send her home, hopefully never bothering the woman again. Then she could call Elio and get him to explain why the cops were pestering her at work. 'I'm going to kick his ass the next time I see him' She thought jokingly.

A loud click echoed through the hallway, drawing Faye's attention back towards the door. Cosimo flung the door open, revealing the interview room. It was nothing like what was shown on tv. No metal table bolted down, no steel chairs, instead it actually looked pretty cozy and inviting. The flooring comprised of a plush gray carpet and the walls were painted a light pastel green. A small white table sat in the middle of the room with three chairs placed around it. Two sat next to each other while one sat at the end. The seats weren't the nicest looking things, but they seemed comfortable enough. Each one had a small layer of padding and was lacking armrests. They almost looked like they came from a doctor's waiting room.

Luciano led Faye over to one of the chairs, pulling it out for her to sit down. Once she did, he took a seat in the one right next to her while Cosimo took the seat at the end. "Can I offer you a drink?" The nicer of the detectives asked with a polite smile. "No, thank you." She answered just as politely, knowing she'd be completely monitored during this whole process.

"Do you know why we brought you in here?" Cosimo asked, getting the interview started. "No." She answered again, internally rolling her eyes at the annoying question. The purpose was to establish complete ignorance in front of the camera, but it was still an idiotic question, regardless. "We brought you here to discuss the shooting that happened Saturday afternoon between two rival gangs and your alleged involvement with the Crimson Kings." He sounded calm and professional, as if he were reading a prompter.

Faye tilted her head in confusion, looking at the detective with wide blue eyes. "What do you mean by involvement? I don't even know what the Crimson Kings are." She was completely sincere in her words, attempting to understand the situation clearly. "The Crimson Kings is the largest criminal organization in Las Pecadora and is believed to be run by Elio." Luciano was the one to explain, sounding as calm and collected as his partner.

The information came as a major shock to her, though she worked hard to hide it, not wanting to give anything away. While it was unbelievable, it made sense, given all that she had been through the last couple of days. Between the warnings that May and Atlas gave her and all the suspicious activity Elio had her doing, it wasn't too farfetched to guess he was a mob boss. That also explained all the terrified looks people gave them. 'Darn, I thought it was because of my alpha aura.' She thought to herself, stifling a chuckle.

She raised an eyebrow in doubt of their words, otherwise her expression showed no emotions to it. "I know this is a lot of information to process, but please bear with us." Luciano's voice was soft and gentle, as if he were breaking bad news to a child. "We want to make sure this information is new to you," Cosimo added in a much sterner voice. So that's what they want, to pin her as some kind of accomplice. This whole setup seemed extremely predatory, almost like they were expecting her to be a ringleader in all of this. Faye had to play it smart and be extra careful with wording. Speaking of which, she just realized they used the term 'believed to be' regarding Elio's position in the mafia. This gave her an idea.

"I really do not know what you're talking about." She said simply, acting both irritated and ignorant. As long as she didn't admit to anything, this should go over just fine. There wasn't any information she could wholeheartedly give them anyway besides the meeting. Elio had her sit through and even then, she didn't actually pay attention. Why would she? It wasn't any of her business what he discussed. The less she said to the cops, the better.

"Did Elio tell you about his work at all?" Cosimo asked, not buying for a minute that she was clueless. "No, we don't talk about work all that much." She retorted calmly, daring him to question it. There was a slight feeling of satisfaction at seeing the detective grind his teeth in frustration. "Didn't talk about work that much? Doesn't that mean you do discuss work?" Luciano spoke up, tagging in. "Yeah, I've vented to him a little about my job and how tough it is, otherwise that's all the work talk we do." She shrugged, explaining away her wording.

The two detectives gave each other a knowing look before turning back to her. "Has Elio ever mentioned his work to you?" Luciano asked for clarification. "All he's ever told me regarding his work is that it's tough, otherwise he has never explained what does for a living." She shrugged, being as honest as she could be without giving too much information away.

There was just so much information being dropped on her it was pretty overwhelming. She didn't know what to believe and really just wanted to call Elio and figure out what was going on. A discussion was definitely in order. Faye just had to think about how she would go about having that conversation. She figured a simple 'hey, so I heard you're the leader of the mafia, crazy,' might be problematic. It'll probably need to be workshopped a little, but right now she was far too freaked out to even think about it.

"Interesting. And how long have you known him?" Cosimo asked the next question. "I've known him for about a week." She answered without thinking. "And how did you two meet?" He was quick to ask the next one. "Through a mutual friend." She retorted with no hesitation. "And who is this friend?" There it was, the first question she knew she couldn't answer. "I'm sorry, but I must respect my friend's privacy. That question will have to go through my lawyer." Her words almost sounded rehearsed, which very much could have been the case.

Mentioning May by name to cops could end in a full on prison sentence, especially if the mafia was involved. That woman was so sketchy, even tweakers tried to avoid her. It was almost idiotic that Faye thought it to be a good idea to date someone who was doing business with her. In her defense, though, she too wasn't of the right mind.

"Do you really think it's a good idea for you to play that game with us?" Cosimo gritted his teeth, seething over her refusal to answer a single question. "I feel I need to remind you I am here of my own free will and am under no obligation to answer every single question you ask. Even if I was being detained, I still have the right to be silent." She remained calm and collected as she spoke, reciting the law to them. "Apologies ma'am, we didn't mean to make you feel uncomfortable. We can move on from that question for now." Luciano apologized, brushing off the grumpy detective's little outburst.

Both detectives felt beyond frustrated at the realization that the young woman was just going to lead them in circles. As much as they wanted to get as much information about Elio as possible out of her, she clearly didn't want to budge. There was no telling if she refused to talk because she was an accomplice, or if she truly did not know who he was and believed they were full of shit. Either way, they needed to switch up their tactics if they were going to get anything out of her.

"Do you remember what happened Saturday afternoon?" Luciano took the lead for this set of questions. "Can you be specific?" She retorted. "Do you remember the shooting?" This was the first question they asked that didn't feel like a trap. "I remember some parts of it, yes." She stated honestly, causing both detectives to relax their bodies in relief. "What do you remember?" Luciano sounded so hopeful that she might actually help them out.

For a moment, she just sat there, staring down at her hands in concentration. "I remember walking down the street with Elio, then this black car pulled up next to us. We heard gunshots and took off running. Elio was carrying me the whole way back." A slight blush dusted her cheeks as she spoke the last part. "Hmm… Interesting…" Luciano nodded along as she explained everything that had happened. "During your walk, did you notice anyone that seemed out of place?"

The questions they were asking were far more genuine than the ones before, which really forced her into thinking up actual answers. "No one that I can think of. Of course, this is Las Pecadoras so everyone is pretty shady." She finally answered after some consideration. "Fair enough." Cosimo mumbled, writing a few notes. While he was annoyed by how little she was willing to tell them, at least she was doing some talking. He just needed to push a little more. Eventually she'll slip up.

"Where did you go after the shooting?" Cosimo asked with an expectant look. "Why does that matter?" Faye wasn't about to answer any question that had nothing to do with the subject. If they wanted to learn about the shooting, they needed to ask about the shooting. "It's relevant because the person you were with could have orchestrated the whole event," He remarked, irritated that he had to explain the obvious to her.

Blue jewels rolled in disbelief at his audacity at assuming her Elio set this whole thing up. She knew for a fact that her boyfriend would never do anything to endanger her life.

"I highly doubt someone as intelligent as Elio would waste his time inviting some girl he barely knew out just to have her shot and killed." The detectives had to admit this was a pretty good point. It's not like Elio to do something so convoluted that didn't have any obvious meanings to it. Usually, if he had a message that needed to be sent, he wrote it in clear handwriting for everyone to see.

"Can I ask something?" Faye said before another question could be asked. "Sure, go ahead." Luciano responded far too quickly. "Do you have any evidence proving Elio is a gang leader?" Her voice came out meek and unsure, almost as if she were afraid to ask. The two detectives gave each other a look as if to wonder where this attitude came from. Just seconds ago, she was brimming with confidence, almost seeming to enjoy just how much bullshitting she could do.

What they didn't realize was that she had been struggling the whole time, attempting to wrap her head around the fact that the man she started falling in love with was a dangerous, sadistic monster with a long history of violence. Luciano and Cosimo practically glazed over that part, expecting her to be okay with that knowledge. "Evidence? You seriously need evidence?" The black-haired detective grew more and more agitated with each word, refusing to believe she didn't know who Elio was.

So that was clearly a no then. They didn't have any proof of their claims. Not that she didn't believe them, she just didn't want to think of him as a monster and ruin the amazing thing they had going. There was a small river of hope in her heart, wanting there to be no evidence so that she didn't have to know the details of his crimes. It was in her best interest to hear it from Elio himself so that nothing came out in the worst way possible. If she was going to have her vision of him shattered, he owed it to her to be the one to shatter it.

"It feels like you're trying to convince me he's a bad person, but he hasn't given me one reason to doubt him." Faye explained with sincerity in her voice. "We aren't trying to convince you of anything, much less Elio being a bad person..." Luciano retorted, trailing off as though there was more for him to say. "Then what's the point of all this? I mean, there's nothing more I can tell you about the shooting, and Elio hasn't done anything shady while he was with me, so why am I still here?"

This was very frustrating that the detectives refused to wrap things up with her. She willingly did this interview and answered every question as best as she could, so why wouldn't they just let her go? What more did they want from her? Maybe they somehow knew she ended up going to his house, but he was pretty smart about blindfolding her so she wouldn't see it. Elio even rushed her through the hallways without giving her a single moment to explore, so there was no way she'd be able to give them any information on his private life. 'Jeez, with all the sneaking around and secrets, I'm starting to think he really is a mob boss.' The humor in her mind was nonexistent.

The two detectives gave each other a look, their lips a thin line as guilt glowed in their eyes. "Look, ma'am, we understand your frustration, but we have to be sure. Is there really nothing you can tell us about Elio?" Cosimo's voice took on a softer tone, no longer trying to patronize her. "No, there isn't. He's been nothing but sweet to me and polite to every person we've encountered. I truly think you've got the wrong person on your radar." Her insistence caught them both off guard.

"It's been a while, hasn't it Cosimo?" Luciano chuckled, his laugh full of sadness and remorse. "Yeah it has, hasn't it?" Cosimo retorted, no longer typing on the computer. Faye looked between the two men, her agitation turning into confusion. "What are you two talking about?" She finally asked, realizing they'd probably never explain without prompting. "It's nothing, just… Well, it's been a while since anyone has ever talked so highly about Elio. Lately, it's all been about how cruel and evil he is. Not one person shares your sentiment." Luciano sounded so nice, and yet his remark was a huge slap to the face.

Her eyes widened in shock as she looked at the two detectives. She couldn't believe they would say something kind of mean about her boyfriend while completely on the record. "What do you mean, no one has anything nice to say about him? He's a really great guy." There was no way that could possibly be true. Every interaction she's had with him so far has been incredible. "He's a liar, killer, and a thief. Do you know how many lives he's ruined? How many he's ended?" Cosimo asked, his voice getting louder with each word.

"No, I don't! Obviously. You keep saying he did terrible things but refuse to give me proof or give examples. How am I supposed to believe you when I have more evidence that points towards him being a good man?" Her anger bubbled as she continued to defend her boyfriend. "Evidence? You really want evidence? Fine! Here's your damn evidence!" Cosimo yelled, turning the monitor around so that she could see it.

'Five dead and fifteen wounded in shooting.' The headline read in bold letter. According to the article, twenty men entered a local drugstore, all wearing red and carrying guns. Without a single warning, they started shooting, aiming for as many patrons as they could. The men were all identified as members of the Crimson Kings who were following the orders of their boss, who held a grudge against the store owner.

Faye skimmed over the article twice, really taking in every word, before she finally looked back up at the detective. "Okay, so I read the article, but what does this have to do with Elio?" She asked with a hint of attitude in her voice. "Are you serious right now? Elio is the leader!" Cosimo was growing frustrated with the girl's refusal to accept the truth about her lover. "There is nothing in this article that mentions him by name." She shrugged, willing to die on this hill. "They have his picture in the fucking article!" He exclaimed while facepalming. "And? You actually believe everything the media tells you? How lame." She scoffed as she took her phone out to 'check the time.'

'Hey, I need a favor.' Her fingers quickly typed before either man could notice. "How can someone be so damn delusional?" He groaned in exasperation. "Look ma'am, every business he owns has alleged ties to the Crimson Kings." There's that word again, alleged. That they couldn't straight up call him a mob boss meant there was still reasonable doubt. "Not believing insufficient evidence doesn't make me delusional. You two are just trying to grasp at straws and throw a little hissy fit when things don't go your way. Now, unless you have actual proof of his crimes, I ask that you don't bring him up again." The arm cross and loud huff meant she was serious.

Cosimo was just about to say something else when a loud knocking sounded against the door. A soft sigh of relief fell from the woman's lips as Luciano stood up and made his way towards the door. "Hello detective Luciano, detective Cosimo." A police officer greeted them, not giving Faye a single glance. "Hello officer Cypress. Is there anything we can help you with? We're in the middle of an interview." Cosimo responded politely, swallowing his annoyance at the interruption. "Yes, actually there is. I'm trying to file the paperwork from your last case, but it seems to be missing a lot of important details. I need you to come and clarify some things for me."

It was almost too funny how irritated the officer sounded towards the grumpy detective, almost as though he didn't like the man. Of course, Faye knew it was all a show to antagonize the two cops so that they might derail the whole interrogation and allow her to leave. The fact that it came to this was ridiculous in itself, especially since they should have let her go the first time she rejected the idea, but they obviously had some sort of vendetta against her boyfriend and were willing to do whatever it took to get dirt on him.

"Can it wait? Like I stated, we are in the middle of something," Cosimo growled, showing clear signs that the plan was working. "Sorry, but it needs to be done right away, otherwise there'll be a serious delay in processing." Cypress explained without missing a beat. "I don't have any more information I can give you." Faye stated calmly, knowing there was no way the two detectives would continue with the interrogation while the officer was in the room.

"Fine." Cosimo resigned, knowing he had no other options but to let her go. "Luciano, can you please take Miss Merci home?" Just as he was about to really break her down, this had to happen. What terrible luck. "Okay!" His partner responded, all too chipper, considering the situation. It almost felt like his chipper counterpart could not care less that they didn't get any good responses out of the blonde-haired woman.

Luciano quickly shot out of his seat, offering his hand out to the irritated woman, who begrudgingly took it. He lifted her out of the chair and gently place the palm of his hand against her back, guiding her out of the room. "Come along, dear. Let's get you home." His overly cheery tone made her want to throw up. She couldn't decide if he was talking to her like a romantic interest or like a child, but either way, it made her feel uncomfortable. A part of her wished they let her either take her own car, or had any other officer bring her home.

Being led out of the police station was a completely different vibe than when she was led into it. Everyone seemed to be solely focused on her, some even offering her a warm smile and a friendly wave. 'Oh, so now you want to act like we know each other?' She thought bitterly to herself, remembering just how two-faced some of her acquaintances could be. Keeping her head high, she chose to simply ignore them and continue her walk of shame out of the station.

Luciano brought her out towards the car, guiding her to the passenger side. He opened up the door, helping her sit down before he entered the driver's side. "These questions aren't meant to incriminate you. We know you're completely innocent." He spoke softly as he started the car, glancing over at her to see her reaction. "I know. It doesn't feel like you're accusing me of anything. It just seems like you're trying to get me to help you make an arrest on my boyfriend." She retorted with bitterness in her tone.

Faye couldn't see it, but Luciano seemed to cringe at that word boyfriend. "Look, we don't want to arrest Elio. Me and Cosimo, more than anyone on this planet, want him to be innocent, but we know that's just not the case." The insistence in his voice caught her a little off guard. "*You* want him to be innocent? Really? Because what it sounds like is that you two are trying to paint him as some evil villain so that you can make a name for yourselves." Her arms were crossed and her frown deepened as she spoke, her rage really bubbling over.

"That's not true! We would never do anything like that to Elio!" He exclaimed, much to her surprise. Until this point, Luciano kept his cool, but he would not tolerate being called a manipulator. "Well then, what are you doing!?" Faye was not about to let him win the argument by being louder. "We're trying to help him!" Luciano yelled back. "Why?!" "Because he's our brother!"

The car went completely silent as the revelation sunk in. "He's your... Brother?" Her voice was soft and quiet, an almost whisper as she tried to wrap her head around the idea. "He's done terrible things. Unforgivable things, but that doesn't make him a bad person. Me and Cosimo, we love him, Cosimo especially, and we want to do right by him. Elio is different than the man we used to know, but we know he's still in there. He's just lost." Luciano sounded melancholic and almost desperate.

"I'm sorry." She apologized sincerely. "I shouldn't have snapped at you and accused you of trying to manipulate the system. I'm just tired and frustrated, and you two sprung a lot of information on me at once." She explained her hostility, which Luciano nodded along to. "I get your point. If someone tried to tell me my significant other was a mob boss, I'd probably look at them sideways too. I told Cosimo this was a bad idea, but with Elio, his logic goes out the window." He gave a dry laugh, regretting his choices.

Faye looked up at him with confused blue jewels that had nearly caused Luciano's heart to stop. "What exactly were you hoping to accomplish?" She asked, no longer sounding hostile. "I guess we hoped to draw him out of hiding, maybe put in prospective what he could lose. I know it was stupid, but we figured... Well, Elio seems to have a huge soft spot for you so we thought..." Shame shadowed him as he realized just how terrible the plan sounded. "So you wanted to use me to get to Elio?" she said softly. "Yeah... I know it's awful. We just wanted to bring our brother back."

A quiet sigh fell from her lips as she gave him an empathetic look. "Now I understand. You're trying to protect your brother, which is sweet, but I think you're going about it all wrong. You want to help someone who clearly doesn't need or want any help. If what you said about me is true, then wouldn't taking me into custody and forcing a confession out of me only push him away further?" His gaze fell down as shame weighed heavily on his shoulders.

"I'm sorry." He apologized, his voice dripping with regret and sincerity. "It's okay, I understand the thought." Her lips twisted up into a genuine smile that offered reassurance and forgiveness. "You know, I have two brothers myself, so I totally get it. I'd probably do something just as stupid if it meant saving them." He couldn't help but chuckle at her statement, finding it comforting at the very least. "I'm glad to know I'm not the only crazy sibling out there." He teased, making her giggle. "There are non-crazy siblings? Where?" She retorted, pretending to sound confused.

The tension in the car grew lighter the more they spoke. It was a strange revelation that they might enjoy each other's company. "You know, there is still a big chance Elio will get sick of you." He said it so nonchalantly, it almost didn't sound like a dig at his brother. "That's always a risk with dating. Hopefully, he doesn't, but if he does, then there's really nothing I can do." She shrugged, trying to pretend the comment didn't bother her at all. "I'm just saying it's a possibility, and seeing that he runs the mafia, he might not leave you alone so easily, even after he's lost all interest. It might end with a bullet in between your eyes. What then?"

"What a stupid question. I'll be dead, so who cares what happens after that?" She shrugged, not wanting to think the worst about her lover. "I'm being serious." Luciano retorted, feeling a little nervous about her response. "He could really hurt you." There was an emotion in his tone that made her feel a little uneasy. "I know, but so can many people. If I only focus on the what ifs, then I'll miss out on all the great things about life." She said in a calm and sweet tone, offering him a reassuring smile. "Besides, I love Elio and I choose to believe he loves me too, so I'm sure it'll work out."

Luciano's expression was unreadable, which made her feel more uncomfortable than when he was overly chipper. The silence only made it worst, forcing Faye to sit there, twiddling her thumbs together while her eyes fell on everything but her companion. As her gaze shifted from place to place, it suddenly landed on the clock in front of her, causing a look of panic to set in.

"Is that seriously the time?" She asked, her voice filled with concern. "Oh, geez, I'm going to be late." His eyes darted over to her, attempting to figure out how sincere she was acting with her sudden worry. "Late for what?" He asked, to humor her. "Feeding my cats. They have to be fed at exactly seven, otherwise they call APS." Her explanation both amused and confused him at the same time. "What is APS?" He asked, tilting his head. "Animal Protective Services."

It took a moment, but once the punchline really sunk in, Luciano burst out into laughter. "Oh God, that's lame! I love it." He said in between chuckles, trying his hardest to focus on the road. "Come on, that wasn't even my best joke." Faye giggled, feeling a little less tense. "Really? You got to tell me more. I love a good joke." He was enjoying her company. "You know, so does my mother. That's why she had me and my brothers."

The two of them continued on with light jokes and small talk, avoiding the topic of Elio at all cost. Neither minded at all, knowing how big and terrifying the elephant was when addressed. Faye felt more than grateful that Luciano wasn't trying to push her either, especially since his counterpart seemed more than willing to do a full-blown interrogation against her will. She couldn't help but wonder what Cosimo's deal was. It seemed like he hated her, though she couldn't think of a reason.

Looking up at the cheery detective, she shrugged her worries away, figuring it wasn't anything personal. 'Maybe he's just like that.' She thought to herself as she relaxed in her seat. Long lashes slowly fluttered shut, sheltering blue jewels. "Let me know when we get there." She muttered, allowing herself to fall into a light sleep.

Faye woke up to the feeling of something softly nudging her. "Hey, hey. We're here." Luciano said a little too cheerfully, causing her eyes to snap open. 'I really got to stop falling asleep in strangers' cars.' She thought to herself with a quiet laugh. "Okay, okay, I'm up, jeez. Don't call the fire department." She joked, unbuckling her seatbelt. "As if I'd ever call those meatheads." He retorted sarcastically, causing her to laugh. "Wow, I didn't think the beef was real." She remarked. "It's not. We just like to have fun. Actually, it's a friendly rivalry built on mutual respect."

There was something sweet and sincere with listening to him talk about the fun side of his job. Luciano had a passion for police work and seemed to get along well with everyone, which didn't come as a surprise. If it wasn't for the circumstances of their first meeting, Faye could have seen them being really close friends.

"You know, it's a shame you and Elio don't get along." Her voice cut through his rambling, causing him to stop mid-sentence. "What do you mean?" He tilted his head in confusion. "We could have been pretty good friends, maybe even teamed up to fuck with Elio, but if he doesn't like you, I have a feeling I shouldn't either? Does that make sense?" As she explained, Luciano's smile slowly dropped. What she said was indeed true. There wasn't a chance in hell Elio would ever let them be friends, no matter how hard he wanted to be.

"You have a point, but I don't think you have to share the same feelings as Elio. I mean, just because you're dating him doesn't mean he gets to control every aspect of your life. He doesn't have to like who you hang out with, but he should respect your wishes." There was something manipulative about his little speech. "I hear what you're saying, but it is disrespectful to go behind my partner's back and befriend his enemies. All I can think is how I'd feel if he went behind my back and befriended Jose or Todd, or even Joey." She said all three names with such disgust it made Luciano wonder who the three might be.

He placed his large hand on top of her head, ruffling her soft, golden locks. "Okay, I get it. We can't be friends because you're crushing on my big bro, but that doesn't mean I don't consider you someone precious. I want you to be safe and take our comments to heart. Believe it or not, Elio runs the mafia and no amount of mental gymnastics is going to change that fact. Please be careful." She rolled her eyes and pushed his hand away. "I'll be fine. Even if what you said is true, it doesn't matter. He loves me and I love him, so there is no way in hell we'd hurt each other." She responded with a reassuring smile as she opened the door. "Thanks for the ride." Faye closed the door before Luciano could say anything.

As he drove off, she made her way towards her house, giving her driveway a quick glance to make sure her car was still there. "Oh thank God, I can still get to work tomorrow." Faye sighed in relief before making her way up the steps. Every bit of that experience was completely nerve wrecking and emotionally draining. All she wanted to do now was go straight to bed and pass out without having to process any of the information thrown at her.

A loud whine on the other side of the door brought her back to reality, forcing her to remember that her cats still needed to be fed. "Hold on one moment, Liggy." Faye cooed gently as she placed her key in the hole, unlocking the door. The moment it opened, the large fluffy cat ran towards her with his ears flattened as though he were prepared to give her a piece of his mind for being late.

"I'm so sorry, my sweet baby boy. I didn't mean to come home late. It's just some stupid cops interrogated me over my mob boss boyfriend…" Just as she explained herself, something in her mind finally clicked. "Wait, a minute…" She thought about everything the two detectives said to her versus her whole experience with Elio, and things made sense.

"Holy shit, I really am dating a mob boss." Her knees buckled under the weight, causing her to fall to the ground, her eyes wide in disbelief. "Meow?" The orange cat cried to remind his master he still hadn't been fed. "Sorry baby…" Faye muttered, patting his head before she returned to her feet. Obviously she'd have to address her boyfriend's career choice, but right now her cats needed her.

'Is everything okay, doll?' She nearly dropped the can of wet food she was holding the moment her phone went off. A look of panic flashed over her face as she realized she hadn't once contacted Elio. How would she even begin to explain where she went and what she learned? Would he be upset with her for learning his secret? Did he even have the right to be upset?

Shaking her head, she cleared her mind of all negative thoughts before dialing his number. "Hello? Are you okay?" Elio answered almost immediately, as though he was expecting the worst. "I'm fine… Just a very weird night." Faye began, not knowing how to explain everything that had happened to her. "Weird? Weird how?" He asked, still very much worried over her wellbeing. "Well… I met your brothers…"

There was a long pause as the air thickened around them. "I guess we have some serious talking to do, don't we?" His voice finally broke through the uncomfortable silence. "Yeah… I guess we do…" she agreed, wishing that instead of acknowledging the elephant, they could just throw a sheet over it instead. "I'm on my way."

Before Faye could respond, he had already hung up the phone, leaving her in a state of anxiousness and self-doubt. More than anything, she wanted to take it back and pretend she never found out, but there was something about Elio that made it damn near impossible to lie. It wasn't anything intimidating, but perhaps his charming and caring personality that made her want to confess her problems to him.

She wasn't worried so much about his profession, but his reaction to her finding out about it. Clearly, he wanted to keep it a secret and didn't feel confident in sharing this information with her. Because of these facts, she couldn't help but worry about him getting upset with her for finding out. Not once did it cross her mind that her boyfriend being upset with her could mean her death, instead she feared he'd abandon her.

'He could only want me because of my ignorance.' She thought to herself, her face turning pale. 'He'll surely get bored with me and leave me for someone better.' Tears welled up in her eyes at the very thought. "Of course, just when I started to fall in love with someone, they leave me…" She laughed bitterly to herself. "Meow?" Banshee cried out softly, rubbing up against her side. "At least you'll always love me." Faye said to her precious cat, gently stroking her soft, silky fur.

The drive was nerve racking as every scenario ran through Elio's head. He expected a lot of screaming and shouting from his lover, possibly a demand that he never contact her again. Surely he'd have to knock her unconscious, tie her up and throw her in the car. He thought about every drug he could get his hands on. He'd need something to sedate her and keep her compliant while still allowing her to maintain her wonderfully addicting personality.

"I need to fake her death and wipe her off the face of the planet. Make sure I'm the only person she ever has contact with." He muttered to himself, deciding on whether he should allow her to keep her pets. "If I try to get rid of them, that might cause her to act even more hostile towards me. At least if they stay by her side, it'll be easier to get her to love me again." Never once did he even think to consider that Faye might still be in love with him, even after finding out the truth.

As she sat on the floor cuddled up with her tailless cat, a loud knock on the door ruptured her train of thought. Her heart beat so fast it nearly popped out of her chest. Slowly, she opened the door, tears forming in her eyes as her large, deadly lover stood towering in front of her. "Elio!" She cried, wrapping her arms around the man, catching him by surprise. "I'm so sorry! I didn't mean to find out! The two detectives! They pulled me from work, didn't give me any choice but to go! I tried to say no, but he insisted… And…"

Faye kept rambling as Elio stood awestruck at the girl, wondering how on earth she thought this whole thing might be her fault. "Doll, it's okay." He finally spoke, silencing the anxious woman. "Let's go inside so we can talk about it." She nodded her head, leading him inside her house.

The moment the door shut closed, Elio had her pulled to the couch where he quickly sat her in his lap. "Now tell me everything from the beginning." He whispered in her ear, loving every bit of her flustered form. Taking a deep breath, Faye explained what had happened from the sudden missing kennel attendant to the two detectives claiming to be his brothers, leaving the part about him being a mob boss for last.

Elio quietly nodded along, offering reassuring squeezes every time she got a little too anxious. "You know, doll, I am the leader of the mafia." He finally spoke, causing her to stiffen. "I figured…" She sighed, figuring she'd have to rip this band-aid off, eventually. "Well?" He asked expectantly. "Well, what?" She responded in confusion. "How do you feel about the whole thing?" His grip on her tightened as he spoke, treating her like a well-loved teddy bear.

Faye thought for a moment, no longer worried that he'd leave her. "To be honest, I was terrified that you would leave me." She answered truthfully, once again catching him by surprise. "You were afraid of me leaving you? Really?" He sounded so unconvinced by her words, and yet her sincerity tugged at his heartstrings. "Yes, of course. I thought you'd get bored with me and leave because I couldn't act dumb anymore."

Cold, rough lips met hers, pulling her into a warm, loving exchange. "I love you so much, Faye Merci. I would never, ever leave you over something like that." He whispered against her, trying so hard to contain his laughter. He just couldn't believe he was the one having to reassure her he wanted to continue this relationship. "I thought you'd be the one trying to leave me."

Faye looked at him with wide eyes, bewildered by his statement. "Why would I leave you?" She asked in confusion. "Because I'm a dangerous criminal." He retorted, just as confused. "So you're sexy, sweet, and a total badass? That's just a bonus in my book." She stated matter-of-factly. Elio's confused expression quickly shifted into a devilish smirk with every word she spoke.

"Oh, really?" He purred against her lips like a cat preparing to play with his prey. Deep down he was still seething in rage at what his brothers had put his poor darling through, but he'd have to deal with those feelings later. For now, he had the cutest girl standing in front of him, admitting that his profession turned her on.

Her bright blue jewels lit up with every kiss he placed on her lips, happy that he wasn't mad in the slightest at her. "Elio…" she mumbled out, leaning into his embrace. "You make me so happy. I just can't help but love you." The smirk softened up completely, turning into a warm smile as he swayed around with her in his arms. "I love you too, my sweet doll. I could never find it in my heart to ever abandon you, especially when you are so accepting of me." His words caused her heart to flutter and her face to heat up.

As they stood there for a few minutes, enjoying each other's company, a silent yawn fell from Faye's lips. "Oh, my poor little doll. You must be exhausted after such an intense day." Elio cooed while he nuzzled her neck. Before she could respond, he already had her in his arms, ready to settle in for the night. He carried her towards the couch and laid down on it, keeping her balanced on his torso.

Slowly, her eyes closed as she took a deep breath, breathing in his wonderfully intoxicating aroma. While she had every reason in to world to want to get away from this monster, she couldn't help the love she held for him. It felt as though the world was fading around them, leaving the two to bask in each other's love.

"I can't believe how calm you are. Not even a little bothered by the revelation." Elio whispered, stroking her hair lightly. "I've dealt with worse..." she murmured with a deep yawn. "What could be worse than your boyfriend being an actual crime lord?" He couldn't help but ask. "I'll... I'll tell you later..." she promised, feeling her body beginning to shut down. "Good night, my love." He kissed her forehead as she went into a deep sleep, happy to be in her lover's arms once again.

Chapter: 20

Tight, muscular arms wrapped around her, constricting her like a python with his prey. His face was pressed against her neck, taking in her amazing scent. His body was the perfect temperature, not too hot and not too cold, just warm enough to keep her comfortable in her sleep. Everything was just right for the two of them. Not a single thing in the world could disturb their peace.

Ring! Ring! Ring! An obnoxious ringing sound brought them out of their bliss, causing Faye to grumble groggily to herself. "Seriously?" She mumbled, grabbing the offending device that was her cellphone. "It's already time for work?" Elio asked, rather annoyed that their time together had been interrupted. "No… Just time for me to wake up." She responded with a yawn, her eyes slowly closing once again.

Ring! Ring! Ring! Only ten minutes had passed before the accursed device went off again. The sudden urge to smash the phone to pieces bubbled up inside her, but she took a deep breath and let it go. "Again with that thing?" Elio grumbled, pulling the blonde girl tighter to his chest. "Sorry, I set quite a few alarms, so I don't wake up too late." She muttered with a yawn. "I see. I mean, it's only 6am, you still have a few hours until work starts."

As he spoke, a realization hit him, causing a wide, devilish grin to appear on his face. "Yeah. Yeah. I know, it's just that mph!" Just as she was about to explain herself, Elio already had his lips over hers, forcing her into a heated exchange. "W-what are you doing?" She squeaked out the moment he pulled away to allow her air. "Taking advantage of the time." He retorted slyly, pulling her back in for another kiss.

He forced his tongue into her mouth, attempting to engage her in a battle for dominance, though through her shock and grogginess, she had no chance of winning. She could feel his groin push up against her as he rocked back and forth, causing the whole couch to squeak. "Elio… Please…" She couldn't help but moan before having her lips attacked again. "Come on doll. How about a quick destresser before work?" His words held so much power over her, it almost felt futile trying to say no.

"Does it have to happen on the couch?" She asked, giving into his request. "Awe, of course not, my love." Elio reassured her as he slowly rose to his feet, picking up the smaller woman. "I'd have you lead me to your bedroom, but I just can't stand not having you in my arms." Why was the scary mob boss so damn cheesy?

Luckily for both of them, there weren't too many rooms to choose from and her bedroom was pretty easy to find. It was the largest room in the house that happened to be at the very end of the hallway. As he kicked open the door, he couldn't help but let out an amused chuckle. The best way to describe her bedroom was pure organized chaos. Everything was neatly placed, but nothing seemed to really match anything else.

Her bed was a small twin sized with large pink sheets covering it that were obviously too big for the mattress. The comforter was even bigger than the sheets and looked ancient, as if she had it for well over a decade. For some reason, she had six large pillows with mix-matched pillowcases covering them and a lot of stuffed animals.

When he looked at the walls, he noticed they were covered in posters and pictures to where the wall was almost completely hidden. A chair sat near the bed with a sewing kit placed on top, two half naked porcelain dolls rested near the kit, an obvious project for the young woman. The fabric box was next to the chair with some patterns already pulled out.

The more he looked, the more curious he became. She had a lot of antiques in her possession that he couldn't help but wonder where she had acquired them from. Old statues of different religious figures stood proudly displayed next to wind-up toys and snow-globes. When he really thought about it, her bedroom reminded him of a museum. 'I could probably take her to one and she'd feel right at home.' He thought to himself in amusement before carefully throwing her onto the bed.

Elio crawled on top of Faye, pinning her to the frame with his body. Big blue eyes stared up at him, anticipating his next move. Not being the type to make his lover wait, he quickly removed her shirt and slowly peppered kisses down her neck towards her chest. A soft cry fell from her lips as she arched her back, pushing her chest into his face.

"I love you so much, doll." Elio whispered against her skin. "I'll do anything for you. Buy you anything, take you anywhere. I'd sacrifice my life for you. I'd even kill for you." Where was all of this coming from? "Please quit this shitty job. Pack up your bags and live with me. I can't stand to see you so stressed out, and I can't stand knowing you're living in a shithole. I need you in my arms." He practically begged her.

She stayed completely silent, unable to respond. As much as she wanted to be with him, she just couldn't bring herself to say yes. Instead, she let out a soft moan, allowing the passion to overtake her. They could always talk about it later.

Though it was quick, it was still exhausting, and so he allowed his body to fall on top of hers, squishing her into the mattress. "So what do you say? Now that the cat's out of the bag, you want to run away with me?" He asked with a goofy grin. "I'd love to… In a month, like we agreed." She reminded him in a scolding tone. Elio rose from his spot, lifting the young woman with him. "Oh, come on doll." He begged as he pulled up his pants. "There's no reason to wait so long. I love you, you love me. You need money to survive. I got plenty of money to keep you going for generations. I even got a nice house with plenty of places for your cats to run around in, so what's the holdup?"

Faye couldn't help but let out an irritated sigh, already tired of this conversation. "It's not that simple, Elio. I mean, there are a lot of loose ends I need to tie up. I still need to pack up, and I don't want to quit on bad terms. Not only that, but there's a matter of mail and what to do with the place." She rambled on and on all the excuses in the book about why she couldn't move in right away. What it really came down to was that Faye just wasn't ready to move in with him, and yet that was the one reason she was terrified of telling him.

Elio, with his keen eyes, saw right through every excuse. "Look doll, if you're not ready, you're not ready. I ain't here to put pressure on you, but I need you to realize how important it is for you to be with me. I mean, anything could happen…" As he trailed off, another alarm rang, signaling that it was time to get dressed. "Can we talk more about this later? I really need to get ready for work." Faye pleaded with the man, hoping for him to drop the whole conversation. "Fine, but this isn't over." He huffed, crossing his arms.

With a lot of difficulty and very little help from her agitated lover, she fully made it off the bed so that she could start her day. Faye had a very noticeable limp as she made her way towards the shower, one that Elio couldn't help but smirk at. Normally, he'd be happy to help his beautiful girlfriend, but since she wanted to be so independent, he figured he'd let her suffer. Faye was not taking it too well, especially when every movement she made caused a lot of discomfort. It made her regret her activities with the extremely rough man.

"I don't think we should have sex right before work anymore." Faye called out from the bathroom, finally crawling her way into the shower. Elio's smirk quickly dropped into a frown at that news. "I still need to move around at work. You damn near almost crippled me." She continued to complain as the warm water hit her aching muscles. "Doll, you know what I'm going to say, so if I were you, I'd stop all the fussing." He practically reminded her she did this to herself. An irritated groan could be heard from the bathroom, causing him to cackle.

It took a little longer than normal, but Faye got fully dressed all by herself. This was a feat she was proud of, given what she had to deal with. Elio, who took up residency on her couch, watched her silently as she limped around the house, collecting all the materials she needed for work. It wasn't until she went for her car keys that he finally moved, swiftly grabbing the keys before she could get to them.

"Elio, give me my keys!" Faye demanded, attempting to jump for them. "No, you ain't driving today." He stated calmly, holding the metal bundle just out of reach. "Please! I need to get to work. I know you don't agree with it, but it's important to me!" She was practically begging with tears in her eyes. "Doll, will you knock it off? I ain't gonna let you be late!" He finally shouted, causing her to stop what she was doing.

"Listen. The cops were the ones who brought your car back, right?" He asked as though he were addressing a child. "Well, yeah, someone had to." She answered, unsure of where he was going with this. "So, obviously, the cops had your car bugged, hoping that they would get lucky enough to catch you talking about me. Now doll, I love you more than anything, but I ain't risking my freedom for some old beat up piece of junk. I'm having my men take it to be scrapped."

Faye's eyes widened at his statement as panic set in. "But Elio, how will I get around? I mean, I need it to get to work, get home, go grocery shopping, and visit my parents. What? Do I have to take the bus again? Because that isn't fair! I worked so hard to get that damn thing." She kept going on, extremely upset at the very thought of having her car taken away.

Elio could feel his anger beginning to rise the more she spoke. He did what he could to quell it, knowing she had every right to be upset. "Look, I get that you're frustrated but…" "No, it's fine." Faye said, taking a deep breath in. "I get it… I just really have to leave right now. I don't want to miss the bus." Just as she reached for the doorknob, Elio once again stopped her, grabbing her by her wrist.

"You're not taking the fucking bus, you idiot. You're the girlfriend of the most powerful mob boss in the city. Do you think public transportation is safe right now? No, it isn't. Not when you have the biggest target on your back." He did everything in his power not to yell at her and yet she stood there looking absolutely dejected. "Look doll... I have your best interests in mind, it's just... Let's discuss this on the way to work. I'll drive you too and from today and then we'll figure out the rest." He promised, softening his voice.

Faye could only nod, knowing that if she attempted to say anything at all, the tears might flow out. She let him lead her out to his car, a beautiful red Cadillac with black and red interior. It looked brand new, as though it were driven straight off the lot. Elio brought her over to the passenger side, opening up the door for her.

"Thanks..." she mumbled, still trying to keep her emotions in order. "Don't mention it, doll." He retorted, trying his hardest to sound chipper after the argument they had just had. He knew it was only going to get worse, especially with how dedicated she was to continuing this arrangement.

"You know, I'm only pushing this hard because I love you, right?" He asked, starting the car, barely receiving a glance from the stubborn woman. "Believe it or not, I don't have the most glamorous lifestyle. It's full of difficult choices and dangerous men that would stop at nothing just to see me suffer. I ain't asking you to move in right away because I want to use you and dump you. I'm asking because I want to protect you from those dangerous men. You're so precious and fragile..."

"I'm not as fragile as you think!" Faye suddenly interrupted him. "I mean, you make these statements about me without really knowing me! It's so frustrating! That's all I want is for us to actually get to know each other. Is that so hard to ask for?" She vented her own problems with his desire. "We can get to know each other by living together! It's far less dangerous that way!" He snapped back. "I don't care about danger! I just want a normal pace for a relationship." She retorted. "You gave up the right to a normal relationship when you agreed to be my girlfriend! I mean, you should have known what you were signing up for!" "But I didn't, did I? Because you hid a very important part of yourself from me."

The moment those words left her lips, regret flooded in, nearly drowning her. Elio gave her a dark look she had never seen before from him. "So you are upset about me being a mob boss, after all. And here I thought you loved me no matter what." His tone held a slight edge to it, urging Faye to back down. "No, that is not what I meant and you know it! I love you regardless of career choices. It's just... You're just so frustrating to talk to sometimes!" She snapped, refusing to back down. "I'm frustrating? You're the one who would much rather live in a shitty run-down shack and work a dead-end job than live with me!"

Hurt washed over her face as tears welled up in her eyes. How dare he judge her life so carelessly without knowing the full story? "I'm a-actually proud of my lifestyle." She stated, trying her hardest not to cry. "Proud? You're actually proud of all that? Really? Are you insane? That is nothing to be proud o..." A soft sob caused him to stop mid rant as he finally looked at the teary-eyed woman sitting next to him.

"Faye? Are you okay?" He asked softly only to be met with a small nod. He let out a sigh, realizing he might have gone a little too far. "I'm sorry. I shouldn't be judging you so harshly. It's just that I care about you. A lot. And I want what's best for you. I think you deserve a nice house and the best car and to not come home stressed out every night because of some shitty job."

As he spoke, the car slowly crept to a stop in front of the small animal hospital. "I also want you to be safe, and I can't guarantee that unless you're constantly by my side." Her emotions were still so high that his words practically bounced off her. "I love you so much, doll." "I love you too…" she murmured quietly, barely above a whisper. "We'll discuss this later. Have a good day at work." He said, pulling her into a soft kiss, which she hesitantly returned.

As she got out of the car, she gave him a heartbroken smile. "I'm sorry for being a burden." She apologized softly before shutting the door and fleeing towards the hospital. Elio could only watch with his fist clenched around the steering wheel. "You ain't a burden…" He mumbled angrily before peeling out of the parking lot aggressively.

Chapter: 21

The moment she entered the building, she quickly made her way to the bathroom, refusing to let anyone see her while she was emotion. She felt so stupid and pathetic for letting herself get so worked up over a small fight. It was just so frustrating that he wasn't able to see her point of view at all. While it wasn't perfect or even slightly ideal, she loved her life, especially with all the struggles she had to go through to get to this point. If he only knew the sacrifices she made, the trauma she went through, the…

'No. I can't go there.' She thought to herself. 'I can't tell him. It's unfair to burden him like that.' Shaking her head of all negative thoughts, she did her best to pull herself together. "I can't let anyone see me like this," she mumbled to herself. "Stupid Elio, making me feel stupid emotions right before work." The sorrow she felt moments ago warped into anger and annoyance towards her dear boyfriend who just earned his rightful place onto her shit list.

"I swear to God if his first words to me are not I'm sorry, then I'll just walk my happy ass home." The thought of being passive aggressive and petty towards him crossed her mind, but she decided not to go that far. The last thing she needed was for a small petty fight to turn into something larger. "Why the hell can't you just wait a month? It isn't that long, and then I'll be all yours."

Pulling herself together, she finally left the bathroom. Marching through the hospital, not bothering to give any pleasantries to the coworkers she passed by. Her mind was too preoccupied to notice or even care about the surrounding people. Not even the mess that was the pharmacy could pull her away from her thoughts.

Taking a seat at her desk, she couldn't help but smack her face into the hard surface, letting out a groan of irritation. "Why is this so hard?" She quietly complained to herself. "If I would have known he'd be this much of a pain in the ass, I wouldn't have agreed to go out with him." She didn't actually mean that, but through her frustration, she couldn't help but vent out loud to herself. "I can't believe I fell in love with such a stubborn and impatient man."

After their little dispute, Elio still felt completely high strung. The moment he saw those tears and that heartbroken smile, he knew he went way too far. He was trying to convince her to live with him, not push her away, so why did he feel the need to insult her? "If she didn't hate me before, she'll hate me now for sure." He said bitterly to himself. "Why does she got to be so damn difficult!? All I want is what's best for her and what's best is that she live with me. Is that so damn hard? She'd be loved and taken care of. Not once would she ever have to lift a finger to do anything. People would kill to have a life like that."

The more he thought about it, the angrier he got. He loved this woman with every bone in his body and he knew she loved him, so why the stubbornness? Why the fighting, why the tears, why the insistence? It made no sense to him at all. She was hiding something from him. He knew it, but no matter how hard he tried, he couldn't get it out of her. "Please doll, just be honest with me. Tell me what's really bothering you and I'll do everything in my power to make it go away." He pleaded.

He drove around the city for a little while longer before finally coming to a stop at an old, rundown dive bar. The parking lot was mostly empty save for one old beat up green mustang which he parked right next to, in-between the vehicle and a large brick wall. "If anyone's gonna fuck with my car, they have to fuck with Maurice's first." He said out loud to himself.

Elio found a little humor in his decision to go to this bar, especially after he insulted Faye's house straight to her face. If her house looked like an old shack, this place looked like a rundown outhouse. It kind of smelt like one too, but he didn't mind too much. He wasn't here for the ambiance, just a hard drink and friendly ear to vent to.

As he entered through the doors, all he could hear was loud, obnoxious country music. The only other patron there was some old drunken homeless man curled up in a corner booth, nuzzling a beer. He couldn't help but roll his eyes at the pathetic display, though it was a little hypocritical. He himself was inside a bar earlier in the morning ordering a drink.

"Ain't it a little too early to be day drinking?" The bartender, a six foot tall dark-skinned man, suddenly spoke up, pulling him out of his thoughts. Elio looked up at the man, taking in his strange appearance. The man in question had green and yellow tattoos riding up his arms and neck and a bright red mohawk on top of his head. His bright amber eyes were covered up by yellow rimmed sunglasses. The outfit he wore, a typical bartender get up with the black pants, white button up and black vest, was a little too tight on his large, muscular figure.

"Shove it Maurice." Elio bit back before ordering a whiskey and coke. "Oh come on now, no need for all that sass," Maurice shot back, quickly preparing his order. "So Elio, what brings you down to my ol' humble abode? It can't just be for the great drink and amazing music, can it?" He gave him a cheeky look, causing the mobster to scoff in irritation. "No, of course not. I can get a decent drink and shitty music anywhere. I just needed someone to talk to." Elio retorted, letting out an irritated sigh.

Maurice tilted his head with a soft smile. "Well, friend, I ain't much of a therapist, but I can lend an ear or two. What's got you down?" He asked, leaning against the countertop. "Got some problems going on with this woman I've been seeing." Elio started going into the whole story as Maurice listened.

"I mean, she acts all tough and mighty, but she doesn't understand what kind of danger there is out there. I'm trying to protect her and all she seems to care about is keeping her independence. What good is independence if you're dead?" He continued on his rant while the bartender listened.

"Damn, it sounds like you got yourself a trouble maker. Why the hell are you putting up with her shit? Just leave her at a whorehouse." Maurice commented with a smirk. "She ain't some streetwalker!" Elio snapped. "She ain't? But I thought you said you got her from

May?" He asked, confused by his friend's story. "I did. It doesn't mean she's a whore. She's just a friend of the crazy ass bitch." Elio explained.

"Actually, my Faye has nothing to do with that type of business. She's got a job in medicine, apparently trying to go back to school to be a doctor of some kind." When he talked about Faye, his eyes lit up and his face softened. "She's so sweet too. Actually cares about her work and worries about the patients." Maurice wanted to laugh at how bipolar the mobster was. One moment he's complaining about the girl being stubborn and a pain in his ass, the next he's practically drooling over the thought of her.

"So, is she a pain in the ass or not? Which is it?" Maurice chuckled. "She's a pain in the ass that I love." Elio shrugged, taking a swig of his drink. "I just wish she'd see things from my prospective." He sighed. "Well, have you tried seeing from her prospective?" The bartender asked. "What do you mean?" He asked in confusion.

"I mean, she ain't like any of the women you deal with. She's honest and clean. You're up there tryin' to get her to run away with you when that ain't what she needs. She's not running away from anything, and she obviously doesn't need no money from you. All it sounds like she's been wanting is a good man to love and support her. I mean, you are asking too much of her to quit her job, move out of her home and cut off everyone she loves for some lowlife gangster she's known for barely a week. The fact that she's even humoring you at all is a God damn miracle. If I were her, I'd run for the hills."

Maurice was blunt with his words, not holding back at how ridiculous Elio sounded. Normally, a lecture like that would get a man shot, but Elio held great respect for the bartender and his wisdom. The words were really sinking in as he realized these were the exact words Faye had been trying to tell him this whole time.

"I've been a real jackass…" He mumbled, angry at himself for not seeing it sooner. "No shit." Maurice snickered, earning a sharp glare from the mobster. "Do you think Faye's going to want to leave me because of this?" He asked, completely defeated. "I don't know, sounds like a question for the little lady, though she didn't seem to mind too much about you be a mob boss, so I have my doubts a tiny little fight is gonna change her mind much." He answered honestly.

Elio thought about it for a moment before pulling out his phone and dialing his lover's number. It rang a few times before going to voicemail. He was about to go into panic mode until a text popped up on his phone. *'I'm a little busy right now. I'll call you back in a few minutes.'* He felt like he was holding his breath, counting down the seconds until finally his phone lit up.

"Hello?" Faye greeted, confused by the random phone call. "Hey doll, I wanted to talk to you about something. You got a minute?" He asked in a soft tone, as if he were trying his hardest not to scare her. "I guess, though, if it's about our argument this morning, I don't want to hear it." She wasn't about to have another screaming match while at work and was more than prepared to hang up on her jerk of a lover.

"I promise I'm not trying to rehash anything. I just wanted to apologize for yelling and insulting you. That wasn't right of me, especially when I know you have a long day ahead of you. There's just a lot going on right now, but that doesn't give me the right to take it out on you." He admitted, hoping to get back in her good graces.

Faye could feel her heart flutter at his little confession, a mix of emotions welled up inside her. On one hand, it was a very petty fight that meant little. But he was way out of line saying what he said and she had every right to be angry at him.

"You know I'm pretty damn scared." He suddenly said, pulling her out of her thoughts. "Scared? Of what?" She wondered. "I'm scared you'll leave me over this. Especially after I was a real jerk to you." Faye couldn't help but groan, irritated by his irrational thoughts. "Of course I'm not planning to leave you, you dumbass. I still love you, even though you are a jerk. It was a petty fight, and it's done. Congratulations to us both. We managed to get through our first fight with each other." She remarked, annoyed he'd even think that to begin with. "I told you once I told you a thousand times, you ain't getting rid of me that easily. Just stop being such an ass."

Elio went silent for a moment before a large grin appeared on his face. "So you really love me?" He couldn't help but ask. "Yes, of course, and I don't say those words lightly, so quit acting stupid." Relief washed over him like rain after a drought. She loved him, even though he hurt her. She still loved him. Of course, that meant he had to tread carefully from here on out and do everything in his power not to hurt her again.

"Is that all you wanted to talk about?" Faye asked impatiently. "Yes," He confirmed. "Good, because I still have a large order to put away and evidently someone left me with a nasty limp this morning." She stated, still unhappy that he had his fun with her that morning and then left her to deal with the consequences all because he was feeling petty. "Sorry about that doll, but you know if it was really that bad, you could have called into work." He pointed out. "And let these idiots put away my order? No way in hell. Last time I did that, I found ursodiol with the pimobendan."

Maurice listened in on their conversation, amused by the whole thing. Never in his life did he ever expect the terrifyingly deadly mob boss to let some young woman chew his ass out like that. It took everything in his power not to burst out laughing, especially when she started ranting about how big of an ass Elio was.

"But I do seriously have to go now. I love you, you jackass." With those final words, Faye hung up the phone, leaving Elio alone in thought with Maurice. "God damn, you caught yourself a feisty one!" Maurice broke down into laughter. "One of these days you ought to bring her down here. I'll give her a drink on the house." Elio rolled his eyes. "Why would you do that?" He asked out of curiosity. "Well hell, I figured if she has to put up with your sorry ass, she more than anyone deserves a damn drink."

Heading back to her desk, she grew irritated all over again with her idiotic lover. He kept flipping back and forth between moods so often it practically gave her whiplash. Of course she loved him and of course she wasn't planning to leave him, it was just obnoxious how persistent he could be. 'Imagine if I rejected his advances at the beginning.' She thought to herself as she got back to work.

"Oh, thank God." Faye mumbled to herself as 1PM finally hit, signaling it was finally time for lunch. It could not come any sooner, especially when this day was starting to really kick her ass. First she starts off her day arguing with her boyfriend, next she gets chewed out, yet again, by her boss for being late. She also had a rather large order come in that day which took forever to put away, seeing as there were back-to-back emergencies, each calling for different medications, a few of which had to be compounded. To say she was exhausted was an understatement.

"I don't even have my car to go hide in… Thanks, Elio." She said bitterly, still very much upset with him. With that hiding spot gone, she needed to find a different spot, fast. The receptionists had no problem at all disrupting her breaks, so the best way to combat that was to disappear. "Where to?" She muttered to herself. "The breakroom is too obvious and the cat room has already been compromised. Hmm…"

With no other options, Faye hid out in one of the kennels, sharing the large cage with a big and friendly saint Bernard puppy. She took a risk rooming with something so adorable, but maybe it'll be far too busy for anyone to actually check.

With her little lunch companion seated on her lap, Faye took out her phone, preparing to dial Elio's number. "Wait, no, I can't call him. I'm still mad at him." She reminded herself, even though it was so tempting. Instead, she dialed Atlas's phone number, figuring she needed a friend to talk to.

"Hello?" Atlas's deep voice came through on the phone. "Hey Atlas, how's it going?" Faye greeted awkwardly. "It's going pretty good, even better knowing you're not in jail. What happened with that whole thing, anyway?" He asked curiously. "Well… To start, I may or may not be dating the deadliest criminal in the city." She responded hesitantly. "Yeah, I could've told you that." He retorted with a snort. "And why didn't you?" She said pointedly. "Because your boyfriend threated to end my life if I spilled the beans."

Faye let out an annoyed sigh at his response. "Of course Elio did that. He's really trying to piss me off today, isn't he?" she mumbled bitterly. "What do you mean by that?" Atlas had to ask, ready for some juicy gossip. "Well, it started with the whole interrogation thing. It really freaked him out, especially when I found out that not only was he, well, you know, but the detectives who interrogated me were his brothers." She sighed, glad to finally have someone to vent to. "Really? Holy crap, that's unreal!" He exclaimed in astonishment.

"Well, it gets worse. The brothers want me to work with them to get Elio arrested. Apparently, they have some weird scheme going where they're going to save him or something stupid like that. I still don't get it. That whole thing really got to Elio and turned him into quite the asshole." She continued on. "Oh? How so?" Atlas asked, prompting Faye to go on. She explained everything that had happened from the night to the morning and even the terrible fight they had got in.

"You've barely known each other for a week. Moving in right now is the worst thing you might do." Atlas ended up agreeing to her point of view. "Honestly, moving in after a month is pretty damn stupid, too, especially if you do not know where you're moving to. What the hell were you even thinking, Faye?" He scolded her for her poor decisions. "I don't know. He was being pushy but also kind of romantic, so I just kind of gave in. You know I have a hard time saying no to people." She attempted to explain herself. "Besides, Elio isn't all that bad. I mean, he's really sweet to me and always fretting over me like I'm fragile or something. Which is kind of annoying but also endearing in a way."

"Faye, you are fragile. I know you hate to think that of yourself, but it's true. Especially when it comes to you living in his world. It's nothing like what you've experienced before." "Not true." Faye interrupted him. "There was that one thing…" she trailed off. "Yeah, and it totally fucked you up. Now, I'm not saying you should move in with Elio right away. In fact, I still think it's a stupid idea, but maybe you two should talk about a compromise. Maybe discuss having a trusted friend or relative live with you until it's time to move."

"I hate to say it, but you might be right." She groaned. "Of course I am," He retorted smugly. "I've been so focused on my ego and prospective I never once thought to consider his. Surely we can work something out." She said thoughtfully. "Or you could just cut your losses and break up with him." Atlas joked. "Interesting suggestion. I can't wait to tell Elio what you proposed." She teased back with a devilish smirk. "No, no. There is no reason to bring me up by name to that brute… I mean, wonderful man. Oh, would you look at the time? I really must get back to work." And with that, Atlas ended the phone call, leaving Faye alone with her thoughts.

"Compromise, huh?" She muttered to herself while stroking the puppy's head. She wondered if Elio would be okay with something like that. "Well, there's only one way to find out." She said, no longer feeling any type of resentment towards her oversized lover. Her finger hovered over his name before pressing the button, dialing his number. It barely rung twice before Elio answered the phone.

"Well hello doll, I was worried you'd never call." He answered, his smile showing with each word. "Hey Elio, sorry it took so long. I had to find a good spot to hide in." She explained with a half-truth. "Oh, and where did you end up?" He asked curiously. "In Buster's cage." She shrugged, petting the puppy in question. "Who's Buster? Someone I should be jealous of?" He joked. "He's a big Saint Bernard puppy who's probably the sweetest thing ever, so yes, you probably should be jealous of him."

Elio couldn't help but laugh, feeling relieved that Faye was joking around with him again. "I take it you're no longer mad at me for being a jackass?" He asked hopefully. "Yes, and no… I think I understand your point. It's just, I need you to understand I'm not ready to move in yet." She explained, trying to remain as calm as possible. "I get it, doll, but my worries still stand." He said sternly. "I know, and I know it's going to be extremely dangerous for me, but I think we can come to a small compromise."

He seemed to really perk up at that word, curious about what exactly she had in mind. "What kind of compromise do you want to make?" He asked, hoping it would really benefit them both in the long run. "Since it's my safety, that's an issue. Why don't I call up one of my friends or family members to move in with me temporally that way they can help when things get to be too dangerous. And if it gets to that point where my life is actually in danger, I'll move in ASAP. How about that?"

Silence fell on the two of them as Elio really thought about what she was proposing. On one hand, a bodyguard would be exactly what she needed if she insisted on doing this for a month. Plus, the moment things get out of hand, he can then insist she live with him and she wouldn't be allowed to say no. This seemed like a great deal to be made, but there was the one problem he had with the whole thing.

"I don't think having your friends or family play bodyguard is a good idea. If we agree to an arrangement like this, I want someone actually trained to protect you, not some rando who owes you a favor. They have no intention of paying back… No offense." He explained, trying his hardest to be nice, especially when he did actually like the idea. "Oh? Do you have someone in mind, then?" Faye asked inquisitively, at least somewhat relieved he didn't shut the whole idea down.

Elio gave it some more thought, thinking about who he could entrust with his precious Faye. "I think I do, in fact, have someone in mind, but we can discuss it later when you get off. Okay?" He responded with a soft smile. "Okay! Sounds great! I can't wait to meet the person who's going to make sure I stay alive." She said cheerfully as she continued to cuddle the large puppy on her lap.

The two of them continued to chat, both being happy that the tension from that morning was completely gone. "I'm so glad I'm no longer mad at you," Faye sighed blissfully as she leaned her head against the metal bars. "Yeah? I'm glad you ain't mad at me, either. I can't stand the thought of you not talking to me again." He responded, equally relieved. If there was one thing he learned about Faye, it was that she was as stubborn as they come. If she truly didn't want to do something there wasn't a force alive that could make her. It was just one thing he'd have to keep in mind if he was going to continue on with his pursuit of her.

They finally ended their phone call, both extremely hesitant to hang up. Unfortunately, Faye needed to get back to work, and Elio had quite a few errands to run, so both parties had no other choice but to end their discussion. "Well, I got to go. See you in a few hours?" She said hopefully. "Of course, doll, not a damn force on this planet could stop me from getting to you. I'll talk to you later. Love you." "Love you too."

The moment she hung up, she felt her heart skip a beat as her face flushed bright red. She couldn't help but smile and squeeze the poor puppy trapped with her lovesick self. "He's just the best, isn't he?" she said aloud to herself. "So sweet, so compassionate, so loving. Ugh, he's just amazing!" As she left the kennel, she started to skip and hum a light, cheerful tune. For the first time that day, she felt positively gleeful. It felt as though a suffocatingly heavy weight had been lifted and she could finally breathe again. With a smile on her face, she made it back to her workstation, fully prepared to take on the rest of the day.

Chapter: 22

Finally, after a grueling final four hours, it was time to leave. Faye shot Elio a quick text message, letting him know she was all done for the day. *'Okay doll, I'll be there soon,'* He replied, probably in the middle of wrapping up a job. With that said, she skipped to her locker and began packing up her belongings. She had to admit it was quite nice seeing Elio right after having a long day of work and knowing she could rest in the car on the way home. "I could get used to this life." She chuckled to herself, quickly walking down the long hallway towards the back door.

"I wouldn't go out there if I were you." A kennel attendant warned with a stoic expression. "Why? What's out there?" She asked worriedly. "Mr. Smith. He's been out there for at least thirty minutes." She let out an annoyed groan, knowing exactly what that meant. "Why?" She asked, though she knew the answer. "His dog is scheduled for a bath today, and you know how he gets. No matter how busy it is, he expects us to drop everything right away and do it ASAP. Fucking annoying old bastard if you ask me."

She knew exactly what her coworker meant, as she had her fair share of encounters with this client. He was old, aggressive, and entitled, one that made his problems everyone else's. She knew the moment she stepped out that door he'd practically jump her like a starved wolf to a defenseless rabbit, more than likely wasting thirty minutes of her time complaining about how slow the employees here are and why his dog should get preferential treatment above all animals. Walking away from the old bastard didn't help either, as he would follow uncomfortably close and pollute the air with his demands.

She paced up and down the hall, thinking up ideas on how to avoid the man completely. Just then, her phone rang, Elio's name lighting up the screen. "Oh, jeez… How the hell am I supposed to make it to Elio's car without getting lectured… Wait a minute, I have an idea!" She suddenly said in excitement at how genius she was.

"Hey doll, I'm here." Elio said cheerfully, probably excited to see his lover again. "Oh thank God, I am so happy to hear your voice." She said, sounding really relieved. "Did something happen?" He asked with concern. "Uh, not really. It's just a difficult client. Do you mind meeting me at the back door?" She requested. "Of course. Is it the old guy standing there? Is he bothering you? I don't mind taking him out if he's going to be problematic towards you."

Faye couldn't help but laugh at how over protective Elio could be with her. "No, no. He's not a threat level problem, just really fucking annoying. I just need you to stand there and shield me from his line of sight. Hopefully, if he can't see me, he'll leave me be and bug one of the other employees." She explained, trying to convince her boyfriend not to call a hit out on some miserable old man.

"If you say so, but just know if any of these assholes give you problems, I won't hesitate to snuff them out." She could feel his sadistic smile through the phone and knew he'd stay true to his word. "I'll let you know if that's needed, but I think I'm good for now. Maybe next time." She giggled, ready to escape this societal prison.

Just like he said he would, Elio went to go stand at the back door, acting as a bodyguard for his beloved Faye. He knocked three times, signaling his arrival so that she could sneak out behind him. Quickly, she did just that, pulling herself into his large coat to cover up her identity. He let out a soft chuckle at how dramatically she was acting towards the whole thing. "You know, doll, you could have just told me from the beginning you wanted to be close to me." He teased as he kissed her on top of her head. "I want to be close to you." She retorted, humoring him. "Now go, go before he recognizes me." She whispered, ushering him towards the parking lot.

The old man did indeed notice and recognize her, but one sharp glare from the mobster made him think twice about approaching. Instead, he found some other unlucky employee to complain to. He more than likely threw in some subtle hints about shady characters hanging around the hospital doors. The man had no clue how lucky he was that Faye was so forgiving, otherwise he might have traveled with them.

The moment Faye's body hit the soft, cushioned passenger seat, a wave of exhaustion washed over her. "Long day?" He asked, starting up the car. "Yeah…" She yawned, using all her might to keep her eyes opened. "You know, doll," Elio started, placing his hand on top of her leg and giving it a gentle squeeze. "You can take a nap. I won't mind." He offered her a gentle smile, which she returned with yet another yawn.

"Okay…" she mumbled, allowing her eyes to slowly fall shut. She put her hand over his, trapping it on top of her thigh, forcing him to drive with one hand. "You really are something else," He whispered as he focused on the road. "You want everything the way you want it and ain't willing to compromise. So stubborn, yet so beautiful and kind." He had a soft serene smile as he spoke, stopping his speech every so often to hear her mumble about what was happening in her dream. "I love you so much doll, I can't wait to have you."

He continued his drive, hyper-focused on his surroundings as he did everything in his power to get them both home safely. Just as he approached a turnoff, he noticed a large black van following closely behind him. "Damn it." He mumbled, trying to keep his voice down so as not to wake up the slumbering woman. "When the hell did the Black Spades start following me?"

Picking up speed, Elio changed directions, not willing to chance the rival gang finding out where Faye lived. "This isn't good." He said, his eyes glued to the windshield. They were gaining on him fast, more than likely attempt to rear end him. They were now going at least ten miles over the speed limit, flying by different cars on the busy roads, nearly wreaking at least a handful of times.

Elio was in a complete panic as the realization set in that they were trying to corner him. Quickly, he pulled out his phone, dialing one of his top men. "Henry, I need you to get a group out on Old Elm immediately!" He all but shouted into the phone, nearly waking up his sleeping beauty. "Right away, boss!" The man responded, no questions asked. As he hung up, he couldn't help but glance over at Faye with an apologetic gaze in his eyes.

"Sorry doll, I won't be able to get you home just yet," He said so softly, still trying his hardest not to wake her up. She mumbled something in reply, most likely attempting to reassure him everything was okay. "You know, this might actually be a good lesson for you about why it's so important to stay by my side." As much as he wanted to see the positive side of this inconvenience, he knew better than to take his focus off of the road.

In an attempt to lose the van, he started making sharp turns wherever he saw fit. One turn nearly flipped the car entirely. "Huh? What's going on?" Faye asked, rubbing her eyes as she attempted to wake up. "We're being followed." Elio retorted, trying his best to remain calm. "Wait what?" She was suddenly fully awake and alert, turning her head behind her to look at the van that was so obviously following them. "Shit, that's not good." She mumbled, though she didn't sound too worried.

"Okay, I've been in this situation before. When you come up to this light, cut in front of that blue car and take an immediate left turn. Don't miss the light." She said, her voice calm and relaxed, as though she were giving simple directions. Elio gave her a side eye wanting to say something, but he decided to instead trust her words and make the turn. Sure enough, the black van couldn't turn in time and ended on the freeway with no way off.

"Wait, that actually worked?" Elio said in surprise. "Of course it worked. These roads are so fucked up and the lights are so short it's pretty easy to lose anyone on them, especially if they don't know where they're going." She shrugged as if it were common knowledge. "I mean me and my family do it to each other all the time. It's actually the best way to start a fight." She giggled, earning a strange look from her lover. "Your family is weird." He said pointedly. "Oh, and you're one to talk?" She shot back. "Fair enough."

"Where are we going?" Faye asked after twenty minutes of driving, now noticing they weren't anywhere near her house. "We're heading to one of my clubs." Elio answered, as though it were obvious. Without words, Faye tilted her head, prompting him to continue on and explain himself. "Just because we lost them doesn't mean there aren't more of them circling the area." He explained. "I'll have my men scope out the area and snuff out any suspicious characters they see. In the meantime, I want to make sure you're kept somewhere safe. If the Black Spades discover where you live, there's no doubt you'll have them knocking on your door."

Faye let out a little huff, obviously not happy about the arrangements. "Oh, don't give me that look," Elio scolded her. "It's either I take you to my club or you get kidnapped and possibly trafficked. Your choice." She rolled her eyes at his dramatics. "Don't threaten me with a good time." She teased, resting her head on his shoulder. "But I suppose since it's not you kidnapping me and using me, I have no choice but to choose the club." She sighed as if it were the hardest decision of her life. "Quit being a little brat." He chided her. "Never."

"Now that I think about it, I really need to make a phone call." She said absentmindedly, pulling out her phone to dial a number. "Okay, this is the second night in a row. Can you stay out of trouble for five goddamn minutes!?" the voice of her best friend shouted on the other end. Click. She ended that phone call rather quickly. 'Welp, that bridge is currently on fire.' She thought to herself. "Okay, let's try this again." She muttered, much to her boyfriend's amusement.

"Hey Faye. What's up?" A pleasantly cheerful voice sang through the phone. "Hey Luca." She greeted, hearing her dearest best friend in the background raging. "Did you just call Atlas and hang up on him?" Luca asked, stifling a giggle. "Maybe... But in my defense, he was being a dick." She explained. "You are such a fucking…" Atlas's voice echoed through the phone. "Fair enough… So whatcha calling for?"

Elio listened in on the conversation, also curious to see what his beloved needed from this strange man. "Well, my dearest friend, I have a favor to ask of you, if you'd be so kind." She stated with a fake posh accent. "Why, of course, my dear, anything for you." He replied with the same fake accent, causing them both to burst out into laughter.

"Do you know how I have the two cutest cats in the world?" She started earning an eye roll from her boyfriend. "Yes, indeed, you do." Luca retorted with a smile. "Well, I need you to go to my house and feed them. Please?" She dropped the accent and got a little more serious at the end. "Wait, are you seriously asking what I think you're asking? You want me to go to your house… And steal your cats." He said the last part so quickly she almost didn't catch it.

"No… I need you to feed them, not steal them." She groaned, already annoyed. "Feed them and then steal them. Got it." He laughed. "I swear to God if you take my cats out of my house, I'll shove my foot so far up your ass you'll be tasting rubber for weeks." She threatened, nearly earning a chuckle from Elio. "Okay, okay I got it, only feeding, no stealing… Maybe…" Before she could retort, he already hung up the phone, probably planning how he'd take her cats before she got home.

"Interesting friends you got," Elio said in amusement. "Yeah, they are… My cats aren't going to be there when I get home, are they?" She sighed in annoyance. "Doesn't sound like it." He responded, giving her thigh a gentle squeeze. "Don't worry, we'll go pick them up after we're all done here, okay?" She nodded in agreement while trying to stifle a yawn.

It took a while, but they finally made it to their destination. A large, brightly lit building stood before them with the words 'Till Dusk to Dawn' lit up on top in huge neon letters. The parking lot was mostly full, with only a few spots left in the reserved area. Elio pulled up to the valet and stepped out, handing the employee his keys. He walked around to the other side, opening the door for Faye before offering his arm to her.

Faye looked around at the crowd surrounding the front door, wondering what on earth they were all doing partying on a Tuesday night. "Don't any of these people have jobs?" She asked, slightly weirded out by the club. "Yes, and no," Elio answered with a shrug. "Most of the people here are a bunch of rich brats living off of mommy and daddy's money. They either don't work at all or they work high ranking jobs at their parents' companies being given more power and freedom than they actually deserve."

A sour look appeared on Faye's face at the sight of all this disgusting greed standing right in front of her. "How despicable." She spat, already hating where he brought her. "It might be, but at least there are plenty of people, plenty of security, and plenty of hidden rooms, so it's safe." He retorted, completely unbothered. Elio could not care less how rich morons spent their money as long as it all went into his pocket.

As they got closer, the loud music plagued Faye's ears while the smell of cigarette smoke, vapes, and booze had assaulted her sense of smell. She felt sick to her stomach by it all and was completely worried she'd throw up. Elio didn't seem to have a care in the world.

He led her inside, cutting the line completely, much to the annoyance of the crowd. The few who recognized him tried to grab his attention, hoping to gain entrance quicker.

Those futile attempts were simply ignored. "Come along, doll, let's get you to a quieter place." Elio spoke just loud enough for her to hear him over the loud music.

Faye followed close by, hanging off of his arm out of fear of getting lost. The overstimulation in this building was insane. Fog and smoke blew everywhere while the music played on full blast. Drunken patrons chattered loudly, splashing their drinks around without a care in the world. She attempted to look around at her surroundings, but the lights constantly flashed blue and purple, making it difficult to see.

The main room had a large bar in the middle with tables decorating the outside. Most of the bartenders and servers were all women wearing flashy, revealing clothing. With a quick glance, Faye could actually see the walls of the establishment were lined with security guards, all wearing red suits. 'He wasn't kidding when he said there'd be plenty of security.' She thought to herself, still clinging to his arm for dear life.

Strangely enough, she felt eyes glaring at her as she moved through the room. It was consistent no matter where she went, as though there were a group of people who kept watching her, seething in anger at her existence. 'Oh great, what did I do this time?' She thought to herself, agitated by the sudden unwelcomed attention. Elio, knowing they were being watched, pulled her along quickly, maneuvering through the crowds with little issue.

He took her past a long hallway towards a door near the end. She noticed the further they got from the main lobby, the quieter the music got. 'Thank God.' She thought to herself, a little too excited that she could actually hear her own thoughts now. "Come on, doll, don't mess around too much here. There ain't any cameras and not a lot of security in this hallway. There will be a single camera in the room, but that ain't really used too much for security." He said in a stern voice as he pulled her along.

"Well, I feel safer already." She mumbled with an eye roll. "Look doll, I know it ain't ideal. Hell, if I could take you anywhere else I would, but this is the closest place to your home and, if needed, to your work. I promise we won't be here for too long. Just until the smoke clears." He gave her a sincere look that nearly melted her bitter, icy heart. "Okay, I'll stop complaining." She sighed, earning a soft peck on the forehead from the gentle giant. "Thank you."

At the very end of the hallway was a door unlike any of the others. While the other ones were blue and purple to match the theme of the club, this door was bright red and seemed to have a very intricate and complex lock. Faye watched as Elio entered a pin of some kind, causing the door to unlock and open on its own. "That's so freaking cool." She mumbled in amazement, much to her lover's amusement. "Is that really what it takes to impress you?" He chuckled as he took her arm and led her inside.

The room inside was huge, almost like it was built to fit thirty men. The design was way different from the club's, with the walls being a darker shading and the lighting being a dim yellow instead of the bright neon lights that ran through the ceiling. The floor was made of mahogany that had a bit of a red tint to it. On one side sat a large brown couch with what looked like a stripper pole in the middle. On the other side was a huge bar carrying a lot of expensive drinks Faye hadn't ever even heard of. There were televisions along the walls that seemed to be linked up to all the cameras in the various rooms.

"This is our most private room, reserved for mostly meetings, though if one of these assholes wants to pay the right price, I don't mind renting it out." Elio explained. "This room will be your sanctuary in case of emergencies. No one can get in without a code and only me and few of my capos have the code. If you need to, you can open the door by pressing that purple button over there, but be careful of who you let in. Drinks are behind the bar, and yes, there are some nonalcoholic drinks, you little saint. The bathroom is in the back and you can use the tv's like normal television sets or you can just watch whatever bullshit these morons get up to in these rooms."

Faye stood there, taking in everything he had to say, unsure of how to respond. "How are you feeling, doll?" He suddenly asked as he picked her up bridal style and carried her over to the couch. "Fine, I guess. Just a little tired is all." She replied with a soft yawn. "I'm sorry to hear that. I promise I'll get my men to wrap up this nonsense in no time so I can get you back home safely." He said, placing a gentle kiss on her lips. "I know you will, my love. You're so fast and efficient. That's one of the many reasons I love you." She mumbled, nearly causing his heart to explode.

As he placed her down, he couldn't help himself. Leaning over the couch, he quickly captured her lips in a heated exchange, trapping her body underneath his. "I fucking love you so much." He murmured against her mouth as she allowed him complete control. Finally, he let up, knowing he was wasting precious time that could be spent protecting his love. "I'll be back soon. Just hang tight, okay?" He said before exiting the room, leaving the exhausted pharmacy tech all alone to sit with her own thoughts.

Chapter: 23

Curled up on the couch, Faye laid there, still in disbelief of everything that had happened to her. One moment she was working her regular shift, the next, bam, she was trapped in the middle of a gang war. "When did life get so fucking weird?" She felt the need to ask herself. Is this what life would be like from here on out? Nothing but stress and worry, as she constantly needed to look over her shoulder again and again.

She shook her head, knowing that if she thought too hard about it, it would only cause her more grief. Besides, it was completely worth every pain in the ass if that meant she got to be with Elio. "What's a little added excitement if it means I get to spend every waking moment with the love of my life?" She giggled to herself, finding that her body finally relaxed against the couch. Looking up at the television screens, she couldn't help but scrunch her nose in disgust.

"So that's what the cameras in the rooms are for. Gross…" she mumbled to herself before turning away to look at her phone, turning on the security cameras just in time to catch her dear friend sneaking off with her two cats. "That son of a bitch." She grumbled before flipping to a social media site so that she could watch cute animal videos instead of whatever sins were happening on the cameras.

Elio stomped down the hall with murder in his eyes, wanting every Black Spades members' head on a plate. He still couldn't believe how easily they tracked him down and caught up to him while he was with Faye. Nor could he believe they were still lingering around her neighborhood, more than likely waiting for her to be left all alone.

"Dammit Faye, why couldn't you just agree to come live with me?" He shouted in frustration, slamming his fist against the wall. "Look at the trouble you've caused me. Now I got to figure out a way to clean this mess up and still keep you happy. You're so fucking lucky you're actually worth it." While he wanted to be mad at her, the most he could muster up was extreme concern for the woman's wellbeing.

"Hey!" He called out to one of the servers. "There is a woman down in the VIP room that I'm keeping locked in there. If she asks for anything, bring it to her, otherwise leave her the fuck alone." He sneered, with a threatening look in his eyes. "O-of course, sir. W-whatever she wants." The server stuttered out, absolutely petrified by the giant beast of a man.

He made his way out of the building and walked towards the back where there was no one there save a few employees taking a smoke break. "Beat it." He ordered, shooing the employees away. Once he was all alone, he pulled out his cellphone and a cigar that he lit rather quickly and skillfully. While he was trying to cut back for Faye's sake, seeing as she had issues with smoke, he really needed one that night, so unfortunately, his love would have to deal.

As he dialed Henry's number, hoping to get an update, he couldn't help but think back on the argument he had with Faye earlier that day. It was so frustrating and heartbreaking, especially when he saw those tears in her eyes. That look she gave him, oh, that look. She could get away with murder just by giving that look. He couldn't bear to even think about that look, especially when it was directed at him. "I swear to God I'll never make you cry again." He promised.

"Hey boss." The capos greeted after the second ring. "Any updates?" Elio asked, skipping past all the pleasantries. "No signs of them anywhere. The damn cowards must have run off the moment you ditched them. How disappointing, and I was hoping for an actual fight." He rolled his eyes at the comment, expecting no less from his top man. "We'll do one more sweep of the area and let you know if anything comes up," Henry said, sounding far too chipper. "Good." Elio retorted. "I also need you to get in contact with Leo. Tell him to get his ass down to 'Till Dusk to Dawn.' I have an important task for him." "Right away, boss."

Elio finally hung up once he was satisfied with the conversation. He felt quite lucky that the Black Spades decided against sticking around. The last thing he needed on his plate was another turf battle, especially in a gray zone. All he wanted to do was get back to his Faye and relax with her for a little while longer, with no interruptions. He just hoped she was holding up just fine in that room.

Faye laid upside down on the couch with her head dangling off the seat and her phone two inches away from her face. She scrolled through different videos, trying so hard to kill the time. She was both exhausted and annoyed about the whole thing and wished for nothing more than to curl up in bed and pass out. "Hell, at this point, I'd even go to Elio's house." She sighed as she continued her mindless scrolling.

A loud knock sounded throughout the room, pulling her away from her phone. "Hello?" She called out, unsure if it was a good idea or not to open the door. While she was locked in this room to keep her safe from whatever threat was looming around, Elio didn't say she couldn't open the door. "Who's there?" She called out again, only to be met with silence.

"Room service." A soft, feminine voice finally called back. "I don't think I need any room service." She replied skeptically. "The boss requested it." She answered quickly and rather rehearsed, as though she expected that answer. Faye thought about it, weighing her options before she figured it couldn't hurt her too much to trust a random stranger. 'It's gotten me this far.' She thought to herself as she got up from her seat, nearly falling on her head, and made her way over to the door.

She could feel her heart racing the closer she got to the button, worry etched on her face. 'If I see more than one person, I'm shutting the door.' She kept repeating over and over in her head. After everything that has happened, she knew this was the dumbest decision she had ever made. Okay, one of the many dumbest decisions she's ever made.

The door flew open, revealing a woman in a purple vest and a blue miniskirt. The woman had beautiful white hair and sparkling violet eyes with the longest lashes. Her long curly hair fell down to both sides of her head, each decorated with a blue bow. Cute little freckles dusted her brown cheeks like glitter, shining bright under the neon light that illuminated over her head.

Faye couldn't help but let out a sigh of relief, seeing as this girl was the only one standing there. "Well, come on in, I guess." She said, leading the white-haired girl inside her temporary sanctuary. As she turned to close the door, she felt the girl's eyes burning holes in the back of her head as though she were trying to set her on fire with just one look.

"So... Elio sent you here?" Faye asked, attempting to break the uncomfortable silence. "Actually, I'm just here to assess the newest little crimson mouse." The girl responded, her tone arrogant and full of spite. "I'm sorry, crimson mouse?" She asked, confused by the statement. "Yeah, that's what we like to call you pathetic sluts that think they can weasel their way into our club just by fucking every member of the Crimson Kings." She snapped.

"What?" Faye was taken aback by the accusation. "You heard me, little mouse. I know all about this little game they like to play with girls like you. Butter you up, tell you you're going to be a star and then drop you off at the nearest club or brothel for you to 'work' your way up to stardom. Well, let me just shatter that delusion before you spend the next few months acting all entitled and prissy. You ain't going to be anyone special. All you are is a cheap fuck."

Faye blinked once, then twice, trying her hardest to understand the strange girl's speech. "Wait, I'm confused... You think I'm here to chase some stardom? I don't get it." She tilted her head in confusion, pleading with the girl to break it down simpler for her. "Jeez, you ain't the brightest. No wonder they got you so easily. Look darling, what I'm trying to say is you're nothing but a common whore, nothing more, nothing less."

"No, I'm not." She finally spoke up to defend herself. "I'm none of what you're saying. I'm not a common whore, I'm not a streetwalker, and I'm not an idiot. What I am is a - tired pharmacy technician waiting for her boyfriend to come back." If she wasn't so exhausted, she'd be seething at this point. Suddenly, the girl burst out into laughter.

"Sure honey, of course you are. Do you even know what happens in these rooms, especially in this one? The gang members bring you in here to break you in. Make sure you're good company for any potential clients." Faye crinkled her nose in disgust as she realized she might be sitting on top of who knows what bodily fluids could be all over the couch. "Great... Now I have the sudden urge to burn these scrubs." She muttered.

"But in all seriousness, I can assure you Elio did not bring me in here to have his men gang bang me. This room just so happened to be the most secure place in the building, which is actually pretty sad," Faye said, finding a bit of amusement in the girl's accusations. "You know, you really shouldn't refer to the boss so intimately. It could get you killed."

Faye, wearing a playful grin, couldn't help herself. "Someone would seriously kill me for calling my boyfriend by his first name? That sounds a little harsh, don't you think?" She retorted in a cheerful tone. "Boyfriend!?" the girl exclaimed. "The boss isn't you boyfriend." As much as she didn't want to believe it, there was not even a single hint of dishonesty in Faye's eyes.

"Yeah, he really is. We've been together for about a week, but we're hopefully going strong." She shrugged. "But if you're his girlfriend, then that means I just..." "Made a terrible judgment call and flat out disrespected someone who could cost you your job..." Faye interrupted her. "And so much more..." the girl finished, sounding as though she were about to be sick. "Look ma'am..." "You can call me Faye." "I am so sorry! I thought you were one of those flashy showoffs that like to talk shit and act tough just because they slept with a gangster."

Faye smiled in amusement, knowing the exact type of girl she was referring to. May used to get plenty of those types of workers in all the time, thinking they're too good for the job. It was a serious pain to deal with and often she'd see some of May's top girls showing the same level of hostility as this girl. She really couldn't blame her for acting this way.

"It's okay. I'm not mad or anything, just relieved the misunderstanding was cleared up." Faye replied with a soft laugh, bringing a little relief to the girl. "Thank goodness. I was worried there for a second. I tend to get a little ahead of myself. Sorry again." The woman shook her head. "All water under the bridge." She shrugged, patting her shoulder. "I just hope the boss doesn't find out."

"Find out what?" Elio's voice echoed throughout the room, catching the attention of both girls. "Elio! You're back! Does that me I can go home now?" Faye cheered as she jumped off the couch and into the man's arms. "No, not yet, my love. They're going to do one more sweep of the area and then call it a day. In the meantime, I figured we could spend a little more time together. Alone." The last word came with a hidden warning towards the unwanted guest in the room. The girl, while terrified, did not overlook the warning and left without a single word.

The door closed behind her, locking the two of them in by themselves, left to enjoy each other's company. "So, doll…" Elio purred, pulling Faye over to the couch so that she could sit on his lap. "What exactly were you two talking about before I got here?" She looked up at him with soft blue eyes. "Oh, nothing in particular. She stopped by to offer me a drink and we got to chatting is all." She lied through her teeth, not wanting to get the girl in trouble.

Elio, as intelligent as he was, did not buy it for a second. "Oh, come on doll." He whispered in her ear, moving his hands up to rest against her sides. "Why don't you tell me what you were really discussing?" His lips moved down to her neck, allowing his teeth to lightly graze her soft spot. "I promise I won't get mad."

He sounded so earnest that she could almost believe him. "I… Ah… Don't know what you're talking about." She tried to play dumb, finding it difficult with the way he was kissing her neck. His hand slipped up the front of her scrub top, landing on one of her breasts. "You'll either come clean right now. Or I'll fuck the information out of you." He growled, moving his lips back against hers. His hand began to squeeze and pinch, kneading the soft bundle of flesh as she let out a string of mewls and moans.

"Elio, please…" she begged as she began to grind against him. It felt as though her body was moving against her will, completely under her lover's control. "No, doll, I won't stop until you tell me the truth." He chided her, going in for another kiss. "I promise it wasn't anything important." She mewled, attempting to escape his tight grip. "If it wasn't important, then you shouldn't have any issues telling me."

His movements grew rougher with every kiss as he flipped her around on her back. There was a dark glint in his eyes as he pinned her to the couch, forcing his knee in between her legs. "I'm not kidding, doll. Either tell me the truth or I'll fuck you right on this couch, and I won't be gentle either." While the threat was more than tempting, all Faye could think about was how many people had sex in this exact spot before her.

"Okay, okay. I'll talk." She finally surrendered both to Elio's joy and disappointment. "Good girl." He praised, nuzzling her face. "You promise you won't get mad?" She asked. "I promise." He agreed. "She thought I was a... Oh, what did she call it? Oh yes, now I remember. She thought I was a crimson mouse." She could feel Elio's grip tighten on her, his nails digging into her skin. "Ow! Elio, you promised you wouldn't get mad!" she whined. "Sorry... It's just... She had no right to come in here and accuse you of being a prostitute." He growled, loosening his grip so that he wouldn't cause any damage.

Faye let out a soft sigh. "It's okay, really. She acted that way to protect your business. It happens all the time. Some pretty young thing comes in clinging on to their pimp's arm, acting all high and mighty. They act like they're in charge and suddenly they get picky on which clients they see, only servicing the top dollar ones and ignoring all the regulars to the point of pissing them off. It's just bad business." She shrugged, as if she were discussing the weather.

"Doll, how do you know about any of that?" Elio asked, sounding rather impressed by her knowledge. "I learned through May. She's taught me a thing or two about the sex industry, probably hoping I'd take over one day. See how that turned out." She laughed as though she didn't have a care in the world. "Interesting..." Elio mumbled, lost in thought.

"You know, doll, May is one of the best in her profession. Gangs everywhere would do just about anything to recruit her, so the knowledge she's given you is pretty sacred. Make sure you keep hold of it and be careful who you tell. The last thing I need is for people to find out you're May's little apprentice. It'll make it much harder to protect you." He warned her. "No need to worry. I try to not tell people I know the crazy Dane, let alone telling people I have been secretly learning her trade over the years."

Elio finally sat up, releasing her from the cuddly prison so that she could sit on his lap. "I still feel like I need to punish her for coming in here." He muttered as he stroked her hair. "Technically, I let her in, so I think I should be the one punished." She teased, leaning her head against his chest. "Oh, really now?" He smirked. "And how would I go about doing that?" He purred, kissing her temple. "however you see fit, my love." As she spoke, he pulled her into another heated kiss.

As he pulled away, a notification popped up on his phone. "Any new updates on when I can go home?" Faye asked hopefully. "No, none right now. Why the interest? Are you already trying to leave me?" He asked with a fake pout. "Maybe. I thought a quick game of hide and seek would be fun." She retorted sarcastically. "Oh, doll." Elio purred. "There isn't a single corner in this world that you could hide in where I won't find you." He smirked. "That sounds like a challenge." She replied.

Large hands wrapped around her, flipping her back onto the couch underneath the large mobster. "Just try to run away, doll." He warned, his face barely an inch away from hers. "And I'll find you and punish you real good for causing me so much trouble." Before she could say anything, he had already closed the gap, forcing her into another kiss.

The taste of cigars and whiskey hit first, giving her the sudden urge to pull away. But he was just so gentle and his underlying taste was so sweet. It was like taking a bite out of a freshly picked apple that was just ripened to perfection. His wandering fingers did wonders against her tense, stressed out muscles. She could feel him grinding against her pelvis, creating a friction that could easily make her see stars.

His sly fingers crept under her scrub top, resting at the sides. Knowing how Faye felt about public intimacy, he didn't dare to go forward. At least not without her consent. She almost wanted to give the go ahead, especially since Elio was the only one who could actually enter the room, but there was one slight issue. She couldn't stop thinking about how many people had sex on this very sofa without cleaning it up.

"Hey Elio." She said mid kiss. "Hmm?" He responded as he nuzzled the side of her neck. "How often is this couch cleaned?" A soft chuckled fell from his lips as he realized what had been on her mind. "So I'm guessing the server told you what this room is for." He said pointedly. "Yeah… I'm guessing you brought me here to break me in and make sure I'm good company." She giggled before wrapping her arms around his neck to bring his face down towards hers. "Oh doll, I already broke you in and you are really good company." He purred as he pressed his lips against hers, taking in her sweet taste. "And to answer your question, we clean this couch after every use."

They switched positions so that Faye could comfortably lie on Elio's chest. He rested his chin on top of her head, breathing in her scent. If he had things his way, they'd be in the position forever. Unfortunately, all good things must end. A loud banging on the door pulled them out of their bliss.

"Who is it?" Elio yelled, his tone deep and menacing. Faye couldn't help but blush at it, finding the sound to be sexy and exciting. "It's me, Leo, sir." The person called out in a shaky, hoarse voice that had a hint of an Irish accent to it. He rose from his seat, gently moving his lover out of the way, and made his way towards the door, hitting the switch to open it up.

"Well, are you gonna come in or just stand there looking stupid?" Elio asked impatiently. In stepped a tall, lanky man with pale white skin and slicked back red hair. He wore a dark red button-up shirt and black slacks. His green eyes darted back and forth nervously, as if to avoid eye contact with the mobster standing in front of him.

Neither Faye nor Elio were all too impressed by the man's appearance, as it all seemed sloppily put together. "Fix your tie and tuck in your shirt," Elio ordered with a heavy glare. The man, Leo, did exactly what he was told, not wanting to face the wrath of the powerful mafia leader. Faye had to stifle a giggle at how ridiculous the scene in front of her was. There was something about a grown man telling another grown man how to dress that was just too comical.

"Doll, I need to have a word with Leo in private. I'll be right back. Don't let anyone else in, okay?" His voice was much softer and held sincerity in it. "Can I at least let the cute server girl in? She's pretty harmless." She asked with pleading eyes. "Fine, but only her, no one else." He gave in, finding it hard to say no to her. "Thank you!" She smiled as she jumped into his arms while Leo watched the display with a confused and somewhat terrified expression.

He gave one final kiss. "I'll be right back, I promise." Faye smiled with a light dust of pink on her cheeks. "I know you will. I love you." With that, the two men left the room, leaving the young woman all by herself once again.

Going back to watching videos on her phone, Faye couldn't help but think about her wonderful boyfriend and the looks of terror he'd constantly received. "I wonder what he's done to get looks like that." She pondered out loud to herself. "Probably something seriously badass." She decided not to think too much about it, knowing how wicked his line of work could be.

Knock! Knock! The loud banging echoed throughout the room once again, pulling her out of her thoughts. "Who is it?" She called out. "It's me, Opal." The familiar feminine voice called back. Faye quickly hopped up onto her feet and rushed over to the door, pressing the button. There stood her newfound friend, the adorable server girl.

"Hello again!" She greeted a little too cheerfully. "Hello Faye, I saw the boss left, so I figured I'd stop by and make sure you are all taken care of. Can I offer you a drink or anything?" Opal replied politely, no longer rude and arrogant. "Oh no, I don't need anything to drink at this moment." For a second the girl looked slightly dejected, but quickly perked back up so as not to worry the young woman.

"You know, I could really use a good friend to talk to if you're willing to stay for a bit. Elio left me all alone again and I can't stand places like this," Faye requested, hoping the girl would say yes. "Of course I can stay. It would be an honor to entertain the boss's girlfriend." Opal squeaked out happily. "Thank you so much!" Faye cheered, pulling her into a hug.

They walked back over to the couch, taking a seat before starting up a conversation. "Does the boss know about our little talk?" Opal suddenly asked, worry in her eyes. "Yeah, but he ain't too mad. At least he's not allowed to be. I told him not to be. But he seemed to understand when I explained your thought process and how you're only trying to protect his business. When I brought up that May would have her girls do the same thing, he brushed off your comments, so all is good in his book."

Opal looked so relieved by her comment, but then something she said really caught her attention. "Wait, you know May?" She asked in disbelief. "Yeah, she's a longtime friend of mine." Faye replied. "Why?" She questioned the sudden interest. "Really!? That's so cool! May is an absolute legend. Us working girls would do just about anything to work for her. What's she like? What's her favorite hobbies? Is it true she's actually planning to retire? I heard she's secretly training someone to replace her. Is that true? Do you know who that person is?"

Suddenly, Faye was ambushed by a plethora of questions that were almost too much for her to handle. "Wow! Wow! Slow it down. I can only answer one question at a time." She sighed, mentally preparing to answer each question to the best of her ability. "To start off, May is a massively crazy bitch with a heart of gold. She's extremely pushy and demanding, but she loves to take care of her own." She started going into detail about her relationship with the mistress.

"So, how did you two meet?" Opal asked with sparkling violet eyes, drinking in every word like it was gospel. Never did she'd think she'd meet someone who is close friends with her idol. "Oh, well, when I was thirteen, she attempted to kidnap me..." Faye answered, deadpanned. "What?" The girl asked, not quite understanding. "I was out walking my dog one day. It was pretty damn hot out so I mostly had to carry the little guy and she pulled up next to me, asked me if I was lost." She stopped to look up, reminiscing about the day she met May.

She was a young teenager walking on an empty sidewalk in the middle of the day with a small little terrier following at her side. It was scorching hot out in the triple digits, and most sane people stayed inside. Unfortunately, the house they were living in was a rental and they weren't allowed to have pets so for the day, while the landlords came to do an inspection, Faye had to make her little dog disappear while her parents and brothers made sure everything was in order.

She wore a large pink backpack filled with dog food, a gallon of water, a plastic bowl, and a couple of extra water bottles, along with some snacks for herself. She held a large umbrella over her head to give her and the small dog some relief from the harsh sun. "Man, this sucks…" she grumbled to herself. "Why'd they have to pick the hottest day of the year to do an inspection?"

As she continued to complain, she didn't notice a small silver Toyota constantly circling her like a shark prepared to attack. It wasn't until the fifth time it drove past her she felt a little worried. "Be prepared, Peanut. You might have to play guard dog." She joked to her companion to quail her nerves.

The car slowed down, creeping towards her before speeding up once again to go off in a different direction. Faye scooped up her small dog and make a run for it, attempting to ditch the suspicious vehicle. Unfortunately, she ran in the wrong direction towards a cul-de-sac, leaving herself completely cornered.

She could feel her heart racing and panic set in at the sight of the strange car. "Shit!" She cursed herself for acting so stupid. A part of her thought to knock on doors and ask to use their phones to call her parents, but the obedient side of her convinced her not to, warning her she'd get in a lot of trouble if she interrupted the inspection.

The window slowly rolled down, revealing a young woman in the driver's seat, her hair was dyed bleached blonde with brown roots showing and she had pretty hazel eyes that didn't seem to hold any hostility in them. "Hello little one." She greeted with a thick European accent. "Is everything okay?" Faye, still suspicious and cautious of this woman, hesitated with her response. "Uh, yeah. Just out for a little walk with my dog." She explained, her eyes darting back and forth for an escape.

The woman looked at her skeptically, taking in her appearance. It was then that Faye realized what she was wearing: a large torn up black shirt with some faded band logo on it and a dirty pair of pink sweatpants. She kind of looked like she was a homeless teenager with her dog. "Are you sure everything is okay? I have a nice house with plenty of space if you and your little friend need a place to stay."

Now Faye was completely weirded out. "Uh, no thanks?" She more so stated as a question than an answer. "I think I'm fine…" "May will you stop bothering this poor girl!" A deep voice shouted from the passenger's side. "She probably thinks you're trying to kidnap her." That man hit the nail on the head with that observation. "But I'm not trying to kidnap her. You can't kidnap someone who doesn't have a home."

Faye felt her left eye twitch as she slowly backed away from the car. "I actually have a home. I'm just out for a walk." She tried to explain again. "Bullshit." She retorted so grotesquely. "If you have a place to stay, you'd be there and not out in this awful heat. Now come on, let me take you home." What the hell? Why was this crazy woman so desperate to kidnap her?

"Please leave me alone." Faye begged, holding her dog close. "No, no, don't look at me like that. I'm not trying to hurt you. I want to help. I promise!" She insisted. "I promise you I have a home. I'm not allowed to have pets, so I'm trying to hide him from our landlords. Please believe me!" She was on the verge of tears, wanting so desperately to get away from these dangerous people.

"Oh! Why didn't you say from the beginning? Look, little one, I'm not trying to steal you. I just want to make sure you're safe." She explained with raised hands. "My boyfriend here is actually a cop, and he was worried, too." Faye tilted her head to look into the car and saw the man who was yelling at her. He had short black hair and almond-shaped amber eyes. He offered her a polite smile and a little wave.

"I promise I'm fine, but thanks for checking in." Faye said, still trying to move away, though this time with far less haste. "You know, if you're not allowed to be home right now, you can come with us. Like I said before, there's plenty of room and it's not too far from this area, so you'll be able to relax in a cool spot for a bit before you have to go home."

She thought about the offer for a moment, weighing her options. "Ah, what the hell…" She shrugged. "What do I have to lose?" The woman happily jumped out of the car and led her over to the backseat, opening the door for her. "I'm Faye Merci, by the way." She said, holding out her hand. "Nice to meet you, Faye. I'm May Saken and this is my Boyfriend Jake Hefflin."

Opal sat with wide eyes, quietly listening to the story. "So you really just got in a stranger's car for no reason?" She asked in disbelief that anyone could make such a poor judgement call. "It wasn't for no reason. You have to understand it was really hot out." Faye tried to justify her reasoning. "And I was a really stupid kid." She shrugged as if that was an excuse on its own. "You know, I kind of wanted to ask how you met the boss as well, but I'm a little scared now." She gave a nervous chuckle. "Yeah, that story isn't any better." Faye replied sheepishly.

The two continued to chat, opening up about their lives and where they came from. Apparently, Opal used to live on the streets working the street corners just to make ends meet. She serviced several shady men, some of which did terrible things to her. It was one of Elio's top henchmen that pulled her out of this lifestyle. He set her up at the nicest nightclub as a server and she's been here ever since.

"I owe that man my life." Opal said quietly. "If it wasn't for him, I'd probably be dead in a dumpster somewhere." Faye gave her newfound friend a sad look. "Oh Opal." She said, pulling the girl into a tight hug. "That's terrible! I'm so sorry you had to go through that." Opal hugged the girl back, giving her a light squeeze. "To tell you the truth, I was hoping the man would take me to one of May's clubs. I guess lady luck wasn't fully on my side." She sighed sadly.

"Why didn't you just go to one of her clubs? She would have offered you a job almost immediately." Faye wondered. "I tried to, but when I went to one, this one girl there turned me away almost immediately. She wouldn't even let me see the head girl, much less May herself." She looked at the girl in surprise.

"Really? May has never turned away a girl, especially one in serious need. It's kind of a promise she made to herself. Who did you talk to?" She asked curiously. "I think her name was AmberRose. Short girl, black and silver hair." Faye narrowed her eyes with an irritated expression. "Ugh her? No wonder you couldn't get in. She's as troubled as they get. That woman is what you would call a crimson mouse, for sure. I just call her a cunt whore.

She was always trouble, even from day one when she discovered the owner was, in fact, a woman. I am so sorry you had to put up with that thing.”

Opal couldn’t help but laugh, finding humor in Faye’s apology. “I’m glad it wasn’t just me. She really was what you said she was.” She sighed. “Yeah, she was. So rude and disrespectful to May. When I say the crazy woman will hire just about anyone, I’m not kidding. I’m surprised the girl lasted as long as she did with the amount of hell she put May through.”

As they continued to chat, Opal suddenly realized the time. “Oh goodness! I need to get back to work!” She exclaimed, standing up from her seat. “Oh man, sorry for holding you up,” Faye apologized, standing up with her so that she could lead her to the door. “Thank you so much for spending time with me. It’s been fun.” She smiled warmly. “It’s honesty been my pleasure. Thanks for putting in a good word to the boss for me.” Opal replied, giving Faye one last hug.

“Come by the club sometime and say hi,” she requested. “I would, but I doubt they’d let me in. I’m not their average cliental.” Opal gave the young woman a strange look. “Honey, your boyfriend owns the club. They aren’t allowed to turn you away.” She reminded her with an eye roll. “Oh, yeah… I keep forgetting about that.” The girl let out a loud laugh. “You’re so pretty.” She giggled as she left the room, leaving Faye all alone once again.

“Elio needs to hurry his ass up.” Faye mutter to herself, pacing back and forth throughout the room. It felt like an eternity passed by and she was bored out of her mind. She couldn’t fall asleep, at least not with what was playing on the television. She was also starting to really miss the big jerk.

Just as she found herself lost in thought, the door flew open. In the doorway stood a stoic Elio and a terrified Leo. “Oh, you didn’t kill him. Neat.” Faye commented almost too cheerfully. “Why would I kill him? He’s your new bodyguard, after all.” He retorted with a smug smile. She tilted her head in confusion as she walked up to the tall, lanky man, observing every part of him.

“So let me get this straight. You don’t trust any of the people in my life, including my two huge, scary looking brothers, but you trust this guy to protect me? No offense.” She scoffed in disbelief. Leo looked very much offended by the woman’s audacity, but made the smart decision to keep his mouth shut.

“He might not look like much, but trust me, doll, he’s the best man for the job. He’s got a keen eye and a quick shot. He also knows quite a few ways to take down a man twice his size and his body count is no joke. He’s perfect. Plus, you need someone that can actually fit inside your small ass house.” Elio hyped him up, much to Faye’s amusement and relief. If her boyfriend thinks he’s perfect, then he must be worth something.

“Alright, I trust your judgement better than my own. But I do have some conditions. I don’t want him at work with me and he is not allowed in my bedroom at all.” Elio nodded along with her requests, finding them reasonable. “Okay, you heard the woman, no snooping in her bedroom and stay on the outside of her work. Anything else, doll?” She thought about it before shaking her head no.

Faye walked up to Leo and held out her hand. “I’m Faye Merci. It’s good to meet you.” He took her hand, giving a light handshake. “My name’s Leo. Nice to meet you too, ma'am." She noticed his hand was rough and callused, more than likely caused by years of hard work. If he was a hard worker and a sharpshooter, he might not be too bad of a bodyguard after all. And what's better is if he pissed her off, she could just go to Elio and have him removed from her life. She could really get used to being a mob boss's girlfriend.

Elio spent a few more minutes going over the details of Faye's living arrangements for the next month until both parties understood it, with no questions asked. While she didn't like the idea of having a total stranger live with her, it was better than being possibly kidnapped by evil strangers. She didn't actually know if they were evil or not, probably just the same level of gray as Elio's gang, but she liked to think they were the bad guys.

"Alright doll, let's get going." Elio said, wrapping his arm around the young woman. He pulled her close to his chest and walked out of the room, with Leo not too far behind. They made their way into the main lobby, past the bar, where Faye spotted Opal. She gave her a small wave, which the young server returned, albeit nervously.

The moment they stepped foot outside, Elio turned to address his doormen. "The girl right here is Faye Merci." He spoke in a quiet tone so that nobody but the two men could hear him. "Add her to the list. She gets entry no matter what." His tone was low and threatening, as if he were daring them to say no. Of course, neither of the big burly men tried to challenge his judgement and instead gave an affirmative nod as they glanced over at Faye briefly.

She looked at Elio with a confused expression. "Why are you making this a big deal so that I get full access?" She wondered. "I want to get it established now, just in case something terrible happens where you need to hide away somewhere. Like if someone's chasing you, or you just don't feel safe at home, I need you to call me and then head here immediately. I'll give you the access code to that room back there so you can hide in there until I show up. Promise me you'll do that." He pleaded softly with the most sincere look. "Okay, I promise." She agreed rather easily.

Satisfied with her answer, Elio continued to lead Faye and Leo towards the parking lot, where they went separate ways. Leo went towards the main lot while Faye and Elio made their way towards the valet parking. "He isn't coming with us?" The young woman asked. "He's taking his own car back to your place. We'll meet him there." Elio explained. "Besides, I'm sure we have one more stop to get to before I can take you home. Isn't that right?" He asked with an amused smirk.

She thought about it before realization struck her. "Oh yeah! We got to get my cats back from that asshole." Elio snickered at her comment before opening the door of the car for her. As she got in the car, she quickly told the mobster her best friend's address.

Chapter: 24

"Hey Elio." Faye spoke as her lover got them back on the road. "Hmm?" He answered, completely focused on driving. "You know how you said May's knowledge is sacred?" She started, unsure if it was the best thing to tell him right now. "Yeah?" He answered, wanting to know where she was going with this. "Well, she's actually been secretly training me to take her place. It's only been for the past two years that she's stopped because of some… Unfortunate circumstances. But mostly, I know practically everything that she knows about the sex trade industry."

For a moment, Elio looked over at her with a quizzical look. "Why are you suddenly telling me this?" He asked confused. "I just want to be open and honest about what I know, just in case it comes back to bite me in the ass." The car went unbearably silent as Elio attempted to process everything she said.

"No worries, doll. As long as you don't run around telling that to everyone, you should be good. I got to say though, it is awfully tempting to get you in contact with the members that I have running the clubs and brothels. I don't think I'll do that just yet, but you never know."

After a long drive, they finally made it to Atlas's house. The house itself wasn't anything glorious, just a small, cute cottage style home. It had a decent sized yard covered in grass and decorated with various statues and plants. The exterior walls had been painted a nice dark blue, making it pop out a little from the rest of the houses on the block.

Faye practically jumped out of the car and ran up to the door. "Luca!" She yelled, banging on the wood. "You have ten seconds to open this damn door before I kick it in!" She could hear snickering on the other side of the door. "I want to see you try!" Luca called back. "No!" another muffled voice shouted out.

Just as she was about to carry out her threat, the door suddenly unlocked, revealing a tall, bulky man. He had short, shaggy hair dyed blue and yellowish green eyes. His pale face had a light dusting of freckles and a well-kept black beard. Tattoos of various shows and styles ran up his arms, stopping at his neck.

The man had an amused smile on his face as he greeted the angry blonde girl in front of him. "Hey Faye!" He chirped happily. "Give me back my cats." She retorted, getting straight to the point. "Can we negotiate?" He asked, trying not to laugh. "Of course." She replied in a sickly sweet voice. "Give me back my cats, or you'll die." Elio, who was standing right next to her, let out a small snort.

"Hmm... Let me think about it... No deal." He crossed his arms and huffed. "How about I keep Banshee and you take Caligula?" He countered. "Absolutely not!" She snapped. "Fine, you take Banshee and I'll keep Caligula." He sighed, trying to reason with her. "No!" she yelled again. "Come on, Faye, you don't need two cats. You're being selfish." He teased. "Luca! Give her the damn cats back!" A voice echoed from inside. "Fine!" He whined, upset that his fun was being ruined.

"Well, come on in, I guess." Luca waved them in, with Faye going first and Elio following right after. "Oh, and who's this?" He asked with a sly smile. "This is Elio, my boyfriend." Faye explained, absolutely loving being able to say that. The man in question gave her a soft smile before kissing the top of her head. "Aw, so adorable." Luca gushed, happy that his friend found someone.

Elio looked around the house, finding it a clear upgrade from Faye's own living conditions. The walls were painted a light blue and decorated with various photos and art pieces. It was very simplistic, but very elegant. 'I wouldn't mind having her live here if needed.' He thought to himself, wondering just how much he could trust the two men who lived here to protect his precious Faye.

Luca seemed to grin ear to ear, happy to have his dear friend in the house. "You planned this, didn't you?" She asked, deadpanned. "We never get to hang out anymore." He whined, pulling her into a tight hug. "And Atlas told me you were planning to move far away, so I'll see you even less." He had the saddest, heartbreaking look, like a kicked puppy.

"Aw, Luca, I might be moving away, but it's not going to be that far away. I'll still be able to come and see you." She promised, pulling him into a tight hug. 'If I allow it.' Elio thought to himself, still unsure of whether Luca could be trusted. "You better come see me!" He cried. "Who else will help me fuck with Atlas?" Faye had a look of determination on her face. "I will come visit! I promise. Not a damn force on this planet could stop me from fucking with Atlas."

"What are you two dumbasses talking about now?" A man called out from the hallway before stepping foot into the living room. He had neatly combed short black hair and beautiful amber colored almond-shaped eyes. His skin was a light olive color that held no flaws or blemishes to it. The man looked like a model, to say the least. On his wrist, he had a heart-shaped tattoo with the different colors of the rainbow on it.

"Atlas!" Faye exclaimed, pulling the man into a tight hug. "My dearest best friend who I'd never torment! Oh, how I missed you." Luca let out a small snicker as Atlas rolled his eyes. "It's good to see you too, troublemaker." He joked, ruffling her hair. "Trouble maker? Whatever are you going on about? I'm practically a saint." She declared. "More like a pain. You're lucky I don't charge you for my legal advice." He huffed, crossing his arms. "And that's why I love you so much." She replied sheepishly, earning herself a light smack on the head.

"Now that that's settled, Luca!" she said, turning to the man in question. "What?" He asked. "My cats! Now!" She snapped her fingers and pointed towards the hallway. "Ugh. Can't you just stay the night and take your cats home in the morning?" He suggested, not wanting to go through the trouble at this moment. "No! I need my cats now. I got work in the morning." Luca rolled his eyes. "Fine, fine. I'll go find them... So mean." He mumbled, walking off towards the back of the house.

Faye turned her attention back to her best friend, offering him a soft smile. "So... How has work been lately?" She asked, trying to break the ice. "Pretty rough, honestly. I was just handed the worst fucking client ever." He replied with a sigh as they moved to go sit on the couch. Faye crawled into Elio's lap and leaned her head back so that he could stroke her hair.

"Really? Why?" she asked curiously. "His case is a pretty simple case, easy to prove he didn't do it, pretty open and shut. The problem is, he doesn't know when to shut the fuck up. The guy is obviously innocent, but he's such an asshole the judge wants to hold him in contempt. I swear these clients just get dumber and dumber. What about you? How's work been treating you?" Atlas was trying to exclude Elio from the conversation.

"It's going well... Just a lot of emergencies lately. Plenty of exotic animals coming in because owners couldn't be bothered to research the animal before buying. You know how it goes..." she replied awkwardly, trying hard not to complain too much about her job in front of Elio. "Don't worry, doll, in a month, it won't even be a problem anymore." He purred, nuzzling her head.

Atlas narrowed his eyes, upset by the reminder that a deadly crime lord would take his sweet friend away. "I don't see her job as a problem. She actually does amazing work for the community. If it wasn't for her, a lot of animals would go without proper medicine and treatment. She's so dedicated to her work, I've seen her research the best medications to use for dogs with severe anxiety. I think it would be a shame to let her knowledge and dedication go to waste."

"I would never allow such a brilliant mind to be wasted." Elio retorted. "I could easily find better things to keep her sharp and functional rather than counting pills and measuring elixirs. She'll be commanding powerful men and women and preventing turf wars from breaking out. She'll be what brings this city peace."

Faye looked back and forth between the two bickering men, wondering what caused them to fight. "Faye!" Luca's voice echoed throughout the house. "Please help! Caligula is trying to kill me!" She let out a sigh of relief at having an excuse for leaving the room thick with tension. "Serves you right!" She shouted back as she stood up from her spot and made her way towards the direction of the voice. A sound of loud hisses and growls followed the sound of footsteps before leaving the two in silence.

"You know, Faye doesn't need to prove anything to you. She's perfectly happy and satisfied with her life as it is." Atlas said a little too bravely. "Oh really? So you don't think she deserves the best of the best. The better house, the nicest car, and the financial freedom to do whatever she wants? Some friend you are," Elio scoffed, wondering where this man grew the balls to talk to him like that.

"She isn't the type to take without giving. She grew up with strong morals about hard work and earning your keep. That lifestyle would only make her feel useless." He argued, already irritated with this conversation. "She wouldn't be useless. She'd be my right hand." Elio insisted. "No!" Atlas suddenly snapped, causing the mobster to narrow his eyes. "What did you say to me?" His tone was dark and gave off a warning. "Please, don't involve her at all in your business! I'm begging you. Faye doesn't understand one bit of what you do, and it would destroy her if she learned..."

"I ain't planning to ruin her innocence!" Elio suddenly interrupted. "I just want what's best for her." His voice went quiet and soft. "So do I." Atlas agreed, as they sat there in silence. Neither man wanted to speak up first. "Look, Mr. Eclisse, it sounds like we both want the same thing, for Faye to be safe and happy. I can admit that, if you can admit that isolating her from all her friends and family will do the exact opposite." "Who said I wanted to isolate her?" He cut in. "I ain't planning to isolate so long as the people in her life keep her best interests at heart."

Atlas had a look of shock on his face as the words sunk in. "Wait? You aren't planning to take her away?" He couldn't help but ask. "No, I'm not. She seems so fond of you people, God knows why, and so the last thing I'd ever want to do is take away something she loves. Why do you think I'm planning to take her damn cats with us?"

The two of them came to an agreement of sorts that they wouldn't interfere in each other's relationships with Faye. Neither one wanted to see the young woman hurt. "Believe it or not, I really love Faye with all my heart. She'll be safe and satisfied so long as I can have my way." That was all Atlas needed to hear to feel somewhat at ease. He still didn't like the idea of his best friend dating a crime lord, but he understood he was helpless to stop it. "Faye never ceases to amaze me." Atlas said with a soft smile. "Getting infamous Elio to fall in love with her. Why is her life so damn weird?"

As the two continued to chat with far less hostility and tension, Faye and Luca finally returned from their battle with the cats. Both came brandishing battle scars, with Luca's being far worse than Faye. "Next time you try to kidnap my cats, leave Caligula at home!" she chided him. "It ain't my fault you fucking raised Lucifer!" Luca retorted. "Next time I'm taking his vicious little ass to church to get exorcised." "Don't you dare! You know how many souls I had to sell to get him?" The two of them broke out into laughter, wincing slightly when they felt the still fresh wounds.

Elio stood up with a worried expression. "Are you okay?" He asked, running to his lover's aid. Taking her arm in his large hand, he observed the fresh scratches that littered her soft skin. "Yeah, I'm fine. You should see the other guy." She joked, pointing towards a carrier now containing a pissed off Caligula. His long orange fur was completely puffed up and his big ears laid flat on his head as he hissed and growled. Banshee seemed fine and content just lying in her cage.

Elio still seemed a bit freaked out by the state of his beloved. "Come on, doll, we need to get these cleaned up and dressed." He said, dragging her out of the house. "Elio, slow down." She warned him nearly dropping the cats. "Bye Faye!" Luca called out to her. "Bye Luca! Bye Atlas!" she called back, attempting to wave at them before being pushed into the car.

"So what happened?" Elio asked once he got her safely into the vehicle. "Oh, nothing too bad. Liggy just got stuck in a cupboard and we had to pull his ass out. Luca actually got the worst of it. Serves the bastard right." She muttered the last part to herself. "Faye, you know how dangerous cat scratches can be. You need to be more careful!" He lectured, causing her to roll her eyes. "Yes, I know, and it's fine. The cuts aren't too deep. They'll probably be all healed by the morning." She shrugged.

"That's not the point. I can't have you going out, letting all these things cut you up. I need you to be more careful." He insisted. "What about the cuts and marks you put on me, huh?" She said slyly. "That's different." He smirked. "Those marks are to show my love."

Faye nearly burst out into laughter at that comment. "Red flags aside… I promise I'll be more careful. Okay?" Elio sighed in relief, happy she was at least able to promise it.

He gave her a tight squeeze and a soft kiss on the forehead. "You know I love you, right?" He said, his voice sweet and loving. "I love you too." She grinned up at him, pulling his face down for an actually kiss. "Meow!" The little orange menace screamed from the back seat of the car. "Well, we better get going. This is going to be a long drive." Faye groaned, knowing the hell they were about to go through.

Finally, after a long journey of loud screams and cries, the four of them made it back home safely. "Doll, can I make one request when we move you out?" Elio asked in the nicest way possible. "What is that, my love?" Faye replied with a smile. "Can the damn cats come in a separate car? I ain't listening to the howling for an hour."

"Wow." She giggled. "I can't believe you want to put one of your poor men through that." She pretended to be shocked. "Oh, most definitely! Those assholes deserve it with the headaches they cause me." He retorted, causing her to laugh some more. "You know, doll, you still have the cutest laugh I've ever heard." He purred, his face inches in front of hers. "I could just listen to it for days." "Meow!" "Goddammit, will you stop doing that?" Elio yelled, angry that he was once again cockblocked by a cat.

They stepped out of the car and went into the backseat to grab the cats. Elio took both carriers, hoping to prevent another accident. Faye looked on at her house, noticing the lights were already on and a dark blue car was parked in her usual spot. "I'm guessing my new bodyguard is already here." She commented. "Yeah. I hope you don't mind, but I had him let himself in." He replied sheepishly. "I guess it's okay." She sighed, still not happy living with a strange man.

Elio, noticing her demeanor, pulled her in for a tight embrace. "I promise he'll stay out of your way. It'll be fine, my love." He reassured her. "Yeah, I suppose you're right. It might actually be nice living with someone again." She sighed. They leaned in for a kiss when suddenly. "Meow!" "Why!?" If Faye wasn't so fond of these damn cats, he would have had them turned into fur coats a mile back.

Faye let out another giggle, feeling way more relaxed now. "Because he loves you." She replied. "Bullshit. I don't even think that thing is capable of love. The bastard is just pure chaos." He whined, really wishing he could kiss his girlfriend with no interruptions. "Well, let's go then, before these two try to cause a prison riot." She said calmly, leading her lover up the stairs.

The moment they entered the house, Faye unzipped the two carriers, freeing the cats. Caligula and Banshee both booked it down the hallway, finding shelter in her bedroom. She looked around before spotting the red-headed man standing in the kitchen with a blank look on his face. 'Creepy.' She thought to herself, eyeing him suspiciously.

"Leo." Elio sneered, causing the man to look up in fear. "You better protect my Faye and not give her any problems." He warned. "If I find even one scratch on her, it'll be your fucking head." After the threat, he turned to Faye with a soft expression. "I got to get going, doll." He gently kissed her on the lips. "Let me know if you have any problems. Okay?" Faye pulled him into a loving embrace. "I will. Love you." She smiled happily. "Love you too." He responded, shooting one more glare at Leo before leaving.

"So…" Faye spoke awkwardly. "Leo is it?" "Yes." He spoke in a deep, grainy voice. "I guess you can take the spare room. There isn't much in there but my art supplies, but I have an old air mattress I can blow up for you." She rubbed the back of her neck, feeling a bit embarrassed. "That's fine." He spoke blankly. 'Jeez, this is going to be a long month.' "Okay, I'll go grab it." She went down the hall, into the closet to pull out the mattress and some blankets. She snatched up the portable air pump as well before swiftly walking into the spare room.

Faye felt herself cringe at the sight of the room, canvases thrown around haphazardly, trash littering the floor, and paint stains covering the walls. She checked the time, 9:30 at night, and hung her head down. She bent over, picking up all the balled up pieces of paper along with a few cat toys that were lying around. "You don't have to clean it up on my behalf." A voice rang behind her, causing her to jump, dropping the trash. "Jesus Christ, you almost gave me a heart attack!" She exclaimed. "I'm sorry." He spoke blankly. "I can set up the bed myself. Just relax." He waved her off. "Okay…" This was way too awkward. She ended up going back into the kitchen to find herself something to eat.

"Are you hungry?" Faye called to the man. "I'm cooking some chicken and rice." She offered, not wanting to just cook for herself while there was another person in her house. "No, I'm fine." He called back, causing Faye to frown. She was having a hard enough time trying to get a read on this guy. Oh well, she only had to deal with it for a month, and at least he wasn't trying to bother her too much.

Faye went to the bathroom, deciding she should clean up the wounds so they could heal faster. She ran her arms under the hot water, wincing at the feeling of it hitting the cuts. Caligula really did a number on her. She took some disinfectant spray out of the drawer, spraying her arms down before wrapping them up with some bandage wrap.

She went back into the kitchen, preparing her food, feeling guilty that she was only cooking for herself and not for her guest as well. As she began cooking, Leo made his way back into the living room, glancing over at her nervously. She noticed the way he eyed the food she prepared, so she pulled out another chicken breast, not saying a word at all. Once she finished cooking, she silently handed him a plate, taking her down to her room. Leo looked like he wanted to say something but decided against it, instead choosing to eat in silence.

Faye sat in her room, her cats both on their respective perches, watching her with slanted eyes. "I'm sorry I've put you two through so much." She spoke gently to them. "This month is going to be hell for us, I can just tell. I know I'm being selfish by making you two put up with all the strangers and the constant handling. Please stay strong."

Banshee perked up at her warm tone, moving out of her spot to walk towards the girl. Faye tore off a piece of chicken, offering it to the older cat. Caligula jumped off his spot as well now that food was involved. She ripped another piece off, offering it to the orange fluff ball. "Please don't hate me." She begged them. "I love you both, but I also love him, so I hope we can all get along." Both cats curled around her feet, purring happily. She reached down, stroking Banshee's head, as Caligula nuzzled against her wrapped up arm.

She finished up, taking her plate back into the kitchen, her cats following close by. She passed by Leo, who gave her a nod, wearing a neutral expression on his face. 'Still really creepy.' She thought, rinsing her plate off in the sink and putting it in the dishwasher. She headed back to her bedroom, changing into something more comfortable to sleep in. She sent a quick goodnight text to Elio before jumping into her bed, her furry babies jumping in with her. They covered her body, their purrs relaxing her till she drifted off into a deep sleep.

Chapter: 25

Crusty, lifeless, blue orbs slowly blinked opened before instantly wincing at the feeling of the bright sunlight blinding them with its morning rays. Faye curled up into herself as she coughed up spit and mucus that stuck to the back of her dried up throat. Her face was paler than usual, save for the tint of red that covered her cheeks. Breathing through her nose was a near impossible task due to the amount of snot that clogged it up. To say that she wasn't feeling very good was a gross understatement. In her current state, all she wanted to do was shut her eyes and never wake up again.

Her morning alarm went off, piercing further through her brain faster than any knife could do. Reaching over, she swiped the screen, silencing her phone for what she hoped would be an eternity. A part of her wondered if it was even worth it to go to work that day. She was miserable enough without having an entourage of employees jumping her at the worst possible times. Just the thought of it made it even more difficult for her to move. Maybe she should just bite the bullet and call into work. She was planning to quit in a month anyway, so what harm could one little write up do to her?

Just as Faye reached for her phone, it buzzed, showing a new notification on her screen. Elio's name popped up with a message that read: *Good morning doll, call me when you read this.* A cute little heart emoji sat next to the image, causing her to gush over how sweet he was. She was about to hit dial when a thought crept into her head. If Elio found out she was sick, it would surely cause him unnecessary worry and pull him away from whatever important business he needed to attend to.

'I've already caused him enough problems this week. I shouldn't give him anymore.' She thought to herself, realizing she might have no other choice but to go into work. Now that she had one of Elio's men constantly watching over her, there would be no way of hiding her illness from him, and judging by how protective he became after she got interrogated, something told her it would be in her best interest just to suck it up for now. In that case, she'll just have to deal with it by staying hydrated and overly medicating until she can make it home to pass out. Faye had been through this song and dance before and knew how to take care of herself, so there was no need for an overly protective boyfriend to step in.

Faye grabbed her water bottle off the shelf behind her and took a decent sized gulp out of it, hoping it would help soften up her voice a little before she spoke to Elio. If the goal was not to cause him worry, then it would be counterproductive for her to sound like she just got done chain smoking five packs of Newports. The cool, refreshing water helped soothe her inflamed tonsils a little, though it still felt like she swallowed a bunch of lit matches. At least her voice was functional now.

Dialing her boyfriend's number, she waited for it to ring as she stared longingly at the bed. "Hello doll. How are you? Did you sleep well?" Elio answered after two rings, his deep sensual voice pleasantly filling her ears. "I'm fine, just a little sore. What about you?" She said in a somewhat normal voice. "Oh, I'm okay, I suppose, would be so much better if you were here." She could practically feel him smirking through the phone as he spoke. "Well, at least you're okay." Faye said with a hoarse laugh, her voice tuning in and out of the speaker.

Elio paused for a moment, gears turning in his head. "Are you sure you're fine? Cause you don't sound too good." He pointed out, noting her rough voice. Damn, was he good, and she hadn't even been on the phone with him for longer than a few minutes. "I'm fine, honestly." She attempted to wave his concerns off, but he was having none of that at all. "Don't lie to me, doll." He growled in warning. "Okay, fine, I might be coming down with a little head cold, but it ain't anything to worry about. I'll be just fine." She finally admitted with a slight huff. "Will you be?" He asked with skepticism lacing his voice. "Yes, I promise. My area is pretty laid back on Wednesdays, so I shouldn't have it too rough at work. In fact, I'm pretty sure the only task I really need to get done today is entering the prescription logs, which don't involve too much movement."

Faye wasn't sure if she was trying to convince Elio that she'd be fine or if she was trying to convince herself. He had already caught her, so there was really no reason to force herself to go to work, but she felt the need to prove some obscure point to herself. Maybe she was afraid of becoming too reliant on her boyfriend to help her out and needed to prove she could take care of herself, or maybe she figured it was pointless to sit in her room all day wallowing in her own misery. Going to work and toughing it out for the day seemed far more ideal than the alternative. Whatever the reason, she stood her ground and not let him convince her to stay home.

"Are you sure you'll be fine going to work? I don't want you to overexert yourself." He sounded so worried, she nearly gave in. "I promise I will be. I know how terrible my body can get, and this isn't even remotely close to the worst I've ever felt." She insisted, not wanting him to fuss over her. "If you say so, but please don't push yourself too hard, and call me if it gets to be too much." The sincerity in his voice caused her face to turn bright red and her heart to skip a beat. He was just so sweet and caring, it was almost impossible to believe he was the same man that everyone labeled as evil and cruel. "Push myself too hard? Honey, I'm a pharmacy tech, not a construction worker. It's a pretty chill gig." She laughed, downplaying just how much energy it took for her to do her job.

Elio was not amusement by her obvious fibs, knowing just enough about the young woman to know that she most definitely would attempt to push herself past her limits. Unfortunately, he also knew arguing with her would be counterproductive. Faye was as stubborn as they came, so there was no way in hell he could ever convince her that going to work would be a bad idea.

"Just be careful, doll. If you get seriously hurt because your fucked up work decided calling in is the worst sin ever, I swear to fucking God I will hunt your boss down and rip her ugly little head off." He got more and more heated with every word, grinding his teeth at the thought of his precious Faye being forced to work in such awful conditions. "Awe... You really love me, don't you?" She retorted teasingly, not at all concerned by his threat towards her boss. "Of course I love you." His voice softened in his reply, sincerity wrapped around his sweet words. "I love you too." She said just as softly, wearing a goofy smile. "I promise if things get worse, I'll call in tomorrow. Just let me tough out today, alright?"

He thought about it for a moment before he relented. "Okay, I won't murder your boss. *Though kidnapping and trafficking her is still on the table.*" The last part was said in a whisper, almost too quiet for Faye to make out. She ignored his comment, knowing she'd be really pushing her luck by mentioning it. "So what did you want to talk about, anyway?" She completely changed the subject, hoping there would be no more lectures about her health.

"Oh, I almost forgot. I wanted to ask you out to a party I'm attending on Friday night." Elio's whole attitude changed to a more flirtatious tone. He went into detail about what type of party it was and who will be attending. According to him, this party was to celebrate an up-and-coming politician's victory and allow networking between different wealthy officials. There would be a fully serviced bar, a gourmet feast filled with priceless delicacies, and high-class entertainment, not to mention just how exclusive this event was. Of course, all Faye heard was blah, blah, rich people showing off. She had absolutely no interest in attending something so boring and fake, though she knew she didn't have much of an option if Elio was going.

"So, why are you going?" She wondered, curious about his role. "Well doll, the nicest way to put it is, I'm going there to observe and network. You see, I practically run this damn city with an iron fist, so it's important for me to keep up to date on any new *puppets* that could either aid or potentially ruin my rule." *'That wasn't nice at all.'* She thought to herself with a slight giggle. "And is my attendance necessary?" While the question sounded harsh, she intended it to be playful. "Of course it is! You think I want to watch a bunch of jackasses stroke each other's dicks and talk boring political shit? Fuck no! I need a beautiful dame there to keep me entertained." His flirtatious and downright sexy smirk practically traveled through the phone with each word.

A breathy laugh, followed by a small coughing fit, sounded through the line as Faye attempted to gather her bearings. "Wow! You are really selling the party to me." She teased, her voice growing raspy. "I ain't one to sugarcoat things. Just want to let you know what you're really attending. Besides, the real selling point is that you not only get to spend the night with me, but you also get to see politicians piss themselves at the sight of me." She could picture his eyebrows wiggling up and down. "Damn, you really know me!" she laughed. "Now I'm actually excited to go."

Those were the exact words Elio was waiting to hear. "Good, for a second I thought I'd have to tie you up and force you to come with me. Though that doesn't sound like a bad time. I might enjoy the sight of you wearing nothing but rope, tied to my bed, completely spread apart for me to do with as I please." His voice went quieter, taking on a much deeper tone as he rambled off all the things he wanted to do to her. Faye's face flushed bright red at his words before she let out a small cough to catch his attention.

"I want to give you a heads up if I'm attending this type of thing. I can't stand crowds of any kind, so I might be extra clingy with you." She gave fair warning, knowing just how annoying she could be at functions where she only knew one person. "How cute. You really think you'll be allowed to wander off on your own. Oh my sweet little doll, you'll be at my side all night." A sinister tone overtook his voice, making Faye question whether he was reassuring her or threatening her. "Fantastic. It's a date then!" She said in the peppiest tone she could muster up.

They went into a deeper discussion on the details of their up-and-coming date, allowing Faye a better understanding of how it will play out. Elio had already decided he'll be picking her up straight from work, figuring it wouldn't cause any problems for the young woman so long as Leo was around to take care of her cats. Faye nodded along with his plans, her eyelids half opened as she attempted to keep herself awake.

Slowly, her body remembered the illness that had crept up on her in the middle of the night. She could feel her already dry throat grow more and more irritated the longer they conversed. Unfortunately, as much as Faye wanted to talk to her beloved for a longer time, she needed to conserve her energy in order to face her grueling workday.

"I have to get going." She sighed, her voice sad and apologetic as she felt her lover's disappointment through the phone. "If I don't start getting dressed now, I probably won't ever make it out the door." Elio's lips fell down into a frown at her words, annoyed by the thought of his girlfriend hanging up on him. "But I can call you again once I get in the car." As if recognizing his annoyance, she quickly promised the last part, hoping it would appease him. "Oh alright, I let you get off the phone for now, but you better call me the second you sit down in that car." He tried to sound playful, but Faye could detective a hint of seriousness in his tone. "I promise!" She chirped happily, finding his worried nature adorable.

Unfortunately, the moment she ended the call, all the pain and fatigue came back with a vengeance. "Why am I even doing this again?" She asked herself, feeling a cough fit coming on. The moment she felt a tiny, fluffy paw gently swipe at her foot, she couldn't help but smile down at the adorable creature. "Oh yeah, I do this so that you can eat. Isn't that right, Banshee?" She cooed sweetly, scooping up the old lady in her arms and peppering her black and white face in kisses.

Slowly, she forced herself to move, taking one step after another out of the bedroom with her baby in her arms. As she made her way into the living room, she decidedly stopped in front of a bedroom door, the one that sheltered her new roommate. Faye bent down, allowing Banshee to jump out of her arms so that she could knock on the door. A quiet, almost hesitant knock sounded against the old, weakened wood, causing her to wince with every noise.

A part of her really didn't want to wake up the gangster that was assigned to watch her, but she knew her boyfriend would grow frustrated with her if she left him behind. Faye didn't want to admit it, but she found it somewhat scary to be living with a complete stranger, even if he was an employee of Elio. *'Keep it together.'* She thought to herself, shaking her head of all negative thoughts. *'He ain't going to hurt you.'*

Realizing there was no response from the other side, Faye grew irritated at how rude the man was acting. Bang! Bang! Bang! She pounded against the door; her knocks were way louder than before. "I'm getting ready now, make sure you're done in ten." Mentally, she celebrated the fact that she hadn't even coughed once, though that was completely short lived. "I'll be out soon." The man's voice travelled through the door. "Okay, just be qui…" Before she could finish her sentence, she went into a major cough fit, feeling as though her lungs were going to fall out.

"Dammit…" she muttered to herself as she walked away towards the kitchen. "This is going to be a shit day." She complained, pouring herself a cup of water, hoping to ease the tickle in her throat. She debated on whether she wanted to make breakfast or just skip it entirely.

Finally, after a few minutes, Leo finally came out of the room fully dressed. "Are you ready, ma'am?" He asked with a stoic expression. "Yeah, I guess." She sighed, already hating everything about this. "And you don't need to call me ma'am. Faye is okay." He gave her a blank look, as though he had his whole brain removed. "Okay ma'am, whatever you say." She felt her left eye twitch in annoyance. "Let's just fucking go." She grumbled, dragging her feet out the door.

Once they got on the road, Faye pulled out her phone to dial back Elio. "Sorry, I know it's rude, but I promised I'd call once we leave." She smiled apologetically. "Do what you must, ma'am." Leo spoke with a shrug. She called Elio back, her smile widened when she heard his voice. "Hello again, doll, miss me?" He purred. "Of course! But I think my aim is getting better!" She joked, laughing when Elio groaned at the terrible joke. "That was fucking awful doll." He chided. "Oh, it wasn't that bad." She giggled. "So, what did you want to talk about, Elio?"

Leo froze at the name, now listening in fully to their conversation. What could the boss possibly want from her? All Leo had known about her so far was that she had been their boss's latest catch. It wasn't abnormal for Elio to have someone keep guard of the working girls, especially the new ones, while they made the transition over.

He found it odd that she still had a normal 9 to 5 job, but he wasn't one to judge, only to follow orders. Leo thought Faye was nice enough, and pretty cute, though she wasn't his type, and he certainly wouldn't go out of his way to find whatever brothel or club she got assigned to. What he found truly strange was how much involvement Elio insisted on having with her. Parading her around like some trophy, threatening anyone who dared look her way. It almost seemed like he was actually dating the girl.

Listening in on how casually she spoke to him only solidified that fact. She seemed infatuated with the boss. 'Poor, dumb girl.' He thought to himself. 'She's only opening herself up to heartbreak.' Elio would never love her, not in the way she obviously loved him. He probably loved the money he'd end up making off her, the clients she'd bring in. She was an asset to him, nothing more, and the second she overstepped her place, he'd throw her away.

"Okay, have a wonderful day. I love you." She smiled happily into her phone, ending the phone call. "What did the boss want?" Leo asked out of curiosity. "Apparently, he just wanted to hear my voice again." She laughed. "And he said my jokes were cheesy. His are just downright terrible." Leo gripped the steering wheel tightly.

"You really should be careful with what you say about the boss." He warned. "Why?" Faye asked. "He doesn't take too kindly to being disrespected. Especially by one of his working girls." Leo spoke rather bluntly. "Dude, I'm not one of his working girls." Faye retorted, growing sick of this accusation. "And I'm getting tired of people mistaking me for one." She rolled her eyes.

"Ma'am, I know it seems like he's treating you like you're something special, but by the end of this month when you get placed, that'll be it. It would be best for you to just keep your head down and be careful." Leo advised. "Thanks for the advice, but I'll be fine." Faye spoke nonchalantly. "Besides, do you even know where I'm being placed?" She questioned him. "No, nor do I really care." He admitted.

"Though whatever brothel or club you go to, you know you can't have those cats with you, right?" Faye burst out laughing at that. "Sorry, but the cats are a packaged deal. Besides, I'm not going to any clubs or brothels. I can't stand crowds." She retorted. "Well, where do you think you'll end up?" Leo played along. "Ah, never mind." Faye smirked. "You wouldn't believe me if I told you." Leo gave the strange woman a confused glance before turning his attention back to the road, taking her to her destination.

After a long, awkward drive, they finally made it to the hospital. Faye quickly hopped out of the car, embarrassed that she was being driven around like a child. "Thanks for the ride, I guess." She mumbled politely. "What time do you want me to pick you up at?" Leo asked, completely ignoring her gratitude. "Five would be just fine." She replied before she made a dash for the door, attempting to escape this uncomfortable conversation.

"What a strange woman." Leo muttered to himself, thinking back on their conversation. "Very delusional too. Oh well, she learn her place soon enough." His lips fell down into a frown. "It's a shame, though. She seems like a really nice girl."

The day went by quickly for Faye, though she felt even more sore than before. She may have overdone it with her tasks. Between restocking and the constant running around she did, Faye felt absolutely sick. She made her way out back, body feeling weak and head spinning around. She wanted nothing more than to go to bed.

As she made it outside, her phone rang. "Hey Elio." She croaked out. "Doll, is everything alright?" Her worried lover responded, concern etched in his voice. "I may have overworked myself today." She admitted sheepishly. She could hear him sigh. "I think you know what I'm going to say." He said calmly. "I know. I'm going straight home to get some sleep." She promised him. "If I don't feel better by tomorrow, I'll call in." It was as if she had rehearsed these lines all day.

"It might be better if you just come over." Elio spoke gently. "So that I could take care of you." It might have been the splitting headache and her aching bones clouding her judgement, but that honestly sounded nice. "I don't want to be a bother." She responded. "Not a bother. Never a bother." He reassured her. "Now hop in that car and I'll have Leo drive you over to me, alright?" He instructed. "Okay." She agreed. "But what about my cats?" She wondered. "Why don't you bring them with you? They need to get used to your new home, after all." He smirked. "That's a great idea." She agreed without a thought in the world. "I should grab some clothes as well." "Wonderful, I'll see you in a bit, doll." He ended the call.

Elio dialed up Leo's number, satisfied that Faye was in no mood to fight. "Hello?" Leo spoke, not realizing who the caller was. "Leo." Elio snapped. "I need you to drive Faye to her house to collect her things, including her cats, and then take her back to the base." He ordered. "Do not let her lift anything too heavy and be careful with her pets." He warned. "Yes, sir," Leo squeaked out, terrified for his life.

Just as he hung up, Faye made her way back to the car, looking absolutely pale. Leo rolled down the window, looking the girl up and down. "Are you alright ma'am?" He asked, a twinge of worry in his voice. She crawled into the passenger side, resting her head against the cool window. She simply hummed, half asleep. "Alright, let's get you home." He patted her head gently, driving off.

They made it back to the house with no issues. Faye got out of the car, her balance a little off, and made it to the front door. Once inside, she grabbed the two carriers still sitting in the living room, calling for her precious fur balls. The two felines ran in, ready to great their master.

"Leo, can you grab the cat treats?" She asked, her voice still rough. Without saying a single word, the gangster did as she asked, handing over the bag labeled Friskies. She shook out a few treats into each carrier, letting the cats walk into them by themselves. She zipped them up quickly before either could protest.

Faye went to her room, throwing some clothes into a bag and changing out of her scrubs. She walked back into the living room wearing a baggy t-shirt and some sweatpants. Leo gave her a look but said nothing. He quickly took the bag from her. "I already put their food in the car." He informed her, tossing the bag over his shoulder as he grabbed the two carriers. "I can carry something." Faye offered, not wanting to be a nuisance. "It's fine." Leo waved her off. "The boss insisted." She could only nod, her head hurting once again. There wouldn't be any use arguing against an order given by Elio. Well, at least not in the condition she was currently in.

 Faye rested her head against the window of the car, the cool glass feeling nice against her burning forehead. "Do you have a blindfold?" She asked groggily. "Why?" He questioned her. "I can't know the location of his home until I actually move in." She muttered, feeling dazed. "You're moving into the base?" He asked.

She hummed an affirmative, lulling her head back and forth. "He wants me to live with him." She said quietly. Leo went silent, figuring asking anymore questions might cause her some problems. Faye fell asleep after a while, allowing Leo to drive in peace. A part of Leo hoped that the things she said about her relationship with Elio were true, because she seemed nice. Only time would tell, though.

Once they arrived, Elio stood outside, waiting for them. He swiftly made his way towards the passenger side, pulling Faye out of the car without disturbing her. He marched into the building, carrying her bridal style as Leo followed at a distance with her bag and her cats. He made it down the hallway to his room, opening the door quickly, and gently setting her down on the bed. He turned around to grab the items from Leo, giving him the order that they were not to be disturbed.

Elio's scowl quickly faded away the second the door slammed closed, as he turned his attention back to the sickly woman who was completely passed out. He leaned over her form, placing his hand against her forehead to check her temperature. She most definitely had a fever, much to his agitation. He only wished he could have convinced her earlier in the day to come and stay with him for the evening. At least she was with him now, completely safe, and curled up on his bed. "Doll, I swear you're going to be the death of me." He mumbled, running his fingers through her hair.

He went over to the carrier and unzipped them, releasing the two cats. Both came out hesitantly, sniffing around their new environment. He walked back to the bed, crawling in next to the slumbering woman, pulling her close to his chest. The fact that she didn't fight him at all about staying with him while she's sick didn't go unnoticed by him. "Maybe you should get sick more often, doll. That way, you can stay here safe with me." He whispered in her ear. She mumbled something incoherent before nuzzling into him.

Just as he got comfortable, he felt something move at the bottom of his feet. Shooting up, he nearly sent the orange cat flying. Elio scowled at the fluffy menace, only to be met with a smug expression. "If it wasn't for her, I would've skinned you alive and thrown you out for the birds to peck at." He lowered his voice to not wake up Faye. Caligula tilted his head at the mob boss, calling his bluff. He grumbled, falling back against the mattress.

He felt a weight shift between him and Faye. Looking down, he could see Banshee sneak up on the bed and curl up against the unconscious woman. He rolled his eyes, giving the old cat a little scratch around her ear. "You two really like pushing your luck huh?" He chuckled. Caligula crawled over to them, climbing on top of Elio, flopping down next to his head as if he didn't have a single care in the world.

A few hours passed before Faye finally woke up. She still felt terrible, her head dizzy and her joints stiff. She felt herself panic, not recognizing her surroundings immediately. The weight of Elio's arm wrapped over her brought her back to reality. 'Oh, I'm in his room.' She thought. 'Wait, why am I in his room? When did I even get here?'

She started sitting up, only to be pinned back down by Elio. "Rest." He ordered, pressing her tightly against his body. She shuffled in his grip, struggling to lift her head up to look at him. "Doll, please go back to sleep." His voice was so gentle, she wanted nothing more than to obey. "So warm…" she quietly spoke, her voice cracked from the lack of moisture.

Elio unwrapped himself from Faye, pushing himself off the bed. "I'll be back. Don't leave the bed." He told her calmly. She nodded, too worn out to argue. Instead, she rolled over, snuggling into the pillows, her eyes closing shut. Elio melted at the sight of her drifting off. He made his way out of the room, locking the door so that no one got any ideas.

He made his way through the base, his men scattering around him, trying to stay out of his way. Elio moved swiftly to the kitchen, deciding that Faye needed to get some food in her stomach. He also wanted to get her some cold water for her sore throat. He went through a mental checklist of what he needed.

Medicine. Was there anything in the building he could give her, or would it be better to send someone out to grab some? He'd figure that out when he got back to her. He took a few moments to prepare a decent meal for her, hoping she'd appreciate the effort. He grabbed a couple of bottles of water and some orange juice as well, making his way back to his room. His men would throw curious glances his way when he wasn't looking, wondering what his plans were for the unconscious girl.

He unlocked the door, balancing the tray of food with one hand. He entered, closing the door with his foot. Elio set the tray down on the nightstand, scanning over Faye's sleeping form. She was sprawled out, the tuxedo cat threaded between her feet. He looked around the room looking for the orange menace but could not locate him. As if on cue, he heard some whining and scratching coming from the bathroom.

He would deal with that later. For now, his attention would be dedicated to his beloved.

Putting his hand against her forehead, his frown deepened. She still had a high fever. He needed to find some medicine for her as soon as possible. "Doll." He gently shook her. "Wake up." Faye groaned, her eyes slowly opening once again, only to be met with Elio's beautiful fiery orange orbs. "Very pretty…" she mumbled, reaching up to grab his face. He smiled warmly down at her, letting her stroke his cheeks.

"Doll, you have a fever. We need to get that under control." He spoke sweetly. She lulled back and forth, eyes completely blank. "I have some Tylenol in my purse." She slurred out. "That should help reduce the fever." Elio scooped up her purse, looking inside but not finding anything. "Front pocket." She told him. "It's where I keep my pharmacy." She giggled.

He opened the pocket, almost doubling over in laughter. She wasn't kidding about the pharmacy. She, at the very least, had a medicine cabinet in there. "Is half this shit even legal to carry around?" He snickered. "Does it matter?" She retorted, knowing that most of the bottles were over-the-counter pills.

He grabbed one of the water bottles off the nightstand and walked back over to her. He sat on the edge of the bed right next to Faye, helping her sit up. Elio handed her the pills, offering sips of water to help get the medicine down. "There you go. Small sips." He murmured, combing through her hair with his fingers. She got the tablets down along with half the bottle. Her body felt heavy as she felt herself fall back against the bed. Elio caught her before she slammed against the headboard.

"I know you want to go back to sleep, but you need to eat something first, doll." He tutted, once again sitting her up. He pulled the tray off the stand, setting it on her lap. Faye looked at the food in front of her, not realizing how hungry she was. He prepared a simple meal of tomato soup and grilled cheese. She happily took small bites of the sandwich and soup, the warm soup soothing her sore throat.

Elio stood patiently by, feeling nervous over her judgement of the meal. "Thank you, it's really good." She smiled at him, finishing the food quickly. The mobster seemed to relax at her words, taking the tray aside to put back on the stand. "I'm glad you enjoyed it." He sat next to her, feeling her forehead once again. "Still pretty high." He said, more so to himself. "It takes some time for the medicine to kick in. My fever will break once I fall asleep." She reassured him.

Scratching and whining sounded from the bathroom once again. "Caligula." Faye sighed. "Get out of the bathtub." He seemed to listen as he came waddling in smugly. "He likes the bathtub." She explained, leaning against Elio. "They're probably hungry." She said quietly. "I should probably…" She tried pushing herself up but almost lost her balance.

He pulled her back into him so she wouldn't hurt herself. "I can feed them, love, just lay back down." He cooed. "Okay." She agreed, her eyes fluttering closed. "Half a can of wet food each, and a quarter of a cup of dry." She mumbled, as Elio settled her back into the pillows and blankets. He fed them as instructed, making his way back to her, pulling her against him. "Good night doll, I love you so much." He purred against her neck. "Love you too," Faye answered, half asleep.

The next morning, Faye's alarm went off, signaling that she should start getting dressed. She went to reach for her phone, but Elio beat her to it. He silenced the alarm and turned off her other ones as well. "How are you feeling today?" He asked Faye, who was currently snuggled up against his chest. "I feel a little better." She responded quietly. "That's good, but I still can't have you go into work today." He reminded her.

"I don't even want to go in right now." She mumbled, nuzzling into him. "Can we just lie in bed all day?" The young woman requested. "No, we can't, but we can stay in bed for a little while longer," He promised. "Alright..." she agreed. "Can I have my phone back? I need to call and tell them I will not be there."

Elio handed it to her without protest, happy to get his way. She called her work, putting the phone up to her ear, listening to the automated prompts. It took a minute, but she finally got pushed to reception. After spending five minutes on hold, a receptionist finally answered, going through the usual script. "Hey, it's Faye." She started; her voice cracked. "I won't be able to make it in today. I'm not feeling too good." There was a pause on the other end. "That's terrible, Faye. I'll let everyone know. Get better soon." The receptionist replied. She gave a quick 'thank you' and hung up, falling back into Elio's embrace.

"You are being awfully submissive lately." Elio joked. Faye's eyes were half lidded. "Do you want me to put up a fight?" She retorted with a yawn. She felt his chest shake with laughter. "Go back to sleep." He chided. "Fine." She attempted to whine, but it came out as a yawn, causing Elio to laugh once again. She drifted off, wrapped around his torso.

He laid there watching her, memorizing every detail. Elio counted down the days until Faye would fully belong to him. He thought for a moment how easy it would be for him to simply keep her here right now. He didn't have to drive her back to her house. Instead, he could make false promises of taking her home later. Maybe have someone collect her most valuable items. Or he'll just replace everything. She already had her pets. What more could she need?

If she questioned him, he could tell her she was still ill. She needed to take an extra day off to fully recover. He could also destroy her phone completely and keep her in his bedroom for a few weeks. That way, she would have no concept of time and had to rely on his words alone.

He ran through the many ways he could keep her trapped safely with him. He carefully pulled her off him, pinning her slumbering form to the bed with his body. He peppered kisses around her face and neck, listening to her soft mewls and moans. "Doll, you are so precious, so perfect." He purred. "Can I please keep you? I'll take such good care of you, I promise." He groaned against her flesh.

Faye whimpered, snuggling into his touches. "See love? Even asleep, you know who you belong to." He pressed his face into her torso. "I've seen and done some terrible things." He sighed. "Everything in this world is fucking awful, including me." He sat up, pulling her into his lap. "I would happily watch this whole fucking city crumble to the ground." He cradled her in his arms. "And laugh at the pile of corpses trapped under the rubble."

He was careful with his movements, trying not to wake her up. "I started this whole damn gang so I could make that dream happen." He leaned against the headrest, pressing her into his chest. "Did you know you're currently ruining that plan?" He narrowed his eyes at her. "It's okay though, I'm not mad." He softened his features, stroking her hair lightly.

"Everything about you is just so perfect, so wonderful. Nothing in this world matters except you." Faye mumbled his name, nuzzled against his chest. "I just want to love and protect you. Keep you by my side." He continued his quiet speech. "I know I've been pushy with you, but it's only because I need you. I can't stand the thought of you being tainted by this cruel world. But if you insist I wait, I'll do it. Just don't be surprised when I take every opportunity I can to pull you back to me." He laid back down, keeping his arms wrapped around her.

He held her for an hour, watching her sleep. He was almost hypnotized by the way her chest rose and fell. Elio actually had a few things he needed to do, but he didn't want to leave Faye by herself. "I'll just have to bring you with me." He decided with a toothy grin. He pressed himself against her, placing his mouth over hers. "Doll, it's time to wake up." He purred, pushing his tongue past her lips. The one thing he could never get sick of was her sweet taste. "Nymph..." she moaned into the kiss, body still pressed limply against his. He ran his tongue over hers, exploring the inside of her mouth. He began to grind into her, forcing moans out of her.

Elio retracted his tongue once he felt Faye shift underneath him, her eyes barely opening. "Elio?" She questioned, trying to adjust to the light. "There's those pretty eyes of yours." He smiled, leaning down to steal another kiss. "Elio..." she moaned again, kissing back with as much passion and delight as him. "Ah..." she cried into his touch. He pulled away, pushing his face against her neck. She tilted her head, giving him more access to her sensitive flesh. "So sweet." He groaned, inhaling her scent.

He drug his fingers up her leg, resting on her inner thigh. He gave it a squeeze, moving up further, watching Faye's expressions. "I... Ah... Please..." she whimpered, unable to speak fluent sentences. "What's wrong, love?" Elio chuckled darkly. "Cat got your tongue?" He slid up to the hem of her sweatpants, slowly pulling them down.

"Please..." she moaned, the pleasure too much and yet too little. "It'll be okay, doll." He planted a soft kiss on her whimpering lips. "I promised I'll be real gentle with you. You're still recovering from that awful cold, after all." As he spoke, he melded his body over hers, making it impossible for her to escape.

Elio flopped down next to her, letting Faye rest her head on his chest. "You sure you're not hurt?" He asked, rubbing her back soothingly. "I'm fine. You've taken good care of me." She reassured him, hugging him happily. "I'm glad..." He smiled, wrapping his arms around her. "You deserve the best."

They snuggled together for a few more minutes, Faye almost drifting off again when Elio's phone went off. He groaned in annoyance at the interruption, causing the young woman to giggle against his chest. "Oh, shut it." He ruffled her hair playfully.

"What?" He snarled into the phone, ready to end the life of whoever disrupted his moment of peace. "My apologies." A deep voice sounded over the phone. "But I was wondering if you were on your way?" The speaker sounded nervous. "I'll be there in an hour!" Elio snapped, teeth bared. "O-okay!" They stuttered quickly, hanging up on him.

He turned his attention back to Faye. "Sorry about that, doll. I hope it doesn't scare you too much when I yell like that." He said sheepishly. "It's fine. I don't find you scary." She mumbled, blushing. She actually found it attractive when he put on his Mob boss persona, but she'd never admit that.

He started pulling himself up, keeping his arms wrapped around her so she'd move with him. "Alright, doll, let's get cleaned up so we can start heading out." He rose from the bed, holding her in his arms, carrying her off to the bathroom. He set her down, shooing off the orange menace.

"He really likes you." Faye hummed. "Yeah, likes to annoy me." Elio grumbled. "Now get your ass in the shower." She stuck her tongue at him before walking in with him following behind, pushing her up against the tiled wall. "You're such a brat sometimes, you know that?" He pressed his body against hers, causing her to squeak out in surprise.

He lowered his head, his teeth dangerously close to her neck as she tilted her head, allowing him more access to do as he pleased. "There she is… My beautiful, submissive girlfriend." He cooed against her neck, biting down on her soft spot. Faye moaned his name, happy to be claimed by him. "Let's get you cleaned up, doll." He purred. "Before you make me even more late."

Chapter: 26

After almost 30 minutes, they finally made it out of the shower, leaving Faye's skin covered in bruises and bite marks, and her legs shaking badly. Elio held a smug expression on his face, pulling the flustered woman back into the bedroom. "Oh look doll, we're going to be really late now because of you." Elio teased. Faye had a hard time catching her breath, so all she could muster up was a scowl which appeared as more of a pout.

"Awe. Don't look at me like that. I might just throw you on the bed and go a third round." Elio patted her damp hair. Faye could only stare wide eyed, still figuring out how to speak again. Her silence only caused Elio's grin to widen triumphantly. She went to her bag, pulling out some pants and a t-shirt, quickly throwing them on, before walking, limping, back over to him. She wrapped her arms around him, leaning into his chest as he straightened out his tie. "Alright doll, let's get going." Elio said sweetly, scooping up the girl and carrying her out of the room.

The two were back on the road, Faye still clinging to Elio, trying her hardest to stay awake. "This guy we're going to see is a real piece of work." He explained, arm wrapped around her. "He trains strippers and escorts, before selling them off to gangs like mine." Faye listened to his every word. The man he described sounded awfully familiar.

"He not only sells whores, he also buys them, too. He is also really fucking persistent. If there's a girl he wants, he'll do whatever he can to have her. Pain in my ass, really. He ain't too kind to his girls either. Heard if they don't perform too well, he'll beat and fuck them till they're holding hands with death." Faye's face darkened, knowing full well who he was talking about. She met him a handful of times when she went to visit May. Often he mistook her for a prostitute, and would treat her as such.

"I will not play nice with him." Faye spoke bitterly, as though she had this conversation before. Elio gave her a look, asking her to explain. "You're talking about Joey, right? I won't let him ever disrespect me again." She informed him. "I wouldn't ask you to," Elio spoke after a moment of silence. "I'll rip his fucking head off if he even thinks about harassing you." She snuggled closer, satisfied with his response, as he stroked her head soothingly.

Once they made it to the meetup spot, Elio jostled Faye awake. He exited the car, offering his hand to help the groggy woman out, pulling her into a loving embrace. They walked into the building, which, by the looks of it, was some sleazy adult toy shop. The smell of sweat, rubber and lube invaded her nostrils, making her face scrunch up. Elio strolled through the shop, nodding at the clerk knowingly before making his way towards a back door with Faye by his side. Two of his men followed close behind, faces blank of any emotion.

Once inside, Faye spotted the object of her disgust. A man in his late thirties sat at the edge of a table, his cold eyes hidden behind sunglasses. He had a mole right under his left eye that Faye secretly wished was cancerous from all his years of tanning. His skin held the texture and appearance of leather, with wrinkles around his face that made him look older than he actually was.

The man held a smug expression that Faye swore was stuck that way. He wore a heavy migraine causing cologne that made her feel sick. This guy was definitely the jackass that would often meet with May, trying to talk her into selling some of her girls to him. He even offered a pretty penny for Faye, though that offer had been turned down for obvious reasons. Faye had always remained polite with this man, not wanting to cause any problems for May, though she had a limit, and he always pushed past it.

"So you want to tell me again why you called me all the way the fuck out here, Joey?" Elio snarled, pulling Faye onto his lap as he took a seat. "Oh Elio, always so crude. Even in the presence of a little lady." He smirked, eyeing Faye up and down. "But for your sake, I'll get to the point. I know you recently got some new properties from May. Well, word is, she got rid of all her girls."

Faye groaned internally, already not liking where this was going. "While I'm bitter that she didn't even approach me with any offers, I managed to track down the majority of her ex-employees." He again eyed Faye up and down, his wandering gaze did not go unnoticed by Elio.

"Keep staring and I'll rip out your eyeballs." He threatened, his grip on Faye tightening. "Sorry." Joey quickly apologized. "I didn't mean to ogle the merchandise, though I am curious how much you paid for that one. I could have sworn May stated she wasn't for sale." He attempted to make it look like he wasn't still looking at her. "I ain't for sale, you scumbag," Faye snapped.

Joey's expression darkened at her words. "You better watch your fucking mouth." He warned. Elio narrowed his eyes, ready to beat this man to death. "Oh, shove it up your ass, patient zero!" Faye retorted before Elio could even move. "Patient zero?" The mob boss questioned. "It's a nickname me and May came up with a while back. Because we're pretty damn sure every STD known to man started with him." She explained, causing Elio to snicker as he rested his chin on top of her head.

"Disrespectful little bitch. Elio, you outta give this one to me. She's obviously not trained at all, doesn't even know when to keep her mouth shut. I can teach her a thing or two about respect." He sneered at her.

"First, I have more respect for cow shit than I do for you. Second, how many fucking times do I have to tell you, I'm not a whore! And even if I was, I'd rather walk into a burning building and let the flames engulf my body than sleep with you. Based on how many women willingly fucked you, I'd say that feeling is unanimous. I've talked to some of the girls you've slept with, and they said they'd rather shove a cactus up their hole than ever see your wrinkly ass naked again."

Joey stood up from his seat, veins popping out of his head, as his face burnt up in anger. He lifted his hand, prepared to swing at her with his fist clenched. Faye glared at the man, daring him to hit her, unaware of the dangerous look Elio was giving him. Joey hesitated. The deadly stare directed at him made his blood run cold.

"I hope you aren't planning on hitting my girlfriend." Elio warned him, his tone held a venomous bite to it. "Girlfriend?" Was all he could manage, fear causing his muscles to freeze up. "Yes, *my* girlfriend." He emphasized, his nails digging through Faye's t-shirt. "And hearing you talk about defiling her is starting to really piss me off." He growled, tightening his embrace.

Joey, a bit shaken up, sat back down in his seat. Faye put her hand on top of Elio's hand, slowly stroking small circles, causing his grip to relax. As much anger and resentment as she held for this man, she didn't want to make Elio to upset, especially on her behalf. Her fights should be her own after all. Also, this was her favorite shirt, and she would really prefer that it stayed in one piece.

"I apologize again, Elio." Joey quickly gathered his bearings, playing off that he wasn't absolutely terrified of the giant mobster. Faye had to give him credit. Joey was pretty good at remaining cool in hostile situations. She could even remember walking in on May, shooting him in the leg, and the asshole laughing it off. If the man wasn't such a shit stain on Satan's underwear, she may have had some respect for that, instead she told May to aim higher next time.

"I only want to talk business with you. I'll leave the little who… Lovely lady." He corrected himself, "Alone. Now, back to the topic at hand. I thought you might need some more girls to fill out your new clubs, and I got what you need. I recently ended up with a bunch of new girls, fresh off the street, completely submissive and willing to do anything." He smirked.

Faye rolled her eyes, sighing softly at his sales pitch. She played with Elio's hands, trying to distract herself from the conversation. "How beat up are the girls?" Elio inquired, not actually interested but keeping an open mind. "Only a bit," Joey admitted, "but it's hardly noticeable, and all their wounds will heal. Ain't nothing a little makeup couldn't cover up." He rationalized. They continued their discussion. Elio, honestly, not wanting to make any purchases from this man. Faye could feel Joey's eyes drift over to her every so often, causing her to shudder in disgust.

"Out of curiosity…" Joey said after fifteen minutes of trying to sell to the mob boss. "Out of all the whores, why did you choose this one? I know she's one of May's, so she's got to have some talent, but that red-headed bitch had way nicer girls to pick from." He rambled on a bit. Faye could feel Elio's nails digging in again as his face turned red with rage.

"You know Joey…" Faye spoke through clenched teeth. "There's this lovely pig farm near my brother's house. Not too much traffic goes out there, and the owners don't get along with the authorities. I go out there with my brother all the time to help them with feeding." Joey felt his eye twitch. Elio simply listened, trying to figure out where she was going with this.

"I'm pretty careful out there. Pigs are dangerous after all, especially when they're hungry." "What the fuck are you talking about?" Joey finally snapped. "All I'm saying…" Faye glared at him. "Is that if you keep talking shit, that's where you'll end up, and I promise it will be during feeding time." She threatened.

The room went silent with all eyes on the woman. Elio eased up his grip, moving his hands up to her shoulders, rubbing them softly. He's never heard her sound so cold before, her threats seemingly genuine. "I think we're done here." Elio finally spoke, causing the eyes to go back to him. "If I spend another second in this room with you, I'll end up smashing your fucking head through the table." He narrowed his eyes, rising from his spot with Faye in his arms. They left without another word as Joey's mouth hung open, his smug expression completely gone.

Once they were out of the building, Elio set Faye down, kissing the top of her head. "I'm so sorry doll, I didn't expect him to get that nasty with you." He spoke so tenderly. "I should be the one apologizing for causing you trouble like that," Faye laughed sheepishly. "I'm usually better at keeping my composure, and I know I shouldn't have gone off like that." Elio let out a hearty laugh, pulling Faye into a tender kiss.

"Are you kidding? Listening to you put him in his place was so fucking entertaining. And that pig farm threat… Fucking hell." Faye shrugged. "Apparently, those pigs could devour a human body within minutes, according to the owners." Elio rolled his eyes. "I know it's weird coming from me, but you should probably stop hanging around criminals."

Faye giggled at his comment, hugging him tightly. "I refuse." She retorted. "Besides, how else will I come up with these weird fucking stories to confuse you with?" Elio laughed at this. "You know, every day I fall more and more in love with you, right?" He sighed into her hair.

He had one more place to be at, debating with himself on whether he should bring Faye in with him. Unfortunately, his only other option would be to leave her in the car, which could put her at serious risk of being abducted. "Alright doll, I just have one more meeting and then we can go home." He promised her, taking her hand in his. They walked hand in hand, Faye trying to match his pace as they entered a warehouse.

Once inside, Elio pulled her close to him, kissing her temple lightly. "Stay close to me, alright. I'm meeting with a couple of members over some missing packages, and it could get pretty messy." She grabbed onto his arm, nodding in understanding.

There were ten men lined up, all looking down, dread etched on all of their faces as if they already knew what their fate was. Elio went stoic, his facial features unreadable. Faye stayed quiet, not wanting to interfere with his business. "Where the fuck did my drug shipment go!?" He yelled at them, anger laced in his voice. "Sir, I can explain." One grunt pleaded. "The shipment came up a few bundles short." He averted his eyes a few times, going into the explanation of how they were shorted by the supplier. 'He's lying…' Faye thought. 'And judging by Elio's grip on me, he knows the moron is lying.' She pressed her face against him, having no intention of witnessing what he was surely going to do.

"Even if I were to believe that shit, you're seriously going to tell me you were so incompetent that you didn't even bother to fucking count the packages to make sure everything was there!?" He blew up at them. "I'm fucking done hearing your excuses! I already had Tony search through your fucking shit! Three fucking bundles! Did you really think you'd get away with fucking stealing from me!?"

'I wonder how things are going at the hospital.' Her mind drifted away from the current situation. Elio pulled out his gun, ready to shoot down the ten men. "You fuckers are lucky I have my girl with me today, otherwise, your deaths would be far more painful." He sneered. "Doll, cover your ears. I don't want the noise causing you any problems."

Faye did as she was told, remaining wrapped up in his arm. Even with her ears covered, the gunshots still echoed in her head, and before she knew it, all the men laid cold on the floor, dead. 'Did I feed the cats this morning?' She asked herself, covering her nose, the stench of smoke and gunpowder surrounding her.

Elio lifted her face up, his eye no longer cold and deadly. "How are you feeling, doll?" He asked, concerned he might have scared her too much. "Tired and hungry." She answered nonchalantly. "Otherwise I'm fine." He was taken aback by this answer, expecting her to be a little more terrified than she appeared to be. His shocked expression quickly turned into a smirk as he pushed her up against his body. "Let's grab some lunch, then we'll head home, okay?" She nodded, letting out a yawn. Elio picked her up, carrying her back to his car.

After grabbing a bite at some diner nearby, they made their way back to the base. Faye was curled up in Elio's lap, in a deep sleep, as he gingerly combed through her hair. "Oh doll, I'm going to have to take you back soon, aren't I?" He murmured, eyes glued to her peaceful face. "Do you really want to go back to that run-down shack?" He asked, not expecting a response. "Want to stay… With you…" she breathed quietly. "What did you say?" He asked her to repeat herself. "Stay with you…" she repeated, still very much asleep. "That's what I thought you said." Elio smirked, a sinister look in his eyes. "Whatever my doll wants, she gets."

Tired blue eyes slowly fluttered open as Faye once again found herself in the bed of the deadly mob boss. The man in question laid underneath her, holding her tight against his bare chest. She attempted to shift around, trying to escape his grasp, but he was far too strong for her. "Doll, would you stop squirming?" Elio Growled into her ear. "You ain't going anywhere."

She relaxed, knowing it was futile to fight him. "What time is it?" She asked, trying to gage how much longer she had left with him. "Does it matter?" He retorted, flipping her over so that she was trapped underneath him. "I mean, kind of." She laughed, thinking he was just messing with her. "I still have work in the morning. You know that, love."

Suddenly, he had his lips pressed against hers, shoving his tongue into her mouth. He tasted of coffee and honey, a whole new flavor profile she'd never tasted on him before. Faye couldn't help but whimper out, begging him to let her breath. Finally, after a couple of minutes, he pulled away, licking his lips.

"None of that nonsense, my love." He murmured against her neck. "You're mine now, and you know it." Her face flushed bright red as the gears started turning. "Oh, you're serious." She whispered, more so to herself than to him. "Yes, I am," He confirmed, diving back in for another kiss. "I got you and your pets here. I don't see any reason for you to leave."

Faye gave him a look of pure shock, unsure of what to say. "Elio, be real… You're not actually planning to keep me here, are you?" She asked worriedly. "Yes, I am," He confirmed again, nuzzling against her neck. "I thought we talked about this." She laughed nervously. "Oh, we did." He retorted as he sat up, pulling her into his lap. "But after your little confession, I realized you really don't want to leave." He started peppering kisses around her jawline, earning soft mewls.

She looked at him with wide eyes, confused at what he meant by confession. "In your sleep, you told me you wanted to stay with me. I am here to please you, so if that's what you want." He smirked, applying pressure to her soft spot. "I… Mph… Never said… I didn't…" she cried out, trying to pull away from him.

"I already told you." He bit down against her spot, causing her to tear up from the pain and pleasure. "You ain't going anywhere." He sat up, sliding her into his lap, as he continued his assault on her neck, leaving marks she could already tell were going to be a pain to cover up. "Elio… Mph… Ah… Please stop… It's too much…" she begged him, but he didn't let up.

"What's wrong, my love?" He asked playfully, sliding his hands up to her chest. "I thought you loved my touch." He began to rub and squeeze her breasts, drawing out adorable little mewls from her. "You're so cute, you know that?" He cooed, messaging her mounds. "I really am planning to keep you here. There's no point in sending you back when you're better off with me." Faye looked at him with half-lidded eyes, faces bright red and tear stained.

"I want to stay with you." Her voice was soft and meek. Elio smiled triumphantly at her words. "But…" She averted her gaze, not wanting to see the look of disappointment he would surely give her. "I need to go back." He narrowed his eyes, his smile falling to a frown. "Why?" He growled, angry that she was still going to argue against him. "Am I not good enough!?" Faye winced, her heart racing.

"Elio…" She gently grabbed his face, pulling his head down to hers. "I really want to be with you, but I have to be careful about it." She sighed. "You're right when you said I don't owe my coworkers anything. And if my only problem was work, I'd quit immediately. I love animals, but I don't feel any real attachment to my work. Some days I actual dread going in. My problem is my friends and family. While the friends who actually matter are aware of the situation, I don't think they understand what it fully entails for me to move in with you. Okay, Atlas and May do, which is why they are so pissed off at me. But all my other friends don't get it. I haven't even told my family yet, and I owe them, at the very least, an explanation." She felt ashamed of herself. "I just don't want to let anyone down."

Elio stared at Faye, his eyes unreadable. "Doll…" His voice was soft and soothing. "All I want to do is make you happy. I hope you understand that?" He kissed her lips tenderly. "I'm not a very patient man, and I'm worried everyday you're not with me." He confessed. "But I'm willing to cooperate if that is what you truly want, but only if you promise me one thing." Faye tilted her head, her beautiful jewels wide with wonder.

"I want you to promise me you won't put yourself in any dangerous situations." He almost sounded desperate. "I don't understand what you're asking." She admitted sheepishly. "Look, doll, I know how you are. As sweet and caring as you are, you have a big mouth on you, and you always seem prepared to fight. I love this about you, and I'll always have your back in any fight, but it gets difficult when you're not with me." He explained.

"You realize I've always been like that, right? I mean, I've been fine so far." She tried to reassure him, though it didn't quite help. "I understand that, but it's completely different now. You're not just going up against random everyday assholes now. There is a much bigger target on your back, which is only going to grow if word gets out that you were May's apprentice. The world is against you now and you're practically cornered. There ain't a single favor in that book of yours that could possibly help. All you can do now is keep your head down and your mouth shut."

He looked terrified when thinking about all the terrible things that could happen to his precious Faye. Her expression softened at that realization. She ran her thumb over his cheek, pulling him out of his panic. "Look Elio, I will not pretend to be terrified, but for your sake, I promise I'll keep my head down and not cause any problems." She agreed, much to his relief. "I love you so much. I hate seeing you so upset because of me." She admitted before softly kissing his lips.

"Okay fine." He relented. "I'll let you go back to your house." He said, nuzzling her neck. "Wait, you really would not let me leave?" She rose an eyebrow at him, causing him to laugh. "Now doll, if I find out you did something fucking stupid that put yourself in danger, there will be consequences." He warned, earning an eye roll from the stubborn woman. She never seemed to take any of his threats seriously.

"Okay, but what time is it?" She asked again, this time getting a real answer. "6PM my love. Plenty of time to cuddle." He purred, pulling her back down to the bed and dragging her under the covers. They stayed like that for who knows how long, enjoying each other's company. She enjoyed these little moments where they could just talk without a care in the world.

She would often go into some ramble about a show she liked or hobby she was into which Elio listened to, loving the sound of her speaking. He never made her feel like she spoke too much and would give his input every so often just to reassure her he was listening. His favorite thing to get her to talk about was her weird dreams she had. The worlds she would find herself in intrigued him. "So you threw yourself off a cliff because you were bored?" He asked in disbelief. "I was 80% sure I was dreaming." She shrugged. "And nothing was happening, so I figured I would wake myself up. Or die…" She laughed. "You're so fucking weird." He chuckled, kissing her neck.

Caligula made his way up on the bed, stalking toward the snuggled up couple. "He knows we can see him, right?" Elio side-eyed the cat. "I just let him have his fun." She nuzzled into the mobster. Just as she spoke, the Maine coon pounced, grabbing Elio's arm with soft paws. He pulled his arm away, much to the cat's dismay, trying to shoo him off.

"Go on, orange menace, leave us alone." He grumbled as Faye stifled a giggle. Caligula wouldn't relent though, and with determination in his eye, he jumped again, climbing onto Elio's shoulders. The young girl burst out in laughter, shoving her face into his chest to muffle herself a bit. "You proud of yourself?" He grumbled to the smug cat. "Told you he likes you." She grinned into his shirt.

Elio begrudgingly brought Faye back to her house, still not wanting to let her go. He made Leo take the cats back in a separate vehicle, not in any mood to listen to them howl. Once they made it to her house, Faye attempted to open the car door, only to be pulled over to the large man. "Doll…" He purred, pressing his lips against hers in a sensual kiss.

"Remember your promise to me. Play nice, or else." His voice took on a more sinister edge, causing goosebumps to run up her arms. "I will." She whined, letting his appendage invade her mouth. "Also, once you get off work, you're staying with me for the weekend, alright?" Faye spoke a muffled okay against his lips, her arms wrapped around his neck.

Elio pulled away, a string of saliva connecting them. "How about one more for the road?" He winked at her, causing her to blush. He leaned against her neck, sinking his sharp teeth into her soft spot. She moaned out, feeling his tongue trace over the bite mark as he sucked against her skin.

"What is… Mph… with… Ah! Ah! Your obsession with… Oh god… My neck?" She cried, pushing herself harder against him. "You just taste so amazing. I can't help myself." He smirked against her bruised skin. "You also make such adorable sounds." He peppered small kisses up and down her neck, making his way to her collarbone. "I can't wait until tomorrow night, when I can have you over and over, begging and crying my name." He groaned against her. "I'll be looking forward to it." She mumbled, smiling yearningly. He let her leave the car, and watched as she entered the house, making sure she got inside safely. "Until tomorrow, doll…"

Once inside, she spotted Leo sitting on the couch, reading one of her books. "How you feeling today, Ma'am?" He asked, not even bothering to look up. "Better than yesterday." She said, walking into the kitchen to grab a cup of water. "Glad the boss didn't get too angry at you." He commented. "Why would Elio be mad at me?" She raised her eyebrow at him. "Getting sick like that before your even placed. When the boss had me bring you to the base, I thought for sure he was gonna kill you."

Faye shot him a glare, flipping the gangster off. "Oh, shove it up your ass. Elio would never hurt me. He loves me too much." She shot back at him, causing the man to snicker. "You keep telling yourself that, crazy lady." She walked back to her room without another word, ignoring whatever look Leo was giving her. 'She better hope that hickey heals before she's placed. That will definitely turn away potential clients.' He sighed, turning his attention back to the book.

Faye woke up the next morning to her third alarm going off. She shot out of bed, running into the bathroom as quickly as possible. "Shit! I overslept." She cursed herself for rushing to get dressed for work. After a quick five-minute shower, she got her scrubs on and began gathering her things. Her phone went off with a notification from Elio. *Good morning my love.'* She smiled to herself, sending back a good morning text of her own before walking into the living room.

There she spotted Leo, sprawled out on the couch, his body twisted up. She rolled her eyes, walking back into the bathroom to grab some ibuprofen from her medicine cabinet and went into the kitchen to grab a glass of milk. "Hey, wake up." She told the slumbering gangster. "I can't afford to be late." Leo nearly fell off the couch, suddenly being awoken by the young woman. She snickered a bit at his clumsiness.

He rubbed his neck, trying to kneed out the stiffness from the position he slept in. "Here." She handed him the pills. "What are these?" He eyed her suspiciously. "Vicodin." She deadpanned, causing him to look at her funny. "It's just ibuprofen. It should help with the pain you'll surely be in sleeping like that. Take them with a glass a milk, otherwise it'll mess up your stomach." She informed him. He took the pills and the glass of milk gratefully.

"You gonna actually walk around with that hickey?" He questioned her. "Hickey?" She asked, pulling out her phone to check herself in the camera. "Are you fucking kidding me!?" she whined in exasperation. "I really don't want to wear a sweater again. It's far too warm." She grumbled. "Why don't you just cover it up with makeup?" Leo suggested. "Makeup?" She tilted her head at him. "You know the thing you wear to in order to look pretty." He teased her. She, in return, threw a pillow, smacking him right in the face. "Jackass." She stuck her tongue at him. "I know what makeup is. I just don't know how to put it on like that." He looked at her funny. "Seriously?" She gave him a look, causing him to sigh. "Alright, come on."

He led her to the bathroom. "Where do you keep your makeup bag?" He asked. "Under the sink." She responded, trying to figure out what he was up to. He grabbed the bag, pulling out some supplies from it. "This'll only take a moment, sis." He told her. 'Sis?' She thought. 'That's a new one.' After some poking and struggling, he finally finished up. Showing off the end results of his work. "Wow, you did an amazing job." She praised him, checking out his handy work. "Thanks, sis." He grinned at her. "But we should really head off before you're late. Again." Her eyes widened in worry. "Shit!" She panicked, running out of the bathroom, grabbing her things, Leo following at a casual pace behind her, giving the older cat a gentle pat on the head before leaving.

Faye ended up being around fifteen minutes late to her shift. She sighed, rubbing her temples to soothe what she was sure would be a headache of a day. Two steps into the building and she got pulled into the office to discuss her attendance. "Faye, I know you're leaving in a few weeks, but you really need to be on time." Rachel scolded her. "And with yesterday's absence, you could face termination, which I really don't want to do." She sighed.

"I know..." Faye looked down. "Yesterday, I was barely able to keep my eyes open." That was kind of true. "And I was extremely sore." Definitely from the sinus infection and not from other activities. "Trying to work in that condition would have been dangerous for the patients." Elio would have never allowed her to, anyway. "But I understand how unprofessional it is and if you feel the need to fire me, there are no hard feelings." She kept calm, not too worried about losing her job. She was quitting anyway. She had little to lose. Rachel shook her head. "No, I think we're good here." She sent Faye back off to work without another word.

"Faye!" The lead kennel attendant, Alice, came running out to greet the pharmacy tech. "Holy shit, you won't believe it!" she exclaimed. "What?" Faye replied, confused by her work friend's sudden appearance. "It's about Chuck." Her voice suddenly went into a whisper so as not to gain any unwanted attention.

Faye's eyes rolled at the mention of that man's name. "Ugh. What is it this time? Did they end up taking his sorry ass back? It was just getting peaceful here, too." She spat in disgust. "No, it's even crazier than that. Apparently he went missing, hasn't been seen since last Friday." She announced like it was the biggest news of the century.

"Well, maybe he ditched town." She shrugged, attempting to remain rational. "I mean, he was a pretty shady guy, always up to something." Alice gave her a sly smile. "I don't think so. There's security footage of him leaving Friday night with a couple of men all wearing red. The cops came around this morning after his wife apparently filed a missing person's report. I could only hear a bit of what they discussed with the manager, but I heard something about the Crimson Kings."

Faye's face went pale at the mention of her boyfriend's gang. "So wait, they really think a gang is involved?" She asked, trying to play it cool. "It's not just a gang, it's the fucking mafia. You know what kind of dumb shit you have to do to piss off the mafia?" She asked, excitement in her voice. "I can only imagine." Faye said, trying not to sound too nervous. "If they're really involved in his disappearance, then the cops might not even be able to find the body. Chuck might be gone forever." Alice was far too excited about this.

"Hey, you know, it happened right after you left. Did you see anything?" She suddenly asked, putting Faye on the spot. "No, nothing. I was kind of in a hurry after the whole Choco incident, so anything after that has nothing to do with me." She spoke a bit too fast.

Alice eyed her suspiciously, trying to get inside her head. "Okay, if you say so. Just don't go around wording things like that. People will think you're weird." She teased, patting the tech's shoulder. "I'll see you around, Faye." She waved goodbye. "See you."

She stood in the pharmacy for a couple minutes with a million questions running through her head. What happened to Chuck? Is he dead? Did Elio kill him? She shook her head, trying to rationalize it.

Elio couldn't have actually killed him, at least not without a good reason. Besides, why would he do something that would send the cops to her workplace? She kept telling herself that over and over as she got to work. She could always ask him later as well, just to ease her mind. She really didn't want to be in that interrogation room again, especially over something that might involve her.

During her shift, she received random calls from an unknown number. They didn't leave any voicemail to identify themselves, and Faye was not too keen on answering her phone to some stranger. As she was getting ready for a break, her phone buzzed, this time with a text. *'Answer your phone. -LE'* As if on cue, her phone rang again with the same unknown number. She fled the pharmacy to go back into the kennel, finding an empty cage to hide in.

"Hello?" she answered politely, unsure if she should be talking to some stranger with all things considered. "Hello! Hello!" A familiarly enthusiastic voice rang through. She couldn't quite place the voice with a name. "Do I know you?" She ripped the Band-Aid off and ask. "Awe you don't remember?" He fake pouted.

"I'm better with faces than voices." Faye shrugged, not sure what to tell the man. "Why don't you guess first? I'll give you three chances and then I'll tell you." Why is this person so insistent on her remembering his name?

"Alright, I'll play. But I get a hint." She gave in. The person on the other end gave a light laugh. "I knew you'd play with me. Alright, for the hint, I'm bright and bring you warmth." Faye groaned internally. "I said a hint, not a riddle." She whined, only to be met with a snicker. She let out a sigh, thinking of who it could be. Bright and brings warmth. "Luciano?" She asked. "Ding! Ding! You got it!" He cheered, causing the young woman to giggle.

"So why are you blowing up my phone in the middle of work, huh?" She held a more casual tone, leaning against the metal bars of the cage she hid in. "Would I have actually been able to talk to you outside of work?" He shot back at her. "Elio doesn't like me too much and I highly doubt he'd ever give me and Cosimo another chance to contact you again." She couldn't argue with that logic.

"That's all fine and dandy, but I only have thirty minutes to chat, so what's up?" She moved the conversation along. "Sorry to take up your time, but there are a few things I wanted to discuss." Faye rose an eyebrow at this. "I feel like I should contact my lawyer first." She retorted. "Oh starlight, there's no need for that. Nothing in this phone call would be allowed in a courtroom, anyway." He tried to persuade her, causing her to roll her eyes.

"It's always comforting to hear a cop say I don't need a lawyer." Luciano chuckled at this statement. "I promise I'm not calling to harass you. I'm just doing a wellness check." He sounded so sincere. "Wellness check?" She questioned. "Yeah, I just want to make sure you're safe, especially with you know who," He explained.

"If you're referring to Elio, I'm fine." She pouted. "He treats me good." Luciano sighed into the phone, expecting an answer like this. "I'm telling you the truth." She insisted. "I'm not calling you a liar." He retorted. "You're implying it." She snapped back.

"Faye." Luciano's voice went serious. "I know you didn't show up to work yesterday." Faye rolled her eyes in annoyance. "And? I was sick. It happens." She replied. "Check your phone." He demanded, as a notification went off. She opened it up, revealing photos of her with Elio from the previous day.

"Okay? Besides the stalkerish pictures, what's wrong with them? Yes, I spent the day with him. I wasn't feeling well, and he offered to take care of me. That is a normal thing for couples to do." She said. "Is it also normal to walk around with all those bruises?" Faye nearly choked on air. "W-what bruises!?" she sputtered out.

"Oh please, I can spot the dark spots all around your arms and neck. Don't pretend those weren't his doing." Luciano spoke the accusation so earnestly. She turned bright red, stumbling on her words. "Are you trying to insinuate that he's been beating me!?" she squeaked out. "The bruises speak for themselves, Starlight." Faye groaned out in embarrassment.

"Oh my god, I'm gonna murder Elio." She mumbled to herself. "He's not beating me!" She exclaimed, forcing the detective to pull away from the phone. "If he ain't hurting you, then how did you end up with all those bruises?" He wondered. "I ain't answering that." She spoke dryly. "Look Luciano, I appreciate the concern, but I'm fine. I know Elio would never hurt me."

"I don't want to argue with you about him." He spoke calmly. "You're obviously in far too deep with him for me to pull you out. I just want you to be careful. Just because he's sweet on you doesn't mean his isn't dangerous." Luciano lectured. "If anything happens, I need you to contact either me or Cosimo immediately so we can get you out of there." Faye was getting tired of these brothers treating her like she's fragile.

"I'll be fine. I don't need any more people worrying about me. Besides, I already promised Elio I would stay out of trouble." Luciano's eyes widened at this. "He wants you out of trouble?" he asked skeptically. "Yeah, apparently I attract danger and he doesn't want me to get myself killed. He even got mad at my cat for scratching me." She replied with a smile. He went into another fit of laughter.

"Wow, you're really turning the big bad Elio into a big old softy!" He laughed. "I knew you'd be a good influence on him!" Faye laughed at this. "Darn, and here I thought I was gonna be the devil on his shoulder." She teased. "Yeah, right!" he snorted. "You're probably the best thing about Elio." She scrunched her nose up at that. "Hardly." She said quietly to herself.

"Well, it was nice talking to you again, but I must get back." She told him. "Alright." He pouted. "Maybe don't tell Elio about this conversation, so he doesn't prevent us from contacting you." He suggested hopefully. "Awe Luciano. You know I'm going to tell him the second we hang up." She retorted. "It would be dumb for me not to." She could hear his disappointment through the phone. "Alright, Starlight, I understand. Just be careful and call us if you're in any trouble, alright?" Faye agreed, pressing the end call.

"Well that, took 15 minutes of my lunch away." She pouted. "Oh well, time to waste the last 15 minutes." She pressed the call button on Elio's number, listening to the ringing. "Hello doll." He answered. "Hi Elio!" she greeted cheerily, her heart racing. "What can I do for you?" Faye felt a little nervous about how he'd react to what she was about to say.

"So your brother just called." She blurted out. Elio went completely still. She could feel him seething on the other end. "Which one?" He growled out. "Luciano." She replied quickly. "He kept blowing up my phone until I answered. I just got done talking to him." Faye explained. "What did he want?" His voice was dark and sinister. "He said he was doing a wellness check, I guess?" It came out as more of a question than an answer.

"Apparently, we were being followed around yesterday. He sent me some pictures of us together." Elio remained silent, waiting for her to continue. "All I said was I was sick, and you took care of me." She shrugged. "Was he trying to imply that I was hurting you at all?" He asked. "Yeah, he accused you of beating me, which is both dumb and insulting." She grumbled, a bit miffed at Luciano for assuming that.

"You know I'd never do that, right?" Worry trickled through his voice. "I wouldn't be with you if I even thought for a second that you would." She reassured him. She could hear him sigh. "I love you so much…" He mumbled quietly. "Did he say why he thought that?" Faye turned bright red from embarrassment. "Yes…" Her eye twitched. "You might have been a little too rough in the shower."

It took Elio a moment to figure out what she meant, but when he did, a wide smirk broke out on his face. "I can hear your smugness." She scowled. "Well, I ain't apologizing for marking what's mine." He purred. "Maybe I can add a few more marks tonight, now that you're feeling better." Faye choked at that comment.

"So no concerns at all with us being followed around then?" She deadpanned. "No concerns for you, doll. I'll make sure it never happens again. But there is another issue we should address." His voice took on a sadistically playful tone. "What issue?" Faye took the bait. "Doll, I told you to lie low, didn't I?" He chastised, his voice deep and gravelly. "I have been?" She responded, confused. "I wouldn't call talking to cops lying low." He tutted.

"I didn't know it was a cop calling me." She attempted to defend herself. "You shouldn't have answered an unknown number to begin with." He retorted. "What you should have done was call me immediately so that I could deal with it." Faye groaned, not wanting to argue anymore.

"Alright, you're right." She relented. "I should have been more careful. I'll do better next time." She shook her head in annoyance. "Oh doll, that's not enough." Elio chuckled darkly. "You broke your promise to me, and I have to make an example." Faye rose her eyebrow. "What are you gonna do? Shoot me?" She asked blatantly.

"Doll, you know I would never hurt you, but you need to be *punished*." He put an emphasis on the word punished. Faye felt a shiver run up her spine at the implications. "What punishment do you have in mind?" She asked sheepishly. "You'll have to wait and see." He grinned. "But don't worry, I won't punish you tonight. I need you to walk, after all." He purred, causing her heart to skip a beat.

'Fucking hell.' She thought. 'He's going to be the death of me.' "Well, I know you have to get back to work, so I'll let you go for now. I'll see you in a couple of hours." He said. "Okay, bye Elio, love you." She ended the phone call and let herself out of the cage.

After the call ended, Elio leaned back in his chair, a murderous look on his face. His brothers were beginning to really overstep. He could understand to some extent their persistence with trying to capture him, but for them to go after Faye and try to turn her against him was unforgivable. It was about time he had a heart to heart with his dear brothers. He called up one of his informants to track down their location. After all, he still had plenty of time to spare before he had to go pick up his doll.

Luciano and Cosimo sat across from each other at a small diner, holding a light conversation. "I reached her." Luciano spoke casually. Cosimo rolled his eyes. "Why bother? She's a dead end. Absolutely delusional and refuses to accept the truth of him." He grumbled, taking a sip of his tea. "I think she's lovely, and I rather enjoy talking with her." Luciano smiled. "Plus, I think she knows more than she's letting on."

"Of course she knows more. Doesn't mean she's gonna tell us anything." Cosimo retorted with a hiss. "She's a lost cause at this point. The only use we'll get out of her is using her as bait for Elio. And that's going on the assumption that he actually has feelings for her." Luciano grimaced at the idea of putting Faye in any danger.

"Maybe we should rethink this plan. We could destroy this poor girl's life and possibly get her killed if we keep doing this." He tried to reason with his counterpart. "Luciano, this may be the only way for us to get our brother back. Besides, she knew what she was signing up for when she got involved with Elio, so anything bad that comes her way is her own fault." He spoke coldly, as if Faye's life was meaningless, which to him, it was. She was nothing more than collateral damage.

After a few minutes of discussion, Luciano's phone suddenly rang, the number showing up as unknown. "Hello?" He answered with his usual cheery voice. "Stay the fuck away from her." Elio's voice echoed through threateningly. "Elio?" Luciano asked, causing Cosimo to look up. "Put it on speaker." The black-haired detective whispered, which he complied.

"You and Cosimo better leave my girl the fuck alone before there are problems!" He neither confirmed nor denied his identity, but instead sent out a warning. "I don't want you texting her, talking to her, and I better not ever see you visit her, or I'll mount your head on the fucking wall!" Angry wasn't enough to describe how Elio felt towards the two detectives.

"Elio, calm down." Luciano started. "I only talked to her. I didn't threaten her or anything." He tried to reason. "I don't give a shit what you did. Leave her alone. She hasn't done anything wrong, and I'll never let anything happen to her. This will be your one and only warning. Stay away."

"Luciano, get down!" Cosimo shouted, pulling his brother under the table. Gunshots sounded around them as the windows exploded, showering the restaurant in glass shards. Luciano reached for his gun, peering over the table, only to find that the assailants had already fled. Bullets and blood covered the floor as a few patrons were shot in the attack.

Cosimo phoned over the radio for backup while Luciano checked on the diners to see if there were any casualties. The two detectives looked towards the road, spotting an unmarked vehicle watching their every move. Elio's message was received loud and clear. He was willing to go to the extremes to insure Faye's safety. Cosimo was convinced, using her as bait was their best option. 'I'll bring you home, you bastard.'

Chapter: 28

The day was long and grueling, but much to Faye's relief, it was finally over. She said her goodbyes to some of her colleagues, wishing them all well, before leaving the building with her head held up high. It felt so amazing to leave after such a stressful week. She didn't even care that she couldn't go home. 'I get to spend time with my wonderful Elio.' She thought to herself, gushing at the thought.

Elio waited for her right outside, refusing to take any chances of her being snatched up. With the police and Black Spades closing in on him, it was only a matter of time before either of them got their dirty hands on his precious Faye. The thought of it all filled him with so much poisonous rage, it made him want to…

The young woman skipped out of the door and straight into his arms, clearing his mind of any negativity. She rested her head against his chest, breathing in his intoxicating scent. "I missed you so much." She mumbled with her eyes closed. "You're so needy, doll." He chuckled, stroking her long golden locks.

He spun her around a few times in the parking lot before waltzing back towards his car. "Here you go doll." He said, leading her to the passenger side and opening the door for her. "Why thank you, my love." She smiled, taking her rightful seat happily.

"So, doll, besides the unwanted phone call, how was work?" Elio asked as he started the car. "It was alright. It could have been better, could have been worse. The good thing is, it's finally over." She chirped, leaning her head against his shoulder. "What about you? How was your day?" She asked.

Elio thought for a moment. The sounds of gunshots and screams echoed in his brain as he tried to figure out a good response to her. "It was pretty uneventful." He lied, refusing to bring up what he did to his meddling brothers. "Snatching you up was probably the highlight of it all." Faye beamed up at him as she felt her heart flutter.

Suddenly, a thought crossed her mind. The conversation with Alice kept playing over and over in her head. "Elio?" She started, unsure if she should ask. "Hmm?" He replied, completely focused on the road. "Do you remember that one coworker that kept bugging me and almost got a dog killed?" A dark expression fell on Elio's face as he ground his teeth together. "I kind of recall. Why?" He hiss out, clearly upset by the mention of that man.

211

She took in a deep breath. "It's just… One of my coworkers came up to me earlier and mentioned something about him going missing…" she trailed off, still trying to work up the courage to ask him. "You want to know if I'm involved, right?" She nodded, unable to verbalize the words. "Look doll, all I can say is that if he's gone missing, it's because he messed with the wrong people. You don't just go missing unless you've done something you shouldn't have. Don't think too much about it, okay?" He patted her leg in comfort.

Once they got further into the city, Elio pulled off to the side of the road. He reached into the glove compartment, pulling out a red blindfold. "Alright doll, you know the drill." He held the velvet fabric in both hands as Faye leaned over. "What's stopping me from pulling the blindfold down?" She asked with a sly grin. "Doll, if I catch you pulling it down, I'll throw you in the car's trunk." He retorted, half joking. "That's all?" She laughed. "May used to shove me in her car's trunk every other day."

She let him tie the fabric around her face. "That's concerning." He hummed, focusing on tying the blindfold behind her head, being mindful of her hair. "There we go doll. Nice and tight." He placed a gentle kiss against her lips before starting the car once again.

They made it back to his base, Faye half asleep from the drive. "Enjoying the view?" Elio teased. "Oh yes, it's quite lovely this time of year." She retorted sarcastically, letting him pull her out of the car and towards the building. "I'll probably be able to navigate this place blindfolded long before I navigate it while being able to see." She laughed, hugging his arm as he guided her inside.

"You make it sound like you'll be going anywhere but *our* bedroom, doll." He smirked. "When I finally get you, I'm tying you to *our* bed so you can never leave." Faye smacked his arm lightly while wearing a soft smile on her face. "Oh, stop that." She giggled. He simply pulled her close to his chest, kissing her forehead. "Let's get you inside so I can see your pretty eyes again." He ushered her in.

Elio pulled Faye along through the hallways of the mansion until they made it back to the bedroom. Once inside the room, he pushed her onto the bed before crawling on top of her. "Oh my sweet, beautiful doll." He kissed her lips tenderly. "I'm so happy to have you in my arms again." He stared down at her lovingly, as if she was the most precious creature in existence.

"Elio…" Faye sighed happily, wrapping her arms around his neck. He planted another kiss on her lips. "Alright, enough playtime. Let's get ready for the party." He pulled her up into his arms, Faye giving him a quick peck on the lips. She was looking forward to these little tender moments with the terrifying mob boss.

"You're too cute for your own good." He returned the peck. "To cute to punish?" She asked slyly. "Oh, doll." He chuckled. You're so cute it makes me want to punish you harder." He spoke huskily. "Now go get dressed." He ordered, setting her on the ground. Faye made her way into the bathroom. Stripping out of her black scrubs, she jumped into the shower to wash away the stress of her workday.

While Faye was in the shower, Elio quickly grabbed her cellphone, unlocking the screen with ease. 'She really needs a better pass code.' He chuckled to himself as he started going through her contacts and apps, wanting to see if her phone was even worth keeping.

The fact that Luciano got in touch with her worried him enough. He didn't want to think about who else could have gotten hold of her contact details. He had a strong urge to smash her phone to pieces and get her one that's harder to track, but he had a feeling she wouldn't be all too happy with that. He could also have someone rework her phone to have all the unknown calls go through to a burner, but he'd need to find someone he could trust enough to do something like that.

As he continued to scroll through her phone, he looked through her gallery, admiring the pictures in there. Most of them were a mix of different exotic animals that came into her workplace and photos of her cats. 'What a dork.' He snickered to himself.

He got to a photo that was taken at some formal event. Faye stood next to two tall men in black suits. The skinnier of the two men had short blonde hair that was neatly combed off to the side and exhausted hazel eyes. He stood in the middle, his arms wrapped around the other two. The bigger of the two men had curly brown hair and cold blue eyes. The smiles they wore seemed fake, as if they were putting on an act.

Besides the awkward smile, Faye looked positively radiant in the photo. Her golden locks were curled up at the bottom, giving them a bouncy appearance. She wore full on makeup, which had to have been applied professionally, and a long, lacy black dress that went down to the floor.

"I remember that day." Faye hummed next to him, causing Elio to jump. She leaned over his shoulder, a large, fluffy red towel covering her body. "Doll, you really shouldn't sneak up on me," Elio chided. "You could seriously get hurt." Faye gave a sly grin, wrapping her arms around his chest.

"You shouldn't go through someone's things without their permission." She teased, planting a kiss against his cheek. She could hear his heart drumming against his chest as his face flushed bright red. "I'm just admiring your photos." He responded sheepishly, causing her to giggle.

"That was taken at my older brother's wedding." She told him. "He's the one in the middle with the stupid haircut." Faye pointed out. "The other man on his left is my little brother. We were his groom's men, hence why I wore black to his wedding." Elio had pulled Faye into his lap, beaming down at her.

"You guys look so happy in this picture." He said sarcastically, causing Faye to snort. "You can thank the lovely camera man for that. Every photo he took, he insisted everyone smile. It was pretty weird, and I think my mother threatened to beat him with the camera if he told her to smile one more time." He chuckled at that. "Does your whole family just choose violence?" He asked. "Only when it's necessary or funny." She retorted.

The two of them got so caught up in scrolling through photos, they nearly lost track of the time. It was a loud knock on the door that brought them out of their blissful moment, much to Elio's agitation. "Who is it!" He shouted, his voice rough and commanding. "It's me, Leo, boss." The lanky Irish man called back through the door. With a stoic expression, he took off his jacket and threw it over the naked woman, engulfing her in the heavy fabric. "Enter!" He ordered as he pulled Faye onto his lap.

Leo did as he was told, entering the large room carrying two pet carriers. "I brought the cats just like you told me, boss." He explained, trying to avoid eye contact. "Well? What are you waiting for?" Elio asked impatiently. "Set them down and get the fuck out!" The gangster, without hesitation, sat the carriers down and fled the room as quickly as possible.

Once the door was shut, Faye slid the jacket off of her before laying back on the soft, plush mattress. "Doll, you better start getting dressed so we don't end up late." Elio told her, his eyes scanning over her nude form hungrily. "Do we really have to go?" She asked, hoping to persuade him against going. "Yes, we do." Elio responded, pushing himself off the bed.

The mobster made his way over to the two carriers, unzipping them so the two fluffy beasts could roam free. "I picked out a few outfits for you." He smirked as he reached into the closet, pulling out a velvet red cocktail dress. "Of course, I'm sure you'll eventually want to wear your own clothes when you live here." He continued on with a slight hum to his voice. "Have you started packing yet?"

"Huh?" Faye responded, confused by what he meant by packing. "Your bags. Have you started packing for when you move in with me? It's only three weeks away, and I might not give you the chance to go back after that." He spoke, the last part quieter, with a sinister tone to his voice. "Oh, uh, not yet..." she answered nervously, afraid of being scolded by him. "But I promise I'll do it next week."

She quickly went back to admiring the outfit he handed her. It was so simple and yet elegant, and the fabric was soft. When she tried it on, the dress fit perfectly around her body. "How do you always get the right size for me?" She asked, doing a little spin in the outfit. "Informants." Elio said plainly, like it was the most obvious answer in the world. Faye didn't want to know what he meant by that.

He stood up from his spot, strolling over towards the beaming young woman. Reaching out his arm, he took one of her hands in his much larger one, pulling her gently into a spin. "Are you ready to go, doll?" He asked lovingly. She nodded, grinning ear to ear. "Alright, let's get going." He picked her up bridal style and walked out the door.

Elio carried Faye out to the car, her eyes once again covered by a soft piece of fabric. He sat her in the back seat, crawling in after her. She reached up for him, unable to see. She gripped onto his shirt, pulling him down to her. The young woman nuzzled into the mobster's chest as he wrapped his arms around her. "When we get there, just relax and have fun, alright?" He ran his fingers through her hair. "I'll try." She responded. "Again, I might end up clinging to you the whole time." He chuckled at that, his grip tightening around her. "I wouldn't have it any other way."

They arrived at a luxurious-looking mansion located just outside of town. "I'm getting Great Gatsby vibes from this," Faye deadpanned, her blindfold long since discarded. "Funny." He kissed her temple, opening the door to the car. He stepped out, offering his arm to her, which she graciously accepted. They made their way towards the building, Faye holding onto him with constrictor like grip.

"Doll, you're going to rip my arm clean off." He teased her, strolling towards the front entrance, a large grin on his face. "Sorry." She apologized, easing up her grasp on him, but remaining close to his side. They made it to the door where a large, burly man stood there at the entrance. Elio gave the man a deadly look, daring him to utter a single word to them. He took the hint and opened the door to them, letting the couple enter the building.

Faye looked around, feeling slightly overwhelmed by the expensive décor surrounding her, alongside the amount of people who are in attendance. "This place sure is fancy." She whispered, more so to herself. "It's the governor's house." Elio whispered backed. "He tends to not spare any expense." She gave the opening another look over. "It feels cold in here." She mumbled. He pulled her close, opening his jacket up to her. "Better?" He nuzzled her neck, causing her to giggle. "Much." She smiled, though in her mind she still felt uncomfortable.

"Elio!" a high-pitched voice cried out, catching the attention of the mob boss. A short, thin woman ran up to him, wrapping her arms around his backside. "I knew you'd be here!" She smiled as Elio awkwardly pulled away from her embrace. "Juniper." He spoke curtly. "How many times do I have to tell you not to touch me so casually?" His voice was bitter and full of venom, which went unnoticed by the overly affectionate girl. "Awe 'Lio, no need to be so shy!" she gushed.

Faye, feeling a little weird being in the middle of this exchange, let go of Elio and stood by his side instead, much to his dismay. Juniper seemed to have just noticed the young woman's presence, giving her a dirty look at how close she was to the mobster. "Oh, and who's your little friend?" She asked in disgust. Faye raised an eyebrow at her sudden rudeness. 'Are we really doing this?' She thought to herself, sighing inwardly. "Hi, I'm Faye." She put on a fake smile, extending her hand out to the girl, who swatted it away like some housefly. "Alright, I'll just go fuck myself." She mumbled to herself, taking hold of Elio's hand.

Juniper narrowed her eyes at the contact that Faye made. Her face darkened. She sauntered over to the woman, leaning close to her. "You really should learn your place." She whispered just out of earshot of Elio. Faye shrugged at her, not at all intimidated by the brunette. "I'm pretty secure in my place." She snarked back, a playful glint in her eye. "Whatever." Juniper rolled her eyes.

"Elio, do you mind accompanying me? There are some things I want to discuss." Elio looked at his beloved, silently asking if it was okay. She gave him a soft smile, letting go of his hand. "I'll just keep myself entertained for a bit." She told him, pulling out her phone and some earbuds. Taking this as a sign to go, he walked off to a more private area, while Juniper seemed to linger around for a moment, waiting for something.

Just as she was about to plug in her earbuds, an older man made his way across the room, taking his place next to Faye's side. "Oh, Uncle Pete!" Juniper smiled. "Hello Juniper." He nodded, his eyes glued to Faye, wearing a predatory smirk on his face. "You have perfect timing, as always. Would you kindly entertain Elio's 'date' while I talk to him?" Faye could tell the brunette wanted to vomit at the word 'date.' "It would be my pleasure." Pete purred, taking Faye's hand, much to her disgust.

Juniper skipped off after Elio, leaving Faye with the sleezy old man who had a death grip on her hand. "So you came with Elio huh?" He asked, his face a little too close to her for comfort. "Yeah…" she answered, trying to pull away from his touch. "Awe, a shy one aren't we?" He laughed. "More antisocial than shy." She rolled her eyes. "Feisty too, I like it." He pulled her closer to him. "Elio picked a good one."

She felt sick and desperately wanted to get away from him. "Look, Pete was it? I really don't need any company. I'm perfectly happy watching random cat videos on my phone." She tried pulling away once again, only for him to tighten his grasp. "Oh babe, there's no need to be scared. I'll take care of you." He cooed. "I think you're misunderstanding my emotions. I'm not scared, I'm creeped out." Faye retorted. "And don't ever call me babe." She glared, though he didn't seem phased at all. Instead, he began pulling her off in another direction.

He walked her towards a bar area, pulling out a seat for her to take. "Let's have a drink before we begin." Pete suggested, snapping his fingers at the bartender. "What's your drink of choice, darling?" She was getting sick of the pet names from him. "It's Faye." She snapped at him. "And I don't drink." Pete chuckled darkly. "Better mind that tone of yours if you know what's good for you." He threatened. She crossed her arms, a clear scowl on her face.

"Now, how about that drink?" He sounded way jollier. "I don't drink." She repeated. "You look like a wine kind of gal. Barkeep, get me a whisky sour and my girl your nicest red wine." He ordered, completely ignoring her. "I'm not your girl." She grumbled. The bartender, with a neutral expression, prepared the drinks, placing them in front of the two.

"So, Faye, where did Elio come to find a girl like you?" Pete attempted to start a conversation as she stared down at her glass in disgust. The wine smelt bitter, which was how she was feeling, and she had no interest in talking to him about her life. "I see, not one to talk, huh? I could live with that." He smirked. "I like my sluts on the quieter side, anyway."

Her eyes widened at the boldness of his statement. "Excuse me?" She said with offense. "Alright, I'm done here." Faye rose from her seat, wanting to leave this creep and find Elio. "You're not going anywhere, sweetheart." He grabbed her arm, tugging her back to her seat. "I don't know who you think I am, but..." she started. "Oh, I know who you are," He interrupted her. "Your some young whore Elio found wandering the streets. Took you in, promised you a good life if you behave." He slurred. "Well, you better behave, darling, otherwise you'll end up back on the streets. Is that what you want?" She crinkled her nose. "The streets sound awfully homy right now." She retorted. "Drink." He ordered her. "Or I'll make your life a living hell."

Elio spent the next half hour listening to Juniper drone on and on about herself, her voice like nails on a chalkboard to him. "I feel like it was fate." She sighed happily. "Meeting you here at this party." He raised an eyebrow at her, unamused. "What are you talking about?" He asked dryly. "It's as if the universe wanted us to be together! Oh, I can hear the wedding bells now!" She squealed, pulling Elio into a hug.

"Get off of me, you fucking broad!" He pushed her away in disgust. "How many times do I got to tell you I ain't interested?" Juniper didn't seem fazed at all. "Awe, you don't have to be like that. We're practically dating, after all." She cooed, taking a step towards him. "We ain't dating you bimbo." He spoke bluntly. "I already have a girlfriend." Her eyes widened in shock at that. "What do you mean, you have a girlfriend?" She shrieked. "Who?" "The girl I brought with me." He told her. "The one that Uncle Pete just ran off with?" Elio nearly flip out at this. "What!?"

'What a pain.' Faye thought, swirling the glass of wine, having only taken a few small sips of the extremely bitter drink to appease the old man. 'I could say something, maybe hurt this asshole's feelings, but that's not really lying low. I need to do something that will get me out of this without breaking my promise to Elio.' She nodded to herself, determination in her eyes.

Luckily, the old sleazebag was far too busy drinking and talking about himself to notice what she was up to. Faye pulled out her phone and shot a quick text. *I need you to call me.* Not even ten seconds had passed when her phone rang. "Hold that thought, Pete. It's my brother, could be an emergency." She told the man, hitting answer.

"Hey Shaedon, what's up?" She said causally. "Wait what? What happened to Mom? Is she okay?" She got out of her seat, panic clear on her face. "Is everything okay?" Pete asked, the alcohol taking effect. Faye's eyes started watering up. "I need to go." She cried, fleeing from the bar, leaving the confused man behind.

"Alright, seriously, what's going on, Faye?" A deep, gruffy voice sounded through the phone. "I just needed an excuse to get away from some creep." She answered with a wince as her head was hurting. "Thanks for having my back, Shaedon." "Where the hell are you?" He asked. "I'm at some weird party with a bunch of rich snobs. Don't ask why." She explained. "Oh no, you can't say that with no context. I'm going to ask why. He laughed. "How did you end up at a party?"

She groaned in annoyance, rubbing her temples. "Alright, I'll tell you, but you can't tell our parents or Bane. I want to tell them myself. Okay?" "Fine." He whined. "What's this big secret that got you trapped at a party?" He asked. "My boyfriend brought me to this party." She admitted. "Seriously? Why are you hiding that? That's great news. Means you're finally planning to fulfill your womanly role in society." He congratulated her.

She rolled her eyes at the terrible comment. "Sexism aside, I'm hiding it because ya'll get really fucking weird when I show interest in someone." She explained with a pout. "Get the fuck over yourself." He laughed. "So who's the dumbass that got with a dumpster fire like you?" Faye felt her eye twitch, kind of regretting texting her brother to begin with. "What did you say? The service is bad here." She said, annoyed. "I got to go, but hey, let's continue this conversation. Never." She hit end call before Shaedon could respond.

Faye made her way into an area of the building that was pretty crowded, her mind foggy and dizzy. She felt worry flood through her, being around so many people, but swallowed it down, deciding to scan the room for Elio. She let out a frustrated huff, failing to spot the tall man but moved on to another area, her body growing difficult to control.

She moved around carefully, afraid she might run into the gross old man again, and in her state of panic, she didn't want to think of what he'd do to her. Faye pulled out her phone once again, this time dialing Elio's number. After three rings, he picked up. "Hey doll, where are you?" He sounded both worried and relieved that she called.

She let out a breath of relief. "I'm in some weird room surrounded by statues of the formere presidents." She told him. "I'm kind of trying to hide from some creepy old man that keeps hitting on me." Faye laughed nervously. "Stay right there, doll. I'll come get you." His tone was calm and soothing, as if to reassure her that everything would be okay. "Alright, I'll just chill by Taft." Her voice was a bit slurred and shaky, but she tried to remain positive.

Elio hung up, rage building up in him as he stomped through the building, patrons moving out of his way to avoid his wrath. The mob boss wanted nothing more than to find the creep that made his doll feel uncomfortable and tear him to pieces, but he needed to find Faye first and make sure she was okay.

He made his way over to the presidential room, opening the door quickly only to find the most heartbreaking sight. Faye sat on the floor, curled up in a ball, trying to make herself as small as possible. He made his way across the room, gently reaching out for her. He placed his hand on her shoulder, feeling her flinch at his touch. "Doll, it's me." He spoke tenderly. She rose her head up, her eyes red and puffy from crying. The second she spotted him, she got up from her spot, wrapped her arms around him, and hid her face in his torso.

"It's okay, my love, I'm here." He hummed, rocking back and forth with her. "I'm sorry. I know it's stupid to cry over something small." She said sheepishly, afraid of him judging her. "It ain't stupid." Elio reassured her. "Some creep bothered you while you were in a vulnerable position. You have every right to be upset. I'm just glad you got away from him." He smiled at her. "Yeah, me too. I just hate that I had to call my brother to bail me out." She muttered against him, lulling her head off to the side.

"You called your brother?" He questioned her. "I didn't want to cause a scene, and I figured if I gave a valid reason, social pressure would make him leave me alone. So I texted Shaedon and had him call me. The little asshole will probably never let me live it down." Elio wasn't too pleased that she felt the need to reach out to her brother, but he let it go for now. Eventually, she would come to rely only on him. He'd just have to give her time.

"Thank you for finding me." Faye sighed against him. He hummed, swaying around with her in his arms. "I'd do anything for you, doll." He told her, dancing around with the young woman.

They walked out of the room, cuddled close together. Elio's arms were wrapped protectively around Faye as she hugged him. "So who was that lovely lady, anyway?" She asked curiously, trying to focus on anything but the dizziness she felt. "Some psycho who's obsessed with me." He grumbled. "She has it in her head that me and her are in love. Something about how we are destined to be together." He sounded disgusted by the thought of her.

Faye gave a mischievous smile, leaning her head against him. "I'd hate to come in between destiny." She teased. "Doll, you are the only one I'm destined to be with." He grinned down at her. "Ugh, so cheesy." She laughed. Elio took her back out to the party, refusing to let go of her no matter who tried to speak to them. Faye was happy with the arrangement, not wanting to ever leave Elio's side in fear that some other scumbag might try to make a pass at her.

He struck up a conversation with some random government official about the upcoming election, though Faye didn't pay any attention to their discussion, finding the topic pretty boring. She stared at Elio's face, admiring every little detail on him. Ever since she discovered he had the cutest freckles, she's made it her mission to count them. She felt so calm and relaxed in his arms, as if she was untouchable. Moments like this made her almost ready to pack up her stuff and live with him.

"And who is this lovely lady?" The man spoke, motioning towards Faye. "This is my girlfriend, Faye." Elio answered smugly, moving his hands to grasp her shoulders. She nodded at the man, not really in any mood to converse with him. "Well, it's a pleasure to meet you." He extended his hand out to her, which she took hesitantly. He placed a kiss on the backside of her hand, giving her a wink. "Nice to meet you too, I guess." she sounded unamused, pulling her hand back.

Elio glared at the politician as his arms snaked back around Faye, pulling her against his chest. "Don't touch her." He warned the man, teeth bared. "I didn't mean to overstep." The man raised his hands in surrender. "She's just so beautiful. It's hard to resist." He gave her a sly smile. "You better do your best to resist if you know what's good for you. She's mine." He growled, pulling Faye away from the flirty politician.

"Is everyone at this party a horny scumbag?" She asked in annoyance, swaying in his arms. "Doll, you're surrounded by political figures. What did you expect?" Elio retorted, causing Faye to burst out in a fit of giggles.

He pressed his face against her neck, nuzzling into her soft flesh. "You're so cute when you laugh." His teeth grazed her skin, begging to sink into her soft spot. Faye leaned back into him, craving his touch, and desiring the marks that showed the world just who she belonged to.

"There you are!" a familiar voice called out, ruining the intimate moment between Faye and Elio. She looked up at the interruption, her eyes darkened at the sight of Pete. "That was pretty rude of you to run off like that." He seemed to completely ignore the large mobster's presence. "Especially when we were just about to get to the fun part." His face was flushed and his speech slurred. Faye felt a pit in her stomach, like she wanted to throw up at the sight of him.

"Pete." Elio snarled dangerously. "Oh, hey Elio." Pete greeted drunkenly. "Didn't see you there." Faye turned around, hiding in the mob boss' grip, trying to disappear into his large form. He couldn't help the feeling of pride knowing that she was depending on him to protect her from the pathetic, drunken attorney. "What do you think you're doing?" He asked the man menacingly. "Just coming to find the little slut and finish our date." He laughed, pointing at the cowering woman.

"Little slut? You mean my fucking girlfriend?" He pushed Faye behind him before he took the attorney by the neck, dangling him in the air. "Give me one good reason I shouldn't gut you like a fucking fish right now?" Elio snarled, his nails digging into Pete's flesh. "I... Um..." He stuttered out, terrified of the crime lord. "I'm sorry! I didn't know she was yours." He pleaded for mercy. Faye watched, unsure if she should stop Elio or not. On one hand, she truly believed the creep had it coming, but on the other, she didn't deem it a safe spot to commit murder.

"Elio..." Faye spoke quietly, gaining her lover's attention. "Please don't... Not here." She requested, fearing that if she didn't step in, there would be a bloodbath that wouldn't go over so well for Elio. His eyes softened at the worried expression she gave him, lowering Pete to the ground. "Consider yourself lucky. I don't want to risk getting your pathetic, disgusting blood all over my beautiful doll, otherwise I'd rip you to pieces." He hissed, his voice holding a deadly edge to it. "Don't think I'm done with you, Pete. I'll make sure you never lay your eyes on another woman again." With that final threat, he picked Faye up and carried her out of the building towards the car.

They got into the backseat together. Faye snuggled close to Elio, not wanting to loosen her grip at all with him. He wouldn't have asked her to anyway, loving all the attention she gave him. "Doll, do you care if that man lives or not?" He asked her, wanting her full opinion on the matter. "No, I don't." She admitted. "But I didn't want you to kill him in there with all those witnesses around. I don't think he would have been worth going to prison for." She explained, her face against his chest. "So smart." He cooed. "I swear you're my voice of reason." She couldn't help smile at this.

Faye fell asleep against him, snoring lightly as he stroked her precious head, lost in thought. He never realized how much he loved protecting her and seeing her in such a vulnerable position. Even now, seeing her curled up in his arms, she just looked so delicate, so fragile, as if even the smallest touch could break her.

Just as he got her to sit in his lap with her head resting against his chest, her phone rang. He hit decline quickly, not wanting to wake her up, but the phone rang again. Elio sigh in annoyance, hitting answer. "Hello?" He spoke, agitation clearly shown in his voice. "This ain't Faye, is it?" A rough voice asked teasingly. "No." Elio deadpanned. There was a silence on the other end.

"Okay, so I called the right number and I know she didn't change her phone number in the last hour, so who's this?" He sassed. "I'm Elio. Who are you, and why do you want to talk to her?" He snapped back. "Name's Shaedon and I just want to make sure she made it out of the party alive or if I need to make funeral arrangements. Can I talk to her?" Shaedon? He must have been the younger brother that she called. It was in his best interest to play nice with this man.

"Ah, you must be her brother. It's nice to meet you." Elio was extra polite with him. "No, I'm afraid you can't talk to her right now. She's had a long day and is currently asleep." He explained. "Well, wake her ass up. She can't be that tired." He retorted. "All she does is play with dogs all day. Her job ain't that hard." He insisted, though Elio wasn't planning on giving in.

"I'm not waking her up." He stood his ground. "Lame. Fine, can you just ask her if she got the number of that old man who hit on her?" He tilted his head in confusion. "Why do you want his number?" "Well, I thought, hell if my big sister ain't going to whore herself out, I just might if it means I don't have to go to work tomorrow." He laughed. "But honestly, I just want to have a little chat with the guy." Shaedon's voice took on a dark tone.

"Don't worry about it." Elio spoke calmly. "It's my fault she got put in that situation, so I'll take care of him." He didn't want to involve this man more than necessary, especially since Elio was planning to keep her all to himself. "Okay, you take care of it. But tell Faye if she ever hangs up on me again, I'm throwing her cats into the pot." He hung up the phone, leaving the mobster with more questions.

As he listened to the sounds of her slow breathing, he couldn't help but feel lucky to be pulled into her strange world. The car came to a stop in front of his base, Faye still deep in sleep on top of him. Elio stepped out of the car, carefully picking her up so as not to disturb her. As he walked inside, he called for a group to meet with him.

He made his way into his office, five gangsters following close behind. Faye clung to his shirt as he took a seat, adjusting her so that she was resting in his lap. He began the meeting, going over which politicians would act as great allies and which needed to be taken care of. The group was tasked with making certain big named political figures disappear without raising any suspicion. They made sure the message was crystal clear. Elio ran the city, and they were all puppets that he could cut the strings to at any moment.

"Finally, Pete Jones is to be gotten rid of immediately." Elio ordered. "Out of town or six feet under?" One of his men chimed up. "Six feet under. Make it hurt." He clarified with his face darkened. "Now go." The men all gave a unanimous 'right away, boss' before leaving the room with haste.

He leaned back in his chair, pulling the young woman against him. "Doll, you are dead asleep." He commented more so to himself. "There's no way you were that worn out from all that." He looked down at her features, noticing how sickly she looked. Elio lifted one of her eyelids carefully, bloodshot, just as he expected.

His frown deepened at the sight of his beautiful girl. "I'll make that bastard regret laying a single hand on you." He spoke softly to her, standing up to carry her back to their room. He laid Faye on the bed, stripping off her dress and shoes to get her ready. He reached for a shirt, pulling it over her as a makeshift nightgown before crawling in next to her, pulling her into a spooning position. "Goodnight, my love." He nuzzled into her hair, taking in her scent.

Chapter: 30

She couldn't move, couldn't speak, couldn't feel. Her feet were glued to the ground as the world around her shifted and changed. Her phone rang, echoing around the empty space, but she couldn't reach for it. It continued to ring repeatedly; the tone going into an earsplitting pitch. Where even was she? Her surroundings seemed both familiar and mysterious.

She felt herself sinking into the ground. Was this dirt under her? It pulled her further and further down, squeezing her tightly. She wanted to scream, cry for anyone to help, but her voice came out as a whisper. *"Relax."* A strange voice echoed around her. It sounded gravelly and monotone, leaving a sinking feeling in her stomach. Panic grew as she attempted to move, but found herself paralyzed. *"If you don't stop struggling, you might never wake up."*

Faye's eyes shot open, beads of sweat running down her face. Her head was spinning, and she felt dehydrated and nauseous. She grabbed her chest, feeling the pounding of her heart. Rarely did dreams terrify her like that, but there was something about this one that shook her up.

"Doll, are you okay?" Elio's voice sounded next to her. She attempted to answer him but found it difficult, like her mouth was stuffed full of cotton. "Here, doll, drink some water. It'll make you feel better." He offered her a bottle, which she gratefully took.

After a few small sips, she found her voice. "Thank you." She told him. "And I'm fine, just a freaky dream. I think I was dying?" She tried to put together the meaning of what she saw now that she had calmed down a bit. He sat up, setting his chin on top of her head. He rubbed soothing circles into the upper part of her back, causing her to lean against his chest.

"What do you remember about last night?" Elio asked, a tone of uncertainty in his voice. She looked up, thinking back at the events from the party, but her mind went blank. The memory felt like a jumbled mess of things out of order. "I think I remember you needed to do something, and then I got pulled to a bar by some guy. He made me drink some wine or something. I don't know." She confessed, feeling kind of ashamed at herself for not remembering properly.

Elio held a solemn look in his eyes. "You were drugged, doll." He told her, causing her to look at him strangely. "Drugged?" She questioned, wondering how that was possible. "Yes." He confirmed. "Pete must have put something in your wine," He explained. "But that's impossible. I didn't let him anywhere near the glass

223

and kept my hand covering it. I wouldn't have drank out of it if he was given even a second to tamper with it."

He looked rather impressed by the extent she would go to not being drugged. "Did you watch the bartender prepare the drink?" He asked her. "No…" she admitted. "It's common at these events that the guests hand off vials to servers and have them lace the drinks of sex workers who tag along." Elio explained, wanting to give her an idea of what had happened. "Once the drug kicks in, they carry them off to one of the guest rooms to have their way with them." He gritted his teeth at the last part, thinking how close that scumbag got to touching his Faye.

She went pale at the thought, tears welled up in her eyes. "I did it again, didn't I?" she spoke softly, regret in her voice. "I did something stupid without thinking and caused more problems for you." She couldn't even look at him. She felt ashamed. Elio turned the girl around to face him, though she still refused to meet his eyes and instead stared at her hands, trying to hold back the tears.

"I didn't mean to." She whispered, begging for forgiveness. "Doll…" He spoke gently. She didn't budge, though. "Faye, look at me," He ordered, tilting her head up to meet his eyes. She expected to see anger and disappointment, but was instead met with compassion, concern, and adoration. "It's not your fault." He assured her. "You did everything right in trying to prevent it from happening. There was no way you could have known the bartender would spike your drink."

He pushed his forehead against hers, nuzzling it sweetly. "You came up with an escape plan that wouldn't cause a major scene on the spot, which is incredible. I'm so proud of you." A tear slid down her cheek as he pressed a tender, loving kiss against her lips.

Faye leaned into the kiss, letting Elio take complete control. "Don't worry about that, asshole." He said, breaking away from the embrace. "I promise you'll never see him again." Faye tilted her head. "You didn't kill him on my behalf, did you?" She questioned. "Doll, I've killed men for less." Elio answered honestly. "I wasn't kidding when I said I'd burn this city to the ground for you."

She felt a twinge of guilt knowing that a man died because of her. He seemed to have picked up on that feeling though, as he mashed his lips against hers once again, invading her mouth with his tongue. "Don't feel bad, doll. The man was a piece of shit." Elio said bluntly. "Deserves everything that's coming to him. You ain't the first girl he's tried something like that on."

He didn't want her wasting a single bit of thought and energy on this man. "You're right." She sighed, her arms wrapped around his neck. "It's just the initial shock of finding out someone died because of me, but I'll get over it." It was pretty endearing the lengths the mob boss was willing to go to make her happy. "I'm glad you see it my way." He smiled.

"I'm just glad I have this big, scary boyfriend to protect me." She beamed at him, kissing his cheek softly. He chuckled earnestly, feelings of pride flowing through him. "Damn straight, doll. Don't you ever forget that either."

While neither wanted to, they both finally made their way off the bed. "Do we really have to get up?" Faye whined as she went to feed her cats, who weren't the happiest beasts in the world. "We got things to do today." Elio retorted as he flipped through the closet, trying to find the perfect outfit for her. "Yeah, but what if we just skipped them and cuddled all day?"

Elio shot her a warning look that she simply laughed off, not quite understanding how dangerous he could actually be. "I was only joking." She shrugged, taking ahold of the dress he held out to her. "You better be, doll. I still have one punishment to hand you. Don't make me dish out two." He gave her a devilish smirk, as though he were daring her to talk back.

"Wait, I'm still getting punished for talking to your stupid brother? That's not fair!" She pouted, crossing her arms. "You're getting punished for talking to the cops, doll." He corrected. "I swear when I see Luciano again I'm going to..." "You won't be seeing him again." His voice went deeper, with a menacing tone to it. "If you ever speak to him again, I swear I'll tie you down and make you watch as I peel off every bit of skin on his body."

Faye stared at him wide eyed and pale, feeling almost like she was in danger. Never had she seen this side of him directed at her before. "Elio... You know I love you, right?" She asked softly, almost unsure if it was the right thing to say. "Yeah, I know doll. I love you too." He sighed, figuring he might have gone too far. He took a step over to her, noticing how she slightly flinched.

"I won't hurt you." He swore, holding his hand out to her. She took it with slight hesitation as he pulled her toward him, smashing her against his chest. Sucking in a deep breath, Faye relaxed against his torso, allowing for his arms to wrap fully around her. "I know you won't hurt me..." she mumbled quietly. "It just freaks me out when you raise your voice like that."

They stayed in that embrace for a few minutes before finally departing. Faye made her way towards the bathroom, deciding that she needed a shower after the night she had. Elio continued to dig through the closet until he finally found the perfect outfit for her.

The moment she stepped out of the bathroom, he quickly stepped in front of her, shoving the outfit into her chest. She looked down to see what he picked: a white blouse with a red Lolita style skirt. "You keep picking out cute outfits like this and I might throw out my whole closet and make you pick out an entire wardrobe for me." She threatened playfully as she slipped on the dress. "You keep looking good in those outfits and I might have to hide you away from the world." He retorted just as playfully, pulling her in for a quick hug before suddenly pulling away.

Faye slightly pouted at the loss of contact, which made him chuckle. "Sorry, doll, but I have a few important meetings to get to." He gave her a small peck. "I guess I'm hanging out in here today." She said, slightly disappointed but understanding. He gave a sinister laugh, his eyes half lidded. "Oh no, doll, you're coming with me." He snickered. "After all, I still need to punish you for the phone call." She looked away from him, cheeks bright red. He wrapped his arm around her shoulders, pushing her to the door. "Time to go."

Elio led her to a room near the back of the building, passing by different gang members who would glance at the two for a second before running off. He opened the door for her, ushering her in. "Welcome to my office, doll." He spoke with a sly grin. Faye glanced around the room, realizing that it was just a typical office, complete with a desk and a large chair up next to a bookcase. Much to her absolute amusement, though, she noticed that the room held the same color scheme as his bedroom.

"What do you think?" Elio asked, drawing her attention back to him. She shook her head, a playful smile on her face. "It's nice and all, but I am a little disappointed there isn't a single head mounted on the wall." He gave a genuine laugh at this comment before flashing her his own playful grin. "Sorry, but that type of decoration is strictly reserved for the red room." He retorted. "Ain't all the rooms in this building red?" She raised an eyebrow at him. He rolled his eyes, pulling the smartass girl in for a kiss, which she eagerly returned.

"I bet you're wondering what your punishment is." He pulled away from her, wearing a large grin on his face. She gave him a nod to continue. "What I'm going to have you do is stay completely quiet during these phone meetings. Understand?" She looked confused. "That's all?" She questioned him. "Nothing else, just stay quiet?" It seemed far too simple. "You'll understand just how difficult this punishment is." He retorted, his grin widening. "Wha..." Before she could respond, he picked her up and carried her to the desk. "Now remember, my love, stay quiet." He held a threatening tone as he sat in the large chair with Faye in his lap.

Faye panted, trying to catch her breath after having to muffle herself for so long. Her body was sore, her legs trembling, and she wanted nothing more than to pass out. "Did you learn your lesson, doll?" He smirked, trailing his fingers across the bruises on her hips. She attempted to glare at him, but the best she could manage was a cute pout which only added to his smugness. She attempted to stand up, but her legs felt like jelly, so she needed to cling to him to stabilize herself.

Elio scooped her up, being mindful not to be too rough with her, and exited the office. "I can walk." Faye whined, her arms wrapped around his neck. "If that were true, you'd still be in my office, on my lap doll. My goal was to make sure you couldn't walk." He retorted, navigating the long hallways with her pressed close to his chest.

Once they made it to the front entrance, Elio set her down for a moment to tie the blindfold around her eyes before picking her up once again to take her away. "How about we stop to get something to eat first before we take care of business?" He asked casually, sliding her into the passenger side. "Okay? I guess." She sounded unsure. "Where are we going?" Elio started the car, paying her no mind. "Don't worry about it doll, I just have some things to take care of is all. All you need to do is stay close and look pretty." He winked at her. "Well, I can stay close, at the very least." She joked quietly.

While on the road, they stopped at a nice little diner to eat lunch and discuss their plans for the day. "So, where are we heading to?" Faye asked in between sips of water. "You'll find out soon enough, doll." Elio retorted, "but I promise you'll find it entertaining." He winked at her, causing her to giggle. "You know, that's a low bar.

I'm easily entertained. I'll stare at Banshee for hours and all she does is stare at the wall." He let out a deep chuckle at her response.

"Hello lovelies! Are you two ready to order?" A waitress spoke with the cutest high pitched voice. Faye looked up from her menu, only to find an adorable young woman standing in front of her. She had short, platinum blonde hair with streaks of pink in it and wore a pink knee length dress with a white apron covering it. She had the prettiest blue eyes that sparkled like sapphires.

"Yeah, I'm ready." Elio replied, not even bothering to glance up at the adorable woman. Faye couldn't take her eyes off her, desiring nothing more than to give this girl a big hug. She used restraint on that desire and instead placed her order before continuing her conversation with her lover.

"That waitress is pretty cute, don't you think?" Faye asked quietly, so as not to gain any attention. "I guess." Elio shrugged. "If you're into prison bate. She looks and acts like a child." He showed absolutely no interest in discussing the waitress at all. "I guess, but the way she does it is adorable." She insisted. "More like annoying. It comes off as fake and trying too hard. That's one of the reasons I like you so much. You're none of that." He gave her a genuine smile.

"That's really sweet, but I still think the waitress is cute." Faye replied while leaning her head on her hand. "Agree to disagree, doll. You're still the cutest thing ever." He smirked, scanning her body up and down.

"Cute enough to tell me where we're going?" She asked slyly. "Why are you so interested?" He wondered, wishing to understand her mind. "You're just so secretive about it, I can't help but wonder why." She explained with a giggle. "My man of mystery." She sighed, leaning further into her hand.

"You two make such a lovely couple." The waitress gushed, pulling the two out of their conversation. "Do the two sweethearts wish to have their picture taken?" She asked, holding out a novelty camera. "I'm not really comfortable being photographed." Faye answered honestly. "No." Elio spoke bluntly, attempting to wave the waitress off who skipped away happily, humming.

After their lovely lunch, they got back into Elio's car, heading towards their destination. Faye laid her head against the cool glass window, watching as the buildings and people passed them by. "You're being awfully quiet." He pointed out, his eyes glued to the road. "Care to share your thoughts?" She looked at him, a soft smile on her face. "There's not a lot going on in my mind, just people watching." She shrugged with a genuine smile.

"Just making sure you're okay. I hate seeing you upset." She felt her heart flutter at his words. "You'd be the first." She spoke quietly to herself. Though Elio still heard it, he opted to say nothing. Instead, he wrapped an arm around her, pulling her against him while he used his other hand to steer. She leaned into his touch, resting against his shoulder.

Elio pulled into a parking spot, having reached the destination. He got out and made his way to the passenger side to open the door for Faye. He pulled her close to his chest, making his way into the building. Two of his men exited a different vehicle to follow behind. Faye noticed the place they were going into was a strip club, though it looked oddly familiar. "Isn't this one of May's clubs?" She asked curiously. "It was." He confirmed, strolling to the entrance. "I bought a few clubs from her, and this is the final one I'm doing a walkthrough for." He explained as she nodded along. "I want to make sure everything is in top shape before we complete the deal."

They entered inside, the building mostly being empty except for a few employees cleaning up. Chairs were neatly stacked on tables, the bar thoroughly cleaned. Not a single glass was out of place. Elio walked around, inspecting each nook and cranny, rather impressed by what he was seeing. A subtle smell of vanilla and lavender filled the air, giving the strip club a wonderful aroma.

"She kept this place in pretty great shape." He hummed rather, impressed. "Believe it or not, she's actually a major germaphobe." Faye responded. "Everything had to be cleaned thoroughly and the building code kept up to date or she would lose her shit." She snickered at the memory of May freaking out over a few bugs found crawling around on stage.

"It's funny, though, that she sold you this one." Faye said thoughtfully. "Why is that?" Elio asked curiously. "This was her first one, the club that started it all. I remember when she bought this building, I was a senior in high school." She thought back to that memory fondly. "She called me at one in the morning, asking if I could help her clean the place up and put some furniture together for her. I didn't know what she was using the space for, so I just said yes and told her to pick me up."

Faye reminisced a bit, walking towards a table in the far back. "This table has a wobble to it." She pressed against it slightly, moving the table back and forth. "Because her clumsy ass husband tripped and pulled me down with him onto the damn thing." The mobster chuckled at the thought, listening to her stories about the club. "Did you know this place was originally just a bar restaurant combo?" She asked rhetorically. "Atlas used to buss tables here his first year of college. Me and Luca would always come by after school just to fuck with him."

Elio pulled Faye back to him as she continued to talk, telling him stories about back when the place first opened. "This is actually where that whole 'I'm a prostitute' thing started, as well. I used to kind of work here back in high school as well when it first opened, long before she turned it into a strip club. I wasn't an actual employee, but now and then May would call me up to lend a hand when she was short staff and pay me for my time. People who found out I worked here would always get the wrong idea."

She shook her head in amusement. "It also didn't help that at one point, May would introduce me to people as her top girl just for a laugh." Elio couldn't help but laugh at that. "That must have been fun for you." He teased. She rolled her eyes, smiling at him. "Oh yeah, so much fun." She said sarcastically. "She did it one too many times, and I finally had enough. I told her either she stops telling people that or I'll just have to straight up kill her." She shrugged, making Elio snicker.

He gave the area one more good look to make sure everything was in place before making his way towards the staircase. "Ready to go finish up this deal?" Elio asked, offering his arm out to Faye. "Yeah, this should be interesting." She replied, grabbing his arm dreamily, allowing the mobster to take her up the steps.

At the top of the staircase sat a room that was set up to conduct meetings in. The room was square and relatively small, acting as a loft area overlooking the strip club. The walls around were painted a light shade of purple and decorated in various photos of the different strippers. On the very back, on a black side table, sat a small framed photo of Faye and Atlas standing in front of a proud-looking May.

In the middle of the room were two white couches facing each other. A weary and tired looking May sat on the couch that faced more towards the club while a tall man similar in appearance to Atlas sat next to her. He looked to be high on something, continuously lulling off onto the mistress's shoulder.

Faye was all too familiar with this setting, having spent many nights in this room with the red-headed woman. Normally, she would sit next to May, having to face whoever she needed to negotiate with. This was a nice change for once, no longer having to put on a show for anyone.

The moment the footsteps hit the floor, May stood up to greet the man, only to be met with the horrifying realization that he had a guest with him. There stood Faye Merci, clinging to Elio's arm with a giddy smile on her face like a love-struck puppy. She wanted so badly to scream, but kept it in, if only for the sake of everyone in the room.

"Well?" she asked hopefully. "Is everything up to your standards?" Elio made his way over to the empty couch, pulling Faye down to sit in his lap. "So far, the place looks good." He nodded approvingly, placing his large hand onto the younger woman's thigh, stroking it affectionately. Every little movement made the Danish woman flinch.

She feared for the safety of her friend, but hoped that with the final property accessed and signed over, the mob boss would leave them alone. May thought Elio was using her friend as a sort of hostage, not quite making any threats towards her, but letting the overall message linger in the air. If that were the case, then Faye might actually come out of this encounter just fine. All she had to do was keep it together and not draw any type of attention.

"Hey that cute girl looks pretty familiar." The man next to her slurred, his face bright red. "She looks like our daughter." May groaned internally, nearly forgetting the nuisance sitting next to her. "We don't have a daughter." She reminded him in a strict, stoic voice. "We don't!?" He sounded surprised. "Well then, who's that strange girl that always comes over to our house and eats our food?"

"That's Faye." May deadpanned, regretting her choice to bring her husband to the meeting. "Oh yeah! Faye! I like Faye. When's she coming over?" He asked, his head leaning against her shoulder.

"I'm right here." The woman in question spoke up with an annoyed eye roll. "Faye? Is that really you?" The man tried to sit up but nearly fell off the couch. May quickly caught the man, pulling him back up on the couch, this time pushing his head into her lap.

"I apologize for my husband. He just got out of surgery, so he's a little out of it at the moment." She explained, stroking the man's head. "What the hell did you do this time, Jake?" Faye asked curiously, with a hint of concern in her voice. "I can't chew gum and walk, otherwise I fall down the stairs." He slurred out a response. "It's okay though, doctors say after pills wear off, I'll be thinking good again." He kept swaying his head back and forth, attempting to nuzzle May's lap.

"How are you not dead yet?" She sighed, shaking her head in disappointment at him. "Same way you're not dead yet. Sheer determination." He lifted his hands up as though to emphasize his point. "Fair enough." She said, going back to playing with her lover's hands.

May and Elio went back to discussing the arrangement of the deal while their respective partners sat idly by. The mistress's eyes kept darting over to the young woman who seemed completely unbothered by everything. If anything, she looked as though she was enjoying the crime lord's company. 'Clear case of Stockholm syndrome.' She thought bitterly to herself.

"Faye!" Jake suddenly shouted, once again pulling them out of their discussion, much to Elio's annoyance. "What?" She asked, already sick of his outbursts. "Have I ever told you how pretty your name is?" The mobster let out an irritated sigh, warning May to silence her husband. "Jake please." She pleaded with him, hoping to break through his drug induced haze. "What? I'm just complimenting my friend. She has a great name. Much better than that awful name those assholes gave her." He laughed.

All eyes turned to the rambling man, curiosity etched on everyone's face. "What name?" Faye asked, unsure of what he was talking about. "Oh, you know the name. So gross and unfitting. Remember? They used to call you the cannibal witch?" He laughed as though it was the funniest joke.

Faye's eyes widened in shock and hurt, while May smacked the man upside his head. "Jake! We promised we'd never talk about it again." She chided him. "Cannibal witch?" Elio repeated, confused about the whole situation. "Yeah! That was the nickname she was given when she..." It was then that Jake's face went pale as realization hit him.

"Shit!" He exclaimed, knowing he royally screwed up. "Faye I am so..." "Shut up." She interrupted him with a dark expression, completely silencing the man. "But I..." "I don't want to hear it, just shut up."

The room went completely silent as the tension rose. Faye's eyes were frozen in a glare directed at the drugged up man, something close to hatred sparked in them. She wanted so badly to jump across the room and strangle him, but stayed still, trying her hardest to disappear.

"Faye..." May said softly, giving the woman a sympathetic look. "It's fine." Faye retorted, hugging Elio's arm tightly. "Just finish the exchange so that we can leave." Elio, who did not know to what they were talking about, couldn't agree more. The fact that this pathetic man had the audacity to upset his Faye was more than enough cause for him to put a bullet in between his eyes.

After an hour of discussing and a little more negotiating, the mistress and the mob boss came to an agreement. He snapped his fingers and one of the gangsters behind him brought out a briefcase full of cash. "You can count it if you want, but everything should be there." He explained, handing her over the money.

May hesitantly took the briefcase while giving Faye a worried look. She knew now that any chance she had at saving her friend was completely crushed by the idiotic outburst her husband made. Even if he was hurting her, there was no chance she'd turn to the couple for help, not with the reminder of what he did lingering over her head.

Elio and Faye made their way out of the building, their moods both being soured by what happened. "Is everything okay, doll?" He asked, his voice soft and gentle. "I'm fine." She replied coldly, looking everywhere but at the man. "You don't sound fine." He pointed it out as he opened the car door for her. "Yeah, I know… It's just, well, Jake can be extremely insensitive, I mean, who is he to crack jokes when it's his fault I'm stuck with the damn nickname?"

He looked at her as he started the car, hoping for her to continue on. "Can I ask?" He wondered, with a look of concern and curiosity. She shook her head, looking out the window in melancholy. "Remember when I told you I'm not fragile? Well, I am stupid and easy to manipulate." She sighed. "Jake took advantage of that."

Fiery orange eyes darkened the moment she spoke, and he nearly turned the car around. "No! Not like that!" Faye swore, noticing the deadly look the mobster gave. "What did he do to you?" Elio growled through gritted teeth. "He lied to me." She replied. "Tricked me into a dangerous situation and nearly got me killed, all to save his friend." There was a bitter sound to her voice as she spoke.

Just as she was about to explain what happened, lights flashed behind them, changing from red to blue back to red. "Shit." Elio muttered, irritated by the disruption. "Friends of yours?" Faye asked teasingly. "Hardly. I'm pretty sure it's one of my brothers."

Chapter: 31

They pulled off in to a parking lot with the cop car right behind them. Elio stepped out of the vehicle after telling Faye to stay put. She watched from the passenger side window as Cosimo exited his car. He walked up to the mobster with an arrogant smirk on his face. She pressed her ear up to the window, listening in on their conversation.

"Elio Eclisse, I need to bring you in for questioning." He spoke in an authoritative tone while holding out a pair of handcuffs. "On what grounds?" Elio asked with a growl to his voice. "Regarding the disappearance of Pete Jones. We have multiple accounts stating you were not only the last person to see him, but you also made threats to his life. There is a suspicion of foul play."

Faye couldn't help but roll her eyes at this. Some rich asshole goes missing and suddenly the entire world has to stop for them. She could guarantee that if it were her that suddenly went missing, not one person would come looking outside of friends and family. 'And even them… They didn't seem to care last time.' She thought bitterly.

She couldn't take any more of this nonsense and finally stepped out of the car. "You know, at my last job, plenty of people threatened me and not one single cop showed up." She spoke up, catching the attention of both men.

"None of those threats were followed through with, obviously, since you're still standing here." Cosimo snarked back. "And his threats weren't followed through with either. We've been together this whole time," Faye pointed out, causing Elio to chuckle. "It's true. We've been together all night and day. Pete probably got lost on his way home last night. We have an alibi for after the party." Elio said as he stepped next to Faye, draping his arm over her shoulder.

"Oh, he made it home just fine." Cosimo said, calmly. "It was when he was supposed to be at work today that he went missing. His vehicle was found parked outside some ally way all beat up, and that girl's word on where you were is as good as mud."

"We have an alibi for today too, actually." Faye spoke up. "Oh really? This outta be good. What solid alibi could you two possibly have? Huh?" the detective asked, rather amused at the woman's claim. The mobster looked down at her slightly, also curious about where she was going with it. "Elio took me to visit my dearest friend who recently got out of the hospital. You might know him. His name is Jake Saken."

232

She gave him an innocent smile, testing if he would recognize the name. Cosimo's eyes narrowed. "If it is the Jake Saken that I am thinking about, there is no way he would involve himself with lowlife criminals like you. He is a highly respected intelligence analyst." He spat. 'You obviously don't know him well enough.' She thought with a snicker. "Are you kidding? I've known him most of my life. He's practically like a second father to me." She retorted, a sly grin daring him to argue.

He shook his head, pulling out his phone. "I can't believe I'm about to humor you." He grumbled, dialing Jake's phone, and placing him on speaker. "Hello?" His voice rang through the phone. "Hello, agent Saken? It's Cosimo." The detective spoke. "Cosimo? I'm currently on leave right now so whatever case you're working on will have to wait until I recover." Jake spoke politely yet groggily.

"I'm aware, and I'm terribly sorry to bother you, but I have a girl here trying to use you as an alibi." He explained, just as politely. "Oh? Who?" He asked. "I can verify if it's true or not." Faye relaxed a little, realizing that the drugs were wearing off on him. "Faye Merci." He responded. "Says she was with you all day for a visit." Cosimo smirked. "Oh Faye? Yeah, she was here since early this morning with her boyfriend. They just left not too long ago."

Jake spoke so calmly and sincerely, Faye almost believed the little fib. "Sweet girl really, came to make sure I was okay and help my beautiful wife. She's like the daughter I never had, and her boyfriend is pretty great too. Helped us do some packing for when we move. Such an adorable couple." She had to keep herself from rolling her eyes. "Is that all you need to know?" He asked. "Yes, thank you, and I hope you make a speedy recovery." Cosimo responded before hanging up.

"So, does our story check out?" Faye asked smugly. "I suppose it does." Cosimo admitted. "Elio, you are free to go." He gritted his teeth. The mobster shrugged, a sly smirk on his face. "Nice seeing you again, brother." His voice lowered into a more dangerous tone. "If I were you, I'd stay clear of diners. Never know what can happen at one."

Before Cosimo could retort, Elio and Faye already made their way back to the car, leaving the detective to seethe. He had to admit, the little pharmacy tech was pretty interesting. But the fact that she could pull a highly respected man out like that made her far more dangerous than either detective could expect.

He pulled out his phone, calling his other brother. "Hey Cosimo, did you get Elio?" Luciano answered cheerily. "No." He retorted through gritted teeth. "He apparently had a pretty solid alibi." He was still in disbelief that agent Saken would vouch for the two. He must have been really out of it to not recognize Elio, but there was no way he would lie about something like that.

"Darn… That's no fun," Luciano tsked. "Oh well, better luck next time." He seems so chill about it, like he could care less if Elio was arrested or not. "What about Faye? How is she doing?" He changed the subject quickly. "She's moody as ever." Cosimo responded. "But I think we should change up our game plan with her." He suggested. "Oh, you mean leave her alone and double down on Elio?"

Luciano grew quite the soft spot for Faye and didn't want to do anything that would cause her harm. He wanted to have more of a relationship with her, but with Elio in the picture, that wouldn't ever happen. He made the decision that so long as she and Elio were happy, he'd stay out of their business for now.

"No, I think we should focus primarily on Faye." Cosimo responded. "Dig up as much dirt as possible on the broad." He decided she was a far greater threat than they originally thought. "Cosimo…" Luciano sighed. "That's a terrible idea. We have already dug through her files and she's completely clean." He really just wanted to leave her alone and let her play house with the mobster.

She wasn't hurting anyone by doing that as far as they could tell. "We've only looked at her files. We need to really start looking into her life. Interview friends, family, and acquaintances, and get some real dirt on her. There is no way she'd end up with a guy like that if she was actually innocent." He decided if she truly wanted to play Bonnie and Clyde with Elio, he'd make her life a living hell and destroy everything for her.

"Look, if you're planning on going after Faye, I will not stop you." Luciano resigned. "But I ain't going to help you either. I don't think she's done anything wrong, and we can't lock someone up for falling in love." He sounded a little melancholy at the last part. "I think hurting the one thing in this world that Elio seems to actually care about is a terrible idea, and frankly, I don't want to be gunned down by him again, so I'll keep out of this investigation." The detective spoke guiltily, knowing he'd be letting down his brother.

"Fine." Cosimo snapped. "I'll deal with the brat on my own." He hung up angrily, baffled that his own brother, who had stuck by his side all this time, was now siding with an obvious criminal. Sure, he couldn't prove she did anything wrong, but she had to have some skeletons in her closet. He just needed to keep looking, regardless if Elio actually tried to kill him or not.

The drive had been silent and awkward. Faye's heart race from the adrenaline she felt moments before. A part of her still couldn't believe Jake would actually lie to a cop like that for her, though after his little outburst it was the least he could do.

"That was pretty clever." Elio suddenly spoke up, breaking the silence. "Using that man as an alibi. How did you know he'd cover for us?" Faye gave a look of boredom, finding the question annoying.

"He has to. It's part of the deal." She answered, as if it were obvious. "What deal?" He asked. "The deal of the book. I told you about it. People ask me for favors and write their names down in the book. Jake has the most amount of favors owed." She shrugged. "What kind of favors does he owe you he'd lie to the cops just to make up for it?"

Faye sucked in a deep, shaky breath, not wanting to answer. "He got me kidnapped and tortured by the drug cartel." She finally said, creating a tense silence. Elio felt his hands tighten around the steering wheel, his anger bubbling up.

"He did what?" He asked her to clarify. "Two years ago, he lied to me and told me I was going on a relaxing vacation to Mexico. It was when I was at my lowest, so I figured it was just a friend trying to cheer another friend up. It turns out that wasn't entirely true." Her eyes went dull as she explained.

"Apparently, a cop friend of his went missing down in Mexico. He believed it was the cartel and well... He sent me down there with a tracker... I... I was there for two weeks before they found me... I had to do terrible things just to survive." Her voice went quiet.

"On the bright side, he's now completely indebted to me. Has to do whatever I say, otherwise May will divorce him." She tried to sound more cheerful, but it was difficult. What Jake put her through was completely unforgivable. It nearly destroyed his marriage and almost got her killed. The fact that he could joke about it so openly was almost sickening, even if he was on high doses of painkillers.

"So how does this whole favor thing work?" Elio asked, attempting to change the subject. "I feel like it's very self-explanatory." Faye answered. "I do people favors and they do me favors back." She shrugged. "I mean, how do you get people to pay you back? There's no way they're willing to do what you say without force." He wondered.

She smiled at this. "I wouldn't ever force anyone to do anything, but a little blackmail never hurt." Elio couldn't help but laugh. "Damn, I never knew my doll was quite the loan shark." He smirked, squeezing her thigh. She giggled at his comment, relaxing as the tension died down. It felt as though a weight was lifted off of her chest.

"So, where are we heading to now?" Faye asked, leaning her face against the window. "Nowhere fancy, just an old bar a friend of mine owns." He replied, pulling up into a nearly empty parking lot of an old, dingy building that had the words 'Maurice's Corner' flashing overhead. He led her out of the car and through the parking lot towards the bar.

Once they entered, Faye looked around, enjoying the rundown aesthetic this place held. The lighting throughout wasn't overly bright, just a nice dim yellow color. The walls were covered with old pictures of the city and historical newspaper clippings. Country music played over the speakers at a low volume that was pretty easy to tune out.

She noticed the bar didn't have too many customers, maybe five people tops, which brought her some relief. "How are you feeling, doll?" Elio checked in on her mental wellbeing. "I feel fine." She smiled up at him. "Great." He grinned down at her, leading the woman towards the bar area, pulling out a stool for her to sit. "I was going to take you to some big fancy place, but I thought you might need a mental break from all that."

The fact that he knew not to take her anywhere too fancy and crowded right now showed just how much he truly loved and cared for her. She held an adoration for quieter, quainter areas that had plenty of interesting items to stare at, and this bar reminded her of the one her grandmother worked at when she was a child. The bar stool sat a little too high, preventing her feet from reaching the ground, though it gave Elio no problems at all.

"Hey Maurice." Elio greeted the tall southern man that came out of a backroom. "Elio." Maurice grunted back in his thick southern accent as he walked towards the couple. "Drinking early again, are we?" He teased the mobster, a sly grin on his face. "Shut the fuck up." Elio snapped with a roll of his eyes. "Eh, no swears in my bar," He teased.

Faye giggled softly to herself at the exchange between the two, causing Maurice to turn his attention towards her. "You didn't tell me you were bringing a pretty little lady in," he smirked, causing Elio to narrow his eyes in warning. "Hello Miss." He purred, taking Faye's hand in his. "The name's Maurice. What brings you here on this fine day?" He gave her hand a soft kiss, irritating the Elio more.

"I'm Faye, and Elio brought me here." She smiled, leaning her head against the mobster's arm. "Ah." He chuckled. "You're the stubborn beauty that has the big bad Elio whipped." He winked at her.

"Maurice, if you keep flirting with my girlfriend, I will rearrange your skeleton." Elio growled menacingly, which only caused Maurice to burst out laughing. "Oh, calm your ass!" He grinned with sharp teeth. "You know I don't want your girl. She ain't my type. I like my women as slutty as can be." He sang the last part. "Whatever." Elio muttered grouchily. "Just keep your filthy fucking hands off her." He warned.

"Fine, I ain't going to touch her, but I owe her a drink." He said smugly. "Owe me a drink? Why?" she questioned. "Cause I ain't never met a single damn person who could put Elio in his place like you. I told him your drinks are on me if he ever brought you in and I am a man of my word." He proclaimed proudly. "Now what's your poison?"

Faye stifled a giggle at the goofy man. "She's not a drinker." Elio answered for her, dryly. "Let the little lady speak for herself." Maurice chided. "He's right." She agreed with her boyfriend. "I'm not a drinker. Causes me too many problems." She explained, resting her cheek on her hand. "Well, it ain't got to be alcoholic." He retorted. After a lot of persuading on Maurice's part, Faye chose a virgin mix, watching intensely as he prepared her drink.

"It's okay, doll. He won't drug your drink," Elio whispered reassuringly, allowing her to relax. The night prior still weighed heavily on her mind, with the creepy old man being one of the few people to shake her up badly. It took a lot for someone to put her in such a helpless position, and she was truly grateful she had Elio to protect her from him. The fact that Cosimo wanted to arrest the man for ridding the planet of that pathetic scumbag made her blood boil. Wasn't there other things in the world to focus on besides the disappearance and possible death of a rapist?

Once Maurice made her drink, being showy about it, he handed it off to Faye, who was pretty impressed. The three got to talking, Faye mostly listening to the two men chat, putting her piece in when needed. This moment just felt so normal to her, as if she wasn't dating one of the deadliest criminals around.

Time went by quickly, and before they knew it, the sun was already beginning to set. "Well, we better head off." Elio said nonchalantly, standing up from the stool. He helped Faye get up before saying a quick goodbye to Maurice. She waved happily at him, which he returned with a giant, toothy grin.

"Come along, doll, let's get home before all the meth heads come out." Elio smirked, pulling her up against his chest. "Meth heads aren't that bad if you don't make eye contact." She pointed out. "I worry about you, doll." He retorted, pushing her gently into the car. "I feel like I've been hearing that a lot lately." She hummed, leaning back in her seat with her eyes closed.

"Well, pretty soon, it'll only be me worrying about you." He ran his fingers through her hair, ruffling her locks a bit. "Please don't kill my friends and family." She requested jokingly. "Alright." He sighed teasingly. "But only if you behave." She giggled at this. "You know, I'm actually not all that attached to them." She opened one eye, a mischievous smile on her face. Elio laughed sincerely at this, starting up the vehicle to head back to the base.

Halfway through the drive, Faye ended up falling asleep, her head against the window. The mobster's eyes scanned over the slumbering woman for a moment, wishing he didn't need to look away to focus on the road. He decided he wouldn't blindfold her since she was deep in sleep, and he didn't want to risk accidentally waking her up after putting her through such a long week.

As much as he was used to the criminal lifestyle, he understood she was not, and the constant paranoia and harassment couldn't have been easy on her, though he had to admit she took it all pretty well. Though the more he learned about her, the more sense it made why she acted how she did. "Poor sweet, innocent girl, thrown into everyone's cruel game." He cooed. "Pretty soon, you won't have to struggle or worry anymore. I'll make sure of it." He promised her, finally coming up to the base.

Slowly, he came to a stop, being mindful not to shake her up too much. He made his way over to the passenger side, picking her up bridal style. She stirred for a second before nuzzling into his chest, her body completely relaxed. He wondered for a second if she slept this well around anyone else, though it seemed obvious that she wouldn't. As he entered the building, he put on a stoic expression, ready to murder the first gangster that dared to disturb him. His only goal was to get Faye to their bedroom and hold her close.

Elio could feel a pair of eyes staring him down while his back was turned. "Keep looking at us and I'll gouge your fucking eyes out, Leo." He snapped at the young gangster, who quickly put his head down and scurried away, not wanting to push his luck.

Leo truly believed that Faye and Elio were in a relationship. He ran out of ways to explain to himself why those two were so close and affectionate with one another. He thought, in the beginning, that Elio was manipulating her into believing he had some sort of attachments to her.

Never in a million years would Leo ever consider that the deadliest mob boss in the city, possibly the country, would ever have feelings for someone, especially someone who was seemingly insignificant. The last few days spoke for themselves, though, with how Elio reacted to every little thing that involved Faye. From taking care of her when she was sick to spoiling her with gifts and luxury outings, it was a safe bet that the mob boss held some adoration for the strange girl. He apparently even placed a hit on some hot shot attorney who got handsy with her at a party.

Leo didn't have a doubt in his mind that Faye was head over heels in love with Elio. The way she clung to him like a little puppy clung to their master spoke for itself. He worried for the woman's sanity a bit, but also he wanted it to truly work out for her. She seemed like a genuinely nice girl and had shown the gangster nothing but kindness, albeit she'd did it in a somewhat sassy way, but her actions were sincere.

In a way, Faye reminded him of his older sister with how she teased him and cooked for him. When he originally believed she was being sent off to some brothel, he felt a sense of protectiveness towards her, ready to transfer over as a bodyguard to whatever place she got sent to. To his relief, Elio explained to him she was to move into the base and live in the boss's bedroom, which meant she would be completely safe and secure. Leo shook his head, smiling at the thought that the weird ray of sunshine would live here, brightening up the otherwise dreary base.

They made it back to the room with Elio nearly tripping over Caligula. Luckily, he avoided the little orange menace right on time. He did throw out a couple of soft swear words in the process.

As he lowered her onto the bed, he stripped her of her attire, hands ghosting over her nude form as he traced every curve on her body. He could sit there for hours watch her sleep, and often did as he found it difficult to fall asleep himself. When the entire world wanted you dead, sleep wasn't the greatest option. Tonight was different. He wanted to fall asleep with her curled up in his arms. Enemies be damned.

Undoing his tie, he made his way back over to the door, locking it so that no one could enter. He then made his way to the girl and sat her up as he took off his shirt. He wrapped it around her, covering up her exposed bosom, and slid it down as a nightgown. She unconsciously wrapped her arms around herself, taking a deep breath to take in Elio's scent with a content smile.

"So cute." He mumbled, moving her so that she was lying underneath the blankets. He crawled in on the other side after turning out the lights, pulling her up against his chest, nuzzling his face into the crook of her neck. "I love you more than anything, Faye." He mumbled. "My beautiful, amazing little doll." For once, he finally let himself fall into a peaceful sleep, his grip on her tightening like a little boy with his favorite teddy bear.

Faye woke up feeling alert and refreshed, ready to take on whatever challenge the day called for. She could feel her lover snuggled up against her, spooning her from behind. His arms were wrapped securely around her torso as he curled up around her. She attempted to move out of his embrace but was met with an expected resistance. "Elio..." she whined, a sweet smile on her face. "I need to feed the cats."

Instead of the snarky, suggestive reply she would normally get from the man, she received a low groan as a response. It almost sounded like a quiet snore.

Wait, was he still asleep? She couldn't help but wonder, but as she shimmied and struggled to turn and face Elio, her theory was confirmed. She couldn't help but admire him in his slumbering form, his facial features completely relaxed.

Faye noted how his normally slicked back hair was a ruffled mess spread out along the pillows. She couldn't help but reach up and stroke his short, soft locks, admiring the amazing color of it. In its natural state, his hair had cute little curls to it that bounced around his face.

Slowly moving her fingers down, she traced the outline of his facial features, lingering right above his scar. She thought for a moment before pressing her hand against the scar, feeling how deep it ran. "Oh Elio." She whispered. "The world has been so cruel to you." She wondered what caused such a large mark.

Her curious fingers moved down, finding the edge of his lips. They were slightly parted, soft breaths falling out as his chest rose and fell. "You know, Elio, I remember the countless times you've woken me up by shoving your tongue down my throat. Maybe I should return the favor." She giggled quietly as she slowly bent over, closing the distance with her lips in a sweet, chaste kiss.

Just as she was pulling away, his eyes slowly opened, being met with the most adorable sight. Faye's bright blue jewels widened with a guilty look on her face. "Well. Well. Well." He tutted in a deep gravelly voice. "What do I have here?" He held a smug grin, loving the look she had at being caught. "Was my sweet little doll trying to pull one over on me?"

Faye gave a sheepish smile, knowing there was no way he'd let her get away with messing with him in his sleep. "I was just admiring your face, is all." She still tried to get away with it. "Oh, really?" He tilted her chin up with his thumb, staring deep into her eyes. "Well, by all means, allow me." He leaned down, mashing his lips back against hers, forcing his tongue into her mouth. She wrapped her arms around his neck, allowing him to deepen the kiss.

He finally pulled away, allowing her to take deep breaths of air as he rubbed her back soothingly. "You better be careful doll, I am a dangerous criminal after all." He teased, giving her neck a little nip. "Oh come now, Elio, I highly doubt that. I don't think you could even harm a fly." She teased back, snuggling into his embrace. "Doll, as much as I admire your faith in me, I did murder ten men in front of you." He pointed out.

"My eyes were closed during it, so as far as I'm concerned, they all passed away from natural causes." Elio couldn't help but chuckle at this. "They each had bullet holes in their heads." Faye rolled her eyes at this comment. "So naturally they died." She jested. "Besides, I didn't actively see you shoot them, so my point still stands." There was no use arguing, so instead he went back to snuggling against her.

The two of them went about their day, arm in arm, as Elio made his rounds around town. He felt a little bad, not being able to take her on a proper date that day, but she didn't seem to mind, happy to at least be with him. Plus, she rarely got to see the city, so she found joy in driving around with her wonderful boyfriend.

According to him, the clubs were all running smoothly, so there was no need to fully involve himself for now. While she didn't fully understand what he was doing, she enjoyed listening to him talk about his work now and then asking him to explain. Faye felt incredibly lucky to be with someone who was both badass and loving, and she truly couldn't wait to spend the rest of her life with this man.

The day went by just as quickly as the day before, forcing Faye and Elio to part ways. As heartbreaking as it was for them, they knew it was only temporary. As the mob boss pulled up to her house, he parked the car, pulling her against him as he peppered kisses all along her neck. He let his hands wander down her back, slithering up her shirt. He moved his lips against hers, leaning over the seat to press her fully against the window.

She turned into a flushed mess against him, submitting to his every move. Elio finally pulled away from her, satisfied with the marks he made. "You better get going, doll, before I change my mind and drive you back to the base." He smirked at the flustered woman. She exited the car hesitantly, almost tempted to take him up on the threat, but decided against it. After all, they didn't have that much longer until she was all his.

Chapter: 32

'It's been a while.' 'Did you think you could fucking hide from me, you bitch?' 'Answer your fucking phone.' 'Did you seriously fucking block me?' 'It doesn't matter. I know where you work now. I'll talk to you real soon.'

Two weeks had passed since their weekend out together, and the two grew closer to one another. Faye spent her time when she wasn't at work, going through her house and packing up the items she wanted to take with her. While she told her family she was planning to move soon, she hadn't quite broken the news to them about where she was going and that she had a boyfriend. She just wanted them to collect whatever things they wanted from her house so she could donate the rest.

It was a Wednesday morning. Faye had gotten dressed for work and was waiting for Leo to finish getting ready so he could take her. She finally got used to the arrangements and actually felt pretty safe because of it. "Ready to go, sis?" Leo asked, car keys in hand. She gave him a nod, shooting a quick text off to Elio about how she'll call him on her first break. *'I'll be looking forward to it. Love you.'* She had the biggest grin on her face, hugging her phone to her chest. "I'm guessing you finally know what whore house he's sending you to," Leo teased her knowingly.

She smacked him on the back of his head lightly, scowling in annoyance. "Awe, don't be like that. You know I'm teasing." He snickered. "I hate you." She rolled her eyes. "Yeah right." Leo retorted. "You don't hate anyone, sis." He ruffled her hair a bit. "You'd be surprised." She huffed, following him out the door.

'Are you still ignoring me you little bitch?' 'You think pretending I don't exist will save you?' 'I'll make your life a living fucking hell.' 'Looks like your cat's leg is all fixed up. Wouldn't want her to have another accident.' 'Unblock me, you fucking bitch.' 'I'll see you real soon.'

Faye made it to work, racing to clock in before she ended up late again. It took her a moment to mentally prepare herself, but after a deep breath, she was ready to tackle the day. She got deep into her work, the amount of pharmacy orders already starting off high. It took her about 50 minutes to get things cleaned up and easier to manage, and just as she was finishing up, a receptionist came running to the back with the biggest smile.

"Faye!" she spoke in a singsong voice. "What?" Faye mocked in the same type of voice. "There's a delivery just for you. Amber's coming back right now with it." She looked at her in confusion. "Pharmacy isn't getting any deliveries until next

241

week. Are you sure it's not treatment's?" She questioned. "I didn't say it was pharmacy. I said it was for you." If it were possible, her grin widened.

Faye looked at her skeptically, not sure she liked the idea of getting some random package. "What is it?" She questioned. "It's flowers. From the wonderful boyfriend you're so obsessed with." She teased lightly. Flowers? It wasn't strange for Elio to give her flowers, but he'd never send them directly to her work. It would bring in too much unwelcomed attention to the woman.

"Are you sure it's from my boyfriend?" She had a strange, uneasy feeling about it. "Well, that's what he told us. Said he was in a hurry but wanted to drop them off real quick and be on his way." Okay, now she was truly skeptical. There was no way Elio would ever show up at her work or home and not stick around to see her, even for a moment. Still, she was mildly curious, plus it was only flowers. How bad could it be? When the receptionist brought back the bouquet, Faye scrunched up her nose, absolutely irritated by the arrangement.

"Yeah, no." She said dryly. "These aren't from my boyfriend." The flowers were a mix of bright orange, neon pink and purple colors, making the whole bundle look like a total eyesore. They were also thrown together carelessly with a few weeds mixed in, as if the sender put little thought into the appearance.

To even pretend Elio would have sent this was an absolute insult towards the man. The flowers contained a mixture of orange lilies, yellow tansies, pink peonies, and the most shocking, monkshood. "None of you guys touched the actual flowers, right?" She asked, worried. "No, just the plastic part." The receptionist answered. "Oh, thank god." She sighed, putting on some gloves before handling the bundle. She took them out to the back dumpster, disposing of them without a second thought. She then quickly made her way back inside, trying not to bring too much attention to herself.

"Who in their right mind would send someone poisonous flowers?" Faye thought out loud to herself. She attempted to go through a list of people in her head, but came up blank. 'Could it be one of Elio's enemies?' She wondered, but just as she reached for her cellphone to call him, another receptionist popped in.

"Call for you on line three." She said sweetly. Without thinking, Faye answered the phone, giving her usual company greeting. "How may I help you?" She said in her best customer service voice. "Did you really think you could fucking hide from me?" A deep, familiar voice spoke, making Faye's stomach drop and face turn pale white.

"No." she whispered to herself. "God no." She could hear the man laughing, his voice like nails on a chalkboard to her. "Did you get my flowers? I thought they would be fitting for a bitch like you." She could feel tears prick at the corners of her eyes. "Please, just leave me alone already." She begged, bile caught in her throat. "Awe, but I did leave you alone, didn't I? I gave you two years to get your affairs in order." He mocked her.

"Besides, I already told you, I'll never fucking leave you alone!" Faye's mouth felt dry and her heart pounded hard in her chest. "Now you better unblock my phone number or else your cute little cats will be going for a swim in some boiling water." As much as she wanted to hang up on him, she knew he wasn't bluffing about his threat. Past experiences spoke for themselves about how badly this man wanted to hurt her. What made it worse was… "And you can tell whoever the hell you want. No one would ever believe you." It was true, no one had ever believed her, or at least didn't take her concerns too seriously.

Faye hung her head, trying her hardest not to cry in public as she went into her phone log and unblocked the man's phone number like he told her to. She felt sick watching the constant stream of messages fly in. "Stop." She cried quietly. "It doesn't look like anyone is home." He chuckled, her eyes widening at the realization. She hung up the phone, her hands shaking. "I need to go." She spoke quietly, walking to the office to grab her things.

She called up Leo after collecting her belongings and made her way to the back door. "Hey sis, what's going on?" He asked, rather confused that she was calling him this early in the day. "Please come get me." She squeaked out, her voice trembling. She sounded so fragile, it freaked him out. "I'm on my way, sis." He confirmed. "Just stay put. I'll meet you at the back entrance." Faye agreed, trying not to cry. Messages still popped up one after another, making it impossible for her to tell who sent it.

She took a deep breath, knowing the only thing left was to tell Elio. She had a hard time dialing his number; her phone now ringing over and over with that terrible man's number. She made the mistake of pressing answer. Panic flooded through her. "Took you long enough to fucking answer. Get my texts? I bet you did. You look so fucking cute when you're sleeping!" He sneered. She couldn't hit end call soon enough, tears now flowing. She had to call Elio, needed to hear his voice. Finally, she could dial his number, the texts still going off.

"Hello doll." He answered within two rings. "Elio…" the terrified woman spoke softly, relief flooding through her. "Is everything okay?" Concern ran through his body. "No." She admitted shakily. "I'm leaving work early, I'm just so…" It was taking every ounce of her willpower not to break down completely. "I'm scared." She finally confessed.

He went quiet, a dark, terrifying look crossed his face. Finally, he spoke up again. "Doll, have Leo take you straight to the club, and I'll be there soon, alright?" He spoke calmly. "But I need to get my cats first!" She panicked. "If I don't, he'll boil them alive!" She pleaded. The mobster wanted to ask her who 'he' was exactly, but didn't want to stress her out more than needed. "I'll have some men head over to your place right now and collect them, alright? I have three scouting your area currently." He reassured her, needing her to be in a safe place. "Okay." She whimpered, having no issues at all with the plan.

After they hung up, Elio told a few of his men to go down to Faye's house and collect her things, giving strict orders to shoot anyone who seems suspicious. A rage boiled up inside of him over the thought of someone harassing his Faye. Whoever this man was, was going to be broken apart in every way possible.

Finally, Leo made it back to the hospital, coming up to the door to knock. Faye peaked her head out, relieved to see the gangster standing on the other side. "Come on, sis, let's get you home." he attempted to calm her down. "Actually…" Her voice trembled a bit. "Can you take me to that one club? Dusk till Dawn? Elio wants to meet me there." He noticed she was constantly glancing around, looking over her shoulder. Her phone still kept pinging with text messages and phone calls. The gangster could only nod, dragging her over to the car to let her in. Whoever had this poor woman so shaken up had to know the world of shit he was about to be in.

'Is that your boyfriend?' 'Do you think he could actually protect you?' 'I can ruin his life too, you know.' 'I can make him hate you.' 'Are you going to ghost him too?' 'I'm watching you right now, you dumb bitch.' "Your little fucking boyfriend can't protect you.' 'Answer your phone again.' 'Answer your fucking phone.' 'If you don't answer your phone I'll set your fucking house on fire and record your stupid cats burning to death.' 'Once I'm done with that I'll bash your fucking brains in until you're nothing but a retarded fucking mess.'

Leo attempted to talk to her, but she was in a catatonic state, clutching her phone with a white knuckle grip. His heart shattered for the girl, wishing nothing more than for her troubles to end. He could only pray that this will all be over soon, at least for her sake.

He made his way to the exclusive club, not wanting to disobey an order from his boss. Once he arrived, he parked as close as possible to the building, still unsure of what she was trying to escape from. Leo made his way out of the car and opened the door for her, helping her out. It had been a demand of Elio that Faye was always the last person to exit the vehicle and the first person to enter, just in case there were potential threats nearby that could bring her harm.

They made it up to the building, skipping past the line to enter. The doormen, for a moment, attempted to give Faye and Leo a hard time, but luckily Opal was coming in for her shift and quickly spotted the trembling woman. "Faye!" She waved at her excitedly, running over to them.

"That's Elio's girlfriend, you know. The one that he said was allowed in whenever she pleased." Opal whispered into the bouncers' ears, terror and shock slapping them in the face. They stepped aside, letting the two come in, not wanting to get in any trouble with the mob boss.

"I appreciate the help, ma'am." Leo thanked the server, walking next to Faye, who still hadn't uttered a single word. "Of course." She smiled, walking on the opposite side of her. "It's great to see you again!" Opal beamed at the shaking girl, only to be met with silence. "Faye?" She attempted to grab her shoulder, but she flinched pretty badly.

"Something's got her really freaked out." Leo explained. "I couldn't get her to talk at all. The boss is on his way to figure out what's going on." Her phone went off again with another message. *'Think you can fucking escape into some fancy ass club? I'll be in there soon.'* She didn't even bother to check her messages anymore, knowing they were going to be from him. She just wanted it to stop, wanted him to disappear.

They escorted her to the private room in the back, away from the crowds and smoke. She fell on the couch, pushing her legs against her chest. Leo and Opal left the room, Opal going back to work while Leo stood guard outside of the room, a stern look on his face. He could only hope the boss would arrive soon to protect her from whatever monster was tormenting her.

'I'm inside.' The message appeared with a picture of the club's inside. Silent tears fell down her face as she curled up into herself. *'You know, the guy who owns this club is pretty brutal.'* She felt so pathetic, desperately needing someone to save her. *'When he finds out some crazy skank is running wild on his property, oh I could get off to the terrible things he'll do to you.'* She was a cornered animal being blocked in by a crazed hunter. *'You better fucking pray that I find you before him. I'll at least be gentle.'* "Elio." She mumbled, unable to stop the tears, "please save me." She let out a sob. *'Uh oh. Looks like he's here. Time to meet your maker, you dumb bitch.'*

Elio exited the car after pulling up to the club, slamming the door shut. He stormed into the building, a murderous look on his face. His beautiful doll was being harassed by some lowlife piece of shit, and now someone needed to die. He had a deadly aura surrounding him, causing people to move quickly out of the crime boss's way.

Making it to the back end, he spotted Leo standing in front of the door, pushing people away from the room. "What the hell happened to her?" Elio demanded. Leo looked up with both terror and relief. On one hand, he was terrified of the mob boss, more so when he was this livid, but Leo felt happy to see the one man who could pull Faye out of her head and protect her.

"All I know is that she was perfectly normal when I dropped her off and I got a phone call from her an hour into her shift asking me to come get her. Her phone has been blowing up since I picked her up, so she's definitely being harassed by someone." Leo gave the full rundown of what happened to Elio before stepping aside to let him in.

Once inside the room, Elio was met with the most heartbreaking sight. There on the couch lay Faye, curled up in a fetal position with tears streaming down her face. She trembled with silent sobs, seeming to not notice the mob boss enter the room. He closed the door carefully so as not to startle the girl.

"Doll." His voice was soft and tender. He approached her slowly. "It's okay, I'm here." He made his way to her side, leaning over to wrap his arms around her in a protective embrace. She flinched at first before melting into his touch, hiding her face in his chest. "Come on, doll." He kissed her head. "Let's go home, okay?" She nodded, still unable to form the proper words.

He collected her things, including her phone, the messages finally ending, and made his way out of the club. Elio carried the trembling girl, worried that if he didn't keep ahold of her, she might disappear. He took her out to the car, setting her down in the backseat before climbing in after her and pulling her onto his lap. The vehicle started up, pulling out of the parking lot and making its way onto the road.

"Now doll." He gave her a light squeeze as she buried her face in him. "Do you want to talk about what got you so freaked out, or do you need a moment?" He didn't want to pressure her too much, but also needed to know what was going on so he could fix it. She shook her head before reaching over to pull out her cellphone and hand it to him. Elio graciously took it from her, opening up her messages to read through everything.

The more and more Elio read, the angrier he became, his sharp teeth bared. He had to keep control of his emotions and strength, afraid of hurting Faye by squeezing her too hard. The threats to her safety and sanity, the insults, and suggestive comments, along with the overwhelming amount of pictures showcasing her in such vulnerable positions. Oh, this man definitely had a death wish.

"When did this all start?" He asked her, successfully masking his rage. "Five years ago." She answered solemnly. "But he left me alone for the last two years. I thought it was finally over." A tear slid down her face, which Elio quickly swiped away. Five years is a pretty long time to be holding onto a serious grudge. "Do you know why he's determined to ruin your life?" He wanted to figure out what kind of grudge he was dealing with. She nodded her head, looking up to meet his eyes.

"We used to chat through some game we were both into. He, for whatever reason, asked me out, and I rejected him. I got a terrible vibe from him, and I tend to listen to my gut on these things." Her voice sounded broken and exhausted. "He didn't take my rejection so well and kept pestering me about giving him a chance, blowing up my messages, having other friends in our party hound me and be an overall pain in the ass to me. Finally, I had enough and blocked him completely."

Elio listened intently, a frown etched on his face. "It didn't stop the harassment though, and I ended up deleting the game altogether to get rid of him. He found my phone number and all my socials and continued to torment me on there. Anytime I tried to get someone to help me, they would brush me off and tell me to quit being dramatic. It was just online, and I should just block him." She sounded so bitter.

"Well, blocking him online only made it worse. He stepped up his game and found where I lived and broke into my house multiple times. One time he came in and broke my cat's leg because I refused to unblock him on my cellphone. Another time, he poured bleach into my fish tank, killing all my fish."

She took a shaky breath before continuing. "Again, no one believed me, not even the police. They said I didn't have enough proof for them to do anything and even if I did, I don't know what this guy looks like or what his name is, so there isn't a lot that can be done against him. Also, because he isn't consistently stalking me, it makes it so much harder to prove it's the same person."

"And what about your family?" Elio decidedly asked. "I mean, from the sounds of it, they seem to look for a reason to fight." Faye gave a soft laugh at that comment. "Yeah, I know, which is why I couldn't bear the thought of telling them."

The mobster gave her a curious look. "Why?" He asked. "Because... I've done so many dumb things and caused them nothing but trouble. I just want to stop being a burden..." she whispered, tears falling from her eyes.

"Doll..." He spoke softly. "You're not a burden to anyone. It's okay to rely on people, especially those that you know and trust. Do you trust your family?" He asked. "Yes, of course. They've saved me from so many things, but I still don't want to involve them…" Her voice went quieter. "Why not?" He asked, though he wouldn't allow her to, anyway. "It's just… They can be overprotective and my parents are getting up there in age. I don't think they can carry a body like they used to."

He let out a hearty laugh, happy that she still had her sense of humor. He obviously would never involve them, but it was nice to hear she did still have people on her side. Even if those people were batshit crazy.

They made it back to the base, Faye's face completely hidden against Elio to prevent her from seeing. Once inside the building, he set her down, taking her hand in his. "The cats are in our room, so you don't need to worry about anything terrible happening to them." He promised. Faye nodded her head in acknowledgement. He brought her inside the room, locking the door to keep anyone else from entering.

She went to sit on the bed with Elio following suit. She looked at him with the most broken, desperate eyes he's ever seen. "Can I please stay here?" She asked, almost begging him. His eyes softened at the request. "Of course doll." He answered warmly, helping her remove her scrub top and shoes. She laid down, resting her head on his lap as he ran his fingers through her hair soothingly. "Stay here for as long as you need. Forever ideally."

She felt so safe and loved cuddled up against him, as if she were untouchable. "What do you want as an outcome of this?" Elio asked her, lying back against the mattress with her still lying on his lap. "I want him to leave me alone." She told him. "Just leave you alone?" he inquired, seeing if he could get her to give him the request. "He just needs to disappear. I want him to vanish completely."

Elio lifted himself up so that he could pick up Faye and lie her down on top of him. "Want him to vanish, huh? Would it bother you if I made him suffer first?" He gave a sinister smile. "No." She said dryly. "He deserves to suffer." She nuzzled against him, feeling completely relaxed in his embrace. He pulled her face up to his, giving her a tender kiss on the lips.

"Don't worry, my love, I'll take care of it." He promised her, ready to show just how far he will go for her. She felt great relief, as if the biggest weight had been lifted from her. Faye loved and trusted Elio and knew nothing could harm her anymore, though she felt a bit of guilt knowing that he once again had to clean up her mess.

"I'm sorry for dragging you into this." She mumbled sadly. "Don't be sorry." He said, his smile softening. "None of it is your fault. You don't deserve any of this abuse." He brought her in for another kiss. "I want to protect you and prove just how much I love you. Please let me prove myself." For the first time since the harassment started that day, Faye smiled. "I love you so much." She sighed against him, not wanting to move away from his embrace anytime soon.

Elio rubbed her back, enjoying Faye's warm, soft body on top of his. The mob boss thought about all the things he would do to that man to assure he fully paid for what he did. "I'll need to keep your phone." He told her, feeling her heart rate go down. "Keep it, smash it to bits. I don't care." She mumbled against his chest. He tilted his head, a crestfallen look in his eyes.

"I promise everything will be fine. Just stay in our room and let me take care of you." He nuzzled into her hair. She only snuggled in closer to him as a confirmation. "I'll be leaving soon, so just stay put and keep the door locked." He spoke softly to her, as she began moving off him. "Okay…" she said, looking dejected. "Don't give me that look." He cooed. "I won't be gone too long. I just need to run a few errands and I'll be back."

He pressed his lips against hers, savoring her taste, while she wrapped her arms around his neck. "I'll be patient." She whispered against his lips, feeling him smirk. "I know you will be, doll." He pecked her lips repeatedly. "You're just so good." He purred, causing her to melt against him.

Elio hesitantly pulled away, moving off the bed. "I had them bring some clothes for you, so they should be in the closet. The tuxedo cat is under the bed, and I do not know where the fucking orange menace is, but he's in here." He explained in a jovial manner, earning a giggle from her. "I love hearing you laugh. It's much more suitable for you than crying." He smiled fondly at her before leaving the room. Faye grabbed a nearby pillow, hugging it close to her chest. She never felt so loved and cared for in her life.

After leaving the bedroom, making sure the door was locked, Elio made his way to his office, slamming the door shut. His scorching red rage burnt so hot it became a black poison, ready to kill anything in his path. The thought of his beautiful, proud Faye being reduced down to a terrified, crying mess…

He slammed his fist down on the desk, nearly shattering it to pieces. That coward… That worthless, pathetic fucking coward made her cry, and that alone would not be tolerated. Elio decided that for every tear Faye shed, he would pull twenty from this pile of shit.

Elio paced back and forth in the office, smashing different objects in his path, trying to concentrate on his work, but finding it difficult to focus. How could he focus when his doll was a few doors down, sitting in their bedroom, absolutely terrified? A strange ringtone went off in his pocket, pulling him out of his destructive rampage. He pulled out Faye's phone and hit answer.

A feminine voice spoke from the other side. "Faye? Where did you go? You can't just leave work early without saying anything!" Elio ground his teeth together, not in the mood to deal with some broad who feels entitled to his doll's time. "Faye won't be back at work. She quits." He spoke bluntly, no longer willing to compromise with his beautiful doll. "Quit?" The woman questioned.

"But she still has the rest of this week and next. She wouldn't just abandon us like that!" He rolled his eyes at this, wondering if this woman was actually serious? "You've had her long enough. It's time to let her go." He sounded way calmer than he actually felt. "She's having some issues right now and it would be in her best interest to take some time away from everything." His words held a dangerous edge to it, warning the woman to drop it. "Can I at least speak to her? I just want to hear it from Faye." she pleaded. "No." Elio ended the call, not wanting to hear another word on the topic.

This whole stalker situation would be the final straw for him. He would no longer allow her to go anywhere without him ever again. He pulled up the messages on her phone once again, reading through every little thing the creep sent her. The pictures he sent were the most vile things ever, showcasing her lounging around her house in very little clothing. So this asshole has seen her body? He couldn't stand another moment of this, knowing his doll's tormenter was running around wasting resources.

He pulled out his phone to call up his men, waiting impatiently for them to answer the phone. They finally answered, luckily quickly enough not to end up on his hit list. "I need a list of every person who entered Dusk till Dawn in the last few hours." He ordered. "Along with the security footage from today. I want it here in the next two hours or I'll fucking bury you alive." He hit end call after hearing the affirmative, feeling himself heat up even more. According to the messages and photos, this creep followed his beloved into the exclusive club with no issues.

Elio needed to make a few rounds, but his mind kept going back to Faye. He didn't want to leave her all alone in the room, but didn't think she would be mentally ready to leave the base. He weighed his options and decided to at least check up on her and see if she needed anything. Now that he thought about it, she more than likely hadn't eaten anything yet, so getting her some food would be a priority. He made another call, placing an order at one of the nearby restaurants to be picked up by one of his men. He then left the now destroyed office, returning to his and Faye's bedroom to make sure she was doing alright.

Entering the bedroom, he looked over the whole room, only to spot her still lying on the bed, not having moved an inch since he left. She seemed to stare blankly at a wall, her two cats both cuddled against her. She held a pillow tightly against her chest, lost in a trance. He walked over to her, a neutral expression on his face, looming over the petrified woman.

Her eyes lit up at the sight of him, a soft, melancholic smile fell on her face. Elio crouched down, taking her chin in his hand so she was looking directly at him. "How are you feeling, doll?" He asked lovingly. "I'm feeling a lot better than I was." She responded, her voice soft and cracked from all the crying she's done.

He stood up, crawling on top of her, causing the cats to both move away from them. He had her pinned to the bed, face hovering right above hers. "You're doing such an amazing job." He told her. "Keeping yourself together." He propped himself up with one arm, trying not to crush her, and gently stroked her cheek with the other. "I can't imagine how terrified you are right now, but I promise it will all be over soon."

He was so sincere in his words; it made her heart flutter. She slinked her arms around his neck, pulling him closer to her as she snuggled into his chest. "I know you'll take care of it." She sighed against him, wanting nothing more than to stay in his arms. She understood that she would have to let him go soon to do his job. Her eyes widened in realization.

"I didn't actually tell anyone at work I was leaving." She spoke in a panic. "I need to call them and explain. I'll probably still be fired, though." She mumbled the last part quietly. "I already took care of it, my love." He pulled her in for a kiss. "But yeah, you have been terminated." He replied sheepishly, figuring he wouldn't tell her how he quit her job for her. "Oh, well..." she replied. "I don't think I'd be able to go back even if they did not fire me. Plus, they kept trying to postpone my end date." He gave her another kiss, glad that she had accepted that her life at that place was over.

"About your living arrangements." Elio spoke against her lips. "I know you want to say your goodbyes and all, but I don't feel comfortable having you be so far away from me." He nuzzled her face affectionately. "I can take you by to pack up and slowly move your things out, but I need you to stay by my side from now on." He would not negotiate with her and was prepared to tie her to the bed if necessary.

"Okay." she agreed, not even trying to put up a fight. "I don't want to be anywhere without you." It sounded almost pleading. Elio knew it was pretty low to take advantage of her weakened mental state, but he needed to do whatever he could to prevent another incident from happening. He also knew that once she was back to her normal, cheerful self, she would more than likely find humor in the situation and poke fun at him. Yet another reason for him to fix this problem as soon as possible.

Elio figured a few more minutes with Faye wouldn't hurt anything, especially since he didn't have too many fires to snuff out that day. He had his mouth against her neck, kissing and biting at her soft, sensitive flesh. He enjoyed every moan and mewl that left her throat as he marked her up. The temptation to rip off her clothes and claim her once again was strong, but he didn't want to risk hurting her even more. He would just have to be satisfied with the little kisses and nips for now. She didn't seem to complain though, as she was reduced to a moaning and giggling mess, enjoying every ounce of attention the mob boss gave her.

Finally, he let up, happy with his work on her skin. He ran his fingers over the fresh marks, checking to make sure none of them caused her too much discomfort. She watched him with half-lidded eyes and a far warmer and more blissful smile. In this moment, she wasn't pinned underneath a cold-hearted, deadly crime boss. Instead, she was in the tender embrace of her warm, caring boyfriend, who loved her more than anything. This would be the man she would spend the rest of her life with.

"I don't want to leave you." He sighed, pressing his face against her forehead. "But some errands I need to run can get rough, and I would prefer you rest and clear your head a bit." Faye pecked him on the lips as if to reassure him she would be just fine. "I'll be back soon doll, until then, just stay put for a little." He kept his lips firmly against hers. "I also ordered some food for you, which should be here soon."

Elio was using every bit of his willpower to pull away from her, wanting nothing more than to keep her underneath him. He kissed her a few more times and gave her neck a little nuzzle, causing her to giggle from how ticklish it was. He finally pushed himself off her, leaving her to pout slightly at the loss of contact. "Don't give me that pout. If you stay under me for a second longer, you might not be able to walk ever again. Is that what you want?" He scolded.

"Maybe." She gave a mischievous smile. "Walking isn't my favorite activity." He chuckled at this comment. "I'm glad you're feeling better, doll. Once this is all over, I'll take you out to someplace real special, alright?" He promised. "Just me and you all day and night." Faye's smile softened, her cheeks dusted pink. "I would love that a lot." Her voice was quiet and adoring. "Now, don't be late to your badass work obligations." She suddenly chided him teasingly, very much to Elio's amusement.

He adjusted his tie before reaching over to grab his jacket, which Caligula decided was the perfect bed for him. Faye had to stifle a giggle at watching the big, scary mob boss attempt to nudge the fluffy loaf off gently. The fluff ball saw it as some sort of game. He rolled on his back, playfully swiping at Elio's hand every time he reached down. After a few seconds of it, he finally picked the cat up and threw him on the bed. Faye couldn't help herself and busted out laughing. "Keep it up, doll, and we'll make a little trip to my office." He threatened in a low sensual voice, causing her to sputter, her face bright red.

Giving her one last glance, he turned to walk out the door, leaving her alone once again. At least she was safe in his bedroom, or hers and his bedroom now. It felt weird calling it her bedroom, her home, as if the reality of everything hadn't yet hit her. But as strange as it felt, it didn't feel wrong. Elio had been nothing but good to her and she truly was in love with the mob boss, so moving in with him was only natural. She just wished it had been on better terms and not at a low point.

She felt so angry with herself for allowing some creep to have enough power over her to reduce her to tears. Faye prided herself on being strong willed and not easily bothered, but this faceless creep was skilled at finding her in her most vulnerable moments and using them against her. He even convinced her friends and family around her that his torment was all harmless fun and that she was acting dramatically.

Faye admitted when the harassment first began, she didn't take it all too seriously, figuring if she simply blocked him and ignored it, it would all go away. He had to have better things to do than chase after some weird girl he barely even knew. For a few weeks, it seemed like she had been right. No more random friend requests on different sites, no more creepy comments, and no more having mutual friends hounding her to give him a chance. But her victory was short-lived as a barrage of texts started coming in, each one more depraved and violent than the last.

One of the worst texts, which made her involve the police, was a picture of her sleeping in her bed, wearing a tank top and some white panties. The text read: *'I'm going to tie you up, slit your wrists and fuck you while I watch you bleed to death.'* The asshole broke into her house while she slept. The police were no help at all. Telling her the best thing to do was change her locks and invest in security cameras.

No investigation, no scouting her neighborhood, not even an ounce of empathy. She was simply told to deal with it. He got cocky knowing that the law wouldn't help her and continued to send her similar messages, even paying people to follow her around. One person in particular actually ran her off the road, nearly landing her in the hospital. It was just a terrible accident caused by some drunk driver, her friends would tell her.

She knew the truth. The stalker made sure she knew. He texted her pictures of the wreck, telling her it was a shame she lived through it with minimum harm, as he always dreamed of sleeping with a mangled corpse. She would have laughed if she wasn't so emotionally drained from it all. His harassment went on and off for three years until he finally stopped, right before her trip to Mexico.

Now, after two years of blissful silence, this sick asshole crawled back into her life so he could finish the job of absolutely ruining her. It was different this time, though. She was no longer alone, with no one willing to believe her. Faye now had Elio to protect her from the torment, and a dark part of her hoped he would make this man's last moments of life an absolute nightmare. For all the terrible things he had done to her, she wanted him to suffer more than anything.

Just as she zoned out again, a knock sounded at her door. At first she was going to ignore it, not wanting any company in the room that wasn't her lover, but a familiar voice followed the knocking. "You okay in there, sis? I got some food for you." Leo spoke from the other side. Her stomach growled as if on cue, and the realization hit that she hadn't eaten anything that day. Faye decided Leo wouldn't be the worst person to talk to right now, especially for a moment.

She went to unlock the door, revealing a sullen-looking Leo holding a bag. He offered it to her, which she graciously took, setting it on a nearby table. "How are you holding up?" He asked, worried about her wellbeing. "Could be better, could be worse." She answered. "Hopefully, it will all be over soon." Leo looked at her, regret in his eyes. "I'm sorry." He apologized. "I should have done better to protect you." He looked positively heartbroken.

She offered him a warm smile. "It's not your fault. You didn't know I was being stalked." She reassured him. "Even if I didn't know, there was still more I could have done. I could have monitored the perimeter of the house to make sure no one was lurking around. I could have stayed right outside your work and monitored every damn person walking in and out of the building." He started rambling off the ways he could have protected her.

"Dude stop." Faye patted his shoulder. "You did everything you were ordered to do and got me out quickly, without question. Leo, you did an amazing job today and I'm super grateful to have you." She smiled at him, his eyes lighting up at her words. "I'm glad you're safe." He said happily. "And I hope the boss gives that asshole everything he deserves." Faye agreed with that.

"I'm heading over to the house to grab some things." Leo told her. "Congrats on moving in with the boss, by the way. Probably the most fitting placement for you." Faye laughed at this. "Want me to grab some things for you?" She thought about it for a second. "Can you grab my sketchbook?" She asked. "Sure thing, sis." He nodded before leaving the room. She closed and locked the door behind him. Wearing a tender smile on her face, she went to sit and eat.

Elio left the base, taking three of his men with him to ensure everything was dealt with swiftly and effectively. The sooner he snuffed out these problems, the sooner he could get back to his wonderful girlfriend. She really had made him softer — well, at least less blood thirsty. Knowing he had her waiting for him made him less likely to take his time with killing his victims. A lot of the deaths lately have been pretty quick, though he still gave special treatment to those who had screwed up big time. He had a pretty creative punishment in mind for a special someone.

As he sat in the vehicle, the corners of his lips pointed down, and his sharp teeth bared, a vibration went off in his pocket. He grabbed for his phone on instinct, only to find there was no notification. He realized the vibration was coming from Faye's phone, which he still kept on him. Elio planned on getting her a new phone anyway and have her number completely changed. He knew he was being extremely controlling of her, but her safety took priority over her independence, and at least he didn't plan on isolating her from her friends and family.

He took one look at the message and nearly crushed the phone in rage. '*You know I was only teasing you, right?*' The same number that had been blowing up her phone all day appeared with the text. This asshole must be really fucking dense with how casually he thinks he could speak to Faye. *'Let's talk about things, alright? It was all just a funny misunderstanding.'* Let's talk? Elio suddenly felt very conversational.

The three men in the car all went pale white, feeling the venomous aura leaking from the mob boss. They all knew to keep their heads down, otherwise they would be the target of his rage. *'Okay, we can talk.'* He texted back, wondering if the creep would be this dumb. *'Let's meet at Maurice's. 6:00. Don't be late.'* Elio's texts to the man were an obvious trap and there was no way he would take the bait. *'Alright, see you then, **babe**.'* He gritted his teeth, a malicious sneer on his face. Oh, this creep was going to regret every ounce of his existence.

The two-hour time frame he gave his men was ending, and lucky for them, Elio got exactly what he was looking for. He scanned through the list of guests, focusing on who entered right after Faye, which narrowed it down to fifty people. He pulled up the messages on her phone, clicking on the photo the moron sent her, and using the time it was sent to match up with the many security cameras he had in the lobby area.

Zooming in, he found a man standing in the middle with his phone raised in the air as if to take a picture. This footage was only done a minute before the text had been sent to her. "Found you." Elio chuckled threateningly, his phone showing the ID of a forty-year-old pathetic looking man with the name Thad Ralston on it. He just gave the faceless man a face along with a name. Now all he had left to do was to meet this man and teach him a lesson he could take with him into his next life.

He finished up all his "errands" and started making his way back home to his love, giving the orders to his men to clean up the messes. Elio felt rather excited to tell her the good news, that he found the man and would have him taken care of by the end of the day. As he made it to the base, he quickly jumped out of the car, making a beeline straight to the bedroom, opening the door and slamming it shut behind him.

Faye, who was watching some old western, got up to greet him. He took the remote off the table, shutting the television off, before scooping up the woman and dumping her right on the bed, causing her body to bounce slightly. She laughed quietly as Elio crawled on top of her, pinning her to the bed for the second time that day.

He nuzzled against her, peppering her skin with love bites and kisses, sending her into a fit of giggles. He held her down, grinding against her to elicit some moans. Elio felt nothing but pure joy and bliss having her underneath him, giving her the attention she deserved. The mob boss finally pulled away after a few minutes of getting her completely worked up, pulling her into his lap.

"Guess what, doll?" He grinned down at her. "What?" She asked, panting slightly. "I found the creep." He sounded so proud of himself. "After tonight, you won't have to worry about him ever again." Faye's eyes widened with a look of disbelief. "Are you serious?" She asked, astounded, which Elio nodded to confirm. She turned around and threw her arms around his torso, knocking both him and her back on the bed. "Thank you! Thank you!" She pressed her face into his chest, snuggling up close to him. "I love you so much!" She exclaimed. Elio held a soft, sincere look on his face as he let the girl hug him tightly, enjoying the affection she showed him.

"Doll." His voice only held love in it as he ran his fingers through her hair. "How many times do I have to tell you? I'll do anything for you." He had proven over and over that he wasn't afraid to get his hands dirty if it meant she was safe and happy. "He attempted to reach out to you, so I scheduled a meetup with him." He explained to her the plan. "I would love it if you came along with me." He finally told her. "Obviously I won't make you face him if you really don't want to, but I think it would do you good to see your tormentor in his last moments of life." Faye looked up at him, her head tilted to the side. "I'll go…" she said quietly. "As long as you're with me." Elio's lips twitched upward, pulling Faye's face down to his, planting his lips against hers. "Of course, my love. I'll never leave your side."

They spent some time together, cuddled up with Faye's head on Elio's chest. She listened to his heartbeat; the sound lulling her into a light sleep. He felt positively ecstatic over having her live with him, no longer worried something terrible would happen to her. He checked the time. 4:59. They should start heading off, so they don't end up late.

"Doll." Elio nudged her gently, waking her up. "It's time to head off." She lifted her head up slowly, blinking away the sleep in her eyes. He found it rather enjoyable to watch her both fall asleep and wake up, seeing her try to fight against her body's natural functions. He thought it was absolutely adorable. "There you are." He chuckled, his chest vibrating underneath her. "What time is it?" She yawned. "Five." He answered, stroking her hair. "We need to get ready." She mushed her face back against his chest, mumbling incoherently. Faye stayed like that for a minute, Elio almost being convinced she fell back asleep, but she finally lifted her head again, rolling off of him.

Elio got off the bed and sauntered over to the closet while Faye watched him sleepily. He pulled out a gorgeous red cotton dress, the top a white button up long sleeve shirt with a collar. The skirt had layered ruffles, with a black lace trim at the bottom. It also had straps that went over the shoulders and a pretty red bowtie that went under the collar. He laid the clothes on the bed for her and pulled out a pair of ruby red flats to set out beside the bed. She gave him a strange look, which he returned with a smirk. "I just want you to look your best for your first hit." He explained teasingly. She rolled her eyes with a knowing smile. He just enjoyed seeing her in dresses.

Faye stripped out of her clothes, feeling Elio's eyes on her the whole time. She'd never admit it, but she gave him a bit of a show while changing. He simply sat on the edge of the bed, a sly smile on his face. She finally got the outfit on, giving herself a little once over in the mirror. Faye thought, much to her delight and amusement, that this dress really made her look like a doll. "Of course it does." He answered her. She might have said it out loud. "My perfect, gorgeous little doll." He wrapped his arms around her, pulling her into his chest. "Ready to go, love?" She nodded. "Yes, I am." He led her out the door, this being the first time she left the bedroom since she got to the base.

He had his arm around her shoulder protectively as they walked down the long hallway, making the message perfectly clear that Faye belonged to him. As they made it to the front door, she shut her eyes, waiting to feel the fabric touch her face. "We don't have to do that anymore," Elio chuckled. She looked up at him, confused. "You live here now and won't be doing any traveling without me, so there's no need to blindfold you." She let out a little oh, almost forgetting about her new living arrangements. He simply led her out of the door, giving her a moment to take in her surroundings.

The building she had been staying in was a large mansion like structure high in the mountains overlooking the whole desert. Looking out, see could see the city in the distance, a bunch of lights glowing brighter as the sun set. Shades of reds and oranges, mixed in with pinks, purples, and blues, splattered across the sky. The natural vegetation of the land had surrounded the place, painting it an olive green with dots of yellows and pinks added.

She could stand there and stare at the scenery for hours, mesmerized by the different colors that seemed to dance around her. If they didn't have somewhere to be, Elio might have let her, but unfortunately, that would have to be done on another day. He led her to the car, opening the back seat door for her to get in with him following behind. Two large men jumped in the front, not daring to utter a single word. Faye climbed on top of Elio's lap as soon as he got comfortable, relaxing into him.

"How are you feeling about this so far?" Elio whispered in her ear, checking in to make sure she wasn't too anxious. "Surprisingly, I'm actually feeling fine." She admitted. "It feels weirdly normal right now." She figured the closer they got to the destination, the more uncomfortable she would feel, but for right now, she was relaxed and content. "That's good." He hugged her tighter. "Just remember, he has absolutely no power over you. When we enter that building, you will be the one in complete control, not him."

She nodded along, staring out the window as he continued to speak. "I'll send some men in first to make sure it isn't a trap. You'll go in next once they give the all clear to say whatever you want to say to him. I'll be right behind you, staying hidden to lull him into a false sense of security. If he sees me right away, he may attempt to run or do something else equally stupid, and I would rather not put you in more danger than absolutely necessary." He explained the plan in the bedroom already, but he wanted to make sure she understood. He planned it out, so that she had four sets of eyes on her at all times, including Maurice's, in order to protect her.

Her face rested against the cool glass of the window, watching the desert pass them by. "It is a really beautiful evening, don't you think?" She asked Elio without looking at him. "Yeah, it is pretty nice out." He agreed with her. "Everything feels so calm and tranquil, like we fell into a painting." He let her ramble a bit, figuring the nerves were getting to her. "I find it wonderful that I get to share a night like this with you." She had convinced herself that they were just going on a normal date together, figuring she could deal with the reality of the situation later. "Every night I share with you is beautiful." He said sincerely, burying his face in the crook of her neck. This was just a normal night with her wonderful boyfriend.

They pulled up to the bar, parking close to the building. Faye sat silently in Elio's lap, her expression unreadable. The mobster let her sit and think, rubbing her hands in soothing motions to comfort her. The two men up front swiftly hopped out of the car, entering the bar while they waited. "I wonder if his apology will be sincere." She finally spoke up, feeling suffocated by the silence. "Would it make a difference if it was?" He questioned her.

"No, it would just be nice to see some decency from him for once." She shrugged. "Honestly, I just want to know what I did to make him go so far and what he hoped the outcome would be." She sighed, laying her head against his chest, her eyes half closed. "If that will bring you peace, I'll make sure he talks." Elio promised, willing to do whatever it took to make her happy.

After sitting around for five minutes, Elio's phone finally rang. "Well?" He answered expectantly. "He's here, alone. No wires spotted." He seemed unimpressed by their statement, a bored look on his face. "Okay, stay close, but don't raise suspicion. I'll send in the bait." Elio ordered, Faye snickering quietly at being called bait. He hung up the phone, putting his full attention on the young woman. He planted a soft, loving kiss against her lips, which she returned in earnest. "Ready to go, doll?" The mob boss asked caringly. "Yes." She answered with determination. He opened the door, helping her out, and against his instincts, let her walk on ahead into the bar.

Faye held her head up high, a neutral expression on her face. She spotted the man sitting at the bar, drinking a glass of whiskey. She gave the area a glance over, seeing the two men that went in first, both sitting a distance away from him, as Maurice stood behind the bar, cleaning some glasses off. Everything had been set up perfectly. All she needed to do was play her part.

Faye took a deep breath, preparing herself mentally before making her way to the man. She took the stool right next to him, paying no mind to him at all. "Faye? Is that really you?" He seemed to notice her almost immediately. "It's great to finally meet you." He greeted her like she was an old friend, attempting to bring her in for a hug. She dodged away from his embrace, otherwise ignoring the man completely. "Awe feeling a little shy, babe? Why don't I buy us a round of liquid courage?" He was obviously already tipsy.

"Hey!" He snapped his fingers at Maurice. "How about a couple shots for me and my lady friend here?" The bartender turned around, a menacing scowl on his face. "Snap at me again and I'll break your fucking hand." He then turned his attention to Faye, placing a drink in front of her. "Here you go darling, a virgin mojito." He gave her a big toothy grin, which she returned, taking a sip of the drink happily.

"So how's lover boy been treating you?" He started up a conversation with her as if it were a casual night. "Pretty well." She smiled endearingly. "Good. Normally I'd say if he ever hurts you, let me know and I'll kick his ass, but that man is so protective of you, I bet he'd kick his own ass if he hurt you." She laughed at this, not disagreeing. She could feel the man seething next to her, not happy being ignored by her. "Well, let me know if you need anything." The bartender turned away from them, going back to his business.

She could feel the man's eyes burning into the side of her head, holding himself back from saying something stupid. It was probably for the best since Faye, too, was holding herself back from going off on this piece of waste. After a few more sips of her drink, she finally turned to the man, a dull expression on her face. "Oh, so now you're ready to acknowledge me?" He snapped at her sarcastically. She raised an eyebrow at him, placing her glass down.

"You want to talk about things, huh?" She said to him, keeping a calm tone. "Yeah, I figured we could reconcile, put our problems aside and be friends is all."

Faye blinked a few times. "What?" He gave her a shit-eating grin. "Well, I did some terrible things to you, you did some terrible things to me…" "I did nothing to you." She snapped at him, interrupting his proposition. "Oh, come on babe, you humiliated me in front of my friends, ghosted me without a single reason why, and continue to verbally attack my character. I think we are pretty even here." He kept playing with his phone as he spoke to her.

Faye clenched her fists, her rage bubbling up at the sheer audacity of this man. "You killed my fish, hurt my cat, broke into my house multiple times, doxed me, photographed me without consent, attempted to ruin my reputation many times, and you think we're even? Just because I didn't want to talk to you?" She needed to take a deep breath, feeling her tears build up. He held a smug expression. "Come on babe, admit it, you love our little game of cat and mouse. Look, you even got all dressed up for me." He said in a flirty tone, but suddenly his face darkened, a cruel look in his eyes.

"Besides, I know all about your big, scary boyfriend and all the crimes he committed. I'm sure the police would love to get their hands on all the evidence I have against him." Faye's heart was racing, though she still kept a calm face, knowing better than to take the bait. "What are you talking about?" She held a confused expression; knowing he had more than likely been recording them the entire time, and was probably hoping to get a confession out of her.

"Oh, babe." He chuckled sinisterly. "Playing dumb? Really? It really brings down your rating. We all know about how you're dating a mob boss. I bet you even brought him down here to rough me up a bit, didn't you?" He started getting a little too cocky as he continued to play with his phone before setting it down.

She tilted her head in confusion, tapping her class three times. "Mob boss? My boyfriend? What the hell are you talking about?" Maurice, hearing the tapping of the glass, glanced over at Faye, who extended her finger out, pointing towards the phone. "I don't know why you think I came here, but I only showed up to tell you to leave me alone." She spoke with a shaky breath.

"I want you to stop bothering me or I will get a restraining order against you!" He laughed at that. "Restraining order? Really? Once I get that boyfriend of yours locked up, you might as well move to a new country. I am going to ruin you…" A loud smash sounded in front of him, a giant bottle of whiskey had been dropped right on top of his phone, shattering both the bottle and phone, making the device unusable as all the liquid flooded the inside, frying it.

"Oops." Maurice said nonchalantly, winking at Faye. She wanted to laugh at how comically bad his acting was. He could have tried to make it look more like an accident, but at least the deed was done. Thad sat there wide eyed and trembling, seeing that his only trump card had been destroyed right before his eyes.

Looking up at the now smiling girl, he realized this had been all planned out. Every move he made played more and more into her hands, and now he was fully cornered. "By the way." She spoke in an overly cheerful voice. "I didn't get all dressed up and pretty for you. I did it for someone else." He could feel his mouth drying up a bit. "Who did you do it for, then?" He sputtered out. "Me." A deep, gravelly voice sounded from right behind him, causing a chill to go up the man's spine.

The two turned around, Faye's eyes lighting up at the sight of the tall man. She stood up, taking her place next to Elio as he wrapped a protective arm around her waist. As Thad stood up, the mob boss snapped his fingers, signaling for his two men to stand up as well. They stood shoulder to shoulder with the man, gripping him tightly so he wouldn't try to escape. Elio went into his pocket, pulling out a hundred-dollar bill, and handed it to Maurice. "For all the trouble." He said bluntly. Maurice laughed. "Anything for the little lady." He winked at Faye, causing her to giggle. Elio led her out the door as she waved goodbye to the bartender.

Thad attempted to scream and cry for help but had been effectively silenced by a punch to the gut, causing him to double over in pain. Elio eyed the man in disgust as one of his men shoved an old rag into his mouth to muzzle him. "Come now." The mob boss spoke in a sinister voice. "Let's go for a drive, shall we?" His men lifted Thad up, shoving him in the car's trunk, using rope to fully bind him.

Elio opened the back door, leading Faye in first before crawling in after, pulling her back on his lap. As the car started up, they could hear pounding and muffled crying coming from the back. Elio smacked the back seat in warning. "Shut the hell up!" He snapped with a snarl, only to turn his attention back to Faye, gently running his fingers over her shoulder blades.

"You did such a good job in there, doll." He praised, purring in her ear. "So brave and clever." She tilted her head up, allowing him to claim her lips, pushing his tongue into her mouth. She didn't fight him for control, letting him do as he pleased. Just as Elio pulled away from the kiss, a hard kick had been delivered against the backseat, causing Faye to jump slightly.

He narrowed his eyes, angry that this asshole ruined his moment in a futile plan to escape. "Stop the car." He ordered, his men obeying almost immediately. Faye looked out the window, seeing that they had already made it into the desert, the car currently being parked on a dirt road. He slid her off his lap gently, exiting the car and slamming the door shut.

She could hear the trunk open up, the muffled screams growing louder. "You might want to cover your ears, ma'am." One of the men in the front seat warned her. She placed her hands over her ears, muffling the sounds out a bit, though she could still hear what was happening.

Curious, she peaked out the window, watching as Elio drug the man out of the car, slamming his face against the ground as the man cried out in pain. "Want to shut the fuck up now and quit squirming?" The mob boss taunted, driving his foot onto the guy's back. The man curled up into himself, only nodding due to the amount of pain he was in. Elio picked him up by his neck, throwing him in the trunk.

He wiped his hands off with a towel that was left in there, making his way back inside the car. Once seated, He wrapped his arm around Faye, pulling her tightly against him. "Now where were we, doll?" He purred against her neck, kissing her soft spot gently. She snuggled up against him, moving her head to grant him more access to her flesh. All the terror and anxiety she felt earlier that day had completely melted away. She only felt love and trust for the man holding her so comfortably tight, knowing that not only would he protect her no matter what, he also knew when to back off and let her remain in control. Even though this technically wasn't a date, she still had fun and kind of enjoyed being used as bait.

They made it back home with no problem. The movement in the trunk stopped after a while. Faye, for a second, thought he died, but when the men pulled him out, bloodied and bruised, he was still breathing and moving, being forced to walk on his own in between the two men.

Elio had his arm around Faye, holding his head up high with a prideful smirk as they walked on ahead. "Take him to the red room!" He ordered, leading her back to their shared bedroom. Once they entered the room, he had her up against the wall, lips against her neck. "Mph…" she moaned helplessly against him. He slid his hand up her leg, letting it linger on her inner thigh. "Elio… Mph…" His lips moved against hers, silencing her completely. "Don't worry, doll, I just want a taste." He smirked against her, forcing his way into her mouth. His hand started moving up her skirt, his sharp nails grazing her skin, leaving beads of blood in its path.

He finally pulled his face away from hers, letting her catch her breath as he kept his hand on her thigh. She clung to his shoulders, afraid her legs would turn to jelly if she let go. "Sweet little doll." He purred, moving back against her neck. "I just want to take you right now." He groaned against her. "Elio… Ah… I love you…" she cried, her mind turning to mush the longer he kept her there.

The temptation to let him have his way with her was strong, but she knew she wouldn't be emotionally ready to do anything of the sort that night. Elio let up completely, pulling her over to the bed so she could rest against him. "I love you too." He responded tenderly, a soft smile on his face. "I know it would be a little too much tonight, so don't worry." He nuzzled against her. "But I need to kill that asshole, so just stay put, okay?" She nodded at him with a heartwarming smile.

After leaving the room, Elio made his way to the red room, his lips twisting up into a sadistic grin. Inside the room, Thad sat on the ground, tied up and gagged. He slowly sauntered over to the man as Thad watched his every movement with dread in his eyes. Elio bent down over him, reaching out to grab the gag and ripped it out of his mouth. "Well. Well. Well. Look what I caught. A disgusting little leech trying to suck the life out of my precious little doll." Elio mocked, relishing the whimpers of the man.

"Please!" Thad begged. "I'm sorry! I'll leave her alone!" Tears and snot ran down his blood caked face. "Oh, you're sorry, huh?" Elio snickered. "You're sorry? Well, I guess since you're sorry, there's no point in keeping you here, right?" His voice lowered to a dangerous tone. "I just wanted to make sure you learned your lesson." He shrugged. "Really?" Thad asked hopefully. "You'll really let me go?" He didn't see the dark glint in the mob boss's eye.

Elio started pacing, his arms crossed behind his back. "Of course, it would be pointless to kill you. I'm mean, all you did was text some broad a few mean things, right?" Thad sighed in relief at this. "Yeah! What I did wasn't nearly that bad! She's just crazy!" Maybe he could turn the mob boss against her like everyone else. "That's what I thought." He eyed him.

"So five years, huh?" He spoke casually. "She must have done something really fucked up for you to be reaching out to her all this time." Thad relaxed into the false sense of security. "Yeah, she wanted to play mean girl and try to ruin my reputation after ghosting me without a single reason. The little bitch thought just because she didn't have her real name out there, she could play games with me, so I had to teach her a lesson in manners."

Elio looked at this man in shock. He truly was a moron, wasn't he? "What outcome were you hoping for?" He wanted to complete his promise to his doll first. "Eventually, I figured she'd finally pull the stick out of her ass and talk to me like a normal person. Maybe she'd be an example for all women around on how to properly act in society, but I can back off and let you take care of it."

Reeling his arm back and swinging it forward, Elio punched the man, shattering his nose, his head smashing against the cold concrete floor. He grabbed Thad by the back of his head, his nails digging into his scalp, and pulled him up. "You really think I believe any of that shit?" He sneered at the man. "That my beautiful doll deserved any of it?" The man went back into whimpering in agony.

"You know, I've been thinking about it all day." Elio spoke thoughtfully, crouching down once again to be at Thad's level. "What would be the most fitting punishment for a creep like you?" Thad reached his bound up hands towards the mob boss. "Please! You said I could leave!" He begged. "Yeah, I did." He chuckled. "And you can. In a body bag." He lifted his foot up, slamming it down on the man's hands, crushing them underneath, the man screaming at the top of his lungs. "Oh no, that won't do." Elio said, picking the gag back up and stuffing it back in the man's mouth.

Lifting his foot, revealed the man's hands, now a broken mess of bloody cartilage, torn up skin, and shattered bones. "That looks pretty nasty. We better clean that up." He teased as he walked over to the door, banging on it as loud as he could. "By the way, do you happen to remember one of your threats from earlier? It really stuck with me because I knew more than anything it would destroy her."

Thad could hardly focus on what was being said. The pain was unbearable. "Something about boiling her cats alive?" His eyes widen, muffled screams fell from his mouth as two men came in holding a pot of boiling water. "Quit your fucking whining!" He sneered at him as he motioned for the men to lower the pot, slowly trickling it over the wailing man, his skin blistering and pealing. It took five minutes to empty the entire pot on Thad, his throat absolutely destroyed from screaming.

Thad was on the verge of passing out, his breathing becoming labored. Elio clicked his tongue in disappointment. "Is that really all you can take?" He asked with a cruel smile. "You put my doll through way more than that." He lifted the man up, carrying him towards a door in the back of the room. "I think you need to cool down a bit." He laughed, pushing the man through the doorway. Inside was a small walk-in freezer, complete with meat hooks. Fourteen huge black garbage bags stuffed with who knows what littered the floor.

Elio took one of the hooks dangling from above and pushed it through the skin on the back of Thad's neck, leaving him dangling in the air, every little movement sending a jolt of pain through the man's body. "So what exactly did you think I was going to do to Faye?" He asked out of curiosity, smacking Thad on his back to send him swinging.

"Were you hoping I'd do something similar? Maybe strip her down and humiliate her in the process? Is that what makes you hard?" More sniveling sounded from the dangling man. "And to think, after everything you've done to spit in my face, you actually thought I wasn't going to kill you! Thought I'd turn against the woman I love more than anything! Because you claim she's exaggerating?"

He laughed at how ridiculous it sounded. "Let me nail one thing through that thick fucking skull of yours. I don't give a shit what you did to make her cry like that. Anyone who hurts my doll dies. If she even says she doesn't like someone, they're dead because anyone who's gotten on her bad side deserves to be put six feet under." The mob boss pulled out a switchblade and dug it into the man's thigh, piercing through his bone.

"Another thing. Those damn cats of hers are under my protection as well. Anything anyone does to the furry assholes, I do to them ten times harder." He dug his hand into the hole, while still holding the blade, and sliced through the tendons and muscles before grabbing onto the bone. With one swift move, he snapped the bone with his bare hand. After, He raked his blade up, cutting through the man's fabric and skin, swiftly pulling his arm away from the man who was barely breathing seconds away from death.

Elio finally left the freezer, slamming the door closed and making his way out of the red room. He looked down at himself. A bloody mess. No way in hell could he cuddle with Faye in this state. Just as he started walking to their bedroom, he spotted Leo walking down the hall. "Leo!" He yelled to the young gangster. "Where the hell have you been?" Leo looked up at his blood-soaked boss, trying to keep his nerves under control. "I went back to the house, boss, to grab Miss Faye's sketchbook like she requested." He held up the book to prove he wasn't lying. Elio snatched it out of his hands, careful not to get anything on it. "I need you to take Mr. Ralston out of the freezer, throw him in a bag, and bury him six feet under. He might still be breathing. I don't care, just make sure he stays down." He commanded the man. "Right away, boss!" Leo didn't miss a beat. "Also, didn't I fucking tell you to dispose of those bodies in the freezer? Clean it up or it'll be you next!"

The moment Leo left out of his sight, his expression softened as he made his way back to the bedroom. He knocked three times before opening the door, giving warning to the woman that he was coming in. The last thing he wanted to do was startle her.

"Elio!" Faye exclaimed, jumping into his arms. Without thinking, the mobster caught her almost immediately, accidentally covering her in some of the dead man's blood. "Yeesh." She cringed at the feeling of the sticky substance leaking through her beautiful outfit. "Sorry, I should have warned you." Elio said sheepishly. "It's okay, at least we're matching now." She laughed, pulling his face down for a kiss.

The two stood there in a loving embrace, enjoying every ounce of their reunion. The mission had gone over perfectly, and now Faye belonged to him. If there was one more thing he could have said to Thad, it might have been a small thank you for forcing his doll to move in. This would be marked as the happiest day of his life so far, and no matter what the future brings, they would be ready to take it on, together, forever.